P

Broken Pieces

"The story's fast pace and the strong female characters reinforce the terrifying nature of [the] villain. It's perfect for the hard-to-scare reader!" —*Romantic Times*

"Carla Cassidy is a magnificent writer [who] sucks you into the story line, straps you in for the wild ride, and doesn't disappoint you in the end. This is one amazing read!"
—The Romance Readers Connection

"The mystery will keep you on the edge of your seat; it was tautly written and fast-paced! Bravo to Ms. Cassidy, as she has created a first-class tale!" —The Road to Romance

"Ms. Cassidy is a talented writer [who] keeps the suspense level high throughout the story and the romance smoking-hot!" —Fallen Angel Reviews

Every Move You Make

"[A] taut, fast-paced romantic thriller . . . [the] romance shines" —*Publishers Weekly*

"[A] breathtaking mystery . . . pulls you in from the first page and keeps you on the edge of your seat. . . . This is an excellent romantic suspense, and one I recommend you rush out to get." —Romance Junkies

"Carla Cassidy has outdone herself with this dark, complex thriller. . . . This is a fantastic story told by a marvelous storyteller, and comes highly recommended."
—*Affaire de Coeur*

"Romance and suspense mix for a sexy, thrilling ride that keeps you superglued to the pages. Carla Cassidy's books keep getting better and better." —Joyfully Reviewed

continued . . .

Paint It Red

"This nicely crafted mystery has a number of believable suspects . . . a cleverly interwoven romance, and plenty of suspense." —*Romantic Times*

"[A] page-turner. Cassidy's balance of detail and action will keep you intrigued. As the story builds, the tension, suspense, and romance explode, making for a great read."
—Romance Reviews Today

"[A] gripping love story . . . Cassidy does an incredible job pacing the tantalizing romance between Vanessa and Christian, and my heart raced during their moments of terror. . . . A thriller that sucks the reader in until the last page."
—Romance Junkies

"[A] new spin on an old story . . . smart and intricate . . . Cassidy knows how to let a mystery unfold and how to draft a heroine. . . . A genuinely worthy addition to the family suspense drama subgenre." —Paperback Reader

"The suspense was so riveting I could not put the book down. . . . This is the first book I have read by Carla Cassidy and it will not be the last. Filled with romance, well-developed characters, suspense, and mystery, this is definitely not a book to be missed!"
—Suspense Romance Writers

Without a Sound

"Tense . . . exhilarating." —*Midwest Book Review*

Are You Afraid?

"Cassidy's sharp new thriller boasts an easy, masterful balance that's rare and ambitious for a suspense novel. Quiet details make Cassidy's novel work.... Smooth, simple prose tells a full story that's equal parts romance, family drama, and sheer terror." —*Publishers Weekly*

The Perfect Family

"[An] exciting thriller." —The Best Reviews

"Gritty and gripping psychological suspense is rapidly becoming Cassidy's hallmark. *The Perfect Family* is creepy and frightening—but really intense, fun reading."
—*Romantic Times*

Promise Him Anything

"Exciting romantic suspense . . . a terrific tale."
—*Midwest Book Reviews*

"Ms. Cassidy grabs you from the first page.... I highly recommend this read to any fan of the romantic suspense genre. You won't be sorry." —Romantic Designs

"Impressive." —*Romantic Times*

"Edge-of-the-seat suspense . . . a dynamic read."
—The Plot Queens

Also by Carla Cassidy

Promise Him Anything
The Perfect Family
Are You Afraid?
Without a Sound
Paint It Red
Every Move You Make
Broken Pieces

LAST GASP

Carla Cassidy

A SIGNET ECLIPSE BOOK

SIGNET ECLIPSE
Published by New American Library, a division of
Penguin Group (USA) Inc., 375 Hudson Street,
New York, New York 10014, USA
Penguin Group (Canada), 90 Eglinton Avenue East, Suite 700, Toronto,
Ontario M4P 2Y3, Canada (a division of Pearson Penguin Canada Inc.)
Penguin Books Ltd., 80 Strand, London WC2R 0RL, England
Penguin Ireland, 25 St. Stephen's Green, Dublin 2,
Ireland (a division of Penguin Books Ltd.)
Penguin Group (Australia), 250 Camberwell Road, Camberwell, Victoria 3124,
Australia (a division of Pearson Australia Group Pty. Ltd.)
Penguin Books India Pvt. Ltd., 11 Community Centre, Panchsheel Park,
New Delhi - 110 017, India
Penguin Group (NZ), 67 Apollo Drive, Rosedale, North Shore 0632,
New Zealand (a division of Pearson New Zealand Ltd.)
Penguin Books (South Africa) (Pty.) Ltd., 24 Sturdee Avenue,
Rosebank, Johannesburg 2196, South Africa

Penguin Books Ltd., Registered Offices:
80 Strand, London WC2R 0RL, England

First published by Signet Eclipse, an imprint of New American Library,
a division of Penguin Group (USA) Inc.

First Printing, April 2009
10 9 8 7 6 5 4 3 2 1

Printed in the United States of America

Prologue

He'd always heard that under the right circumstances anyone was capable of anything. He'd never really believed it until that day in May when the skies grew dark with the approach of a dust storm and the wind screamed like a cat in heat and she'd pissed him off so much he'd snapped.

Fury and rage. It consumed him as the wind outside screeched and the day grew dark as night. A bird, disoriented by the swirling dust, slammed into the front window. The sound of sudden death only stoked the flames of rage inside him.

When it was through and he saw what he had done, the booze that he'd drunk roared up the back of his throat. Horror filled him, a horror twisted with crashing grief.

Oh God, if only she hadn't made him so mad. If only the hatchet hadn't been on the table by the door. If only he hadn't drunk so much. But all the *if only*s in the world couldn't undo what had been done.

Joleen Donovan lay on the floor near the sofa, decapitated. Near the front door ten-year-old Johnny Donovan and his seven-year-old sister, Jennifer, were crumpled piles of colorful clothes, their eyes staring unseeing at the ceiling.

He reeled around the room in the semidarkness of the storm, apologizing to Joleen, to the children, to God.

It was then he realized the storm had passed and the wind seemed to hold its breath. The abrupt cessation and the unusual silence that followed screamed inside his head.

The sound of dusty brakes squealed from someplace outside. He raced to the front window and saw that a school bus had pulled up down the lane. He watched as sixteen-year-old Allison Donovan got off the bus.

He hadn't thought about her, hadn't realized it was time for her to come home.

With an anguished sob he hid behind the front door, knowing that it wasn't over yet.

Chapter 1

Fifteen years later

The wind screamed a lot in Crow's Creek, Kansas. Old wives' tales spoke of pioneer women driven stark raving mad by the ever-present shriek of the wind across the prairie grass. Tumbleweeds skittering across the plains, a nuisance that was cursed on a daily basis, caused more car accidents than drunk drivers.

The town of Crow's Creek was barely a blip on the map, located forty miles east of the bigger city of Goodland. Main Street ran two blocks and still boasted some of the original buildings from nearly a hundred years before.

The town was semifamous for its Pioneer Days celebration in the spring, for Aunt Emma's Homemade Pies and for Uncle Gus's Tumbleweed Museum. It had once made national news for a particularly heinous murder that had occurred fifteen years ago.

Dust storms still occurred in the small town, as did tornadoes, goofy parades and an occasional bar brawl involving pool cues, bottles and the questioning of parentage.

None of that was on Allison Clemmins's mind as she stepped out of the high school door and the wind whipped her long dark hair around her face.

She clutched her pile of papers against her chest and started down the front stairs toward her car in the distant parking lot. She'd gone only a few steps when a familiar voice called from behind her.

She turned to see Michelle Keller hurrying toward her, her short blond curls bouncing like miniature Slinkys in the wind. "I'm so glad it's Friday," she exclaimed as she caught up with Allison.

Michelle taught American history and Allison taught English, and the two had been best friends since third grade. "You're always glad when it's Friday," Allison said with a laugh.

"I'm not sure I'll survive another month of this group," Michelle exclaimed. "Want to grab a quick drink down at Crazy's?" Michelle had been divorced for two years and often trolled the bars on the weekends, looking for the new Mr. Right.

"Can't. I've got to pick up Sam and get over to the karate studio. He's testing for his brown belt this evening." A surge of pride filled Allison's chest as she thought of her twelve-year-old son.

"Ms. Clemmins!"

Both Allison and Michelle turned at the sound of the high-pitched male voice. Eric Grant ran toward them, his thin, gangly arms and legs appearing disconnected from the rest of his body. Beau Kelly and Patrick Johnson, Eric's two best friends, walked slowly behind him, shaking their heads from side to side as if admonishing Eric for whatever he was about to do. All three boys were juniors in Allison's third-period class.

As Eric reached the two teachers, he jammed his hands in his pockets and hunched forward as if afraid the wind might blow him away. "I was just wondering," he began, his voice riding the octave scale from tenor to bass and back again. "Have you ever heard of Mary Kay Letourneau? You know, she not only dated one of her students. . . . She married him." His watery blue eyes gazed at Allison adoringly as Beau and Patrick reached them.

"Yes, I've heard of her," Allison replied. "Eric, find a nice girl your own age and ask her to prom."

Beau slung a well-muscled arm around his best friend. "Come on, Eric. We told you this was stupid." He gave the two teachers a pained look.

Eric cast Allison a lovesick glance over his skinny shoulder as his two friends led him down the stairs to where Beau's car awaited them.

"Makes you feel all warm and fuzzy inside, doesn't it?" Michelle said dryly. "That the boy most likely to become the next Unabomber has a crush on you?"

Allison laughed. "There are some who gracefully slide through the teenage years. Eric isn't one of them. My biggest hope is that before the school year ends, I can teach him the difference between a preposition and a proposition."

"Good luck with that," Michelle said with a grin. "Call me tomorrow." The two women parted ways, Michelle to her car and Allison to her own.

As Allison slid in behind her steering wheel, she thought of the three boys who had just taken off. The friendship between them was remarkable in that the boys were so different, both in life circumstances and in temperament.

Beau was an only child; his father, Dane Kelly, was the sheriff of Crow's Creek. Beau was good-looking and athletically inclined, with an easy charm that made him popular with both the girls and the boys in school.

Every school had a Patrick Johnson, the boy who would do anything for a laugh. He was an underachiever who Allison suspected hid a well of pain beneath his clown antics. His parents' breakup had been bitter and acrimonious, and even though it had been six years since their divorce, their continued fighting was legendary in the small town.

Then there was Eric. Scrawny and an easy target for ridicule, Eric was smarter than most of the kids, but painfully socially inept. He lived with his father on the edge of town in a ramshackle farmhouse where NO TRESPASSING signs served as a coat of paint.

As Allison pulled away from the school, she emptied her head of thoughts of her students. She turned onto Main Street to head toward her son's school. Because the town was so small, there was no middle school, only the high school and the grade school.

There had been many times over the past ten years when Allison had thought about moving from Crow's Creek. There was no question that this place had been the site of unspeakable horror for her. But it had also been the place of life-renewing joy. She'd married her childhood sweetheart in the Methodist church on Main, then a year later buried him in the cemetery on the south side of town.

There had been plenty of tragedy for her here and yet she stayed, sustained by an aunt and uncle who loved her and by the townspeople who had rallied around her in her darkest hours, and perhaps chained here by the memory of all that had been lost, all that had been stolen from her.

Crow's Creek felt safe and familiar to her. There was only one place she never went and that was an abandoned farmhouse on the western outskirts of town. It was the place where she'd grown up, the house where horror and death had visited one dusty afternoon. She went there now only occasionally in her nightmares.

A smile curved her lips as she pulled up near the playground at the grade school and spied her son tying the shoelaces for a younger boy. Martha Hunter, the after-school monitor, sat on a nearby bench, her blue-gray hair glinting in the spring sunshine.

Martha was almost seventy years old and a widow. She'd been hired by the school to work two hours every day after school watching the kids whose parents worked. Martha loved her job and the kids loved her. She waved at Allison as Sam ran to the car, his usual cheerful smile lighting his face.

He got into the passenger seat, bringing with him the scent of sunshine and the slight tang of boyhood sweat. "Hi, champ," she said as he buckled his seat belt. "Good day?"

"Pretty good. I got a B on my spelling test and Jimmy Simms brought Mrs. Radom an apple that had a big, fat, hairy worm in it." He giggled. "She almost puked in the cafeteria."

Allison smiled. One of the things she was most proud of was the fact that she'd managed to keep Sam a normal, happy boy rather than one growing up too fast in an effort to become the man of the family. It was so wonderfully normal for a twelve-year-old boy to find the subject of vomit funny. Although he was bright and generally a good kid, he still wore his favorite socks too many days in a row, occasionally argued with her about bedtime and sometimes forgot to do his homework.

"I thought we'd head over to the café and get an early dinner before your testing at six," she said.

"Cool," he replied. "Can I get a piece of chocolate pie?"

"After you eat something a little more substantial," she replied. "Your brain doesn't work as well if it's loaded down with nothing but sugar."

"Yeah, Sensei Wayne says 'Balance in all things,' whatever that means."

Allison smiled again. Sensei Wayne was Wayne Fenton, an auto mechanic by day and enigmatic karate teacher by night. He was a strange man in his late thirties who had never married. He was quiet and unassuming until he put on his white *gi*; then he became something other than just Wayne who could troubleshoot an engine simply by hearing it run. Like Clark Kent, when he put on his costume, Wayne became a hero to the kids, commanding respect and demanding that each of his students strive for perfection.

He'd asked Allison out a couple of times, but she'd always declined his invitations. Allison didn't date. After burying her husband, she'd decided to devote herself to her work and to her son. There wasn't time for a man in her life.

As Allison drove to the café, Sam chattered about his day, filling her in on all things important to a twelve-year-old. She listened absently, her thoughts divided between Sam and lesson plans for the next week. She'd never planned on being a teacher, but when she found herself a single mother of a three-month-old, she knew it would be up to her to provide the kind of life she wanted for her son.

Teaching seemed the logical choice for a career. She'd have summers off to spend with her son, and once he started school, their schedules would be almost the same. It had been the best choice she could make. Not only did her job allow her to spend a good quantity of time with Sam, but it also had the added benefit of paying well enough that she'd been able to buy a modest home in a pleasant treelined neighborhood.

Life is good, she thought with satisfaction as she pulled in front of Aunt Emma's Café, home of the best pies in the country. Even though it was still early, just after four, several pickup trucks and cars were parked outside the building. The dinner crowd wouldn't start arriving in earnest for another hour or so, but Emma's was rarely empty.

Short, plump Emma greeted them as they walked through the door. Although Emma had made a fortune with her pie franchise, she still got up every morning to open the café and worked until closing time, at ten on the weekdays. The only concession she'd made to her wealth and success was that she now took Sundays off and on Friday and Saturday nights, when the place stayed open until two in the morning, she had somebody else close up.

"Booth or table?" she asked as she picked up two menus.

Allison looked at her son. "Booth," he said, just as she knew he would.

As always, any stress Allison felt melted away in the café. The air smelled of home cooking and the floral chintz curtains at the windows gave the aura of being invited into somebody's home. The cutlery was everyday and rarely matched, and familiar faces smiled in greeting as Emma got Allison and Sam settled in a booth near the back of the room.

"I'll be back in a jiffy," she said as she handed them the worn menus.

"Thanks, Emma." As the older woman hurried back to the cash register, where a customer waited, Allison and Sam opened their menus. Sam looked at his only a minute, then closed it.

"Let me guess," Allison said to her son. "A burger and French fries and a piece of chocolate pie."

"And don't forget a glass of chocolate milk," he said with a grin. "I can guess yours, too. A salad with chicken in it and a glass of iced tea."

Allison closed her menu and laughed. "We've become too predictable, Sam. Maybe I should have a burger and you should get a salad just to shake things up a bit."

"No way," he replied, his blue eyes twinkling with humor.

For just a moment he looked so much like his father, Bobby, an unexpected grief stabbed through Allison.

Bobby had been her hero, walking her through a time in her life that she almost hadn't survived. His strength and love had steadied her after the tragedy that had sent her reeling, and it had felt right when they married the week after his high school graduation.

At nineteen Bobby was a husband and a father and yet a teenager prone to the same foolish mistakes and errors in judgment that Allison saw in her students. There were times when Allison wondered whether she and Bobby would still be married if he hadn't died while hot-rodding down Main on that rain-slickened April night. Feeling invincible, he never wore his seat belt, and on that night he'd lost control of the car and crashed head-on into a large oak tree. He'd been killed instantly.

As Sam got older, he looked more and more like his daddy. His dark hair had the same hint of curls that Bobby's had, and when Sam smiled, his daddy's dimples danced in his cheeks.

Emma returned to the booth to take their orders as Marianne Bloom and her son, Greg, entered the café. Sam waved wildly at the two, who joined them. Greg was a year younger than Sam and tonight was testing for his yellow belt. Marianne's husband, George, worked nights at a factory in Goodland.

"Be nice if we'd get some rain, wouldn't it?" Marianne asked once she was seated next to Allison, and Sam and Greg engaged in a karate discussion. Western Kansas was just coming off their driest winter of the past twelve years and already there was concern about the dry summer to come.

"We sure could use some," Allison agreed.

Talk of the weather turned to the great sale going on at the boutique and the upcoming Pioneer Days celebration. By that time their food had arrived. As she enjoyed the good food and the company, Allison was grateful that she hadn't chosen to leave Crow's Creek.

Despite everything that had happened here so long ago, this was home and she and her son were happy here.

She looked happy and she had the kind of infectious laugh that made others smile. Seth Walker sipped his coffee, his gaze focused on Allison Clemmins. He'd been seated in the back booth when she'd come in with her son, and he relished the opportunity to study her.

He knew almost everything there was to know about Allison Donovan, the girl. He knew she'd been popular and outgoing, that she had loved her little brother and sister and old Beatles songs. He'd been told about her laugh and how her blue eyes could be as warm as a summer sky or as cold as Arctic air, but he knew very little about Allison Clemmins, the woman.

She was more beautiful than he'd expected. She looked younger than her thirty-one years. Her long dark hair framed her heart-shaped face and complemented those blue eyes. In the brief time he'd been in Crow's Creek, he'd learned that she was a respected teacher and a great single parent.

More than that, she was a survivor.

He glanced at her boy, Sam. He was a good-looking kid with a smile as nice as his mother's. Seth knew she was a widow and had raised the boy on her own.

"How about a warm-up?" The waitress appeared at Seth's booth with the predatory smile of a woman who'd like to take him home with her and lick him like an all-day lollipop.

There had been a time in his life when he'd have not only allowed it but encouraged it. She wasn't a bad-looking woman, probably about thirty years old, with hair bleached an unnatural blond. But he wasn't interested in meaningless, passing relationships anymore.

At thirty-five years old, he didn't know exactly what

he wanted from life, but he definitely knew that the woman wearing the name tag that read BETTY wasn't it.

He pushed his cup toward her but didn't make eye contact. She released a sigh, filled up his cup and then left the booth with a swish of hips as if to show him what he was missing.

He took another sip of his coffee and once again focused on Allison Clemmins. She was a survivor, but he was about to find out just how strong she was. She didn't know it yet, but he was about to wreak havoc on her life.

Chapter 2

"Take notes," Sheriff Dane Kelly told his deputy Rick Solomon.

Rick pulled a notebook and pen from his pocket. If there was one thing he'd learned in his three months of working with Dane Kelly, it was that the man was obsessed about getting everything down on paper.

Rick might have bitched about it if Kelly merely dictated to his deputies, but he knew that the sheriff spent at least as much time as his men writing reports and memorializing on paper everything that happened while they were on duty.

He often wondered if Kelly was the same at home. Were there notebooks scattered around the house detailing every movement he made during the course of a day? He could just imagine the notes. *Got home at six. Ate a meal of mashed potatoes and meat loaf. The meat loaf was dry and the potatoes thin. Watched* The Simpsons *on television, then banged the wife and slept without dreams.*

The two were now walking in Floyd Baxter's pasture, heading toward a stand of trees near the pond that was a popular place for teenagers to light bonfires and drink beer. Normally Baxter was a laid-back kind of guy who rarely got his feathers ruffled about anything. But when he'd called the sheriff's office twenty minutes earlier, he'd sputtered half incoherently that those kids had gone too far.

"I've got to leave here to take my wife into Goodland for a doctor's appointment," he'd said. "But I want somebody out here right now. These kids have really done it this time."

So here they were in his pasture, trying to figure out what had gotten Baxter so riled up. "Make a note of the time," Dane Kelly said as they walked. He glanced at his watch. "Saturday morning at nine thirty."

"Got it," Rick replied as he quickly scribbled it down on his pad. Later he would write up an official report with all the details included. If all the details weren't there, Kelly would kick it back to him for a redo.

Dane Kelly was a big man with muscles beginning to soften with middle age. His hazel eyes radiated intelligence and his features were weatherworn, with deep lines cut across his broad forehead. At forty-four years old, the sheriff was seven years older than Rick. Rick knew Kelly had been elected sheriff sixteen years ago at the age of twenty-eight and was well respected and liked by the people of Crow's Creek.

So far Rick had found him to be a fair and pleasant boss, except for the damned paperwork issue. Still, Rick figured it could be worse.

As they drew closer to the stand of trees, the unmistakable scent of death rode the air. Rick's stomach clenched in response. In his years as a homicide detective in Chicago, he'd smelled that odor far too often. It never portended anything good.

"Smells like we got us a dead animal," Kelly observed.

As the two men stepped into the small clearing among the trees, the source of the odor was instantly realized. Rick's stomach cramped harder as he saw the headless cat carcasses thrown in a pile.

He knew they were missing their heads because those particular body parts were stuck on sticks in the ground, as if they were some sort of exotic hors d'oeuvres offering. The expression on the cats' faces varied from anger to outrage. Sharp little teeth shone in the dappled sunshine as blue and green eyes stared unseeing at the two lawmen.

"Looks like a few of the kids had a little too much to drink and got stupid," Dane said. Rick didn't want to contradict his boss, but as far as he was concerned, this looked far more serious than just stupid. Dane cast him a sideways glance as if able to read his mind. "I suppose you think we ought to start looking for bed-wetting arsonists, nip a serial killer in the bud, right?"

Rick was somewhat surprised to realize that Dane knew about the three precursors that identified the personalities most likely to become serial killers: bedwetting, fire starting and animal cruelty. Dane grinned. "We don't get serial killers in Crow's Creek, but we get a lot of drunk and stupid."

Dane used the toe of his boot to nudge the pile of bodies. Flies took to the air, buzzing at the interruption of their lunch. Six bodies. Six heads on sticks. He knelt to get a closer look.

Rick remained standing as Dane pulled on a plastic glove, then picked up one of the headless forms and examined it carefully. "Looks like they were beheaded by an ax or a hatchet," he observed. He dropped the cat and stood. "Why don't we bag all this up and I'll take it to the dump. I'll ask my boy about it."

Rick looked at him in surprise. "You think Beau had something to do with this?"

"Course not, but if it's some of his friends, he'll know who is responsible." He rocked back on his heels and frowned thoughtfully. "He knows all the kids in school and I know he hangs out here with his friends. You know how teenagers are—they can't keep secrets, especially among themselves. When I find out who is responsible for this mess, I'll see him doing community service for the next month," Dane said. "He can sweep sidewalks and pick up trash. Why don't you get a bag from the back of the car and let's get this mess cleaned up."

As Rick walked back to the patrol car, the spring sun was hot on his shoulders, but the warmth didn't reach the icy place inside his gut. As far as he was concerned, anyone who abused or killed helpless animals was right up there with baby killers and rapists. It took a special kind of person to not only behead a half dozen cats but to then display their heads like trophies.

Rick had a bad feeling. No matter what Dane Kelly said, this was not the result of drunk and stupid.

Chapter 3

"Come on, Sam. They're here," Allison yelled down the hallway toward her son's bedroom. It was just after three on Saturday afternoon, and Sam had a birthday party sleepover to attend.

Sam raced out of his room clutching both a backpack and a wrapped present in his hands. "Bye, Mom. See you tomorrow," he said as he flew past her and out the door.

Allison followed him to the minivan waiting in the driveway. Suzanne Welch sat behind the steering wheel, looking as if she was suffering the headache of all headaches. Three boys were already in the van as Sam climbed in, and Allison knew that Suzanne still had one more boy to pick up.

"You're a better woman than I," Allison said as she walked around to the driver's window.

Suzanne offered her a pained smile. "I must have been out of my mind when I agreed to this."

Allison laughed. "Just think, by this time tomorrow it will all be over."

"Right, all I've got to do is survive the night," Suzanne replied dryly. She put the minivan into reverse. "I'll drop him home sometime tomorrow afternoon." As she backed out of the driveway, Allison waved at her son, but Sam was already engrossed in his friends and didn't wave back.

She sighed. No kiss, no "I love you." Sam had finally reached the age when he abhorred displays of affection if anyone else was around. That's the way it's supposed to be, she reminded herself, but it didn't mean a child's independence didn't cause just a tiny ache in a mother's heart.

She returned to the house, noticing as she went through the front door that the flowers she'd planted the weekend before desperately needed water and the lawn wasn't greening up like it should be this time of year. It was going to be a miserable summer if the dry, hot spring was any indication.

Walking through the living room, she admired the new sofa that had been delivered two weeks before. They'd moved into the house a year ago with the sofa that had displayed the stains of Sam's childhood. She'd finally decided that with Sam now twelve it was safe to buy something new, although she'd chosen a dark green and burgundy floral pattern that would hide most twelve-year-old's mistakes.

As she went into the kitchen, the silence of the house pressed in on her. Funny how Sam filled the house with noise, and when he was absent, the house seemed to hold its breath, waiting for his return.

Normally Allison didn't mind being alone, but now the silence pressed in on her. She fixed herself a Diet Coke, then grabbed the cordless phone and punched in the number to ring her aunt's house.

It was customary for her and Sam to have Sunday dinner with her aunt Maureen and uncle David. She needed to let them know that she and Sam wouldn't be coming the next day.

Maureen answered on the second ring, sounding as out of breath as if she'd just finished a ten-mile run. It wouldn't have surprised Allison if she had. Maureen Donovan was one of the most competent women Allison had ever known.

Fifteen years ago when Allison found herself at sixteen years old without a family, recovering from a mental break and reeling from the crime that had stunned the entire community, her aunt Maureen had stepped in with her calm efficiency and taken control.

It didn't matter that Allison was a niece by marriage, nor did it matter that the man arrested for the heinous crime was Maureen's brother-in-law. She simply did what needed to be done, providing Allison a place to live and an abundance of love.

Allison had lived with her aunt Maureen and uncle David until she'd gotten pregnant at eighteen and married Bobby. After Bobby's death she had found herself living once again with her aunt and uncle, who provided all kinds of support while she got her degree.

"Aunt Maureen, I just wanted to let you know that we can't make it tomorrow for lunch. Sam has a slumber party tonight and won't be home in time," Allison explained.

"Come by yourself," Maureen replied. "I'm planning on doing a roast with all the works and I've got a half a dozen loaves of bread rising right now. I was going to send a loaf home with you."

Allison hesitated. She always enjoyed visiting with them, but the idea of sleeping late in the morning and not having to attend to anyone's needs but her own seemed more agreeable at the moment. "Freeze my bread and give me a rain check? To be honest, I'm thinking maybe I won't even get out of my pajamas tomorrow."

"Ah, I love those kinds of days," Maureen replied.

Allison smiled. She would bet a month's paycheck that Maureen had never enjoyed a pajama day in her life. When Allison lived with her, she'd never seen her aunt in her nightclothes. It was as if Maureen stepped out of her bed with her hair perfectly styled, her makeup impeccable and her heart rate pumped for taking care of whatever business the day might bring.

She worked part-time in the mayor's office, served on a dozen committees and kept her home running with an efficiency that put most women to shame.

The two visited for a few minutes, made plans to have dinner together on Tuesday night, then hung up. Allison carried the phone into the living room, too restless to sit, and contemplating the night to come. There was a stack of papers on the coffee table waiting to be graded and as usual all the furniture could use a good dusting. She could organize a closet or curl up with a book, but all these things held the appeal of a root canal.

As she wandered to the front window, she punched in Michelle's number. Maybe they could meet and see a movie or have a drink. Michelle had finally gotten over the heartbreak of her divorce two years before and had rediscovered her love of life and wicked sense of humor.

She saw the man as Michelle's answering machine picked up.

He stood across the street and appeared to be staring in the direction of her house. He was tall, and even from the distance she could tell he was well built with broad shoulders beneath the white dress shirt, and slacks that perfectly fit his long, lean legs.

What was he doing just standing there? He didn't appear to be particularly menacing, but she could almost feel the intensity of his gaze, and a whispering chill swept across the back of her neck.

"Michelle, it's me," Allison said into Michelle's machine as she stepped away from the window. "Sam has a sleepover with a friend tonight and I was wondering if you wanted to get together and do something. Call me back if you're available."

She clicked off and turned back around to look outside. The man was gone, vanished as if he'd been nothing more than a figment of her imagination, and she dismissed him from her mind.

It was after four when Michelle called her back and they agreed that Michelle would pick her up at eight that evening and they'd go to Crazy's, a popular bar where the drinks were cheap and the music was loud. It had been months since Allison had been out without Sam, months since she'd had a night of strictly adult conversation.

As she pulled on a pair of jeans, she was surprised by how much she was looking forward to the evening. Sam was at the age that it seemed like most of her free time was spent driving him to where he needed to be. Karate classes, baseball, playdates with friends—it was almost depressing that Sam had a much more active social life than she had.

She chose a peach-colored blouse that complemented her dark hair and blue eyes, and then tied her hair back with a matching ribbon. One thing the women of Crow's Creek learned early in life was to fashion hair for the wind.

Most of the older women in town chose the helmet-head approach, keeping hair short and sprayed with enough Aqua Net to make their heads lethal weapons. One of the reasons Allison kept her hair long was that it was easy to tie back or pull up.

She applied more eye makeup than usual and added a pair of dangly gold earrings for the night out. She was in the process of searching her cluttered dresser top for her favorite bottle of perfume when her doorbell rang. She stuck her head out of the bedroom doorway. "Come on in, I'll be ready in a second," she called, and then returned to the dresser, vowing that in the morning she was going to organize the clutter.

Finding the bottle of perfume, she heard the front door open and close. She spritzed herself with the clean floral scent, then grabbed her purse from the bed and left the room.

"Michelle," she called as she headed down the hallway to the living room. She froze as she saw the man standing just inside her front door.

"You said come in," he said.

He was the same man she'd seen earlier standing across the street from her house. A lump of fear lodged in her throat as she stared at him. "I thought you were somebody else," she managed to say, surprised that her voice sounded calm and steady. "May I help you?"

"I hope so." He took two steps toward her, his hand stretched out in greeting. "My name is Seth Walker."

He was extremely attractive, with dark hair sporting the hint of a curl and a pleasant smile that curved a nicely shaped mouth. It was only as she stepped closer to grasp his hand that she noted that the smile that lifted his lips wasn't reflected in his eyes. He had eyes the color of a wintry gray sky, cold but with an intensity that did nothing to alleviate her apprehension.

She took his hand in hers and gave it a quick, perfunctory shake, then released it and stepped back, more than a little bit wary. "What can I do for you, Mr. Walker?"

"I'd like to talk to you about your father."

Her heart seemed to stop beating and a roar sounded in her head.

Her father.

The monster in the closet.

The bogeyman in the shadows.

She'd spent the last fifteen years of her life not thinking about him unless it was to damn him to hell.

No! The word screamed inside her as ancient emotion pressed hard against her chest. "Who are you? A reporter?" She didn't wait for him to reply. "Get out of my house."

"I'm not a reporter, Allison. Please, hear me out." He held out his hands, as if in supplication.

"Get out of my house before I call the sheriff," she exclaimed.

He backed toward the door. "Allison, I'm here on behalf of your father. We believe he's an innocent man. We need your help to exonerate him." He opened the door and stepped out on the porch, but held the door open to continue speaking to her. "Please just give me a few minutes of your time."

"My father should have gotten the death penalty. If there were any real justice in this world, he'd be as dead as my brother and sister and mother. Get off my property." She jerked the door from his grasp and slammed it shut, then leaned against it weakly as her knees threatened to buckle.

She drew several deep breaths as the internal shaking slowly stilled. One of the benefits of remaining in Crow's Creek was that everyone knew her story and in all the years after the murder nobody had spoken Hank Donovan's name in her presence.

She'd spent the last fifteen years of her life pretending he was dead and now a handsome stranger showed up on her doorstep and breathed life into the man who had left her for dead along with the rest of her family.

On wooden legs she moved to the window and peered outside and breathed another sigh of relief as she saw that he was gone. She walked over to the sofa and sank down. Who was Seth Walker? Who was the "we" he'd spoken of?

It didn't matter. She didn't want to know. Hank Donovan was dead to her. He'd been convicted by a jury of his peers and found guilty on three counts of murder and received a sentence of life without the possibility of parole. He was seven hours away from Crow's Creek by car, incarcerated in the Lansing prison. In her mind he was a million miles and another lifetime away, and she resented the fact that Mr. Seth Walker had brought him back into her world, even if for only a few minutes.

She jumped as a knock sounded at the door, then relaxed as she heard Michelle's voice. "Who's ready to party?"

Allison jumped up off the sofa and ran to the door. "I am," she said with forced cheerfulness. "And I hope you're in the mood to be a designated driver because I'm in the mood to get sloppy drunk."

Michelle looked at her in surprised amusement. "You've never been sloppy drunk in your life."

Allison grabbed her purse and linked arms with her friend. "Tonight just might be a first," she replied. She wanted nothing more than to erase the last fifteen minutes of her life and a half dozen gin and tonics might just do the trick.

By ten o'clock Allison was feeling the pleasant buzz that came from three drinks, good company and raucous music that spoke to the soul. She and Michelle sat at one of the round, scarred wooden tables in Crazy's.

Smoke created a blue haze that hung just beneath the ceiling, and peanut shells crunched underfoot. The band was local and played oldies that had people sliding and twisting on the dance floor. Michelle was in rare form, cracking jokes and making Allison laugh harder than she'd done in a long time. And God, she'd needed it after the brief conversation with Seth Walker.

"Uh-oh, look out. Here comes Wayne," Michelle whispered to Allison, who saw the karate king / mechanic approaching from the bar. He smiled, the stiff grin of a man not quite comfortable in the company of women.

"Hey, Wayne, have you come to rev our engines?" Michelle asked with a saucy grin. Allison kicked her friend under the table.

"Hi, Wayne," she said.

"Allison. I was wondering if you'd like to hit the dance floor with me," he said.

"Thanks, Wayne, but I think I'm going to have to pass. I've had enough of these"—she touched her half-finished drink—"that I just might really hit the dance floor."

Besides, she didn't want to encourage him in any way. He seemed to be a nice man and his students adored him, but he just didn't attract Allison and she didn't want to lead him on.

"Maybe another time," he said, then drifted away from the table.

"He reminds me of Norman Bates," Michelle said. "I keep imagining his dead mother in a rocking chair in his bedroom."

Allison laughed. "He's a little odd, but I don't think I'd go that far. You just think he's creepy because he's never shown any interest in you."

"You'd think after all this time he would have noticed that you never dance with anyone," Michelle exclaimed.

The band announced a break and music began to play softly from a jukebox in the corner. The change in music volume made it easier to talk.

Michelle leaned back in her chair and sighed. "That's the problem with living in a small town—all the men my age are either weird or married." She sat up straighter as the outer door swung open and Deputy Rick Solomon entered. "Now, that's a man who can handcuff me to the bed any day of the week."

The two women watched the man take a stool at the bar. Rick Solomon was a good-looking man with sandy brown hair and green eyes that held a hint of sadness. He'd been in town for only a couple of months, but already he was in the sights of every unmarried woman in Crow's Creek.

"I heard that Glenda Nicholson took him one of her famous chicken casseroles the other day. That woman is such a slut," Michelle exclaimed.

Allison grinned. "If she took him the chicken casserole, I'm thinking she'll never get him interested in her. Last time I had a bite of Glenda's chicken casserole, it took me a month to get the strange taste out of my mouth."

"He reminds me of Don," she said, referring to her ex-husband. She cast Allison a wicked smile. "He reminds me of Don before Don became a dick."

"So go talk to him. He's sitting at the bar all by himself. Maybe he'd like your company," Allison suggested.

"You wouldn't mind? I mean, I'll go over there for just a few minutes. You'll be okay here alone?"

"Do I look like I need a babysitter?" Allison countered dryly.

Before the words were out of her mouth, Michelle was out of her chair and heading toward the bar. Allison took a sip of her drink and smiled as she saw Michelle slide onto the stool next to Rick. Michelle was a woman who needed a man in her life. She was happiest when she was part of a couple.

She'd been blindsided by her husband Don's announcement that he not only wanted a divorce but was in love with Sally Jennings, whom he'd been having an affair with for over a year. To make matters worse, Sally was an old nemesis of Michelle's from high school. It was only when Don and Sally had moved to Goodland right after the divorce that the local gossip about the affair had finally died down.

Although Allison had gone on a couple of casual dates when Sam had been a toddler, she'd not allowed another man into her world in any meaningful way and had stopped dating at all when Sam turned two.

Sure, there were moments of loneliness, especially at

night when Sam went to bed, and there were times she missed sharing laughter with a man who knew her almost as intimately as she knew herself. She didn't even miss sex, in truth rarely thought about it, much to Michelle's perpetual shock.

"May I join you?"

The deep voice shot an icy current through her veins as she looked up to see Seth Walker standing at her table. "You know I mind," she replied. This time she felt no fear. They were in a public place and if he harassed her, one of the local men would gladly tell him to take a walk.

He sat in the chair next to her as if he hadn't heard her. "I'll just take a minute of your time."

"Are you following me?" Resentment left no room for any other emotion inside her. "I already told you I have nothing to say on the subject of my father. Now leave me alone and go away."

He leaned forward and she caught a whiff of his cologne, a clean sandalwood scent that filled her head with its sexy attractiveness. This close she could see the long length of dark eyelashes that framed his gunmetal eyes. "I believe your father is an innocent man. I'd like to have your help, but with or without it I intend to reinvestigate the murder of your family." He placed a business card on the table and stood. "Call me, Allison. I'm staying at the Super 8 motel here in town. If nothing else, don't you want to be absolutely sure that the monster who committed those murders is really behind bars?" He didn't wait for her to reply, but walked away from the table.

She watched him until he disappeared out of the door and into the night. It was only when he was no longer visible that she heard the screech of the wind in her ears, smelled the blood in the air and remembered the horror of that day so long ago.

Chapter 4

The Super 8 motel room had been transformed into a temporary office space. Files, folders and notes were arranged in neat piles and hid the top of the spare double bed. A computer and printer sat on the small dining table the room contained. A fax machine stood ready on top of the dresser, the small green ready light the last thing Seth Walker saw each night before he fell asleep.

He'd spent all day Sunday inside the four walls of this room, waiting, hoping that Allison would call, but the phone had remained silent. He now sat at the table with the Monday morning sun shining through the windows. He took a sip of his coffee and glanced at the clock radio on the nightstand. Seven forty-five.

She wouldn't be calling him any time soon. She'd be at work by now and wouldn't be back at her house until later today. He'd hoped to find her agreeable. He'd hoped that she'd work with him. Certainly it would be easier to reinvestigate a crime by talking to one of the victims. But she'd made it clear she wanted nothing to do with him.

He hoped like hell she changed her mind, but even if she didn't, his investigation would continue. The easiest way to get Hank Donovan a new trial was to find new evidence that cast doubt on his original conviction. A daunting task after all these years, but Seth had a driving need to save Hank, who he believed was an innocent man.

Today he needed to introduce himself to the sheriff and see what Kelly had to tell him about what he remembered. Dane Kelly had been a twenty-nine-year-old newly elected sheriff when the crime had occurred.

There had been little investigation into the crime, as Hank Donovan had been found on the scene drunk, covered in blood and clutching the hatchet that had been the murder weapon. He'd been immediately arrested and the town had breathed easier knowing there wasn't a crazed killer in their midst but rather a man who, for whatever reason, had snapped and killed his wife and kids.

But Seth believed there was a killer out there, somebody who had gotten away with murder, and he didn't intend to leave Crow's Creek until he knew who had committed the murders and why.

A vision of Allison Clemmins filled his head. He was attracted to her, though it was clear she wouldn't be returning the feelings.

At the bar on Saturday Seth had wished he were approaching her strictly as a man interested in a woman. He'd wanted to take her by the hand and lead her out to the dance floor, wrap his arms around her and sway to the music of the band.

He'd expected Allison Clemmins to be more fragile considering the fact that she'd suffered through the trauma of the violent death of her family members, the arrest of her father and the loss of her husband. But there hadn't been a hint of vulnerability or fragility in those gorgeous eyes of hers. The tragedies in her life hadn't broken her. In fact they seemed to have made her strong.

He liked that about her. He knew all about drawing strength from tragedy.

He got up from the table, too restless to sit. Maybe he'd take a drive by the scene of the crime. He hadn't done that since arriving in town. He'd been surprised to learn that the old farmhouse had never been sold and was now owned by Allison.

He knew he probably wouldn't be able to get inside the place, but he'd like to get a feel for the location. Decision made, he grabbed his car keys from the top of the dresser and left his room.

Despite the early-morning hour a warm stiff breeze buffeted him as he headed toward his car. The weathermen were predicting severe drought conditions for the area, and by the time Seth got into his car, he felt as if he'd swallowed a mouthful of dust.

As he drove, he thought about Hank Donovan. In the interviews he'd had with the man, Seth had found Hank to be a quiet, intelligent man whose eyes radiated, not the pain of incarceration, but the anguish of the loss of his family and the life he'd once known.

He'd gone into prison as an uneducated carpenter, but he'd used his time in there to obtain a degree in architecture. He worked in the prison woodworking shop and, according to the warden and the guards Seth had spoken to, Hank was a model prisoner.

Seth's father had been a model prisoner, too. He'd been a model prisoner until the afternoon he'd been stabbed to death by another inmate. Seth shoved these thoughts from his mind. He couldn't focus on what might have been. All his energy, all his focus, needed to be on seeing that Hank Donovan was saved.

Apparently there wasn't a rush hour in Crow's Creek. Seth passed only four cars on his way to the west edge of town. The biggest congregation of vehicles was in front of Emma's Café.

It didn't take him long to reach the end of the town proper and travel the two-lane highway toward the old

Donovan place. He slowed as he checked each mailbox he passed, and when he finally came to the right address, he turned off the highway and onto a narrow gravel lane that was the driveway. He drove halfway to the house when he encountered a gate impeding his way. He parked the car and got out only to discover that the gate was padlocked shut.

He returned to his car and shut off the engine. He pocketed the keys, then climbed the gate and dropped to the ground on the other side amid the tall brush and weeds. Ahead of him the house sat on a small hill, looking desolate and lifeless. Tall trees crowded the sides of the house, obviously planted years ago to provide a windbreak.

The house was a ranch with a detached garage in the back. It had once been white, but had weathered to a pale gray. The front screen door had disengaged from its top hinge and hung askew, adding to the sense of abandonment that clung to the house.

What surprised Seth more than anything was that the windows were intact and there was no sign of any kind of vandalism. He had thought the abandoned property would have become party central for the teenagers of the town.

Maybe it was the ghosts of the dead who kept the teens away, that or a respect for the three people who had been slaughtered inside the walls. He peered into each of the dusty windows to see empty rooms. According to city records, nobody had lived here since the Donovan family.

He stood on the porch and stared out in the distance where the nearest neighbor's home was barely visible. He was struck with a fierce sense of isolation. On the day the murders had taken place, nobody would have been able to hear the last gasps of breath; nobody would have been able to hear the terrified screams of the victims.

He thought of all the crime-scene reports he'd read

and all the notes from the trial, and tried to imagine what it had been like that day when Sheriff Dane Kelly walked into the house. The young sheriff must have been horrified. Seth knew from the reports that initially Kelly had told the coroner that there were four bodies. It was only when the coroner had checked Allison that he'd discovered a weak pulse and she'd been rushed to a hospital in Goodland.

She'd been mentally unable to testify at her father's trial. As far as Seth knew, she'd never spoken to anyone about what had happened that day.

Somehow, someway, he had to figure out how to make her talk to him.

Rick stood on the high school steps, waiting for school to be let out for the day. Sheriff Kelly had requested that he unofficially question some of the kids about the cats found in Baxter's pasture. Since the questioning was unofficial, Rick wasn't in uniform. The goal was to talk to the kids informally without stirring up their parents.

Personally he would love to find the little shit who had killed those cats, but he had serious doubts that they'd ever know who was responsible. But this definitely beat sitting in the office, where the air conditioner was on the fritz and the other two deputies spent most of their time talking about sex and football.

Rick couldn't remember the last time he'd watched a game and he didn't even want to think about how long it had been since he'd had sex. Oh, he'd had plenty of opportunities since coming to Crow's Creek and there had been a few times his body had been willing, but his mind wasn't there yet.

Grief was a funny thing. You started feeling better, hopes and dreams began to play in your mind and then it came crashing back, destroying any hope for happiness in the future.

Rick was continually amazed at how the smallest of things could bring on his grief. Over the past three years the list of things that brought back painful memories and had become taboo had grown to mammoth proportions. Peanut butter, the sound of the *Scooby Doo* theme song, pirate costumes and bright purple petunias all evoked the kind of intense emotional response in him that was almost debilitating.

The sun was hot on his shoulders as he waited for the bell to ring and the students to leave the building. His plan was to grab hold of Beau as he came out. The sheriff had apparently given his son instructions to see what he could find out at school today about the cats. Kelly would have been here himself, but he'd had a meeting at City Hall concerning the annual Pioneer Days celebration.

The bell rang and Rick learned a valuable lesson. Never stand in front of the entrance of a high school at dismissal time. The doors exploded outward and kids poured out. The girls looked older than Rick remembered from his high school days, and the boys looked like they had all the secrets of the world in their swaggering walk and confident gazes.

There was nothing better than youth, when the most important thing on your mind was what girl you'd ask out on Saturday night or whether you'd make the track team.

The teens continued to pour out through the door, their laughter ringing in the wind. It was easy to laugh when life hadn't kicked your ass so hard you woke up whimpering in the night.

He'd begun to think he'd missed Beau Kelly as the crowd thinned and cars roared out of the parking lot. Maybe Beau had some kind of after-school activity, he thought as he entered the school doors.

The scent in the hallway brought back distant memories of school dances and student-council meetings and a brunette named Holly who had eventually become his wife.

Don't go there. He needed to focus on the matter at hand and not on the distant past. He'd taken only a few steps when he saw Beau and two other boys come out of a classroom.

The three jostled against one another, hitting arms and slapping shoulders in typical horseplay fashion. It was the tall sandy blond who noticed him first. "Yo, hide the weed, it's the law," he exclaimed with a snicker.

"Knock it off, Patrick," Beau exclaimed as he cuffed his friend on the back of the head. "Hey, Deputy Solomon."

"Hi, Beau," Rick replied.

Beau motioned to the two standing next to him. "This fool," he said, indicating the blond, "is Patrick Johnson." He slung an arm around the shoulder of the skinny, dark-headed boy. "And this punk is Eric Grant."

Rick nodded at the two, whom he'd seen around town in Beau's company. He focused his attention back on Beau. He was a good-looking kid, had his father's square jaw and intelligent gaze.

"You here about that cat thing?" Beau asked.

"Yeah, your dad told me to check in with you and see if you heard anything about it today." Rick shifted from one foot to the other, strangely uncomfortable as he noticed Eric watching him intensely.

"Nah, everybody knew about it, but nobody owned up to it," Beau said.

"You know Jeffrey Dahmer used to behead cats and dogs and frogs and impaled their heads on sticks," Eric said. "And Albert DeSalvo, the Boston Strangler, used to put dogs and cats into orange crates and shoot arrows at them." He offered Rick a crooked smile that momentarily shifted his sharp, pointed features in a way that showed that someday he might be a handsome man.

"Don't mind him," Beau said hurriedly. "Eric thinks he's going to be the next great FBI profiler."

"Yeah, he studies serial killers while the rest of us are making out with our girlfriends," Patrick said with the snicker that Rick already found irritating.

"I don't think it was a kid who killed those cats," Beau said. "I mean, if somebody in school was responsible, I would have heard about it. Somebody would have spilled their guts by now."

Rick hadn't really expected to learn anything and it was obvious the boys were eager to leave. He thanked them for their time, then watched as they hurried past him toward the exit. He'd head back to the office and write his report, and the crime would probably remain unsolved and in Dane Kelly's drunk-and-stupid file.

He turned to head out, but before he reached the door, he heard a familiar voice call his name. He turned to see Michelle Keller hurrying toward him, her blond curls seeming to have a life of their own and her blue eyes sparkling with a lust for life he found almost scary.

"What are you doing here in my world?" she asked as she reached where he stood.

"I had to talk to Beau Kelly."

"Oh." There was a wealth of disappointment in that single expression and he realized she'd thought he might be here to see her. She'd certainly made it clear Saturday night at Crazy's that she wouldn't be averse to him asking her out. "Did you find him?" She recovered quickly.

"Yeah, I just talked to him and two of his buddies."

"That would be Patrick and Eric. They're like the Three Musketeers." They both began to walk toward the exit. "I'm making a big pot of spaghetti Friday. Maybe you'd like to come over and share it with me?"

Rick waited until they stepped out of the school doors; then he turned to look at the pretty blonde he'd enjoyed talking to in the bar. "Look, Michelle, you're a nice, pretty lady, but I don't date."

"Then it won't be a date," she replied easily. "It will just be new acquaintances getting together to share a meal and some friendly conversation."

There was no question that Rick had been lonely since landing in the small town. While he'd had plenty of opportunities to go out with a variety of the single women in town, most of the time he'd felt like a swimmer in shark-infested waters.

There was no predatory gleam in Michelle's dancing blue eyes, only that lust for life that he'd once possessed.

"Come on, lawman, what have you got to lose?"

"What time?" His words surprised him as he thought he had no intention of accepting her invitation.

"Around six? Do you need my address?"

He smiled, the gesture foreign to his facial muscles. "As a lawman I should be able to figure out where you live."

"Great, then I'll see you Friday." She danced down the steps toward the parking lot, her hair glinting in the late-afternoon sun. He stuffed his hands in his pockets and headed toward his patrol car, parked in the lot opposite Michelle's car. He already regretted the acceptance of her invitation.

He'd call her later in the week and cancel. It wasn't fair to her. She couldn't know that she'd just made a date with a dead man.

Chapter 5

Seth Walker's business card was like one of those portrait paintings that, no matter where you stood in relationship to it, looked as if the person in the picture were staring at you.

The card lay on Allison's nightstand, where she'd placed it after coming home from Crazy's on Saturday night, but throughout Sunday, Monday and today she'd seen it in her mind no matter where she'd been or what she'd been doing.

She'd seen no more of the man himself since Saturday, but it was as if he were a ghost following her around the house and to and from work. She wondered why, after all these years, her father's conviction was suddenly getting a second glance. She'd filed away her personal history a long time ago, placed the crime and her father in a box she'd hoped to never open again.

More than anything, she hated the fact that Seth Walker had her thinking about any of this, that he'd tugged a small thread in the fabric of her life and if she wasn't careful, it would all begin to unravel and eventually leave her naked and shivering.

"Come on, Sam. We've got to go," she yelled from the front door. "You know Aunt Maureen hates it when we're late."

Dinner with her relatives was just what she needed

to take away the half-queasy feeling she'd had since first meeting Seth Walker. Maureen and David were wonderful at grounding her and making her feel safe and secure.

Sam's footsteps thundered down the hallway. "I hope Aunt Maureen made something good for dinner. I'm starving," he exclaimed.

Allison laughed and ruffled his hair. "You're always starving. Besides, when has Aunt Maureen ever made a crummy dinner?"

"Never," he agreed as they walked out of the house.

She locked the door and then glanced around the area before heading to the car. Although she hadn't seen Seth since Saturday night, every time she'd walked out of her house the last couple of days, she'd gotten a prickly feeling at the nape of her neck, the crazy, uncomfortable feeling that somebody was watching her.

The only person outside was her neighbor, an elderly man who lived alone. "Hi, Mr. Jacobs," Sam yelled to the old man, who was watering a bed of wilted flowers. The old man, remained focused on his task.

"He can't hear you, honey," Allison said. Ed Jacobs refused to get a hearing aid and was as deaf as a stump. He was a nice man with a pleasant smile, making Allison wonder if tuning out the world led to happiness.

"Aren't we gonna walk?" Sam asked as she pulled her car keys from her purse. It was customary when the weather was good for them to walk the two and a half blocks to Maureen and David's house.

"Not tonight," she said, and motioned him toward the car. "I don't feel like walking tonight." She couldn't shake the odd feeling of somebody watching her, a threat hovering just outside her vision.

"I heard through the grapevine that Uncle David got a new bunny," she said once they were in the car and on their way to the two-story house where Allison and Sam had lived for the first five years of his life.

"Cool," Sam replied. "What kind is it?"

"Aunt Maureen didn't say, but you know the rule. Dinner first, then you can visit the rabbits."

The bunnies were something of a joke. David had bought his first rabbit as an Easter surprise for Sam three years ago with the understanding that the bunny would reside at David and Maureen's house. David was so taken by the furry little creature that he'd become something of a bunny collector with a heated shed in his backyard devoted to the pets.

As they drove the short distance, Allison felt the tension of the past three days begin to ebb away. Sam chattered about his upcoming baseball practice on Saturday and the Pioneer Days celebration that would be taking place at the end of the month.

"You've got to ride the Hurricane with me this year, Mom," he said, referring to one of the more thrilling carnival rides that was set up every year for the town's celebration.

"Oh, I don't know about that, Sam. That ride gives me the willies just looking at it."

Sam giggled. "You're just a big chicken, Mom."

She clucked and smiled as Sam's giggles turned into full-blown laughter. There was no sweeter sound in the world, she thought as she pulled into Maureen and David's driveway.

Although Maureen and David's house was only a couple of blocks away from Allison's place, the two neighborhoods couldn't be more different. Allison's neighborhood was working-class, the homes modest by any measure. On the other hand Maureen and David lived in the affluent neighborhood of Crow's Creek, where the homes were bigger and yards were expansive and most of the wives didn't work unless they were volunteering their time for one project or another.

Maureen answered their knock and opened the

screen door to allow them entry. "Perfect timing," she exclaimed. "I just pulled the chicken out of the oven and everything is ready to serve." She air-kissed Allison's cheek, then patted Sam on the shoulder. "Run along and wash your hands, Sam. Uncle David is already at the table."

Maureen Donovan was a handsome rather than pretty woman. Her salt-and-pepper hair was cut short and worn brushed back from her strong facial features. She had worked as a secretary to the mayor for years and had even entertained the thought of running for mayor several years ago, but had decided she could do more good in the town by not being in office.

David, on the other hand, had worked a variety of jobs that included selling insurance and working at the hardware store, and the year before had officially retired. He was a quiet man who puttered around the house and seemed most at ease when in the company of his rabbits.

He rose from the table as Allison entered the dining room. "Hey, doll," he said, and pulled her into a bear hug. "Where's Sam?"

"Washing his hands." Allison took a seat at the table, knowing better than to offer any help to Maureen, who never accepted help and always had things well under control.

The table was, as always, set with the good dishes, and a fresh bouquet of flowers graced the center. The burgundy blossoms matched the wallpaper border in the room and added a touch of elegance to an ordinary Tuesday night meal.

Sam raced in from the bathroom and greeted his uncle with a quick hug, then took his place at the table. The food was excellent and the conversation was light and easy.

Maureen headed a committee in charge of the Pioneer Days celebration. "We've got fourteen floats in the parade this year," she said. "The parade is going to be the biggest ever."

"I know the junior class is working on a float," Allison replied. "It's going to be a huge crow and several of the teachers have been dyeing chicken feathers black for the last couple of weeks to attach to it."

Maureen frowned. "I hope it's not too Edgar Allan Poe–ish."

"Only if Poe wrote about a smiling raven wearing a hat in the school colors," Allison replied.

"Sounds goofy," Sam said.

Allison laughed. "I think it is going to be kind of goofy," she admitted.

"The sixth grade isn't making a float, but we're all gonna ride on Mr. Baxter's hay wagon," Sam said. "We're supposed to wear school T-shirts and wave to everyone. It's gonna be fun."

"Did you hear about Baxter's pasture?" Maureen asked.

Allison nodded. She'd heard about the cat heads found there. The kids in school had all been talking about it for the past two days. It was positively creepy to think that one of her students, or anyone else in this town, could have done such a thing.

"What about it?" Sam asked curiously.

"It's full of cow poop," David said, and Allison shot her uncle a grateful smile.

Sam finished eating first and looked at his mother with an appealing gaze. "Uncle David, is it okay if Sam goes out to visit the rabbits?" she asked.

David smiled at Sam. "Go on with you," he said. "You know the rules, only one out of the cage at a time and keep the shed door closed."

Before David had finished speaking, Sam was out of his chair and heading for the back door. The adults lingered at the table over coffee, small-talking as their food digested.

Allison hadn't mentioned Seth Walker to anyone. She hadn't even told Michelle about the handsome man who'd haunted her every thought since the moment he'd introduced himself to her. But sometimes in outing the monster, the monster became impotent, and she had a feeling the longer she didn't speak about him and what had brought him to town, the bigger he was growing in her mind.

She wrapped her fingers around the delicate porcelain of her coffee cup, seeking the warmth to battle the sudden chill that the very topic created inside her. "There's a man in town," she said. "His name is Seth Walker. He contacted me because he intends to reinvestigate the incident at the farmhouse."

The incident. That's the way Allison always thought about the horror of that day. The incident. Those words were so much easier for her mouth to form than *the massacre of my family.*

"What?" Maureen stared at her in stunned surprise. "Who is this man and what does he want?"

"His business card says he's a lawyer and a private investigator and works for Freedom Inc., whatever that is," Allison replied. "He told me with or without my help he's going to dig into the case, because he thinks Hank is innocent." There was no way Allison could refer to her father except by his proper name. It somehow made it less painful if Hank, not Daddy, had committed the horrible crime.

David shoved back from the table with such force his water glass overturned. "I won't have this," he shouted, the cords in his neck popping out. "It's over and done, has been done for years. I won't have some stranger come here and dredge it up all over again." He left the room, his feet stomping hard enough to shake the Waterford collection in the nearby curio cabinet.

Allison stared after him, vaguely aware of Maureen leaving the table to go into the kitchen. Allison hadn't considered what Maureen's and David's reactions might be when she told them about Seth Walker, but she was stunned by David's violent reaction.

Maureen reappeared with a towel that she used to dab up the spilled water. She didn't speak until the mess was cleaned up; then she returned to her chair and offered Allison a tight smile. "You must forgive your uncle. This has all been tremendously difficult for him."

"There's nothing to forgive," she replied.

Maureen ran a perfectly manicured finger around the rim of her coffee cup, her smile falling into a troubled frown. "We never talked about it. David was so devastated by what his brother did, he refused to discuss it with me or anyone else." She held Allison's gaze for a long moment. "And you and I never talked about it."

"I didn't want to talk about it. I didn't even want to think about it," Allison said vehemently.

"Do you want to talk about it now?"

"What's there to talk about? It happened a long time ago. Life goes on and there's no point in rehashing anything."

Maureen nodded in approval. "You're right. There's never any point in looking backward unless there's something you can learn from it. And nothing can be learned from that particular tragedy. Besides, if I were to guess, I'd bet this Seth Walker is working on a book or talking to a movie producer. At the time the crime happened, there were plenty of those kinds of people who showed up in town." She straightened her back. "But we shut them down. Nobody spoke to them. Nobody gave interviews or discussed anything with them. Crow's Creek protected its own."

Allison nodded and picked up her coffee cup, but the tepid liquid did nothing to banish her chill. "From my brief meeting with Mr. Walker he appeared to be a man determined to investigate with or without anyone's help."

"I'll do some checking and find out exactly what he's all about," Maureen said curtly. "Hank's guilt was never in question as far as Dane Kelly and his men were concerned. I don't know how much you know about how and where they found your father that day. You were indisposed at the time."

Indisposed. That's the way her aunt always referred to the time Allison had spent in the mental hospital, as if she'd been suffering a mild case of the flu. In reality Allison had consciously chosen to remain in the hospital until people stopped talking about the crime, until her father had been sent away, until life had felt somewhat safe again.

"I don't know a lot of the details," she finally replied. "They never seemed important before."

"And they aren't now," Maureen said briskly. "Why don't you run outside and look at that new rabbit with Sam. I'll take care of the dishes."

Allison didn't bother to protest. Maureen always cleared the dishes after they shared a meal. She couldn't stand anyone else puttering around in her kitchen.

The rabbit shed was half the size of a garage and better insulated and heated than most houses. Allison opened the door to find Sam on the floor with a large gray, lop-eared bunny. David stood at one of the cages, filling a bowl with pellets of food.

"Mom, isn't he cool?" Sam asked as he stroked the bunny's back.

David turned and offered Allison a sheepish smile. "Sorry I got a little excitable in there."

"It's all right," she replied easily. She had a feeling she and her uncle shared many of the same emotions where Hank Donovan was concerned. Allison's feelings for her father were conflicted at best.

She hated him for what he'd done, for how he'd destroyed everything she'd once held dear, but there was a tiny piece left deep in her heart that remembered the rich sound of his laughter, the scent of sawdust and Old Spice that clung to him whenever he gave her a hug. There was a little girl who'd desperately loved her daddy still inside her, and Allison hated that part of herself.

"Mom, Uncle David said if I get a cage and I promise that I'll take care of it, maybe I could have this bunny. He said we could even train it to use a cat litter box. Isn't that awesome?" Sam exclaimed.

Once again a sheepish smile crossed David's features. "I probably shouldn't have said anything without talking to you first."

Allison sighed. She'd known this was coming for a long time. Sam had become as enamored of the furry little creatures as David. "We'll talk about it," she said to her son. "And now it's time to put the bunny away and head home. If I recall, you still have homework to finish before bedtime."

Reluctantly Sam rose and picked up the bunny and carried it back to its cage. "I'll work on her, Uncle David," he said.

And he did. All the way home in the car Sam made promise after promise. He'd keep his grades up. He'd be responsible for cleaning the cage and feeding and watering Bugs, which he'd named the gray bunny he hoped to make his own. "He doesn't bark and he could stay in my room."

"We'll see how I feel about it this weekend," she finally said as she pulled into their driveway. Maybe on Saturday they could go to the pet store and check out the cages.

Over the past couple of years Sam had asked for a variety of pets, a dog or a cat. He was even taken by the idea of owning a goat after a visit to a petting zoo one year. Maybe a bunny was the best way to break him in as a pet owner.

She punched the remote to open the garage door and pulled inside. "Get busy on the homework," she called to Sam as he bounded out of the car and headed for the door that led into the utility room.

As she got out of the car, she felt that prickling sensation again, the impression of cold invisible fingers whispering against the nape of her neck. Instead of walking into the house, she stepped out of the garage and onto the driveway, half-expecting to see an obscure figure hiding in the bushes or lurking on the sidewalk.

She saw nobody. It was only then she realized she'd been waiting for Seth Walker to show up again, to try to talk to her again. She didn't even know if he was still in town, but she felt his presence everywhere like a thick shadow trying to consume her.

She'd never been curious about the details of what had happened that dusty day in the farmhouse. She'd always told herself that she knew all that she needed to know, that the man she'd trusted, the man she'd loved more than anyone else in the world, had, for whatever reason, snapped and become a murderer.

In all the years since the moment she'd awakened in the hospital and learned the full extent of the crime, she'd never entertained a moment's need to know anything more than that her family was dead and her father was responsible.

She hated Seth Walker. She knew little about the man, but she hated the fact that for the first time in fifteen years a tiny bit of curiosity had been stirred inside her.

He leaned with his back against the tree and held his breath, hoping she hadn't seen him from across the street. It was only when he heard the squeak of her garage door lowering that he breathed a sigh of relief.

Allison Clemmins. He found her fascinating. What was it like to survive what she had? Did she ever dream about that day? Did she wake up in the middle of the night screaming with nightmares that were memories of death?

He left the tree and hurried down the sidewalk away from the Clemminses' house, a smile curving his lips. Everyone in Crow's Creek had forgotten about what had happened fifteen years ago, but he hadn't.

The details of the murder were etched forever in his mind, bloody details that filled him with a thrilling exhilaration. He'd thought the cats would ease his hunger for the scent of blood. He'd believed it would be the kick of adrenaline he'd needed for so long, but the cats hadn't been enough. In fact, they had been only the beginning.

Chapter 6

The high school football field was deserted except for the three teenage boys who sat on the bleachers. In the height of football season the wooden bleachers would be filled with proud parents and students, despite the fact that the Crow's Creek Ravens had been a losing team for the past ten years. But football season had passed long ago and this was the second-best place to come to smoke a little dope and mellow out. The best place was Baxter's field, but Beau had worried that Deputy Solomon might be lurking around there trying to catch the crazed cat killer.

The football field was lit only by the spill of moonlight and the faint illumination from a nearby light pole. The April night was unusually hot, with an arid breeze that provided no relief.

They had driven to the ball field in Patrick's car, a five-year-old Chevy his father had bought him three days before. It had been bought after Patrick's mother had told him he didn't need a car.

Patrick took a deep draw off a joint and passed it to Beau. "I still can't believe your dad bought you a car," Eric said.

Patrick grinned, a wreath of smoke escaping through his teeth. "It's one of the bonuses of having divorced parents who hate each other."

"What did your mom say?" Beau asked as he passed the joint back to Patrick. They never offered it to Eric, who they knew from past experience refused to imbibe. If and when Eric became a cop, he didn't want to have to say that he'd smoked pot when he'd been a teenager.

"Mom screamed at him, telling him he was undermining her authority and shit like that. But if he would have bought me a candy bar, she'd say all the same things. I can't wait until I'm eighteen and don't have to listen to either one of them." He scowled and took another hit of marijuana.

For a few minutes they were all silent, the only sound the intake of breath as Beau and Patrick shared the dope. It was usual for the teens to spend their Friday nights together, but on most Saturday nights Beau or Patrick had a date.

"Did you see Callie Winston today?" Patrick asked, and then continued without giving anyone a chance to respond. "I swear her tits get bigger every day. With that tight T-shirt she had on, she looked like she was sporting twin bazookas in her bra."

"Fake," Beau said. "She wears bras that are full of some kind of gel."

Patrick clutched his chest. "Jeez, I wish you hadn't told me that. She was gonna be my fantasy woman for the night." He looked at Beau. "And how do you know this?"

Beau grinned. "I screwed her a month ago."

"If I got laid as often as you do, my dick would be as skinny as a pencil from all that wear and tear," Patrick exclaimed.

"Your dick *is* as skinny as a pencil," Eric replied dryly.

"Ha, very funny," Patrick replied, and elbowed Eric in the ribs. Patrick looked at Beau once again. "I guess that's one of the bonuses of being the sheriff's son. All the girls want to screw you."

"I like to think it's because I'm charming and good-looking," Beau replied, then frowned. "It would be nice if people called me by my name. Half the people in this town always call me the sheriff's boy."

"Don't feel bad," Patrick said. "I'm always the son of crazy Linda and crazier Peter. At least your parents have never had a screaming match in the middle of Main Street, and my parents do that as often as they change their underwear." He took the last puff on the joint, then stubbed it out on the wooden bleacher next to him. "Let's go get some burgers. I'm starving."

It was almost one in the morning when Rick entered Emma's Café. Besides the waitress, who looked tired and cranky, there was only one other person in the place. Eric Grant. The scrawny teenager sat in one of the booths in the back, a cup of coffee in front of him.

"You're too young to be drinking that," Rick said as he scooted into the seat across from Eric.

Eric grinned. "I'm too young to drink a beer, but I'm not too young to drink a cup of coffee."

"What are you doing here all alone so late on a Friday night?" Rick asked, and signaled the waitress for a cup of coffee.

Eric's eyes flashed with something wild and dark. It was there only a moment, then gone beneath his crooked smile. "I never go home on Friday nights. Emma pays me to sweep the floor and clean up when this place closes at two. Then she has a cot in the back and I always crash there for the night."

The waitress arrived with a mug and the coffeepot. "Anything else I can get for you?" she asked as she poured the coffee. It was obvious by her tone of voice that she would have preferred he go anywhere else but here for whatever he wanted.

"No thanks, this is fine," Rick replied. As she left the

booth, Rick picked up the mug and took a sip, unsurprised to find the coffee strong and bitter and tasting as if it had been in the pot far too long.

"Bad, isn't it?" Eric said.

Rick nodded. "Not good," he agreed. "Your parents, don't they worry when you stay out all night?"

Eric traced an old scar on the wooden booth top with the fingernail of one of his index fingers. Rick noticed that the fingernail was both neatly trimmed and clean. "It's just my dad and me. My mom left a long time ago. Anyway, Dad's payday is Fridays. He usually spends his Friday nights at Terrible's Tavern. By the time he gets home, he doesn't know if I'm there or not."

And doesn't care. Although Eric didn't actually say the words, something in his tone of voice implied them.

"So, what are you doing out at this time of night? You aren't in uniform, so you must not be on duty." Eric grabbed a packet of sugar and tore off the top, then dumped it into his half-filled mug.

There was no way Rick could tell the young man that he'd been driven from his bed by grief and guilt, that the simple act of sharing a spaghetti dinner with Michelle Keller had evoked the weight of broken dreams, the weary ache of loss, making sleep impossible.

"Couldn't sleep," he finally said. "I tossed and turned for a couple of hours, then decided to get up and take a walk and here I am."

Eric took a sip of his coffee, his eyes studying Rick over the rim of his mug. "I heard you were from Chicago," he said as he lowered the mug back to the table.

"That's right."

"You must have seen a lot of bad crime there."

"More than I like to remember," Rick replied. "Is it true what your friends told me, that you want to be a profiler someday?"

"Definitely, but even if I don't make it as a profiler, I

want to be an FBI agent and investigate serial murders. I've been studying famous killers for the last year. Did you know we had sort of a famous murder right here in Crow's Creek years ago?"

"No, I didn't know that." Rick hadn't had time since coming to town to study all the files of past crimes in the small town.

"The Donovan case. Hank Donovan killed his wife and two of his kids with a hatchet. You know Allison Clemmins, the teacher?" Rick nodded and Eric continued, his voice squeaking high, then tumbling low as his eyes burned almost feverishly. "It was her family, but she survived the attack. She's totally awesome and she's beautiful."

It was obvious the boy suffered a heartfelt crush on Allison Clemmins. As he continued to talk about how nice she was, how he liked her smile, Rick felt a pang of sympathy as he remembered his own first high school crush. The girl's name was Belinda. She'd been a hot, blond cheerleader a year older than him, and despite the fact that his heart had burned with love for her, she'd never acknowledged his existence in any way.

Rick wanted to tell the boy to hang tight, that eventually the right girl would come along and it would be the right time to build a future together, but then he remembered that sometimes the right girl came along and tragedy occurred and the future exploded into pieces of what might have been.

Just that quickly Rick was beyond weary. He drained his coffee cup and stood. "Guess I'll head back home. I'm on duty in the morning and it's going to be a short night as it is."

"You sure you have to go?" Eric asked, a touch of hunger in his blue eyes.

You sure you have to go, Daddy? Stay home with me today. The inner childish voice haunted Rick, bringing with it a rush of regrets and the grief that never, ever completely went away.

"Yeah, I really have to go," he replied. He needed to be away from this teenage boy, who oddly reminded him of what he'd lost. "I'll see you later, Eric."

He walked away from the booth and out into the dry, hot night, chased by the ghosts of bad decisions, cruel fate and the eyes of a little boy who hadn't lived to see his eighth birthday.

Chapter 7

The bunny operation, that's how Allison saw her Saturday unfolding.

Her uncle David had shown up that morning with a load of wood and a roll of wire and had announced that instead of purchasing a cage for a rabbit, it would be much better if he and Sam built a hutch in the backyard.

Sam had decided building a hutch would be a much better way to spend his Saturday than playing baseball, so Allison had called his coach to say he wouldn't be at practice.

For the past two hours the air had rung with the sound of hammering and laughter. More than once as Allison had gone about her morning chores, she'd paused to stand at the back window and watch the work, enjoying the smiles on both male faces as they chattered about bunnies and the hutch.

Now it was time for her to call a halt to the work in progress. Before David had unexpectedly shown up that morning, Michelle had called to ask Allison and Sam to meet her for lunch at Emma's Café. It was now a quarter until twelve and Allison hadn't been able to get hold of Michelle to cancel.

She opened up the back door and stepped outside. "Sam, fifteen minutes and then you need to clean up. I promised Michelle we'd meet her for lunch."

"Ah, Mom," he exclaimed, obviously dismayed. "I don't want to go to lunch with you and Ms. Keller. You guys will just talk about girl stuff." It was true. Allison had a feeling Michelle wanted to tell her about her dinner date with Rick Solomon the night before.

"Why don't you go ahead?" David said. "Sam and I can fix ourselves some peanut butter and jelly sandwiches if we get hungry, and I was thinking maybe when we finish up here, he could just come home with me and spend the night. I've got some books on rabbit care that Sam hasn't read yet."

Sam's face lit up. "Can I, Mom?"

"You could pick him up tomorrow when you come for lunch," David said. "And we'll have Bugs ready to come here to his new home tomorrow."

"Awesome," Sam exclaimed.

Allison laughed. "How can I possibly be the one to throw a monkey wrench into such plans? Sam, make sure you get clean underwear and socks for tomorrow. And, Uncle David, if you could be sure and lock up here when you guys leave."

"No problem," David agreed as he laid a hand on Sam's shoulder. "I think your aunt Maureen has some meeting or another tonight, so you and I can have a real male-bonding night."

"Cool," Sam replied.

Fifteen minutes later Allison was in her car and headed for the café, knowing her son would be well taken care of for the night. It was another hot, dusty day despite it being only April. She kept her windows rolled up tight and turned the air conditioner on high, feeling as if she might melt before she got to the café.

As much as she adored her son, it would be more pleasant to lunch with Michelle without his presence. Sam was usually well behaved, but he couldn't help the flashes of impatience that often decorated his handsome little face and the overburdened sighs he emitted when she and Michelle got together for a gabfest.

As she drove down Main Street, she passed beneath a colorful banner stretched from one light pole to another advertising Pioneer Days. Prom was next weekend and the Pioneer Days celebration was the following weekend. Before she knew it, school would be out for the summer.

Usually summers were spent here. She worked on the yard and Sam spent his days at the community pool or with friends, but this summer she was thinking about maybe taking a week and driving to Durango, Colorado.

She and Sam could rent a little cabin, visit the historic town and take the coal-fired steam engine up the mountain to the old mining town of Silverton. Sam would love the experience and Allison thought a week away from the promised drought and heat sounded like heaven.

As she found a parking space near Emma's and pulled in, she made a mental note to do a little checking on the Internet about rooms and things to do in Durango.

It was only as she walked from her car to the café door that she realized why Durango had popped into her mind. When she was twelve, her family had all gone on vacation together to the mountain town.

She could still remember her father patiently showing her how to bait a hook with a fat night crawler, his laughter warming her as she squealed. For a single moment the memory of a campfire and her mother's singing while they all made S'mores burned bright in her head, deep in her heart.

She'd felt her father's love that night, not just for herself and her two siblings, but she'd seen his eyes gleam with it as he'd looked at his wife. In that moment, with melted chocolate and gooey marshmallow on her chin, she'd believed nothing could touch them, that they would all be together, loving one another forever.

She snapped the memory from her mind and decided

she'd rather go to Iraq than back to Durango, where those haunting memories of her father's love and her family's happiness might find her. In the aftermath of the murders, those memories felt only like hurtful lies.

At this hour on a Saturday afternoon Emma's bustled with customers. "You alone today or are you meeting somebody?" Emma asked as she greeted her.

"I'm meeting Michelle, but she's always late," Allison replied.

The booths were all full, but Emma found an empty table and led Allison to it. "I'll send one of the waitresses over when Michelle gets here," Emma exclaimed, then hurried back to the cash register, where a patron was waiting to pay.

Allison leaned back in her chair to wait for her friend. Michelle was always one of the first teachers to arrive at school for the workday, but she'd never been on time for any social event, no matter how big or how small.

Allison smiled and nodded at several people she knew, then picked up the menu and looked at it even though she'd memorized the fare years ago.

As she stared unseeing at the words, a sudden sense of loneliness slammed into her. It was the same kind of loneliness she'd felt in the days and weeks immediately following Bobby's death.

The return of the emotion surprised her. She closed her menu and reached for her water glass. As she took a sip of the ice water, she wondered what had brought it back.

Six months after Bobby's death she'd consciously willed that emotion out of her life. With a baby to raise and a degree in education to obtain, she didn't have time to indulge the ache that at times threatened to consume her.

Maybe she was feeling it now because Sam was growing more independent with each passing day, or perhaps that unexpected memory of the family vacation to Durango had stirred up an incredible feeling of loss and loneliness inside her.

In any case she was immensely grateful to see Michelle fly through the door, blond curls bobbing and lips curved up in a ready smile. "Sorry I'm late," she said as she joined Allison at the table. "Where's Sam?"

"With my uncle David. They're building a bunny hutch in the backyard. Then Sam is spending the night over at their place."

"Then you want to get drinks later? Go to Crazy's?"

"No, thanks," Allison replied without hesitation. The last thing she needed was a drink or two on top of the melancholy mood that had settled like an old shawl around her shoulders. Right now the thought of going to Crazy's tonight was about as appealing as cleaning a toilet.

"I'm just planning a quiet night. I have papers to grade before Monday and tonight is the perfect opportunity to get them done."

The conversation was interrupted by the appearance of the waitress to take their orders.

It wasn't until their meals were served that Allison brought up the topic she knew Michelle wanted to talk about most. "So, how did it go last night with Rick?"

Michelle frowned thoughtfully. "I'm not sure."

Allison looked at her friend in surprise. "What do you mean, you aren't sure?"

Michelle set her fork down as if she couldn't eat and talk at the same time, which Allison knew was ridiculous because Michelle could talk and do everything at the same time.

"Things were a bit awkward at first. You know how first dates always go—there's the initial floundering around. I could tell he was nervous, but by the time we started eating, he'd relaxed a bit."

She picked up her fork once again and speared a slice of cucumber from her salad. "He told me a little about being a cop in Chicago and I told him a little about my divorce. Not too much, but just enough that he'd know that I've put it all behind me and am ready to move on. We finished eating and even though I protested, he insisted he help clean up the kitchen."

"Sounds like a great first date," Allison observed.

Michelle's frown deepened. "I like him, Allison, I really do. He gives me butterflies in my stomach."

"I don't know about butterflies," Allison replied.

Michelle popped the cucumber into her mouth and chewed. "Bobby didn't give you butterflies?"

Allison shook her head. "No butterflies. From the moment we met in third grade, we took one look at each other and knew we were going to be best friends and someday marry and spend the rest of our lives together."

A whisper of dark depression nudged into her head and she straightened her shoulders as if to cast it off. Never look back; that had been her motto from the moment she'd come to in the hospital following the slaughter of her family. The past held nothing but pain.

"So, what happened with Rick?" she asked in an attempt to drive the conversation back on track.

"I'm not sure. After we cleaned the kitchen, I poured us each a glass of wine and suggested we move into the living room. He sat for about ten minutes; then all of a sudden he insisted he needed to leave. It was so strange, so abrupt, and he had such a sadness in his eyes." Michelle leaned back and sighed. "I can't figure out what I did wrong."

Allison smiled. "Why does it have to be something you did wrong?" For months after Michelle's divorce she had obsessed about why her husband had cheated on her, on what she could have done differently to keep him happy and at home. She didn't seem to understand that the problem was that she'd married a man who was morally corrupt.

The two ate in silence for a few minutes. Allison felt the melancholy inside her transforming to something different, something edgy and tense. This was a feeling more familiar. She'd felt it off and on since the moment Seth Walker had shown up at her front door. It was the expectation of something happening, something unforeseen and not necessarily welcomed.

"You need to be dating," Michelle said when she'd finished her salad.

"Why?" Allison asked.

Michelle's eyes flashed with impatience. "Because that's what single people do, because Sam isn't always going to be a little boy. What are you going to do when he grows up, goes to college and has a life of his own?"

"Get a cat," Allison replied with a grin.

"You're allergic to cats."

"Then I'll get a dog."

"What do you have against men?" Michelle pressed.

Allison laughed. "I don't have anything against men. I just don't need one in my life."

"Well, I don't *need* one, but that doesn't mean I wouldn't like somebody to look at across the breakfast table in the mornings, or cuddle me on a cold and windy wintry night."

"Don't look now, but the man you'd most like to cuddle just came in," Allison said as she saw Sheriff Kelly and Rick enter the café. The two men took a booth by the front window.

Michelle's hands flew first to her hair, then to the front of her blouse. "Damn, I knew I should have put on that cute little pink blouse instead of this old thing. Did he see me? Is he looking over here?"

"No, he's not looking and I don't think he saw you. Just

relax—you look fine. Besides, that pink blouse of yours makes you look pregnant." Michelle looked stricken and Allison laughed. "Just kidding. Jeez, you are wound tight about this guy."

"He's the first man I've really been interested in since my divorce," Michelle replied.

"Then I hope things work out for you with him." As the door to the café opened again, Allison felt the breath whoosh out of her as Seth Walker entered.

Thankfully he didn't see her, but rather walked directly to where Dane and Rick sat in the booth. Allison felt as if she'd been kicked in the gut by a mule. She'd hoped he'd left town. She'd hoped he'd dropped his insane plans to investigate the murders. But as she watched him shake hands with both men and slide into the booth, the edgy anxiety that she'd fought for the past week exploded inside her.

A roar like the rush of the wind filled her ears and she wanted to jump up and run, run from the man who had haunted her for the past week, who'd brought back nightmares of images she'd thought she didn't possess.

"Allison, are you all right? You're white as a sheet."

Michelle's voice seemed to come from very far away. Allison nodded as the wind finally hushed. "I'm fine. Could you excuse me for just a minute?" She balled up her napkin and stood.

At some point during the brief rush of the wind through her brain, she'd made a decision. She walked over to where the three men sat. As she approached, Seth saw her and straightened his shoulders, as if in anticipation of a battle.

"May I speak to you in private for a moment?" she asked.

He nodded and stood. She'd forgotten how tall he was, how solid and imposing with his broad shoulders and long, lean legs. She'd also forgotten how the coolness of his gray eyes reminded her of winter skies. He followed her toward the register, where at the moment nobody stood.

"I'd hoped you'd left town," she said.

"As you can see, I'm still here."

"I can only assume you're talking to Dane and Rick about the murders." The word felt ugly on her lips. She didn't wait for his reply. "If you intend to go around town talking about me and my family, then I think maybe it's time you and I talked. Can you come to my house this afternoon, say around five?"

His eyes warmed a bit. "I'll be there."

Allison nodded curtly, then strode back to the table, fighting her impulse to turn back and cancel the plans, the impulse to run home, pack her bags and get out of town and away from Seth Walker.

She was grateful to slide back into her seat at the table. Her legs had begun to wobble as a burst of nerves assaulted her. "Who is that?" Michelle asked.

"His name is Seth Walker. He wants to reinvestigate the murder of my family."

"Why?" Michelle's eyes had widened.

"He thinks my father might be innocent."

"And what do you think?" Michelle asked softly.

"I think by the time he's finished here in Crow's Creek, I'm going to wish I'd never heard his name." Allison picked up her water glass and took a sip, wishing the cold liquid could wash away the crushing dread and fear that consumed her.

Seth had kept a low profile for the past week. He'd used the microwave for most of his meals and spent his time reading over the reams of paperwork he possessed concerning the Donovan case.

He'd hoped to hear from Allison. Twice he'd driven

back to the Donovan farmhouse and sat on the porch thinking about the crime that had taken place so many years before.

He'd seen the crime-scene photos and they were the most gruesome pictures he'd ever seen. The first one of Joleen Donovan seated on the sofa with her head in her lap had been bad enough. But it had been the photos of ten-year-old Johnny and seven-year-old Jennifer that had ripped Seth apart, that had haunted him months after he'd first viewed them.

Jennifer had been found in her bed, her arms wrapped around a stuffed dog and the blankets pulled up to her neck. She might have looked as if she were peacefully sleeping if it hadn't been for her protruding tongue, her bulging eyes and the red dots of petechiae that had mottled her face due to the rupture of blood vessels where she'd been strangled.

Johnny had been strangled as well, but he'd also suffered a tremendous blow to the head. He'd been found propped up at his desk, as if preparing to draw a masterpiece with one of the colored pencils in the packet next to his hands.

Then there had been Allison. She'd been hit hard enough in the back of her head that she'd been rendered unconscious for three days. She'd been found in her bed. Her neck bore the marks of strangulation, but somehow she had survived.

The reports indicated that they had all been attacked near the front door and in the living room, but the bodies had been moved postmortem. The reports also stated that school for the younger children had dismissed early for a teacher planning day, and it was suspected that the killer hadn't expected them to be home.

As Seth returned to his seat in the booth next to Rick Solomon, the last thing on his mind was the crime-scene photos. He'd finally called Sheriff Kelly that morning to set up this meeting. The sheriff had agreed to meet him during his lunch break.

He'd been stunned by Allison's invitation to her house. What had changed her mind about talking to him? He shoved thoughts of her away and eyed the man who had been the first responder on the scene.

"Before we were interrupted, you said you wanted to discuss the Donovan murder," Dane said. "What's your interest in that old case?"

"I think Hank Donovan is innocent. I'm hoping to find some new evidence in order to get him a new trial," Seth replied.

Dane shook his head. "That's a tall order. I've never seen so much evidence pointing to one man in all my years in law enforcement."

"This is the second time in two days that the Donovan case has come up," Rick said. "Eric Grant mentioned it to me last night."

Dane grinned. "In his next life Eric would like to come back as the Jodie Foster character in *Silence of the Lambs*. That boy has got murder on his mind. Of course, if he's interested in the Donovan case, I imagine it's because it involves Allison Clemmins. According to Beau, that boy has a first-class crush on his English teacher."

"I was wondering if you had any old notes, maybe things that didn't make it into the official case file, that I could look at," Seth asked.

Dane's smile fell away. "Everything I had was in the case file. That was my first murder case as sheriff and I did everything by the book." There was an edge of defensiveness in his voice.

"I'm not questioning your competency as an officer of the law," Seth assured him. The last thing he wanted to do was step on toes that might make his investigation here more difficult. "I was just wondering if maybe there was something, anything, you might have remembered since then that didn't get into the official report."

The sheriff suddenly looked haggard. The corners of his mouth turned down and all his facial muscles relaxed into a general sag. "Every moment of that terrible day is burned into my memory. Until then all I'd had to deal with was breaking up fights down at Terrible's Tavern and a robbery at the convenience store out on the highway. Nothing prepared me for what I found when I walked into the Donovan house that day."

"Catch me up to speed," Rick said. "I hadn't heard anything about it until last night when Eric mentioned it."

Dane sighed and reached for his coffee cup. He picked it up and stared into it, as if wishing it were something stronger than Emma's special blend. "It was six o'clock in the evening when I got the call. It was Hank Donovan. He sounded drunk or drugged or both. He told me he had a situation at the house and I'd better get out there." Dane took a sip of his coffee, then continued. "There was nothing in that phone call to prepare me for what I found when I walked through the Donovan front door."

He set his cup down. Both Rick and Seth waited patiently for the big man to gather his thoughts. The waitress approached the table, but Seth waved her away, not wanting Dane's train of thought to be broken.

"I walked in that front door and Hank was sitting on the sofa next to Joleen. He had a hatchet in one hand and was holding her hand in the other. There was no question she was dead. Her head was in her lap and there was blood everywhere." He shook his head. "I thought that was the worst of it and then I found the kids."

Again a long silence ensued. It was Seth who finally broke it. "And there was never any question in your mind that Hank was responsible?"

"Hell yes, there was a question. I wouldn't be a good lawman if I rushed to justice and formed an immediate opinion," Dane replied with a flash of irritation. "Hank was incoherent the night of the murder and for some days afterward. We couldn't get any kind of a story from him. What we did know is that eyewitnesses put him at home at four thirty. The coroner estimated the time of death for the victims between three and five. There was no forensic evidence indicating that anyone else had been in the house, no strangers lurking about in the area, no sign of forced entry anywhere. My team followed the evidence, then turned over what we had to the prosecuting attorney. We couldn't help that all the evidence pointed to Hank Donovan. Now, you want to tell me why you think we got it wrong?"

There was no way that Seth could say that he *did* believe there had been a rush to justice, that he thought the entire town had been willing to lynch a man so they could sleep easier at night knowing the vicious murderer was behind bars.

He couldn't tell Dane Kelly that he thought the evidence-collection process had been less than stellar and that leads had not been followed to their conclusion. Seth believed Dane Kelly and his men had done the best they could, but youth and inexperience couldn't be denied.

More than anything Seth couldn't explain to the sheriff that believing in Hank Donovan's innocence was a gut feeling he had, one that had grown stronger each time he'd interviewed the convicted killer.

Seth already had his story in place, a story that absolved him from any tension with the locals. "I work as an investigator for a firm called Freedom Inc. Apparently Hank Donovan contacted the agency and asked for their help in getting him a new trial. I don't know what criteria was used to determine his eligibility for our services. All I know is that I was sent here to investigate the old crime and that's what I intend to do."

This explanation kept him from being the enemy. He was just a working stiff following orders.

"Folks aren't going to be happy with you stirring up old memories," Dane observed. "Those were dark days for this town. Damn dark days."

Seth nodded. "I'll tread as lightly as I can. I'm not expecting much to come out of this, but I wanted to talk to you and let you know what I was doing here. Professional courtesy and all that."

"I appreciate it," Dane replied. "You need anything while you're here in town, you come to me or Rick, and we'll see what we can do to accommodate you."

"Thanks." Seth rose from the table, the politics done for now. "I'll just let you finish your lunch in peace. I appreciate you taking the time to meet with me."

As Seth left the restaurant, his thoughts immediately went back to Allison. She'd stunned him with her invitation to meet her at her house. He tried to tamp down his excitement. It was possible she had agreed to meet with him to serve him with a restraining order or to tell him to drop dead.

There had been a fire in her blue eyes that had been impossible for him to read in those brief moments she'd spoken to him. He glanced at his watch.

He had three hours to kill before he found out if Allison intended to help him or kick him in the ass to help him on his way out of town.

Mary Kelly had first fallen in love with Dane when she'd been a freshman and he'd been a junior in high school, and all these years later she was still as madly, desperately in love with him.

He was a complicated man who could be gregarious and charming, but was also given to long silences that often made Mary feel left out and abandoned. She told herself that it was probably because of his job. She could look back in time and pinpoint the exact moment that those long silences had been born, and it had been on the night he'd returned from the death scene at the Donovan house.

The horrendous nature of the murders had forever scarred the man who had investigated them. Although he'd never discussed the murders with her, she'd seen the horror reflected in his eyes, heard the sounds of his tortured dreams for nights afterward.

She now stood in front of the stove, one eye on the clock and one on the pot of boiling spaghetti noodles. Using a wooden spoon, she stirred the sauce that warmed on the burner next to the cooking pasta, then set the spoon down and glanced at the table.

Dane would be home within the next ten minutes and he would expect the evening meal to be on the table. He was an orderly man, most comfortable with routine when he was home. Mary understood. In his work as sheriff he was at the whim of fate with rarely a warning of trouble, with no way to prepare for what might be around the next corner. That's why it was important that when he was home there were no surprises.

Saturday night was always spaghetti night. Dane always arrived home between five fifteen and five thirty. He wasn't officially on duty on Saturday nights, although he wore his uniform until bedtime just in case he got a call from one of his deputies or an emergency arose.

"Don't you ever get tired of cooking the same stuff all the time?" Beau asked as he came into the kitchen. Felix, the small brown mutt that had been a member of the household since Beau had been five, stood and crossed the room to where Beau stood.

Mary turned to smile at her son as he bent down and scrubbed the old dog around his ears. If there was anyone she loved almost as much as her husband, it was the tall teenager standing in front of her in a pair of gym shorts and without a shirt. "Your father likes the things I cook."

"Oh yeah, and we always have to keep King Dane happy." Beau straightened and grabbed a bottle of Gatorade from the fridge. Felix returned to his position next to the chair where Dane always sat for dinner. "Guess I'd better go pull on a shirt 'cause I know the king doesn't like to see me bare-chested at the table."

"I don't like you without a shirt at the table," Mary exclaimed. "It isn't good manners."

Beau walked over to her and looped an arm around her shoulder. He gave her a smacking kiss on the forehead. "Don't worry, Ma. You've raised me right. Nobody ever says Beau Kelly is bad mannered."

She laughed and playfully smacked his cheek. "I'd better not ever hear anyone say that. Now, get that shirt on before your father gets home." She pushed him toward the kitchen doorway.

As he left the room, her heart expanded with pride. Beau hadn't been a planned pregnancy. At least, not planned for by Dane. She and Dane had dated all through high school; then upon graduation he'd joined the army and found his niche working as an MP.

For the four years he'd been away from Crow's Creek, Mary had stayed true to him, writing to him every day, hoping and praying that when he returned home, he'd still be in love with his small-town girlfriend.

They'd resumed dating when he'd returned, but he seemed in no hurry to make things legal between them. She'd been twenty-four when she'd decided to stop taking her birth control pills. She wanted Dane's baby, but more, she hoped that if she got pregnant, it would force him to make the commitment she wanted from him.

Her plan had worked perfectly. She got pregnant, they got married and within a year Dane had been elected sheriff.

She'd never confessed that she'd intentionally tried to get pregnant to force his hand. There were some secrets you didn't even share with the person you loved most in the world. Besides, it had been the right decision. They were happy and had a good life together.

The back door creaked open and Dane came inside on a breeze of hot dry air. "Hmm, smells good," he said as he walked to where she stood, and kissed her cheek. Felix danced at his feet, his little butt wiggling with happiness at the sight of the man who had saved him from a cardboard box when he'd been a puppy.

"I'll have it on the table in about two minutes," she replied. "How was your day?"

He smiled. "Nobody got shot or robbed, so I suppose that makes it a good day." He reached down to pet the dog and then headed for the doorway. "I'm just going to go wash up."

As he left the kitchen, Mary bustled about, draining the noodles, then pouring them into a serving bowl and adding the sauce and meatballs on top. Once that was on the kitchen table, she grabbed a salad from the refrigerator and the garlic bread from the oven, then filled the water glasses at each plate.

By that time Beau had drifted back in, now clad in a pair of jeans and a T-shirt advertising one of his favorite bands. He sat at his place at the table and tore off a piece of the bread. "I'm starving."

Mary smiled. "You're always starving."

"It's a characteristic of a teenage boy," Dane said as he entered the kitchen. He clapped a hand on Beau's back, then took his seat. Felix took his place at the foot of Dane's chair, waiting for the table scraps that the dog knew Dane would sneak to him. "We need to keep Beau well fed and strong, because as soon as school is out, I've got him set up with a job."

"You've set me up with a job?" Beau looked at his father in horror as Mary joined them at the table. "If you wanted me to get a job, I can find my own."

"I've already got it set up," Dane replied firmly. "Wayne Fenton has agreed to take you on as his assistant in the garage at the gas station, said he'd be happy to have the sheriff's boy working for him."

Beau's face flushed red. "Wayne is a freakin' weirdo."

"Beau!" Mary admonished her son with a stern look.

"Well, he is," Beau replied with mulish stubbornness. "He thinks he's some kind of superhero when he teaches his karate classes. You never see him with a woman. He's never married. I think he's some kind of perv."

"He's no more a pervert than you are," Dane exclaimed as he served himself a mound of spaghetti. "Only problem Wayne has is that he's shy. Besides, working will be good for you, and working at the garage will teach you some basic mechanic skills. I don't want you hanging around all summer long without purpose. Idle hands are the devil's work and all that."

"By the way, I picked up your tux for the prom today," Mary said to her son. "White, just like you wanted."

Dane groaned. "Let's not talk about prom. I'll probably have to work all night long corralling underage drunks and breaking up fights." He looked at Beau. "And you better not be one of the drunks I have to get under control. You know that you're a reflection of me no matter where you are or what you're doing."

"I know, Dad. I don't have any intention of getting drunk and stupid," Beau exclaimed.

For the next few minutes the talk turned to other things, the upcoming Pioneer Days celebration, the end of the school year and the drought that was predicted by all the weathermen.

"I heard your newest deputy had a date last night," Mary said.

Dane raised an eyebrow. "Rick?" She nodded and Dane leaned back in his chair and grinned. "He didn't mention a word about it to me. How come you stay home most days and still always know more gossip than me?"

She laughed. "Because there's nothing the women of Crow's Creek love more to do than gossip."

"Who did he go out with?" Beau asked.

"Michelle Keller," Mary replied.

"She's hot," Beau exclaimed.

"I thought it was Allison Clemmins that all the boys had a crush on," Dane said.

"She's hot, too," Beau agreed.

"Speaking of Allison, I had an interesting talk with a guy named Seth Walker today at lunch," Dane said. "He's from Kansas City and he's here in town to reinvestigate the Donovan murders. Seems the organization he works for thinks Hank Donovan is innocent."

"I'll bet you're nervous," Beau said with just a slight edge of glee in his voice.

"Why would that make me nervous?" Dane asked his son. "I did my job to the best of my ability. As far as I'm concerned, Hank Donovan is right where he belongs, in prison for the rest of his life, and there's no way Seth Walker is going to change that."

Mary couldn't help the niggle of fear that sliced through her. She hoped Dane was right. She hoped Seth Walker just went away. The last thing she wanted was for the Donovan murders to be reinvestigated.

Chapter 8

Allison stood in the kitchen and stared out the window at the newly constructed bunny hutch. She'd arrived home just in time to say good-bye to Sam and her uncle as they left, their mission accomplished and a night of male bonding ahead of them.

She'd spent the past two hours wondering what on earth had possessed her to talk to Seth, to invite him here. She didn't want to go back where he wanted to take her, had spent most of her adult life consciously not thinking about the things Seth most wanted to discuss. So why had she invited him into her home, into her life even briefly?

Curiosity. There was no other answer. Since the moment he'd first introduced himself to her and told her why he was here, he'd stirred a curiosity inside her she'd never entertained before.

"And everyone knows what curiosity did to the cat," she murmured aloud as she turned away from the window. Her gaze went to the clock on the oven. Fifteen minutes and he'd be here. In fifteen minutes her curiosity would be sated and hopefully she could put this all behind her once again and never look back.

She went into the utility room, where the load of towels she'd put into the washing machine was finished. It took her only a minute to transfer them from the washer to the dryer; then she drifted back into the kitchen.

She fixed a pot of coffee even though she wasn't sure she had any intentions of offering him a cup, then went into the living room and sat on the sofa and stared at the wall across from her. There was nothing she could tell Seth that would help him in his investigation. She hadn't seen anyone on that terrible day before she'd been knocked unconscious.

Nervously twirling a finger through a strand of her hair, she wondered what Hank had said or done that had made a man like Seth Walker and the agency he worked for go to the trouble of reinvestigating. He certainly would have proclaimed his innocence, but didn't every man in prison loudly and frequently proclaim innocence to anyone who would listen?

As she thought of the past week, she remembered those moments when she'd felt as if she was being watched. There had been a part of her that had thought Seth had left town and had suspected that Eric Grant was stalking her, but now she was back to thinking maybe it had been Seth watching her . . . waiting for her to break.

And she had broken.

And she hated him for making her remember that day, for making her think about the father she'd written off as dead. She hated him for producing the knot of tension that had clenched in her stomach for the past week, the feeling that something horrible was going to happen at any moment.

She winced as she pulled her hair and dropped her hand back into her lap. If Sam had been home, she would never have invited Seth here. Sam knew very little about what had happened on that dusty day fifteen years ago. He knew that his grandpa had done something bad and was in prison and that his grandmother and Allison's brother and sister had all died. She'd had to tell him that much in case the subject ever came up from somebody in town, but he didn't know the details. He didn't know the brutality of the kill, and he'd never asked questions about it.

Sam had been far more curious about Bobby. Allison had given her son as much information about Bobby as she could, hoping to give him an intimate glimpse into the man who was his father.

Even though she was expecting it, when the doorbell rang, she jumped. She rose to her feet and drew a deep breath, afraid she was about to be taken back to the moment of her worst nightmare.

He'd changed clothes since she'd seen him in the café. The blue dress shirt gave his slate gray eyes a warmer hue than she remembered. That was her first thought when she opened her door to him.

His smile was hesitant as he shifted a bulky file folder from one arm to the other. "Regretting your invitation to me?" he asked.

She lifted her chin. "What makes you think that?"

"You have a death grip on the door and I'm not sure if you intend to open it wider or slam it in my face."

She opened the door to allow him inside. As he passed her, she caught the scent of his cologne, a spicy fragrance with that hint of sandalwood that she might have found appealing under different circumstances.

Mistake. This is a big mistake. The words played in her head as she gestured him toward the kitchen. She didn't want him sitting on the sofa, as if he were a welcomed guest. He could sit at the table, where her insurance agent sat when she renewed a policy or where her banker sat when he wanted to discuss new investment opportunities.

The kitchen table was for business. The living room was for friends. And Seth Walker was not a friend.

He lowered himself into a chair at the table and set the folder in front of him on the table. She moved to the cabinet. "Would you like a cup of coffee?" she asked grudgingly.

"Is this something like the wicked stepmother offering Snow White an apple?"

She knew he meant the ridiculous quip to break the tension, and in a way it did. She felt her lips begin the start of a smile, but quickly halted it. "The coffee is fine, but if I were you, I'd worry about any fruit offering while you're here," she replied.

He flashed her a smile—a killer smile. At that moment she recognized how attractive he was with his square jaw and straight nose. His gray eyes were heavily lashed beneath bold black eyebrows. His dark hair was just a bit shaggy, as if he'd missed his last visit to the barber, but it enhanced rather than took away from his handsomeness.

Not that she cared what he looked like or that his smile gave her a tiny punch in the pit of her stomach. She just wanted—needed—to hear what he had to say.

She poured them each a cup of coffee, then joined him at the table, the tension once again twisting in her stomach. A conversation, she told herself. They were just going to have a conversation, that's all. There was nothing to be afraid of, nothing to worry about, and if she didn't like what he had to say to her, she could escort him out the door. This thought eased some of the tension.

"So, what changed your mind?" he asked.

"Curiosity." She cupped her hands around the warmth of her coffee cup. "I want to know why you're here. I want to know why you think Hank is innocent."

He leaned back in the chair and she resented the fact that he looked relaxed. "There's no easy answer to those questions."

"Then give me the not-so-easy answers." She was determined to be in control, to be the one asking the questions, not answering them.

"Six months ago the agency I work for got a letter from your father. We get hundreds of letters from convicts crying foul and proclaiming their innocence, but something about your dad's letter captured the interest of my boss. Some initial investigation was done and then I was sent to Lansing prison to meet with your father."

She wished he'd stop referring to him as her father. Hank Donovan had stopped being her father on the day he'd murdered his family.

"And he told you he was innocent and now you're here? Gosh, if I ever get convicted of a heinous crime, I'd better give you a call." She couldn't help the edge of sarcasm that crept into her voice.

"I told you the answer wasn't easy," he replied. "We've studied the court papers, checked and rechecked the investigation that took place at the time, and we have questions both about the investigation and the defense case Hank's attorney provided."

He'd apparently caught the fact that she never referred to Hank as her father. "What kind of questions?" she asked.

He leaned forward, his gaze seeming to pierce through her. "For one thing, Hank doesn't fit any profile of a man capable of committing such a crime. We had him evaluated by one of our top psychiatrists and he tested in the range of normal. He has no history of violence, wasn't described as odd or a loner by friends or neighbors."

"And because he doesn't fit into one of your square boxes, you just assume he's a regular peg?"

"A profile is just a place to start," Seth explained. He paused and took a sip of his coffee, then continued. "Dane Kelly was a young, inexperienced sheriff. This was his first murder case and even though he believes he did things by the book, he made some mistakes."

She so didn't want to be intrigued and yet she heard herself ask, "What kind of mistakes?"

He hesitated a moment and although she wouldn't have thought it possible, his gaze grew more intense. "Did you know that your father suspected your mother was seeing somebody? Another man?"

Shock sizzled through her. "That's ridiculous," she said forcefully, a new burst of anger welling up inside her. "That's a story he's manufactured to point suspicion in another direction. My mother was a good woman."

"Good women sometimes make mistakes. They get lonely or unhappy and they have affairs."

"Not my mother." Allison shot up from her chair, unable to sit passively as she battled the raw emotion that tried to choke her. "Blame the victim—isn't that how it's done nowadays? Drag her name through the mud, make everyone think that just perhaps she deserved whatever happened to her."

"That's not what this is about." His voice was even and measured, in direct contrast with her raspy, emotion-tensed voice. "Nothing your mother could have done warranted her death. I'm looking for the truth, Allison, not to make your mother a sacrificial lamb." He waited a moment, as if to give her time to calm down. "That particular lead was never followed. As far as I can tell by reading the reports and such, nobody tried to find out if your mother was seeing another man."

"That's because there was no man to find." Allison drew a deep breath and returned to her seat at the table. Once again she wrapped her fingers around her cup. "Why are you doing this?" she asked. "What's in this for you?"

"Justice. Nothing more and nothing less. I'm not sure Hank Donovan got justice and that's why I'm here." He reached across the table and touched the back of her hand. It was a soft, quick touch; then he drew his hand back. "I need your help, Allison."

"I can't help you. I didn't see anything, anyone, on the day of the murders." The knot in her stomach was so tight she felt as if she couldn't get enough air. "I can't tell you anything about it. I was hit over the head. I was knocked unconscious." She knew she was rambling but was helpless to stop. "I was in a coma for two days. Then after I got out of the hospital, I went to a mental hospital in Goodland for almost a year. I don't know what happened that day. All I remember is that there was a dust storm. Then I got off the school bus and walked into the house, then nothing."

Once again she was out of her chair. She paced the floor next to the table, wanting—needing—him to understand. "When I regained consciousness in the hospital, Dane Kelly came to see me. He asked me if I'd seen anything that day, if I knew who was responsible. I told him no, and that was the last time anyone mentioned it to me. That was the last time I spoke for a year."

She dropped back in her chair and drew a deep, tremulous breath, wishing he would take his gorgeous gray eyes and killer smile and go away. "This was a mistake. I shouldn't have invited you here. I can't help you."

"But you can," he protested. "Allison, everything about your mother's and brother's and sister's deaths is in here." He tapped the folder on top of the table. "I don't need you to talk about their deaths. What I want is for you to talk about their lives. That's what's missing. I need to know about your family before that day."

She frowned and looked at him in confusion. "How will that help?"

"Because in the lives of murder victims you can usually find clues to their deaths."

"There's nothing you can find in Jennifer and Johnny's short lives that would give you any hints." The thought of her little brother and sister forced a dark cloud of grief to momentarily steal her vision. She no longer saw Seth. Instead, images she'd spent the last fifteen years trying to forget flashed through her head.

Johnny on the floor just inside the front door. The back of his head bashed in and his favorite blue shirt untucked from his jeans. He hated it when his shirts came untucked.

Then there was Jenny, in a pink pair of shorts and a pink-striped blouse. She lay next to her brother, staring up at the ceiling with a deathly quiet she'd never known in life.

Finally there had been Allison's mom, seated on the sofa as if ready to watch her favorite afternoon soap opera.

Blood.

So much blood.

And her head.

Dear God, where was her head?

It wasn't where it belonged.

"Allison?"

The deep voice seemed to come from someplace far away. She grabbed on to it, halting her fall into the depths of a grief she knew would consume her. She found herself staring into his eyes and wondered how she could ever have found them cold.

At the moment they were filled with warm concern and when he reached across the table and took her hand, she held tight to his. It didn't matter that he was a stranger, that it had been his questions that had evoked those horrendous visions.

All that mattered was that his hand was amazingly warm, his fingers strong enough to anchor her in the here and now. "Are you all right?" he asked. She gave a curt nod and his fingers tightened around hers. "I'm sorry. I don't mean to hurt you, but I need you, Allison."

She tugged her hand and he released it. For several long minutes they sat without speaking. She stared at the wall just behind him. She could hear the clink of the ice maker in the refrigerator spitting cubes into the tray, the hum of the dryer from the utility room. Normal sounds. Reassuring, familiar noise.

She wanted to lose herself in it, in the mundane world of clean clothes and icy drinks, in fighting with Sam about doing his homework and enjoying Sunday dinners with Aunt Maureen and Uncle David. What she didn't want to do was go where Seth attempted to lead her.

"Hank told me you were stubborn," Seth said, finally breaking the uncomfortable silence. "He told me that even at sixteen you had a strength of character that awed him."

Allison didn't want the words to resonate inside her, but they did. "What's he like?" she asked grudgingly.

"He's a model prisoner, well liked by the guards. He works in the prison woodworking shop building furniture. He's completed a degree in architecture and also does some counseling work with new inmates."

"You've told me what he does, not what he's like," she observed.

Seth frowned thoughtfully and stroked one of his hands down his jawline, as if testing for a five-o'clock shadow. "He's kind of quiet, but has a good sense of humor despite the grimness of his situation. He talks a lot about all that he's lost, your mom and the kids. It's obvious he loved you all very much. He doesn't complain about being in prison, but he's tortured because the person responsible is still free. I think he's a complicated man. I've met with him a dozen times and I like him. I like him a lot."

The man he described was the man she remembered, and she'd have much rather heard that he was a pathetic loser who whined about false imprisonment or a pumped-up brute who terrorized the other inmates. That would have been far easier for her to swallow.

"Allison." Once again Seth leaned forward and the scent of his cologne eddied in the air around her. "If we do this, if we reinvestigate the crime and all the evidence still points to Hank's guilt, then nothing changes. He stays in prison and you continue your life as it is. But if we find evidence that leads us away from Hank and to another person, wouldn't you want that pursued?"

"I guess you believe in that saying about 'better a dozen guilty men go free than one innocent man be behind bars,' " she said.

"I do. Although in the utopian world I'd like to see, no guilty man would go free and no innocent man would spend a day behind bars."

"Ah, so you're one of those dreaded idealists."

He grinned, and once again the charm and warmth in that gesture lit up a warm place in her stomach. "Guilty as charged."

In another lifetime, under different circumstances, this might have been the man who could have changed her mind when it came to relationships and the pleasures of sex. He definitely possessed more than his share of simmering sexual appeal.

Not that she cared. She was perfectly satisfied with her life alone. She'd been perfectly happy in her life before he'd come to town. Once again an edge of resentment pressed up inside her. It was a resentment tinged with fear, the fear that when Seth Walker left town, the calm, well-controlled life she knew would be irrevocably changed.

"You know after Hank was arrested, in all the years since, there hasn't been another murder like that in Crow's Creek. If there was a crazed killer running around who had never gotten caught, don't you think he would have killed again?"

"Maybe. Maybe not. It's obvious the murders were committed by somebody who knew your family."

"What do you mean?"

"Johnny was killed just inside the front door. Then he

was moved to his desk, where he liked to sit and draw. Jennifer was also killed at the door, but she was dressed in her pajamas and tucked into bed with her favorite stuffed animal. And you were placed in bed and Beatles music was playing on your cassette tape player. There had to be somebody who knew Johnny liked to draw and Jennifer loved her stuffed dog."

"And that I loved old Beatles music. You mean somebody other than my father." She picked up her coffee cup and took a sip of the tepid coffee, hoping it would wash away the taste of bitterness, of fear, that still lingered in her mouth.

"This is a small town, Seth. Almost incestuously small. I imagine almost everyone knew that Johnny loved to draw. He never went anywhere without a pad and pencil in hand. And Jenny dragged that stuffed animal everywhere we went. As far as my Beatles music, I blared that music whenever I drove the car into town. Any number of people would know those things about us. Even a stranger would only have to observe us for a day or two to know those things, but the person who would definitely have that information is Hank Donovan."

Once again Seth ran a hand down his jaw and his eyes narrowed slightly with obvious frustration. "Like I told you, if all the evidence continues to point to your father's guilt, then I leave here and go back to Kansas City and nothing changes. Just like I don't want to see an innocent man sit in a jail cell, I'm no more eager to see a guilty man let free."

He paused a long moment. "What if Hank is innocent and you could get back a member of your family, one who had been as much a victim as you had been?"

Old Spice and new-cut wood, the scents swept back to her on a rush of memories. Her dad patting her back and telling her she was the prettiest girl in the whole entire world. The sound of his laughter filled her heart, squeezing it so tight it hurt.

Was it possible that the sheriff and his men and the jury had all gotten it wrong? Had her father simply been a man at the wrong place at the wrong time? A man who had been the pawn in a killer's game?

She thought it more likely that Seth Walker was a nice man, an idealist by his own characterization, who had gotten caught up in a killer's lies. But the handsome idealist with his sexy smile and powerful eyes had planted a tiny seed of doubt in her mind, a damnable seed that would haunt her forever if she didn't do something about it.

"Okay, I'm in," she said with weary resignation. "I'll do what I can to help you." With these words she knew she was facing a journey back to that day of screeching wind, choking dust and the horror that had waited for her at home.

Chapter 9

"Hello? Anyone home?" Allison called as she opened the front door of her uncle David and aunt Maureen's home.

"In the kitchen," Maureen called. She was taking meat loaf from the oven as Allison walked in. "The rabbit nut and his protégé are in the shed."

"I guess I'm taking home a rabbit today," Allison said as she sat at the small table.

Maureen smiled. "Try to get out of here without one and you'll have a war on your hands." She set the meat loaf on a hot pad on the counter, then popped in a baking sheet of rolls. "This will all be ready in about ten minutes." She washed her hands, dried them on the towel tucked into her waistband, then turned back to look at Allison. "So, did you do anything exciting last night?"

Allison considered her answer carefully. She had every intention of telling her aunt and uncle that she was going to help Seth, but now wasn't the time. "No, pretty much just the usual."

Usual other than the fact that after Seth had left, she'd tossed and turned until dawn, wondering if she'd regret her decision. Immediately after she'd agreed to help him, as if sensing her utter and complete mental exhaustion, Seth had left. They'd agreed to meet again Monday evening at her place.

"Was Sam good?" she asked in an effort to keep her mind off Seth Walker.

"You know he's always good for us. You've raised him right, Allison, with a firm hand and consistency. I always worried that he'd take after his father's side of the family." Maureen tempered her words with a benevolent smile, but she'd never hidden the fact that she hadn't liked Bobby or his family. She'd believed the Clemmins family was from the wrong side of the tracks and that Bobby had a wild streak that boded ill for his future. In that, she had been right.

At that moment the back door opened and Sam and David came inside. "Hey, Mom!" Sam greeted her with a quick kiss. His cheeks were flushed with excitement and he smelled of sunshine and a hint of sweat. "We've got Bugs all packed up and ready to take to his new home in our backyard,"

"I hope you know what to do with him once we get home, because I don't know anything about rabbits," Allison exclaimed.

Sam grinned and swung an arm around his mother's neck. "Don't worry, Mom. I'll teach you everything you need to know."

"He knows what to do," Uncle David said, his face wreathed in a proud smile. "He's a quick study."

"Forget about any lessons right now," Aunt Maureen said. "You and your uncle need to wash up. I'm putting everything on the dining room table right now."

Within minutes the four of them were seated in the formal dining room, where the talk was of the high school prom the following Saturday night. "Sam is spending the night with his friend Greg and I'm on chaperone duty that night," Allison said.

"Ugh, I can't think of anything worse than chaperoning a bunch of hormone-driven teenagers," Maureen exclaimed.

"One of my students actually asked me to be his date for the prom," Allison said.

Maureen raised a perfectly arched eyebrow. "And who would that be?"

"Eric Grant," Sam quipped. "He's in love with Mom."

Allison looked at her son in surprise. "How do you know that?"

" 'Cause he told me," Sam replied as he loaded his plate with more mashed potatoes.

"And when did he tell you this?" Allison asked.

"It was last week, I think. I was outside playing catch with Billy and he was walking by. He stopped and talked for a minute." Sam shrugged. "It was no big deal, Mom. Eric is kind of geeky, but he's a nice guy."

"That boy hasn't been taught right from wrong or any kind of social graces," Maureen said, her voice laced with tight disapproval.

"Who's going to teach him? That drunken father of his?" David said. "That man is a disgrace." David shut his mouth as Maureen gave him a warning glance.

"Don't worry, I have things with Eric under control," Allison assured them. "He's just lonely. He doesn't quite fit with the rest of the kids, but I'm sure he'll grow out of it."

"Doesn't he run around with the Johnson boy and Dane's son?" David asked.

Allison nodded. "They're like the Three Musketeers."

"Or the Three Stooges," David said, making Sam giggle.

"They're all fairly good kids," Allison said. "But I have to confess I won't be sorry to see the school year end and summer vacation begin. I've been thinking that maybe Sam and I might go somewhere for a real vacation."

"Really? Maybe Disneyland?" Sam asked.

Allison laughed. "I don't know. We'll have to sit down one evening and see what we can come up with."

The rest of the meal passed with light conversation, and while the adults lingered over cups of coffee, Sam returned to the shed to check on Bugs once again.

Allison knew this was the perfect time to tell her aunt and uncle about her decision to work with Seth. She didn't want them hearing about it through the very healthy and active grapevine that Crow's Creek possessed.

"You know that man I talked to you-all about last weekend? Seth Walker?" she began. She couldn't miss how both her aunt's and her uncle's facial features tightened. "I've agreed to help him reinvestigate the murders."

Maureen gasped aloud. "Why on earth would you agree to such a thing?"

David's fingers tightened around his coffee cup to the point that his knuckles whitened, although he didn't say a word. Allison looked at him, then back at her aunt. "Because for the first time in fifteen years, I'm curious. Because if there's any doubt at all concerning Hank's guilt, then I think it should be explored."

"Oh, Allison, I beg you to reconsider. Nothing good can come from this. That was a dark time in Crow's Creek history and nobody will want to revisit that terrible day."

"I don't think it was any darker for anyone else than it was for me," Allison said dryly. "And if I can handle going back to that day, then nobody else should have a problem with it."

"For God's sake, Allison, you spent almost a year in a mental hospital. What makes you think you can handle all this now?" Maureen protested.

For a long moment Allison didn't answer. There was no question that the possibility of returning to that horrible day frightened her, that she feared the trauma might take her back to the place where she'd curled into herself for protection.

"For one thing, I'm not a helpless sixteen-year-old anymore." She leaned forward in her chair, wanting them to understand, somehow needing their approval. "Besides, what if mistakes were made? What if there was a rush to judgment and the wrong man went to prison?"

"Nonsense," Maureen exclaimed. She swiped her mouth with her linen napkin and threw it on the table beside her plate. "If I were you, I wouldn't go getting any hopes up. You'll only be setting yourself up for a new heartache. This man, this Seth, has turned your head, filled it with thoughts of a nice family reunion between you and your father."

"Don't you think that if I thought my brother was innocent, I would have moved heaven and earth to keep him out of prison?" David asked, his voice thick with emotion. "I wanted to believe in his innocence so badly, but I sat in that courtroom every day and listened to the evidence and I knew in my heart he'd done it." He drew a deep, weary breath. "Hank and I were close. We weren't just brothers. We were best friends and it killed me when he was sent away, but I knew that's where he belonged. I was just grateful that at least his lawyer managed to keep him off death row and instead got him life."

"But what if we were all wrong?" Allison asked. "What if evidence was missed? What if Dad's lawyer didn't do the kind of job he should have done? Wouldn't you want to know?"

"All I know is that I've spent the last fifteen years of my life trying to protect you from the horrid details of those deaths," Maureen exclaimed. "And it breaks my heart that now you're choosing to pursue all this."

Allison reached out and covered her aunt's hand

with her own. "Believe me, I appreciate everything you've done for me and I know how protective you've been. There was a time when I welcomed that protection, when I didn't want to think or talk about what had happened. But I'm not a child anymore and I think I need to do this."

Maureen pulled her hand from beneath Allison's. "I suppose it doesn't matter what we say. You're going to do what you want to, just like you did when you married Bobby." She stood and grabbed her plate from the table and carried it into the kitchen. "And look how that turned out."

Allison didn't need to be a rocket scientist to know that her aunt was angry with her. She'd lived through many of Maureen's temper fits in the past. Allison would be punished with a cool shoulder and curtness until Maureen forgave Allison for having a mind of her own.

David once again released a deep sigh. "You know we love you, Allison, but nothing good can come from all this. We just don't want to see you get hurt."

Love buoyed up inside her for the quiet, gentle man who had opened his home, his heart, to her all those years ago. "I know." She got up from the table. "I'm just going to get Sam and go home. Tell Aunt Maureen to call me when she's ready to talk again."

David nodded and remained seated at the table as Allison went out the front door and around to the back of the house where Sam had Bugs and everything the bunny would need ready to take home.

As she drove home, she couldn't help but wonder if she was making a mistake. She'd thought she'd made peace with her past. She'd asked her aunt only once why her father had done such a thing, and Maureen had simply replied that the only person who could know the reason for the crime was Hank and he wasn't talking.

Although Allison would never understand the reasons for the deaths, she'd believed she'd accepted what had happened and moved on with her life.

The fact that she'd agreed to help Seth with his investigation let her know that wasn't true. There was a part of her that needed to go back, that wanted to understand what had led up to the slaughter of her family.

Chapter 10

"Just the person I wanted to talk to," Michelle said as she joined Allison in the teachers' lounge on Monday morning. It was early and the two of them were alone in the small room where teachers often started the day with a cup of coffee before the first class began.

Allison grinned at her friend as Michelle poured herself some coffee, then sat next to her at the table and pulled an oversized cinnamon roll from a brown paper bag. "It's disgusting that you can eat like that and never gain a pound," Allison observed.

"I'll split it with you if you want."

Allison held up a hand in protest. "No thanks. That five pounds I've been fighting to take off has grown to ten. I'm trying to be good."

"That's not what I've heard," Michelle replied.

Allison lifted an eyebrow. "And what exactly have you heard?"

"That you've fallen under the spell of that hot new guy in town."

"And where did you hear that?"

Michelle tore off a piece of the roll and popped it into her mouth, then reached for her coffee cup.

"Quit stalling," Allison exclaimed.

Michelle grinned sheepishly. "Okay, your aunt Maureen called me last night. I also heard it from a couple of people this morning. Anyway, Maureen told me what was up and asked me to try and talk some sense into you."

"I don't need any sense talked into me," Allison protested.

"Allison, do you really intend to do this?" Michelle asked with a frown. "I mean, you never even talked to me about that day in all these years and I'm your very best friend."

Allison took a sip of her coffee before replying. By the time she'd gotten out of the hospital, the crime had been a year old. She knew that she'd gone into the hospital partly because she hadn't wanted to face the crime, but she also hadn't wanted to face the town.

She hadn't wanted to see the looks of pity, hear the whispers that halted abruptly whenever she drew near. Even at the age of sixteen she'd known there would be those who would take a perverse pleasure in grilling her about the details.

By the time she'd left the hospital, a year had passed and the gossips had turned to other victims, fresh rumors and scandals. She suspected that Maureen, who wielded considerable power in the town, had warned everyone to leave Allison alone and they had.

"I think it will be easier to talk about it with somebody who wasn't around then, with somebody who isn't personally in my life," she finally said. "I can't explain it, but it's like I didn't want what happened to me, what happened to my family, to taint my relationships with my friends and the people here in Crow's Creek."

"It couldn't taint anything," Michelle protested. "Nobody believes that what happened that day was your fault."

Allison nodded, but sometimes in the very depths of the night when she lay in bed cloaked in darkness, she wondered. Had her mother and father fought over something she'd done? Had she been the topic of an argument between her parents? An argument that had somehow careened out of control?

Her father hadn't been overjoyed by her relationship with Bobby, while her mother had been fine with it. Had they fought about it and had the argument escalated? She never allowed these thoughts to play for too long in her head, for they filled her with a despair that was nearly crippling.

While she'd been in the hospital, a psychologist had talked to her about survivor's guilt and offered various coping mechanisms to deal with the emotional baggage, but it wasn't as easy to assuage that guilt as the doctor had made it sound.

"So, you really intend to do this?" Michelle asked, pulling her from her thoughts.

"I do," Allison replied firmly. "And Aunt Maureen will just have to get over it. I don't mean to upset anyone in this town, but I want to do this. If there's a chance in a million that Hank isn't guilty, then I want to know about it." She paused as a wealth of emotion rose up to press painfully tight against her rib cage. "What if we've lost all this time that we could have had together?"

"Oh, Allison, I'm just afraid for you," Michelle replied, and placed a hand on her friend's arm. "Have you considered what this will do to Sam? That you're going to have to explain it all to him?"

Allison frowned. "He already knows some of it. I'll just have to be more open with him. He'll be okay. I'll make sure of it."

"I don't want you to get your hopes up, then be crushed. You've already had more than your share of tragedy," Michelle exclaimed.

"And you were crushed when your husband cheated on you, but you're out there looking for love once again, knowing that it's possible you could suffer another heartache," Allison countered. "And speaking of that, have you heard from Rick?"

"No." Michelle leaned back and pulled her hand from Allison. "I was hoping maybe he'd call me over the weekend, but he didn't." She tore off another piece of her cinnamon roll. "And don't think I didn't notice how you changed the subject."

Thankfully the bell rang, signaling that it was time for teachers and students to get to their first-period classes. "Just be careful, Allison," Michelle said as the two of them walked out of the lounge together. "Don't let your heart get too involved in this, so if the outcome is bad, you aren't devastated once again."

Monday night as Allison waited for Seth to arrive at her house, she thought about Michelle's words. She'd be a fool not to believe that her heart might be involved in this process. Hank Donovan wasn't some stranger she'd read about in her morning newspaper. He wasn't an unfamiliar person who had been profiled on a crime show.

He was the man who had walked her to the bus stop on her first day of school, the man who had rocked her all night when she'd suffered an earache. According to her mother, she'd been a daddy's girl from the moment of conception and nothing had changed that in the first sixteen years of her life.

After the murders, she'd believed she hated her father. She'd damned him to hell a thousand times in her mind. But there was no question that erasing the first sixteen years of love had been perhaps the most difficult thing she'd ever done in her life.

She was expecting Seth at eight thirty. She hoped to have Sam ready for bed before Seth arrived. It was going to be a difficult meeting, but it would be a little less complicated if Sam was asleep.

Her natural motherly instinct was to protect her son from all this, but Michelle had made her aware of the fact that there might come a time when he'd have to know what was going on in her life and more of the details of what had happened in her past.

She now sat on her small back patio with a cup of coffee in hand, watching the sunlight of day fade into night. Thankfully, the wind had died down with the coming of twilight, and although the heat of the day still wrapped around her like an overly warm blanket, without the wind blowing it was almost pleasant to just sit and breathe.

The sliding glass door to the patio opened and Sam stepped outside. "All finished with your homework?" she asked.

"Yeah." He sank down on the chair next to hers and released a deep sigh. " I think Mrs. Reeder is trying to kill us with homework before school ends."

Allison laughed. "I'm sure that's not her intention."

"I think it might be," he exclaimed.

"You remember I told you I'm having a guest over this evening?"

"Is it like a date?"

Allison was surprised to hear a slight wistfulness in her son's voice. "No, honey, it isn't a date. Mr. Walker and I are working together on a project."

"What kind of project?" he asked.

"Adult stuff."

"That means boring." He got up from his chair. "Guess I'll check on Bugs before it's time for me to go to bed."

Allison watched him walk to the bunny hutch and her heart expanded with love. Crow's Creek wasn't like a lot of big cities where families with single parents were common. In Crow's Creek there were far more two-parent families than not and Allison felt that there was no question that Sam had been deprived when it came to having a man in his life.

But giving Sam a father meant inviting a man into her life, and no matter how much she loved her son, she simply wasn't at a place where she wanted to go there.

"Hey, Mr. Jacobs," Sam called to their neighbor, who, as usual, didn't hear him. Sam returned to the patio and once again sat in the chair next to Allison. "He never hears me."

"I know, honey."

Sam looked at the house on the other side of theirs. "You think anyone is ever going to buy that house?"

Allison looked over to the dark two-story. "I don't know." The house had been for sale since she'd bought her house.

"I hope a family buys it and they have a boy my age. It would be cool to have a friend right next door."

"That would be nice, but you have Greg."

"Yeah, but Greg lives so far away that we have to depend on you or his mom any time we want to hang out." It was true. Greg lived with his parents in a farmhouse on the east side of town, too far away for the boys to walk or even bike back and forth.

"Just think, in a few more years you'll have your driver's license and you can drive back and forth to Greg's any time you want," Allison said.

Sam's eyes lit up. "That's going to be so awesome!"

"And now it would be awesome if you'd go get into the shower and get ready for bed," Allison said.

Sam raised an arm and sniffed his armpit. "I really don't need a shower. I don't stink."

"Trust me, when you're a twelve-year-old boy, you need a shower every night. Besides, if you don't shower tonight, maybe Brittany Waverly won't smile at you tomorrow."

Although it was growing darker by the moment, it wasn't so dark that she didn't see the vivid blush that splashed up into her son's cheeks. "Jeez, Mom." He jumped up from the chair. "Okay, you win. I'll go take a shower."

Allison was still smiling as he disappeared back into the house. Although he hadn't told her in so many words that he had a crush on the pretty, blond Brittany Waverly, a mother knew things when it came to her children.

As the last gasp of the sunlight disappeared, she left her chair and went inside. The air-conditioning felt nice after the time outside, but a glance at the clock shot a taut tension inside her. Seth would be here in a little over half an hour.

She had no idea what to expect, exactly how he intended to investigate. She wasn't sure exactly what her role would be in all this and the unknown was nerve-racking.

She hadn't heard from her aunt since Sunday and could only assume that Maureen was still angry at Allison's decision. Allison had spent most of her adult life trying to please Maureen. Now that she thought about it, she realized that she'd never been completely sure that Maureen's love was unconditional.

"My way or the highway"—that's how Maureen functioned, but this time Allison didn't care. Her aunt could either get over it or not. At some point between the time Seth Walker had first introduced himself and now, Allison had become firm in her conviction that this was something she wanted—no, needed—to do.

For the first time since the murders, she wanted answers. If her father was guilty, then perhaps she could find out why, what had happened to cause him to snap to such a degree he not only killed his wife but also murdered two of his children and tried to kill her. It was the one question that had sprung into her mind at odd times of the day and night.

Why?

She felt that if she knew the answer to that, she could

really finally put it all behind her. As it was, Seth's arrival into her life had made her realize just how much she hadn't put the past behind.

She'd believed she'd made peace, but now that sense of peace had exploded apart.

Bobby used to tell her she was the queen of compartmentalization.

He insisted that she had the ability to put all her bad stuff in a file in her head, then rarely go back to access it. That had been true until Seth had shown up. Now the bad file contents were bleeding out and she couldn't seem to stop them.

Blood.

It had been everywhere.

Jenny's eyes staring up at the ceiling.

Johnny with his shirt untucked.

"Mom?"

A scream escaped her as Sam's voice called her back to the present. She turned to see him standing in the doorway, clad in his pajamas, his damp hair slicked back from his face.

"Gosh, Mom. I didn't mean to scare you. Are you okay?" He stepped closer to her, bringing with him the scent of minty soap and citrus shampoo.

"I'm fine," she said as she caught her breath.

"Can I have some chips before I go to bed?"

"As long as you eat them right here at the table," Allison replied. At that moment the doorbell rang.

Allison had a wild urge to turn out the lights and pretend she wasn't home, to forget this whole thing and Seth Walker. But she didn't. As she left the kitchen, she drew in a deep, calming breath, then opened the front door.

He greeted her with a warm smile and as he entered the hallway, she was conscious of the scent of him, a clean masculine scent of cologne and shaving cream.

Once again he held a fat folder and she wasn't sure if it was the sight of it or the sight of him that provoked a small knot of tension in her chest.

"Come on into the kitchen," she said. "You can meet my son before he goes to bed."

He walked in front of her, his broad shoulders in perfect proportion to his slim hips and long legs. There was no question physically the man affected her on a level no man had for a very long time, not that it was anything she intended to follow through on.

When they reached the kitchen, she introduced him to Sam, who stood and held out a hand. "Nice to meet you, Mr. Walker."

"Seth. You can call me Seth."

Sam shot a glance at Allison, who nodded her head. "Then it's nice to meet you, Seth. Want some chips?" Sam returned to his seat at the table.

"No, thanks." Seth took the seat next to Sam and before Allison knew it, the two were talking about karate and acting as if they'd known each other all their lives.

Sam's face was lit with animation as he listened to Seth, then talked about his classes with Wayne Fenton. Apparently Seth had been a black belt when he'd been younger and there was no question the information impressed her son.

As they talked, Allison watched the exchange. Sam appeared surprisingly at ease with Seth. Maybe it was because Seth spoke to him like he was an equal, without the studied efforts of a man trying to get somebody to like him.

When it was quarter until nine, Allison told her son it was bedtime. The routine was that Sam was in bed by nine and could read a book for half an hour.

"If you'll just excuse us for a minute," Allison said as Sam got up from the table. "Help yourself to the coffee and I'll be right back."

She followed Sam down the hallway to his bedroom. Sam's room contained all things boy. The walls were decorated with posters of Bruce Lee and Jackie Chan, and a bookcase held a variety of books. Allison had fostered a love of reading in her son, knowing it was one of the most important gifts she could give to him.

Along with the books there was an array of items considered treasures by a boy—a petrified piece of wood, a model of a dinosaur, a green-bean can transformed into a pencil holder, and a collection of stones. In the center of the bookcase was a small tumbleweed that he'd discovered in their backyard last summer. At Christmastime he'd spray-painted it gold and tied a red ribbon on the top.

As usual, his room smelled of dirty socks. "You need to do a sock check in here," Allison said as he got into bed and turned on the lamp on his nightstand. "You must have some nasty socks hiding out in here because I can smell them."

"I think maybe they're under my bed," he admitted.

"Get them into the laundry hamper tomorrow." She leaned down and kissed him on the forehead. "Lights out at nine thirty."

"Mom? It's too bad it isn't a date. Seth is cool."

"He is nice," she agreed. "Good night and sweet dreams. I love you, Sam."

"Love you, too."

When she returned to the kitchen, Seth had a cup of coffee in front of him. "Sorry about that," she said, and went to the counter to pour herself a cup of coffee.

"No problem. He's a great kid."

"You certainly made a hit with him. He thinks you're cool," she replied as she joined him at the table. She couldn't help herself; she glanced at his hand, looking for a wedding ring. There was none. Not that she cared.

"I guess we're the talk of the town," she said. "My

friend Michelle told me people were talking about why you're here."

"I figured once I spoke to the sheriff, word would seep out." He gazed at her with a directness that was disconcerting. "Are you okay with it? With people knowing what we're doing?"

"Sure, although I got a lecture this morning from Michelle, and my aunt Maureen isn't speaking to me over this."

He frowned. "I'm sorry. The last thing I wanted was for this to cause you problems."

"Don't apologize. Aunt Maureen will get over being mad. She's just afraid for me, afraid that I won't be able to handle talking about it, thinking about it."

"Can you handle it?"

She raised her chin a notch. "I wouldn't have invited you here if I thought I couldn't. But I'm not sure how this works," she said. "I'm not sure what kind of help I can be to you."

"What I'd like to do tonight is just ask you some questions." He opened up the folder and withdrew a legal pad, then pulled a pen from the pocket of his short-sleeved light blue shirt.

Instantly the knot of tension was back in her chest. "What kind of questions?" The last thing she wanted was for him to ask her about that moment when she'd walked into the front door, when she'd seen her brother, her sister and then her mother.

"About life before the murders," he replied. "About the relationship between your mother and father and what kind of parents, what kind of people, they were."

She relaxed a bit. "Life was normal . . . good. We were a close-knit family."

"You were quite a bit older than your siblings," he observed.

She nodded. "According to what Mom told me, she

thought I'd be enough, that having me had satisfied her maternal need, but by the time I was in school full-time, she realized she wanted more kids."

"Was she a good mother?"

She wanted to be offended by the question, but she knew he was simply gathering facts, not making judgments. She leaned back in the chair and allowed her mind to fill with visions of Joleen. She couldn't help the smile that curved her lips as she thought of the woman who had been her mother.

"Mom was different than other mothers. First of all, she was absolutely stunning. She had the kind of beauty that made men stop in their tracks and stare, and part of her charm was that she seemed completely unaware of it. She was a free spirit, always singing, always dancing. She loved romance novels and believed in fairy tales." Allison wrapped her fingers around her coffee cup. "In a lot of ways she was more child than woman, but yes, she was a good mother."

"And what about Hank?"

Pain pushed up inside her, the pain of betrayal and broken trust. "He was a great father, very hands-on. He was patient and rarely lost his temper. He was demonstrative, giving hugs easily and telling us all how important we were to him."

Seth frowned. "And yet you never doubted his guilt?"

"I was sixteen years old, and even when I was in the hospital, I heard things, snatches of conversation among the nurses."

"What kind of things?"

Her fingers squeezed painfully tight to the coffee mug. "That he was found covered in blood and clutching the hatchet in his hand, that he'd left work early and nobody could account for his time that afternoon, but witnesses had placed him at the house sometime that afternoon. I figured there were people older and smarter than me working the case and they would get it right." She picked up the cup and took a drink, needing to wash the bad taste out of her mouth.

"Your mother didn't work outside the home?"

Allison shook her head and lowered her cup. "No, she was a stay-at-home mom. Jenny and Johnny got home from school around three thirty and she liked being home to meet them at the door."

"How did she spend her time during the days?"

"She went shopping in town, had lunch with friends. She didn't do a lot of cooking and she hated to clean. She was a room mother for both Johnny and Jenny. She loved planning school parties."

"Your father and your mother, they had a good marriage?"

She shrugged. "They had their occasional fights. It wasn't perfect, but I would say it was better than most."

"What kinds of things did they fight about?" he asked.

"Sometimes money, but mostly they fought about Dad going out of town to work. When I was fifteen, he got a job with a home builder working on the other side of Goodland. Lots of times if they worked late, he'd just get a motel room for the night instead of driving all the way back here. Mom hated those nights. She didn't like being alone."

For the next hour and a half they talked about life before that terrible day. Allison hadn't realized how hungry she was to talk about the family she'd lost until she began to share stories with Seth.

She told him about Johnny's talent as a budding young artist, how he acquired a lisp when he got excited and tried to talk too fast. She talked to him about Jenny with her sweet nature, Jenny, who had idolized her big sister and who used to sneak into Allison's bedroom in the middle of the night to sleep with her.

It was as if a dam had broken loose, a dam of memories she'd never been able to share with anyone else. Some of the memories made her laugh, and some of them made her weep.

Seth let her talk, reaching for her hand as the tears formed and sharing her laughter when they stopped. It was well after ten when he scooted back his chair and tucked his legal pad into the file folder. "I know it's a workday for you tomorrow, so I'm going to get out of here and let you get some sleep."

"I feel like I've wasted your time tonight," she said as she walked with him to the front door.

"Not at all." He reached the door and turned to face her, and once again she was struck by his attractiveness. His eyes weren't a plain gray as she'd originally thought, but rather flecked with silver shards that added dimension, and more than once, she'd wondered what his mouth might feel like on hers. He had a great mouth, his lower lip slightly fuller than his upper one.

Stress, she thought. That could be the only excuse for such an alien thought.

"I do have a favor to ask you," he said as he opened the door. "I'd like you to make a list of your mother's friends, the women she had lunch with or went shopping with, friends she might have confided in."

"I'm assuming you intend to talk to them?"

He nodded. "Maybe there was somebody giving your mother a hard time, somebody who she'd snubbed or rejected. Maybe her girlfriends can give us a name, something that we can sink our teeth into. I'd also like a list of men your father considered friends, men he had a beer with occasionally, went fishing or hunting with."

"That will be a very short list. Dad didn't really hang out after work or on the weekends with anyone other than the family. The only person I can think of would be his brother, David. Why would you need that? Didn't he tell you who his friends were in all those talks you had with him in prison?"

Seth smiled. "I don't take anything for granted, Allison. You think it's possible your father had a girlfriend?"

The question came at her from left field. "I can't imagine, but then I couldn't have imagined anything that happened at that time." She stared at him for a long moment. "But surely you don't think a woman was responsible for the murders?"

"Like I said, I don't take anything for granted."

Allison's head reeled with this new possibility. It had never entered her mind that a woman could be capable of such brutality. But then it had never entered her mind that anyone other than Hank Donovan was responsible.

"I can have a list for you of my mother's friends tomorrow," she finally said. "Sam has his karate class tomorrow evening. Why don't I drop him off for his lesson and I can meet you at Emma's Café at six o'clock? Would that work?"

"Perfect," he replied.

"I'd like to be with you when you talk to them."

Those eyes of his watched her intently. "Are you sure? Allison, I don't want to cause you any more pain than necessary."

"I'm positive," she replied. "I've spent the last fifteen years with my head in the sand. I'm thinking maybe it's time I pull it out and take a real good look around."

"It's your call. I'll see you tomorrow night at Emma's." As he swept out the door, Allison had a desire to call him back, to make him sit a little longer and talk about movies or favorite foods, of politics or anything that might take away the visions of the family she'd lost.

Instead she closed the door after him and locked it, then went into her son's room and sat on the chair just inside his door. This was what was important, the sound of her son's easy breathing as he slept in peace, the scent of him that lingered in the air.

She couldn't get obsessed with the remnants of the past and she couldn't be attracted to Seth Walker. She doubted very seriously that anything about the past could be changed, and Seth Walker would eventually get the answers he sought and be out of this town and out of her life forever.

Seth parked in the lot of the Super 8 motel where he'd been staying, his thoughts on the woman he'd just left. He'd spent far too much time this evening not thinking about what he was doing in her home, but rather wondering if her long dark hair was as soft as it looked, if her eyes would deepen in hue with desire or if she'd make low throaty moans when she made love.

His thoughts would have stunned his ex-girlfriend, who had often accused him of not being able to think of anything but men with jailhouse stink on them and court cases full of holes.

"Why can't you just be a normal lawyer?" she'd whined. "Hang your shingle, chase some ambulances or get traffic tickets taken care of. Do corporate work and make tons of money so we can travel and have some fun for a change."

Brianna had been a high-maintenance woman, and for a while he'd been able to ignore not only her incredible neediness but also the rather large streak of spoiled selfishness that ran rampant in her.

She was blond. She was hot and she loved sex. The last trait alone was enough for him to forgive a little selfishness. But it hadn't taken long for Seth to realize that it was impossible to have great sex with a woman you didn't really like.

He liked Allison. She was obviously not high maintenance, was independent and strong. Her tears had moved him and her laughter had been infectious.

He knew it was important that he stay focused on his job, that he not get distracted by her, but he had a feeling that might be easier said than done. He felt a kind of desperation as he thought of Hank Donovan. This was the kind of case he'd been waiting for, the opportunity to save a man he believed in his heart was innocent.

But what if you're wrong? A little voice niggled in his head. What if Hank had committed the crimes and had managed to fool him? He shook his head to dislodge the thought. He needed to believe in Hank's innocence.

He'd chase any new evidence he could find, see what the local law enforcement might have missed and present it all to Freedom Inc. After that, his job here would be done and Hank's future would be in the hands of another lawyer and a new jury.

And if he didn't find any evidence that would open the door to a new trial, then Hank would remain where he was, in the Lansing prison, living with the consequences of his actions.

Seth grabbed his folder from the seat next to him and got out of the car. The parking lot of the motel was deserted except for Seth's vehicle and a rusty black pickup parked at the other end of the complex. The place was usually busy on the weekends, but during the week Seth rarely saw another person.

He fumbled his room key from his pocket, but froze as he reached the door and saw that it was slightly ajar. He pocketed the key and backed away, back to his car, where he kept his gun tucked under the front seat.

He'd bought the gun two years ago when an ex-con hadn't liked his line of questioning and had stalked him. Since that time, he always had it with him, but didn't carry it on his person.

Placing the file folder on the driver's side, he then reached beneath the seat and pulled the small revolver from the cloth he kept it wrapped in. He tried to remember if he'd locked the door when he'd left earlier in the evening.

Maybe it was nothing. Maybe when he'd left earlier, he hadn't pulled it shut all the way. Yeah, right, and maybe next week he'd buy some panty hose and wear them down Main Street.

He returned to the door, the weight of the gun reassuring in his grip as he clicked off the safety. He stood for several long moments, holding his breath and listening for any sound that might indicate an intruder inside.

He heard nothing and with every muscle tensed, with his heart pounding, he used the barrel of the gun to push the door all the way open. It was too dark to see anything, but he didn't sense the presence of anyone there.

A flip of the switch just inside turned on the light overhead and as the room was illuminated, Seth gasped. The papers that had been in neat piles were strewn everywhere. The top mattress of the bed had been yanked off. Drawers had been pulled out of the dresser and overturned, their contents spilled to the floor.

The fax machine cord had been cut and his laptop was smashed beyond repair. A glance in the bathroom told the same kind of story. The few things he'd placed on the shelves had been tossed to the floor.

Tossed. The room had been tossed. Somebody had been looking for something. He clicked the safety on and stuck the gun into his waistband. He'd need to eventually call Dane Kelly to report the break-in, but instead of reaching for the phone, he sat at the table where his laptop was in pieces, and stared thoughtfully at the light overhead.

It was obvious whoever had come in hadn't been after the official court files, for they were thrown around the room. Besides, anyone could get a copy if he was willing to pay the copying fee to the court.

I guess we're the talk of the town. Allison's words

played back in his head. This wasn't a robbery attempt; otherwise the laptop and fax machine would have been stolen. Nor was it just a case of senseless vandalism.

In his gut Seth believed that this destruction was the result of one of two things. Either somebody had been looking for something, or somebody had sent the message that he wasn't welcomed here.

He got up from the table and went back out to his car, where he retrieved the file folder, then went back into the room and returned to his chair at the table. The folder contained his thoughts since his arrival in town, along with his theories and the avenues he wanted to explore during his investigation.

Was it possible that this was what the intruder has been seeking? Was the person who had broken in trying to discover what kind of information he'd already uncovered?

Or was this a blatant threat?

A hum of electricity zinged through Seth's veins. The real question was, if Hank Donovan was an innocent man, then whom was Seth making nervous?

Chapter 11

Allison arrived at Emma's Café at quarter after six to find Seth waiting for her at the table in the back. He stood as she approached and she felt a ridiculous wave of pleasure wash over her at the sight of him.

Once again he was dressed casually, in jeans and a short-sleeved white shirt that emphasized the sleek darkness of his hair and the width of his shoulders. This would be so much easier if he'd been a slob with bad teeth and a surly personality, she thought.

"Sorry I'm late," she said as she sat.

"No problem," he replied easily, and took his seat once again. "You doing okay?"

"Fine. I'm late because Sam couldn't find his *gi*. It was supposed to be hanging in his closet, but somehow it never made it there." She shook her head ruefully.

"When I was ten, I lost my best blue dress slacks. I wore them to school on picture day with the strict instructions from my mother to change them right after I got my picture taken. I did exactly what she said and changed into a pair of jeans, but I got home from school that day without the dress slacks and with no idea what had happened to them."

She smiled and leaned back in her chair. "I told you so much about my family the other night and didn't ask you any questions about yours."

"There isn't much to tell. I'm an only child and both my parents are dead."

"I'm so sorry," she said.

He smiled. "Don't be. They've been gone a long time. My father died when I was eighteen and my mother passed away when I was twenty-three."

"Is there a significant other back in Kansas City?" She hoped the warmth of her cheeks didn't show in blooming color.

"No, not even a casual girlfriend. For the past year I've pretty much focused on work."

The conversation halted as Cassie Burkhart appeared at their table, her order pad in hand. "Hey, Allison, Mr. Walker," she said with a cheerful smile.

"Haven't I been telling you for the last week to make it 'Seth'?" he said teasingly.

The young woman's cheeks colored a vivid pink. "You're just a big flirt, Mr. Walker."

Seth grinned at Allison. "I have no idea what she's talking about."

"What can I get for you two?" Cassie asked, her eyes sparkling overly bright.

"Just coffee for me," Allison replied, certainly understanding how easily a man who looked like Seth could cause a young woman to feel a bit giddy.

"How's the apple pie today?" Seth asked.

"As good as it was yesterday when you had a piece," Cassie replied.

"Then I'll have a piece of apple pie and a cup of coffee," he replied.

"Got it and I hope your tip today is as good as it was yesterday," she said with a cheeky grin.

He laughed. He had a deep, rich laugh that resonated in the pit of Allison's stomach like the boom of a bass drum. "You're a big-city boy who could easily turn the heads of us small-town girls," she said lightly.

His smile faded and his gaze seemed to peel away the layers of any facade she might present. "Could I turn your head, Allison Clemmins?"

He not only could—he did—but she wasn't about to let him know that. She ran a finger over the rim of her water glass and smiled. "It's been a very long time since a man has turned my head, Mr. Walker. I wouldn't get your hopes up."

"Ah, but I'm a man who likes a challenge," he replied. There was no question there was a flirtatious heat in the depths of his eyes.

It was heady, the fact that he apparently found her attractive, the fact that she found him equally attractive. She couldn't remember experiencing this crazy excitement with Bobby, but maybe that was because she'd known everything there was to know about the man she'd married, but knew little about Seth Walker.

"I'd say it would be a foolish woman who, under the circumstances, would allow her head to be turned by you, and nobody has ever accused me of being a foolish woman," she finally said.

He sobered and nodded. "Of course you're right." He leaned forward and she was engulfed by his scent. "But I'll tell you this: If you were a foolish woman, I definitely could be a foolish man." He leaned back as Cassie arrived to serve their coffee and his pie.

"I have that list for you," she said when Cassie left. She opened her purse and withdrew the sheet of paper that held the names of the women her mother had been friends with at the time of her death.

"And I have some news for you."

"What kind of news?"

"When I got to my motel room last night, I discovered that it had been broken into."

She stared at him in stunned surprise. "Was it a robbery?"

"No, nothing was stolen. In fact, my laptop and fax machine were smashed. I think maybe our investigation has already made somebody nervous."

Allison tried to fight against the crazy burst of hope that attempted to find purchase in her heart. "But that doesn't mean that Hank's innocent."

"Right now I'm just viewing it as an interesting development," he replied.

"Did you call Dane?"

"I made a report and he came to look at the damage." He picked up his fork and cut off a bite-sized piece of the pie. "I have a feeling I'm not one of his most favorite people."

She smiled. "What makes you think he'd like you? You're here to second-guess him, to punch holes in his investigation. I wouldn't like you, either."

He laughed and again a ball of warmth expanded in her stomach. "Yeah, unfortunately I don't make many friends in my work with Freedom Inc."

"How long have you been working for them?"

"Two years. This is the third case I've been involved in. The first two we investigated didn't result in new trials."

"So the third is a charm?"

"We'll see, won't we?" He picked up his cup and took a sip of the coffee, then continued. "What you need to understand is that I have no desire to help a guilty man go free. Freedom Inc. is truly interested only in helping men we believe the justice system failed."

"Is this all you do? Work for the agency?" she asked, intrigued to find out whatever she could about what drove Seth Walker.

"By profession I'm a lawyer, but I don't get involved with the legal work of Freedom Inc. I'm also a licensed private investigator and that's the talent I offer the agency."

"Who pays for all this? It can't be cheap."

"Freedom Inc. runs on donations, both money and through volunteers. I volunteer my time and services."

"Are you a wealthy man?"

He smiled. "I do okay." He looked down into his coffee cup and when he raised his gaze to look at her, once again there was a darkness to his eyes. "Years ago I came into a large sum of money, an inheritance of sorts, and I've been very smart with that money. It's given me the freedom to do what I want, not what I need to do to survive. Now, that's enough about me. Let's take a look at that list of yours."

He took the sheet of paper she'd laid to the side, and opened it. It was a short list, four names of women Allison could remember her mother having lunch with, calling on the phone on a regular basis.

"Do you know where any of these women are now?" he asked.

"Rebecca Roberts works in the dress shop on Main. Janet Cook works in the library. Both of those women still live here in Crow's Creek. Megan Tindale and her husband moved to Goodland right after the murders occurred, so I'm not sure where they are now, and JoAnn Kellerman passed away last year."

"Of these women, was there one who was particularly close to your mother?"

"Megan. I remember my dad teasing Mom that she and Megan were like Siamese twins who the doctor hadn't quite successfully separated. But I have no idea if she's still in Goodland or not."

"You know what her husband's name is?"

"Dennis. Dennis Tindale."

"I'll find them," he said with self-confidence.

Allison checked her watch. "I'm going to have to go. Sam's class will be over in ten minutes." She grabbed her purse.

"You going to have any time later in the week?"

Allison frowned. "I don't think so. We've got prom on Saturday night. I'm on chaperone duty, and every night between now and then I'm helping with decorations. But, please, keep me informed of what you're doing and if you find out where Megan and Dennis are now."

She stood, then had another thought. He started to stand as well, but she waved him back into his chair. "I do have to buy a dress for Saturday night. If you want, maybe you could meet me at the dress shop and we could speak to Rebecca then. The name of the shop is New Rags and I'm planning on being there around four tomorrow."

"Then I'll see you at four, and Allison, pick something blue. You'd look stunning in blue."

The man was definitely part devil, Allison thought as she returned to the karate studio. He seemed hell-bent on making her think of hot kisses and tangled sheets, of wild, mind-boggling sex. And that's the last thing she needed to be thinking of.

When she pulled up in front of the karate studio, Sam was walking out with Wayne. The mechanic looked almost handsome in his pristine *gi* with the black belt.

As Allison got out of the car, both males smiled at her. "Hey, Mom," Sam said. "Sensei Fenton wanted to talk to you about something."

The self-confidence that had ridden Wayne's shoulders as he'd left the building ebbed as he faced Allison, and a hint of a blush colored his cheeks. "Hi, Allison."

"Wayne," she said in greeting. "What's up?"

"Wayne wanted to talk to you about maybe me doing competitive karate fighting," Sam said, his eyes lit with excitement.

Allison's head instantly filled with a vision of her sweet son's face bruised and bloody. "Oh, I don't know about that," she exclaimed.

Wayne smiled. "I know what you're thinking. It's what all the mothers think when I mention fighting, but it's very safe. The boys all wear protective gear and the competitions take place under strict rules of engagement."

"Please, Mom, at least think about it," Sam begged.

Wayne looked distinctly uncomfortable. "I guess I should have spoken to you first," he said with apology. "It's just that I've been watching Sam closely and I think he has what it takes. I don't see it in all the students, just the rare few."

"I'll think about it," she agreed.

"It would be cool, Mom," Sam said as they drove home. "I could win trophies and ribbons and stuff. Wayne says I'm good enough. He says all I really need is to get a killer instinct."

Allison's fingers tightened around the steering wheel as the words sizzled through her like an uncomfortable electric shock. "That's the last thing you need to get," she snapped. "And I can't believe Wayne Fenton told you such a thing. You're a nice boy, Sam Clemmins, and you care about people, and I don't want anything or anyone to change that. Do you understand me?"

"Sure," he said in a quiet little voice.

It took about two seconds for Allison to realize she'd overreacted. "I'm sorry, honey. I didn't mean to snap at you."

Sam shrugged. "I didn't mean to make you mad."

"You didn't." She eased her grip on the steering wheel and tried to find a good explanation for why she'd gone off on him. The last thing she wanted to tell him was that she was struggling with the question of whether his grandfather had possessed some kind of hidden killer instincts.

"I'd never want you to do something that inflicted pain on anyone else, then feel good about it," she finally said. "We agreed that you'd take the karate classes for fun and to learn discipline, not to learn how to fight with anyone." She pulled into the driveway and punched the remote to open the garage door.

"Mom, if you don't want me to do it, then I won't," Sam said as he unbuckled his seat belt. "I just thought it would be cool to get a trophy."

Allison smiled at him. "You deserve a trophy for being the best kid I could ever want."

He grinned. "That's not what you say when you find my dirty socks around the house."

She laughed. "Maybe I'll get you a trophy for being the kid who never picks up his socks. Now, get inside and into the shower. I'm going to give the flowers out front a little spritz with the hose."

He jumped out of the car and entered the house through the interior garage door. Allison pulled the car into the garage, then punched the code to lower the door. She stood on the sidewalk and gazed at the straggly flowers in the bed just beneath her front windows.

She set her purse on the front stoop, then went around to the side of the house and grabbed the hose. As she stood and watered the flowers, she steamed over what Wayne had told Sam. Killer instincts, indeed. It both troubled and surprised her that he was not only teaching some of his students the art of competitive fighting, but apparently attempting to instill in them a certain level of brutality.

Who would have thought that the mild-mannered man who blushed when talking to women would encourage his students to gain a killer instinct? But then again, who would have thought that soft-spoken Hank Donovan could kill his entire family?

She shut off the water and coiled the hose back where it belonged, then walked back to the front door. As she reached into her purse for her house keys, she felt it—that sensation of somebody near, of somebody watching her.

Seeking a reason for the prickly sensation that shot a rush of cold air through her, she whirled around to look toward the street, toward the neighboring homes, to see if somebody was outside.

"Hello?" she called in a voice faint enough that the wind immediately snatched it away. "Hello? Is somebody there?" she said more loudly. She felt silly, but she couldn't shake the feeling that somebody was close, perhaps hiding while staring at her.

"Eric? Is that you?" She thought of the skinny boy with the big fat crush on her. When she'd felt this way before, she thought it might be Seth skulking about, but Seth was at Emma's, probably finishing up his apple pie and indulging in some harmless flirting with Cassie.

So who was watching her? Although she saw nobody and there was no direct evidence that anyone was close by, the wind felt like a malevolent whisper against her neck, and totally creeped-out, she hurried inside the house.

Chapter 12

"I can't believe I've got to go dress shopping with you," Sam said as he got into the car at his school. "Can't I go to Greg's or stay home by myself while you get a dress?"

"No, but I'll make you a deal. You dress shop with me without complaining, and on the way home we'll stop at Emma's and I'll buy you a triple-chocolate milk shake," Allison replied.

"And a piece of pie?" Sam asked.

Allison laughed. "Sure, and a piece of pie."

For the duration of the drive Sam talked about his school day and Bugs. The bunny was usually a source of conversation. Sam thought it the smartest, cutest rabbit in the entire world.

"We'll have to get a cage for the winter," he now said. "I can keep him in my room and maybe I can train him to use a litter box like a cat. Uncle David said they'll do that."

"Winter is a long time away," Allison replied. "We still have to get through the whole summer." As hot as it had already been, it felt as if summer had descended upon them two months early.

As they pulled up in front of the New Rags dress shop, Seth's car was already parked out front and he sat on a wooden bench next to the front door. "Hey, look, there's

Seth," Sam exclaimed with excitement. Seth stood up from the bench as Sam got out of the car.

"Hi, Sam," Seth said with a smile. "How was school today?"

"Okay, but what are you doing here?"

Seth smiled at Allison as she joined them, then looked back at Sam. "Didn't your mom tell you? I'm here to help her pick out a dress for the prom."

"Are you going to the prom with her?" Sam asked.

"I don't know. I was kind of hoping to finagle an invitation from her today."

Sam turned to Allison, whose cheeks were warm as Seth's sexy eyes teased and flattered her. "Come on, Mom. Put the guy out of his misery. Ask him to the prom."

"I can't imagine why you'd want to go," she said to Seth. "A bunch of teenagers, screeching music and icky punch. I'm there just to make sure nobody gets out of line."

"Sounds wonderful. I never made it to my own prom and I'm pretty good at keeping teenagers in line," he replied.

"Then it's a date," Sam exclaimed with satisfaction. "Now, let's get this dress-buying stuff over with."

The three of them entered the store, where Rebecca Roberts greeted them with a cheerful smile. She was a plump blonde who managed the store for an out-of-town owner. She eyed Seth with unabashed interest and then turned to Allison. "I'll bet you're here for something to wear to the prom. It seems like the only time I see you is the week before the big dance at the school."

It was true. Most of the time whenever Allison went clothes shopping, she drove into Goodland. It was only now as she looked at the woman who had been one of her mother's best friends that she realized she'd consciously avoided Rebecca because of the stir of memories the woman provoked.

She'd once spent a day with her mother and Rebecca in Kansas City. The three of them had ridden the bus into the big city and had gotten a hotel room for the night. Hank had babysat the younger kids and had teasingly told Allison to keep her mother and Rebecca out of trouble.

The two women had been sillier, more giggly than Allison and her friends, but it had been a magical weekend of fun and new experiences.

"I've got all the prom stuff in the back room. It's gotten pretty picked over, but there's still a few nice things left," Rebecca said. "If you two gentlemen want to have a seat." She gestured toward a tufted bench in front of a floor-length mirror.

As Sam and Seth sat side by side on the bench, Rebecca led Allison to a back room where dozens of dresses were hung on racks. "Size eight? Ten?" Rebecca asked.

Allison thought of those pesky ten pounds she'd been trying to take off. "Ten," she replied, and realized now was the perfect opportunity to ask Rebecca some questions about her mother.

Rebecca pointed to the section that held Allison's size. "I remember you coming to our house and playing cards whenever my father was out of town," Allison said as she flipped through the dresses.

Rebecca sat on a nearby folding chair and smiled. "Your mother was the best poker player I'd ever known. Ruthless, she was, when it came to playing cards." A shaft of pain twisted her features. "I miss her, you know. After all these years I still miss her."

Allison didn't even pretend to continue to look at the dresses. She turned away from the rack and gazed at Rebecca, noting the wrinkles that were etched into the skin around her eyes, that trekked across the woman's broad forehead.

Joleen would have been fifty-three years old this

September. Her skin would have begun to show signs of the natural aging process. Perhaps a gray hair or two would have appeared in her dark tresses. Of course she was forever frozen in Allison's mind as the vital, beautiful thirty-seven-year-old she'd been on the day of her death.

"You were close to Mom. Did she ever tell you about anyone hassling her? Somebody in town who hated her?" Allison heard the throb of her heartbeat inside her head.

Rebecca's eyes narrowed slightly. "In fifteen years you've never asked me anything about your mama. Is this about that man in there with Sam? I heard some man was in town and had talked you into asking questions and such."

"When you heard the news about the murders, were you sure that Hank had killed them? Did any other name of a potential suspect ever enter your mind?" Allison's heartbeat was a Chinese gong, a solo drum and rapid booms of thunder all at the same time.

Rebecca leaned back, the wrinkles across her forehead deepening with a frown. "I never in my heart thought that Hank did it. Even with all the evidence they had against him, I was stunned. He was crazy about your mother and you kids." She shrugged. "But you see it all the time on television, men who go crazy and kill the people they say they love the most."

The thunder and gongs died, leaving only a slow bang of a drum left in Allison's head. "So, you don't know anyone else who might have wanted my mother dead."

"Your mother and I were card-playing buddies and we occasionally went out to lunch or went shopping. We were friends, but we didn't share secrets—she didn't confide real personal things to me. She and Megan Tindale were really close. If she told anyone about somebody hassling her, it would have been Megan."

Rebecca stood and gestured toward the dress rack. "Did you have a particular color in mind?"

It was obvious she didn't intend to discuss Joleen anymore. It didn't take Allison long to find a dress. Although it was a stunning sapphire, she told herself her choice of color had nothing to do with Seth's statement that she should wear blue. She tried it on, pleased that it fit perfectly, but before she could carry it to the outer room and pay for it, Rebecca stopped her.

"Allison, we've got the prom coming up and after that the Pioneer Days—good times for the whole town. Nobody wants to be reminded of what happened to your family. In the days following, people were scared, looking at each other in suspicion. Sometimes it's just best to let sleeping dogs lie."

"I'll keep that in mind," Allison replied.

Minutes later Allison stood on the sidewalk with Seth and Sam, her dress hanging under protective plastic. "Me and Mom are going to the café for milk shakes," Sam said to Seth. "Wanna come?"

Seth looked at Allison, who nodded. "Okay, a shake sounds pretty good."

"Just let me get this dress in my car," Allison said.

"I'm going to go get us a table," Sam exclaimed. He took off running toward the café, obviously following the siren song of a triple chocolate shake.

Allison stowed the dress in the trunk, then joined Seth on the sidewalk. "I asked Rebecca some questions," she said as they started in the direction of the café.

"I thought that was something we were both going to do," he said in surprise.

"It was, but it just sort of came up naturally while we were together in the back room." She quickly told him what Rebecca had said. "Actually, I think the women would be more apt to talk if it was just me asking the questions," she said. "You're a stranger in town and besides, nobody seems too eager to have this whole thing revisited. I just think they'd open up easier with me."

"Maybe you're right," he agreed. "But I'd like to be around when you talk to them. And speaking of that, I've located Megan and her husband. They still live in Goodland and I was wondering when it might be convenient for you to take a drive with me there."

Allison frowned thoughtfully. "Sam is spending the night with Marianne Bloom and her son, Greg, on Saturday night while I'm chaperoning at the prom. Maybe I could ask her to keep him late in the day on Sunday and we could drive there Sunday morning."

"That works for me," he replied. "And speaking of the prom. Sam and I kind of pressured you into me tagging along with you. If you want to rescind your offer, I'll understand. I'll be incredibly disappointed, but I'll understand."

She smiled up at him. She liked him. God help her. She wanted to hate him for what he was doing in her life, for what chaos he might leave behind, but she didn't. It was impossible to hate him with the slightly devilish shine in his eyes and that smile that could melt an iceberg.

Most of all it was impossible to hate him because when he looked at her, she remembered that she was more than just Sam's mom, more than just the high school English teacher. He reminded her that she was an attractive woman, a woman who had been alone for a very long time.

"I guess I don't mind if you want to tag along with me," she said teasingly. "Especially since this will be your very first prom."

"What time does it start and what's the dress code for oversized teenagers?" he asked.

She laughed and it surprised her, that he of all people could make her laugh. "Most of the adults wear suits and it starts at seven thirty," she replied. "I need to be there about fifteen minutes early."

"Then why don't I pick you up at seven?"

"Sounds perfect," she agreed. She'd chaperoned the prom for the past six years, but for the first time she was looking forward to it with an eagerness that surprised her, and for some reason, that frightened her almost as much as what they might uncover as they dug into the past.

Chapter 13

The prom was just a prelude to the night as far as the teens were concerned. They'd begin here at the high school, but would eventually end at an after-prom party at somebody's house or in a motel room or in Baxter's pasture. This was the night that curfews were extended or banished altogether for them, and they looked forward to it all year long.

Crow's Creek High School did prom the way prom had been done for fifty years. It didn't take place in a community center or a high-dollar hotel, because neither of those things existed in the small town. Instead, the prom took place in the high school gym, where the decorations were worked on for weeks prior, and the Stanley Boys, a local band, provided the music.

The theme this year was Camelot and the theater department had provided backdrops painted to look like castles and stone walls. Flowers burst forth from pots and trailed down the sides of the backdrops, their scent almost managing to overpower the faint smell of sweat and gym socks that the room normally contained.

A disco ball hung above the room, sending sparkly shards of light like starbursts around the room. A table at the back held a large punch bowl and a variety of cookies and little cakes. The women who worked the cafeteria during the school day manned the table.

Mr. Berber, the school principal, was dressed as King Arthur and stood at the door to greet people as they came inside. As Allison said hello to her boss, she still felt the giddiness of Seth's presence at her side and the way he'd looked at her when he'd first seen her in her blue dress.

He'd told her she looked beautiful with his mouth, but it had been the way he gazed at her that had made her feel truly beautiful. The sight of him in his perfectly fitted charcoal gray suit had been enough to stir her senses on a number of levels.

He'd surprised her with a corsage of white baby's breath and tiny rosebuds and as he'd pinned it on her dress, she'd felt the shuddery excitement of a girl half her age.

"Pretty hokey," she said as they stepped into the gym, where the band was finishing setting up on the stage at the far end of the room.

Seth smiled. "Hokey isn't always a bad thing. Besides, since this is my very first official prom, I don't have anything to compare it with."

"Why didn't you go to your prom?" she asked curiously. It certainly wouldn't have been a lack of a female companion.

His eyes darkened and his jaw bunched with a small knot of tension. "Another story for another time."

Whatever the story was, it wasn't a pleasant one, she thought. "Even though I've been coming to the prom for the last six years as a chaperone, I didn't go to my prom, either. My junior year I was in the mental hospital."

"What about your senior year?" They moved to stand against a wall as they waited for the kids to begin to arrive.

"After I got out of the hospital, I didn't return to school. I was eighteen when I got pregnant with Sam, then married Bobby. I think maybe it was a desperate attempt to build a family as quickly as possible."

Seth touched her elbow, but before he could respond, Michelle joined them. She looked like frothy cotton candy in a pink ruffled dress that complemented her blond coloring.

"You must be the new guy in town," she said to Seth, and held out her hand. "I'm Michelle Keller, Allison's best friend in the entire world, and if you do anything to hurt her, I'll have to break your kneecaps."

Allison gasped in horror as Seth laughed. "Don't worry, the last thing I have in mind is doing anything to hurt Allison," he assured Michelle. "The worst that might happen is that at some point during the evening I might ask her to dance with me."

Michelle grinned at him. "If you can get her out on the dance floor, then you will have accomplished something nobody else has done, because Allison never dances."

Any further conversation was impossible as the band struck up a song and the lights dimmed, indicating the official start of the dance. Within minutes the dance floor was filled with girls who looked older than their years in sparkly dresses and with sophisticated hairstyles. The young men swaggered with bravado in their colorful tuxedos and shiny dress shoes.

"So, exactly what is it you do as a chaperone at one of these things?" Seth asked, leaning close to her to be heard above the din.

"Watch to make sure none of the kids wander down hallways unsupervised, make sure the punch doesn't get spiked, watch for mischief that might get out of hand." She smiled at him. "It's usually pretty boring stuff."

"Why don't you dance?" he asked.

"Long story for another time," she replied.

They stood side by side for the next half an hour, finding it nearly impossible to talk as the band cranked out song after song and the noise level in the gym reached new heights.

"Mrs. Clemmins!" Eric Grant approached her when the band had stopped for a ten-minute break. He was in an ill-fitting tuxedo, the fabric old and shiny and the cut from another era, but he wore a bright smile and a fresh haircut that exposed ears that looked too big for his head.

"Hi, Eric. You look nice this evening," she said.

"You look . . . you look amazing," he exclaimed, his eyes shining overly bright.

"Eric, this is Seth Walker," she said. "Seth, this is Eric, one of my students."

"Nice to meet you, Eric." Seth held out his hand and the two shook.

"I know who you are," Eric said. "You're that guy who's been asking questions about . . ." He shot a quick glance at Allison. "About stuff."

"Tonight I'm just here as a cochaperone," Seth answered smoothly.

Allison placed a hand on Seth's arm. "Seth is here tonight as my guest." Eric's smile faltered, but Allison felt it was important that the young man know that she was not available in any way where he was concerned. "Did you bring a date tonight?" she asked.

"Nah, Beau and Patrick and I all came stag. Beau says it's more fun to pass around our charms to all the girls instead of being tied to one date."

"Sounds like a good plan," Seth said.

"I guess." Once again Eric's smile faltered. "I mostly just came to eat some cookies and listen to the music. None of the girls are much interested in me, but I'm still gonna have a good time." With a nod, he ambled away, nearly tripping on the pants that were two inches too long.

"There's something about Eric that breaks my heart," Allison said.

"You know he has a major crush on you."

She nodded. "I know. I'm hoping eventually he'll find a nice girl who will appreciate the good qualities he possesses."

"I went to school with a kid like Eric. Scrawny with bad skin and bullied by the more popular kids. At my ten-year high school reunion he'd bulked up, he'd made a fortune in computer programming and he had the best-looking wife of anyone there. It was the old adage of 'He who laughs last, laughs best.' "

"I'm hoping that will be the case for Eric," she replied, and wondered if he was the person she had felt watching her from the cover of shadows or brush. Surely a teenage crush couldn't last long if unrequited. And surely she had nothing to fear from Eric.

At that moment the band resumed playing and the noise made it impossible to talk and almost impossible to think.

Rick Solomon stood by the back door of the gymnasium, watching the explosion of youth on the dance floor, and he felt ancient. Many of the dancers on the floor moved in ways he would have thought impossible for the human body.

He hadn't been thrilled to pull this particular duty and suspected he'd been handed the honor because he was the new kid on the block. Across the crowded room he caught a glimpse of Allison Clemmins and Seth Walker standing together and watching the dancers.

Dane had been in a foul mood since Seth had introduced himself and told them what he was doing in town. Dane had told Rick he suddenly felt like he was on trial, as if all the work he'd done on the Donovan case was somehow now under suspicion.

The whole thing had managed to stir up a surprising dose of curiosity in Rick. He'd pulled the files on the old Donovan murder, and for the past couple of evenings before going to bed, he'd studied them. He'd found no red flags, nothing that should cause any real concerns for Dane. The man had done an adequate job and the arrest of Hank Donovan had appeared, at least on paper, to be solid. But Seth Walker seemed to have left a bad taste in the mouth of the sheriff, and an unhappy sheriff trickled down to create harassed deputies.

As the band took a break, Rick released a sigh of relief. He was stationed close enough to the band that he feared after tonight he'd be deaf. He forced a smile as he saw Eric Grant approach him. The kid looked like he was wearing a tuxedo he'd picked up in a thrift store and his face was shining with perspiration.

"Hey, Deputy Solomon," he greeted him.

"Hi, Eric. Are you having a good time?" Rick asked.

Eric shrugged, the shoulders of his jacket remaining in place. "It's okay."

"You headed out to a party afterward? I hear there's a bunch of them taking place."

"I don't think so. I'm probably just going to head home, although I'm sure my buddies are going to do the party thing."

"And you don't do the party thing?" Rick asked.

Eric offered him a slightly pained smile. "I'm just invited to the parties because I'm friends with Beau and Patrick. Nobody really cares if I come or not."

Daddy, Billy Broadbent says I'm a stupid dork. Rick's head filled with a vision of his son's sad face and for a moment Eric's face washed away as a vision of Brian was superimposed over it. He shook his head to dispel the image.

"I know right now this high school stuff feels like it's the most important thing in your life, but trust me, Eric, this isn't the real world and you're going to be just fine."

There was a quick flash of pain in Eric's eyes; then

he offered Rick one of those smiles that hinted of what he might someday become. "Don't worry, I know there's going to come a time when everyone in Crow's Creek will be talking about me. I'll see you later."

Rick watched as he ambled off toward where Beau and Patrick stood near the punch table. The kid got to him, touched him someplace that he hadn't accessed for a very long time. It was a place of compassion that pulled him out of a well of self-pity that he'd entertained so long it felt normal.

He saw her then. Michelle Keller, her pink dress snug around her curves and her blond hair sprung from around her head in charming curls. She approached him, two glasses of punch in hand, and as he saw her tentative smile, a wave of embarrassment washed over him as he thought of how abruptly he'd run out on her the night she'd had him to her place for spaghetti.

"Hey, Deputy Rick," she greeted him. "I thought maybe you could use a glass of punch." She handed him the plastic glass of pink punch.

"Thanks," he said.

"I'd ask you if you were having a good time, but you look like you're about to face a firing squad."

Rick smiled. "I've never been in a room with so many teenagers before."

She moved to stand next to him and looked out at the crowd. "Just think, some of these kids may someday be running the country." She looked at him again. "Scary thought, isn't it?"

He laughed and suddenly remembered how much he'd enjoyed her company, and along with the memory of pleasure, there was also how he'd bugged out on her. "Michelle, about last week at your house," he began.

She held up a hand to stop the apology he'd been about to make. "I had a great time with you, Rick, and if you ever want to spend time together again, I'll be available." She smiled, a wicked little gleam in her eyes. "Excuse me if I'm being too forward, but you strike me as the kind of man who might need a kick in the pants."

Again a burst of laughter escaped him and he realized that at this moment, with this woman, the cold knot that had taken the place of his heart had warmed. It was both an old, familiar feeling and a terrifying new one at the same time.

"I just want you to know that if you need a friend, or something more, then I'm interested," she said. She didn't wait for him to respond, but instead turned on her shiny silver high heels and walked away.

Rick stared after her, a crazy yearning building inside him. Was it possible he was ready to put the past behind him? To let go of the grief that had marked his life for the past three years?

Maybe he could use a friend. He frowned, wondering if it was normal to admire the ass of the woman you were thinking of making your new friend.

Chapter 14

For Allison there was always something sad about the end of prom, when the room emptied of the energy of the teens, and the decorations looked gaudy and abused instead of magical.

There was no question that it had been the best night she'd had in a very long time, and it was because of two things. First, there had been no problems with the kids. Everyone had been on good behavior for the night, but more important, she'd enjoyed the evening because of Seth's company.

She wasn't supposed to like him. She wasn't supposed to feel that crazy electric tingle when he touched her. Did she find herself attracted to him because somehow he'd become a symbol of hope in her mind? She didn't think so.

Even though he believed in her father's innocence, she was still a nonbeliever. She refused to allow herself to get caught up in his fantasy that they would somehow discover critical evidence that had been overlooked and that would exonerate an innocent man.

What she felt for him had nothing to do with what he was doing in town and had everything to do with the chemistry between a man and a woman. Just her luck that the man to jump-start her chemistry was also a man who very likely would break her heart if she decided to follow through.

Maybe it was just the magic of prom that filled her as she and Seth left the high school. It seemed only natural that he reached for her hand as they walked toward his car and it seemed equally natural that she allow it.

It was just after midnight and the night was hot. "On a scale from one to ten, this prom was a ten for me," he said.

She laughed. "Considering the fact that it was your first and only prom, you don't have anything to compare it with."

"Still, it was definitely a ten."

"And now you're going to tell me why you didn't go to your prom when you were in high school," she said once they were settled in the car and pointed toward her house.

"It's a long story," he warned her.

"Then I'll make coffee when we get back to my place," she replied.

"Sounds good," he agreed.

They fell silent for a moment and Allison wondered what in the hell she was doing. Inviting him in for coffee? Wanting to learn about his past? It was like sleeping with the enemy, but for the life of her she was having problems thinking of him as her enemy.

During the ride back to her house they chatted about the kids, about how dress codes and dance styles had changed through the years. When they reached her house, Seth settled in at the kitchen table as she fixed a pot of coffee.

"Are we still on for the trip to Goodland tomorrow morning?" he asked.

She nodded. "I've made arrangements for Sam to stay with the Blooms until late tomorrow afternoon. That should give us plenty of time to drive in, talk to Megan, then get back here."

"You realize you might not like everything that

Megan might tell us," he said as she set their coffee on the table, then joined him there. "Everyone has secrets and children aren't always privy to the secrets of their parents."

"I'm prepared for that," she replied, although she knew she probably wasn't. She wanted her parents to be just what she thought they'd been for the last fifteen years. Her mother had been a tragic victim and her father the man who'd snapped. She'd grown comfortable with them in these boxes and didn't want to disrupt things. But that's what Seth was bringing into her life, shades of gray that would forever change the color of life as she'd known it.

"Tell me about your prom," she said, wanting for just a few minutes not to think about her parents or her past.

He took a drink of his coffee and when he looked at her once again, his eyes had taken on a dark glint. "When I was thirteen, my father was arrested and sent to prison for the rape of a sixteen-year-old girl. Even though he proclaimed his innocence, she'd identified him as the man who'd attacked her. Supposedly she'd showered away any evidence and it was strictly a case of 'she said, he said.' But she was the daughter of a prominent businessman and my father was a groundskeeper with dyslexia. When he was convicted and sent to prison, I was like you. I believed that people smarter and older than me must know the truth and because he'd been convicted, he must be guilty."

He paused, his eyes growing impossibly dark as he released his cup and instead clenched his hands into fists on top of the table. "Dad worked as a groundskeeper at an apartment complex. The teenager lived there with her father. Anyway, he went to prison and my mother fell apart."

His knuckles turned white as he clenched his hands

tighter. "I hated him, Allison. I hated him for doing what he'd done and for destroying our family. He tried to reach out to me time and time again from prison, but I threw away his letters, refused to speak to him on the phone. I lived to hate him. It was that simple."

Allison reached over and covered one of his hands with her own. "Trust me, I know." He nodded and she felt his hand slowly relax. She knew well the kind of hatred he was talking about. It had filled her for a very long time after the murders at the farmhouse. Sometimes she thought that it was her hatred of her father that had kept her putting one foot in front of the other during those terrible days just after the crime.

He turned his hand over to capture hers, his eyes still dark and tormented. "The worst part of all was that four years later the girl recanted her story. She'd made it all up, couldn't live with the lie anymore."

"But why?" Allison gasped.

He shrugged. "Wanted attention, worried that her father might find out she was having sex with a boyfriend. She had a million reasons why she'd lied. Anyway, she went to the appropriate authorities and the wheels of justice began to turn to get my dad released. On the day before his release he was stabbed by another inmate and died."

His pain radiated from his hand up Allison's arm and straight to her heart. "Oh, Seth," she said softly, unable to form more adequate words.

He let go of her hand and forced a smile. "It was a long time ago. Anyway, my mother didn't handle any of this well, and to answer your question, on the night of my prom I was in the emergency room with her as they pumped sixty of her antidepressant pills out of her system. She lived through that, but over the next four years she kept herself either drunk or drugged and finally passed away from a cocktail of cocaine and booze."

He smiled and wrapped his hands around his coffee cup. "I didn't mean to end the night on such a sour note."

"You didn't. I mean, I asked."

"Your father reminds me a lot of mine," he said. "He has the same quiet inner strength, the same sense of humor. He's a simple man like my dad with a strong sense of right and wrong. But enough about all this," he exclaimed. "I've just had a wonderful evening with a beautiful woman and we can pick up all this in the morning."

"I'm glad you enjoyed yourself tonight," she said. "I was afraid you'd be bored to tears."

"How could I possibly be bored? I had you to keep me company."

She smiled at him as her heart stuttered slightly in her chest. "I think Cassie is right about you. You're just a big flirt, Mr. Walker."

He laughed. "I only flirt with waitresses and beautiful women in blue dresses." He glanced at his wristwatch and sighed with reluctance. "I guess I should get out of here. I'm assuming we're taking off early in the morning."

"Whatever time you think is best," she replied. She, too, was reluctant for the night to end, but the rational part of her brain recognized that there was really no viable reason for him to remain any longer.

"Why don't I pick you up around nine? We should be at the Tindale house just after ten or so." He got up from the table and carried his cup to the sink. Then she walked with him to the front door.

When he reached the door, he turned to face her, a frown creasing his forehead. "Allison, I don't want you to think that every time I go out on one of these cases, I become personally involved with somebody. I usually manage to maintain a detached objectivity pretty easily.

But for some reason this time is different. You make it different."

She didn't know what to say, how to respond to him. He didn't seem to expect a reply from her. He opened the front door, then turned back to her. "I suppose a good-night kiss would be a stupid idea."

"Incredibly stupid," she replied, her mouth suddenly dry.

He dropped his hand from the doorknob and took a step toward her. "My mother never told me I was overly bright," he murmured as he gathered her into his arms.

She didn't fight the embrace but went willingly into his arms. "I guess I'm not very bright, either," she managed to say just before his lips claimed her.

The kiss was soft and gentle at first, what would be appropriate for the end of a date between two people just beginning to explore a relationship. She relaxed into his arms, allowing her body to lean into his. Instantly the kiss transformed from something simple into something far more complicated.

Hot and demanding, his mouth opened to deepen the kiss and she encouraged it, yielding to him by meeting his tongue with hers. His body was solid and warm against her and at each point of contact a tingle of electricity sparked.

Just when she felt as if she'd melt into him completely, he halted the kiss and dropped his hands from around her. He took a step back from her, his eyes glowing darkly in the light of the entry. "It would have been so much simpler if that had been a terrible kiss," he said, his voice holding a huskiness that hadn't been there before. He ran his hand down his jaw in a gesture that was now becoming familiar to her.

"It would be easier if we just kept this on a professional level," she said, surprised that her own voice held a slight tremor.

"I agree." He raised a dark eyebrow. "Think we can do that?"

She smiled, still warmed by the kiss, by those moments when his arms had held her tight. "Ask me again in the morning."

He returned her smile, then opened the door. "Good night, Allison. I'll see you at nine."

She stood at the door and watched him climb into his car. It was only when the car's taillights disappeared down the quiet, dark street that she closed her door and locked it.

With the taste of him lingering on her lips and a smile playing on her mouth, she went into the kitchen and shut off the coffeepot, then went into the utility room just off the kitchen.

Carefully she removed the corsage he'd bought for her. He'd had no way of knowing, but this was the first corsage she'd ever been given. There had been no flowers at the wedding ceremony when she'd married Bobby in front of the justice of the peace. Using a clothespin, she hung it upside down on the rack just above the clothes dryer, hoping it would dry nicely.

She knew it was silly, to want to save it, as silly as it had been for them to share a kiss. She turned out the lights in the utility room and headed for her bedroom, her thoughts still filled with Seth and that kiss.

They'd been like two teenagers unable to resist a moment of inappropriate temptation. In the bathroom she changed into her nightgown, then washed her face and brushed her teeth and headed for bed.

If the kiss had gone on for too much longer, if things had escalated, he might have been in this bed with her now. The very idea of a man in her bed, of Seth Walker in her bed, both stunned and thrilled her.

What was she thinking? She punched her pillow and willed away all thoughts of that kiss, of how wonderful it had felt to be held in his arms, to feel his hard body against her own.

Instead she focused on the tragic story of his father. Under the skin she and Seth shared more than just a mutual attraction to each other. The sins of their fathers, that's what they shared. Their early lives had been tainted by the purported crimes of their fathers.

In Seth's case, his father had been found innocent, but the case of Hank was still very much up in the air. *Your father reminds me a lot of mine.* His words whirled around and around in her head. *Your father reminds me a lot of mine.*

It had been obvious that Seth had been tormented by how things had played out for his father. What if Seth had taken up her father's cause to symbolically save his own father and rewrite the tragedy of the past?

He stood near the farmhouse, staring at the darkened windows. Almost three o'clock in the morning. Marianne Bloom and her son, Greg, would be sound asleep. Marianne's husband, George, would be at his factory job in Goodland.

The wind had picked up, whining across the plains like a lost, soulless spirit. He raised his face and closed his eyes as the hot wind blew across him, bringing with it the smells of cow manure, dirt and the faint tang of something dead. Hell. It smelled like what he imagined hell might smell like.

He opened his eyes once again and looked down at the hatchet he held in his hand. The moonlight overhead sparked off the sharp edge—sharp enough to cut through a tree trunk—or through bones.

Despite the wind he could hear the sound of his own breathing. Fast. Excited. And with just a touch of fear.

Was it time?

Was he ready?

He gripped the hatchet more firmly in his hand, liking the weight of the wooden handle, the sense of power that infused him as he swung it in the air. Once again he directed his gaze toward the house. It would be so easy.

One woman.

One kid.

Was it time?

Was he ready?

His heart banged and he breathed so quickly he was dizzy. It was as if the dizziness was the sign he'd waited for. Not yet. Not tonight.

But soon.

Chapter 15

The night had been relatively calm, considering the teenage parties taking place all over town. Rick had spent most of the night in his car, cruising the streets and looking for potential problems. He'd been called out to only one residence to issue a warning to turn down the music, as it was disturbing neighbors.

He was now parked in the motel parking lot, keeping an eye on a room where at least two dozen kids were packed inside. So far there hadn't been any need for Rick to get out of his car. It was almost four in the morning, but there didn't seem to be any end to the party.

He'd seen Seth Walker return to his room hours before and that had gotten him thinking about the Donovan case. During his years working as a cop in Chicago, Rick had seen terrible things, but nothing he'd been involved with in Chicago had compared with the brutality of the Donovan case.

He'd pulled the file and when he'd seen the crime-scene photos, he'd felt physically ill, and strangely enough, he'd thought about the scene in Baxter's pasture with the cat heads. There was absolutely no reason for one to evoke images of the other, but that had been Rick's reaction.

In the last week he'd heard grumblings from several people about Seth stirring up memories of the worst crime to hit the small town. The man was making enemies with his probing questions and by digging into the past.

It wasn't really surprising. The biggest celebration of the year was coming up in one week. According to what Dane had told Rick, Pioneer Days always brought an influx of visitors to town, visitors who spent money. Nobody wanted to think about or discuss something horrendous that had happened fifteen years ago.

His radio crackled and Dane's voice filled the air. "Rick, you there?" He sounded both sleepy and irritated.

"I'm here," Rick replied.

"Where, exactly, is here?"

"I'm parked at the Super 8, keeping an eye on a party."

"Well, pull out of there and head over to Terrible's. I just got a call from Wally, the bartender, and he tells me Leroy Grant is giving him a hard time, drunk as a skunk and wanting to drive himself home."

"Should I bring him in?"

"Nah, I don't want to hassle with the paperwork. Just drive Leroy home and tell him he can pick up his car keys in the morning at the station. And tell Wally to stop calling my home." With another burst of static the radio went dead.

Rick started his car and pulled out of the motel parking lot and headed toward the west end of town where Terrible's Tavern was located. Crazy's Bar was the kind of place where people went to socialize and have a good time. Terrible's was the kind of place people went to drink alone.

Located next to a dry cleaner, the tavern had blinds at the windows all drawn shut. There were only two vehicles in the parking lot when Rick pulled in, a Ford Escort and an old rusty pickup with a wooden toolbox built into the bed. Rick knew the Escort belonged to Wally. That meant the pickup belonged to Leroy Grant, whom Rick had never met.

During his time in Crow's Creek, Rick had been to Terrible's a dozen or so times, usually to break up a fight or to settle a dispute over a bar tab.

Terrible's was a small establishment, the walls painted black, the wooden floor warped and scuffed. A long bar stretched from one end to the other, and several wooden tables and chairs dotted the center of the room. There was no dance floor, no band to liven things up, just an old jukebox that sat in one corner and played songs of loss and heartache.

Rick heard Wally's voice before he got the door completely open. "Dammit, Leroy. You aren't getting your keys. You can't drive home in your condition."

It took Rick one look at the drunk at the bar to realize he must be Eric Grant's father. The man had the same slender build, the same dark hair and, as he turned to look at Rick, the same intense eyes, only in Leroy's case there wasn't a hint of needy friendliness. He glared at Rick with a drunken belligerence, then looked back at Wally.

"What'd ya do, call the law on me?" The words slurred together, nearly incomprehensible as Leroy attempted to stand from the stool.

"Actually, Sheriff Kelly told me you might need a ride home, Mr. Grant," Rick said as he walked closer to where the man had fallen back to the stool.

"Don't need no ride, just need my keys," Leroy said sullenly.

The man stank of body odor and cheap gin, and Rick held back a weary sigh and wondered what it was going to take to get the drunk in the back of his patrol car.

"Come on, Wally, give me my keys or I'm gonna kick your big, fat hairy ass," Leroy exclaimed.

"No ass is going to get kicked while I'm here," Rick replied. Reluctantly he stepped close enough to Leroy to place a hand on the man's shoulder. He felt the man's muscles bunch into ominous knots. "Come on, let me drive you home. You can pick up your truck tomorrow when you're in better shape."

"Yeah, Leroy, for God's sake, let Deputy Solomon take you home. I'd like to get home to my wife before morning." Exasperation filled Wally's voice.

Every muscle in Leroy's body seemed to sag and he would have fallen off the stool if Rick hadn't reached out to support him. "Least you got a woman to go home to," he muttered. He allowed Rick to pull him up and help him to the door.

He half turned to face Wally. "Next time I see ya, I'm gonna kick your fat hairy ass," he said, but it was obvious that all the fight had gone out of him.

"Yeah, yeah. Go home and sleep it off, Leroy."

Thank God Leroy was a slender man, Rick thought as he half carried, half dragged the stinking drunk to the car. He got Leroy into the passenger seat, where the man slumped against the door in a stupor.

"She was the only woman I ever loved," Leroy said as Rick pulled away from the tavern. "And she's gone. Dead. I don't got anything to live for. I wish I was dead." His head thumped against the passenger window with a thud.

Rick wrote the book on loss and he felt the man's pain. He knew the gnawing emptiness and the need to attempt to fill it with booze, drugs or whatever might give a temporary respite.

"At least you have your son," Rick finally replied. "I've met Eric. He seems like a pretty decent kid."

When there was no reply, Rick looked over at his passenger to see him passed out, mouth agape and a thin line of drool sliding down his chin. Rick sighed, not looking forward to the pleasure of trying to get the comatose man out of the car and into his house.

Rick had never been to the Grant place, although he knew where it was located. The gravel road that led off the highway was dark, with only a sliver of moonlight piercing through the thick stand of trees that lined either side. The road led to the house, a dismal ranch faded to a weathered gray and with hand-painted NO TRESPASSING signs nailed to the trees nearest the house.

Light peeked out from the broken blinds at the front window and as Rick turned off his car engine, he was surprised to see the door open and Eric step out on the sagging front porch.

He was still clad in the tuxedo pants and the white shirt that he'd worn to the dance, but had removed his jacket, cummerbund and tie. He squinted and held a hand over his eyes against the glare of Rick's headlights.

"Deputy Solomon?" he said tentatively as Rick got out of his car. Eric's thin voice battled with the wind that rustled through the trees.

"Hi, Eric. I've got your dad here in the car with me."

Eric's shoulders slumped as he approached the car and gazed into the passenger window. "Where did you pick him up?" Shame kept Eric's gaze not quite meeting Rick's.

"Terrible's. He wanted to drive home, but Wally didn't think it was a good idea. Can you help me get him inside?"

Eric nodded and opened the passenger door, his father nearly falling to the ground. They managed to get the drunk man between them and carry him up the porch and in though the front door.

The first thing that struck Rick was that although the furnishings in the living room were old and shabby, everything was neat and tidy and it was obvious that an attempt had been made to make things nice. A colorful blanket hid the back of the threadbare sofa and an artificial flower arrangement was in the center of a highly polished coffee table.

"Where do you want him?" Rick asked.

"Down to the bedroom at the end of the hall."

They passed a bedroom Rick assumed was Eric's. He caught a glimpse of a twin bed neatly made with a navy spread, a desk with books lined up across the back and a dresser with several bottles of cologne on top.

The bathroom they passed was equally clean with a flowered shower curtain and a spotless sink. There was no question that the interior condition of the house surprised Rick. He'd expected the interior to be a reflection of the exterior.

It was only when they reached the bedroom at the end of the hall that Rick's expectations were met. As Eric elbowed open the door, the stench of sour laundry and food, of booze and sweat, filled the air. In this room was chaos and hopelessness. It didn't take a rocket scientist to realize who maintained things in the rest of the house.

They dumped Leroy on the bed. "Motherfucker," he muttered, then began to snore.

Eric followed Rick out of the room and pulled the door closed as if to keep the ugliness from seeping into the rest of the house. "Sorry about this," Eric said as they walked back up the hallway.

"No need for you to apologize. Shit happens."

Eric offered him a small smile. "With Leroy shit happens a lot. You want a cup of coffee or something? It would just take a moment for me to make some." Almost four in the morning and there was still such loneliness that resonated in his voice.

"I can't hang around, Eric. I'm on duty until seven," Rick replied as the two of them walked to the front door. "But, you know, if you ever want to talk or just hang out,

I'm living in the yellow house on Maple Street. You can stop by anytime."

"Really?" Eric's eyes lit up. "We could talk about police stuff, maybe kick around old cases, like the Zodiac killer."

"Sure," Rick agreed. He hesitated at the door. "When did your mom pass away, Eric?"

Eric frowned. "My mom? She's not dead. She's remarried and living in Florida. Why would you think she's dead?"

"Just something I heard that I must have misunderstood," Rick replied. "Will you be okay?"

Eric glanced down the hallway to the closed bedroom door. "Sure, I'll be fine."

With a murmur of good night, Rick walked outside, where the hot night wind, like a hungry beast, nearly sucked the air from his lungs. He started the engine and looked at Eric, a lonely boy with a drunken father who had apparently loved a woman who hadn't been his wife.

Chapter 16

She dreamed of her father. Well, not really dreamed, but rather recalled an ancient childhood memory that had been long buried inside her head. Before there had been Johnny and Jenny, while Allison had been a little girl, her mother had awakened her each morning for breakfast.

Allison would tumble out of bed and still clad in her pajamas and half-asleep, she'd go into the kitchen and crawl up on her daddy's lap. She dreamed of those moments, when the beginning and end of her safe little world had been in the scent of frying bacon, the pleasant sound of her mother's singing and the snug security of her daddy's arms holding her tight.

She'd awakened surprised to find tears still damp on her cheeks. They were the first tears she'd shed for the life she'd once had, for the man who had been arrested for the death of that life.

Minutes later she stood beneath the hot spray of a shower and was surprised to discover that the tears had not ceased. She slumped against the back of the shower stall and allowed the hot water to beat against her, hoping to wash away the pain of those night memories.

For sixteen years her father had made her feel as if she was the center of his universe. Even though he'd loved Jenny and Johnny, he'd always made Allison believe that the firstborn was special, that she was special.

She was ashamed to admit that her anger at her father over the deaths of Johnny, Jenny and Joleen was not quite as raw and painful as the idea that he had tried to kill her, that he'd hit *her* over the head with a killing blow, carried *her* into her bedroom, then wrapped his hands around *her* neck to steal the last gasp of life from her.

From *her*.

From his firstborn, the child he'd cuddled in the mornings, the little girl he'd said he loved more than life itself. How could he have stared into her face and wrapped his hands around her neck and squeezed? And how arrogant she must be to think that he might be capable of killing the others, but couldn't possibly have been capable of killing her.

These thoughts sickened her and by the time she got out of the shower, she felt drained and wanted nothing more than to crawl back into bed and not face the day with Seth.

She felt better after she was dressed and at the kitchen table with a cup of strong coffee in hand. She watched the sun rising, a bright orange fireball that portended another day of heat and dust.

The phone rang at eight and Allison jumped up from the kitchen table to answer, wondering if Seth was calling to cancel the trip to Goodland. It was her aunt, whom she hadn't heard from for nearly a week.

"I heard you took a guest with you to the prom last night," Maureen said, her voice holding a touch of coolness.

"I did, and we had a wonderful time," Allison replied, refusing to feel guilty about the choices she was making where Seth was concerned.

"I was calling to see if you and Sam were coming over this afternoon for lunch."

"I haven't heard from you this week, so I've made other plans for the day. Besides, Sam is staying with

Marianne Bloom until late this afternoon." Allison fought her desire to apologize to her aunt, to somehow bow to Maureen's iron will.

Maureen sighed audibly. "I don't like this, Allison. I don't like us being at odds with each other."

"I don't like it, either, but I intend to help Seth investigate what happened to my family. In fact, we're driving into Goodland this morning to see if we can find Megan Tindale and ask her some questions about Mom."

"Megan Tindale was a lush who encouraged your mother's silly fantasies. You won't find any truth by talking to her. Besides, justice has already been done for your poor mother and Johnny and Jenny. You never asked questions, Allison. Ask them now if you must. Ask your Mr. Walker about all the evidence that pointed directly to your father's guilt. Then maybe you'll see that you're on a fool's errand and none of this is making you any friends in this town."

Allison sighed. What a way to start a morning. "I can't help what people think about me or about Seth. Maybe this is a fool's errand, but all I can tell you is that it's something I have to do. I thought I had closure, but what I've had for all these years is ignorance. I need to do this, Aunt Maureen, for true closure."

There was a long silence and for a moment Allison wondered if her aunt had hung up on her. A wealth of guilt swept through her. She owed her aunt and uncle so much. They had been so supportive of her over the years. She knew bringing this all back had to be almost as painful for them as it was for her.

"Just don't get hurt," Maureen finally said. "I can't help but worry about you. You were so fragile before."

Allison smiled into the phone, relief coursing through her. "Aunt Maureen, you've helped to make me a strong woman. Don't worry. I'm not about to let any of this get to me."

With plans made for next Sunday's lunch, the two women hung up. Almost immediately the phone rang once again. This time it was Marianne Bloom. "I know tonight is a school night and all, but the boys and I were wondering if maybe Sam could go ahead and spend the night again tonight. I'll get him to school in the morning on time and I promise I won't let them stay up too late tonight."

"Are you a glutton for punishment or what?" Allison asked.

Marianne laughed. "To be honest, I don't mind a bit. With George working weekends nights, Greg and I get sick of one another's company in the evening. Besides, I thought I might take them to a seven o'clock movie, and by that time it would be bedtime anyway."

Allison hesitated. Normally the rule was no sleepovers on school nights, but there was just a couple of weeks left of school and Sam was certainly in no danger of failing. "Could I speak with Sam?" she asked Marianne.

"Sure. He's standing right here at my elbow," Marianne replied.

"Can I stay, Mom?" Sam's voice filled the line.

"You aren't overstaying your welcome?"

"Gosh no, it was mostly Mrs. Bloom's idea," Sam replied.

Allison almost laughed out loud. She knew the two boys had planted the bug into Marianne's ear about another night together. "Well, then I guess we wouldn't want to disappoint Mrs. Bloom."

"For real? I can stay tonight?"

"As long as you understand that this is an exception."

"I understand." Sam's voice drifted away. "Hey, Greg, she said it was okay! Then I'll see you tomorrow after school, okay, Mom?"

"Okay, and Sam, I love you."

"Yeah, okay," he replied, and then Marianne was back on the line finalizing the plans.

When they hung up, Allison returned to the table and her coffee and stared out to the backyard, wishing she'd said no and Sam would be home with her tonight. The memories that had haunted her sleep and lingered still, memories of what she'd once had, made her want to cling tight to Sam, so nothing could happen that might take him away from her. She wanted to cherish each moment with him, every laugh, every smile, because she knew how quickly it could all be stolen away.

By nine when Seth arrived, she had managed to get her emotional footing, and the images that had plagued her sleep had been pushed back to a place in the far reaches of her mind. She opened the door to greet him and her first thought as she looked at him was of the kiss they'd shared the night before.

Amazing that the man who had begun her trek back into dangerous territory, the man responsible for the tension between herself and her aunt and uncle, and for the faint stir of hope that she refused to embrace, stirred her on a level no man ever had in her life.

"Ready for a road trip?" he asked as he stepped into the foyer. He smelled of shaving cream and minty soap and that spicy cologne that played havoc with her senses.

"I don't think an hour-long drive qualifies as a road trip," she said with a smile. "Just let me grab my purse and I'm ready to roll."

Minutes later they were in his car and headed out of Crow's Creek. "Did you sleep well?" he asked.

"I slept okay. What about you?"

"Like a baby. Nothing like a high school prom and a kiss from one of the chaperones to give a guy pleasant dreams."

Her cheeks warmed. So, that kiss wasn't playing in

just her mind this morning, but apparently his as well. She didn't want to think about it, felt the need to gain some distance, not only from the kiss, but from the man himself.

Ask your Mr. Walker about all the evidence that pointed directly to your father's guilt.

Her aunt's words played in her head. Maureen was right. Allison had never asked questions at the time of the murders or at any point afterward. She'd believed the answers were self-evident in her father's conviction.

"I realized this morning that you never told me why you don't dance," Seth said, breaking the silence that had momentarily descended between them.

Allison fought the impulse to reach up and twist a finger into her hair, a habit she had whenever she was stressed. "There are two reasons, both ridiculous and emotional."

He flashed her a quick glance. "Emotions are never ridiculous." God, not only did he have incredible kisses, but he didn't think emotions were stupid. Where had such a man come from?

She sighed and looked out the window, where dust swirled across the plains, adding to the desolate scenery on either side of the highway they traveled. "My last memory of my mother was the night before the murders. She had the radio tuned to music, my father was sitting on the sofa and Mom was trying to get him to dance with her. She was wearing a pink flowered dress with a full skirt that swirled around her as she pirouetted in front of him. Dad always said he had two favorite dance partners, my mother and me."

The memory was burned into her brain, a final freeze-frame of the family she'd lost. The flash of the flowers on her mother's skirt as she moved, Johnny's and Jenny's high-pitched giggles and the lines of exhaustion that had been etched into her father's face.

"Johnny and Jenny were dancing around the room and we were all laughing and encouraging Dad to get up, but he wouldn't. He said he was too dog-tired, but he promised that the next night he'd dance with both his favorite partners, but there was no dancing the next night."

"And there hasn't been any dancing since," Seth replied softly.

She nodded. "Even Bobby couldn't get me out on the dance floor when we went out."

"Tell me about him. What was he like?"

A smile lifted the corners of her lips as she thought of the man who had been her husband so briefly. "He was brash and bold. He loved parties and fast cars and me." A lump rose in her throat. "He was too young for marriage and fatherhood when we got married, too immature to shoulder the responsibilities, but he had a heart of gold and meant well. Following the murders, when I was in the hospital in Goodland, every day after school Bobby would drive in to see me. He'd sit with me in the courtyard at the hospital and hold my hand and tell me about things that were happening in school and what flowers he saw on the drive. He talked to me about normal, everyday things and for that year he was my lifeline."

"You loved him a lot." It was more a statement than a question.

She smiled. "I loved him with all the love that a teenage girl going through a trauma could possess. With the wisdom of age and life experience, I'm not sure Bobby and I would have made it through many anniversaries. The qualities I liked in him as a teenager aren't the qualities that would have endeared him to me as an adult woman."

"And there's been nobody since?"

"Nobody." She cast him a wry smile. "I figure the two most important men in my life betrayed me, my father by his actions, and my husband by dying. I haven't been willing to give another man an opportunity to let me down. And speaking of my father, I'd like you to do me a favor."

"What's that?"

"I want you to play the role of prosecuting attorney and tell me all the evidence that pointed to my father's guilt."

He cast her a sharp look. "Why would you want me to do that?"

"Because I know the evidence was compelling enough to get him convicted and I want to hear exactly what it was. Maybe by hearing it, I can understand why you think he might be innocent."

Seth frowned thoughtfully, the gesture doing nothing to detract from his attractiveness. "I told you that your father did everything wrong that day and if I'm going to give you the points of evidence, I'm also going to tell you your father's explanation of things."

"Fair enough," she agreed.

"According to your father, on the day of the murders he got off work early. It was just after noon when he left Goodland to drive back home. He arrived back in Crow's Creek around one, but instead of going directly home, he stopped in at the Gas and Go and bought a twelve-pack of beer. The prosecutor's office obtained a security tape in the store that shows your father making the purchase at one fifteen. After that, nobody saw your father until after the murders."

"So there's no evidence to put him anywhere else at the time of the murders," Allison replied. A knot of tension formed in her stomach. "So, what's his story as to where he was that afternoon?"

"Your father told me that he and your mother had fought the night before the murders. Your mother wanted him to quit the job in Goodland and get something closer to home. Your father liked his job—not only the financial stability it provided, but also the men he worked with. The tension between him and your mother was still there that morning when he went to work."

He paused a moment as he changed lanes, then continued. "Anyway, that day he bought his twelve-pack, but instead of going straight home, he told me, he went to Baxter's pasture to think, to try to figure out how to solve the issue of his job. He spent the afternoon there, just him, his beer and his thoughts. When the dust storm hit, he ran to an old shed on the property and waited it out. He was more than a little drunk, but managed to drive home when the storm passed, and that's when he made his second mistake."

"Which was what?" The knot in Allison's stomach twisted tighter.

"He found the hatchet on the porch by the front door and he picked it up, obscuring any other fingerprints that might have been on the handle."

"So he had no alibi for the time of the murders and his fingerprints were on the murder weapon. Doesn't sound good for your team."

"It gets worse," he replied, and she noticed that his fingers clenched tightly to the steering wheel. "Your father was under the influence and reeling with grief when Dane Kelly took him in for an interview. During that interview your father kept mumbling that it was all his fault."

The knot tightened to a point where it threatened to cut off Allison's air in her lungs. "And you don't think he's guilty?"

"Your father felt guilty at that point in time. He believed that if he hadn't stopped at Baxter's pasture to kick back with his beer, the murders wouldn't have happened. It's a guilt that will live in his heart for the rest of his life."

Allison's fingers found a strand of her hair and worried it as her thoughts raced. "Now, tell me again why you think this case is worth reinvestigating."

"The theory was that your father bought his beer and went home. He proceeded to get drunk and then a fight ensued and in a drunken rage he killed your mother."

"And Johnny and Jenny?"

"Happened to walk in either as the murder was occurring or just after. Your father was still in a rage, they were witnesses and so he killed them, too. Then you arrived home—another witness that had to be silenced."

Thick emotion crawled up the back of her throat, making her feel like she needed to throw up. She dropped her hand from her hair and stared at him. "How can you possibly entertain any thought of his innocence with the facts laid out so completely?"

"Because those aren't facts. They comprise a theory and I believe the theory is faulty," he replied. "I think there are other theories that should have been explored and weren't."

"Like the one where my mother had a lover?" The word left a bitter taste on her lips.

Once again he shot her a glance, the expression in his eyes inscrutable. "It's another theory." It was his turn to sigh. "Allison, the worst mistake you can make is to view your mother as a saint and your father as a devil. They were both human beings with strengths and weaknesses. I don't know if your mother was having an affair. I can't know for sure if your father was having an affair. I don't know if the murder was a result of some psychopath passing through town. The problem I have is that from the minute Dane Kelly walked into that scene and took your father into custody, the investigation was, for all intents and purposes, done."

"What about Dad's defense attorney? Didn't he raise these questions?"

"Your father's defense attorney wasn't exactly Racehorse Haynes or Johnnie Cochran. He was an overworked, underpaid court-appointed attorney whose main goal was to keep your father from getting the death penalty, and in that, at least he was successful."

"So far this conversation has done nothing but create chaos in my head," she exclaimed.

He gazed at her sympathetically. "Sorry, that wasn't my intention, but you asked."

"I did," she agreed.

"I've asked myself a million times in the last couple of months why your father would commit these crimes, then sit on the sofa and call Dane Kelly. If he were truly the cold-blooded killer he was made out to be, then he wouldn't have called to get somebody out at the ranch. He wouldn't have taken the time to report the crime. He would have been out of there and on the run."

"But if it was done in the heat of the moment, maybe he was remorseful," she replied.

"There are two compelling things that make me believe your father's story. The first is that his story has never wavered. He was in Baxter's pasture at the time of the murders and he hid in an old shed during the dust storm. Oftentimes guilty people change their story, trying to fit pieces of the puzzle together that just don't fit, in an effort to prove their innocence. Your father has never done that."

"You said there were two things. What's the other?"

"When your father was found sitting on the sofa next to your mother's body he had the hatchet in his hand, but there wasn't a drop of blood on him. He was wearing the same shirt that he'd worn when he'd bought the beer hours earlier."

"How is that possible?"

"It isn't, not unless he stripped naked to commit the crimes, then washed up and redressed when he was finished."

"And that would make it premeditated," Allison said. She tried to imagine the man who had ushered her into each morning within the safety of his arms blasting into a rage, then calmly stripping naked so he wouldn't get any blood on him when he killed his family with a hatchet, but there was no way she could reconcile the two faces of Hank Donovan in her mind.

She leaned her head back against the seat. "I thought I had it all figured out before you showed up in town. Now all I feel with each moment that passes is more and more confusion."

"Maybe Megan Tindale will be able to give us some clarity," Seth replied as they passed a sign that indicated they had just entered the Goodland city limits.

She fought a shiver of apprehension as she stared out the window at the passing scenery and wondered what secrets Megan might have to tell.

Chapter 17

"Take notes," Dane said to Rick as they walked across the high school parking lot and headed to the back of the brick building. He checked his watch as he took long, stiff strides across the dry earth. "Ten ten on Sunday morning. I should have known we couldn't get through prom night without some sort of nonsense. Don't put that in your notes."

At the moment they weren't sure what the "nonsense" was that they'd been called out to investigate. The school janitor had come in for some extra cleanup in the gym following the dance the night before, and had called the sheriff to tell him he'd better get over there right away, that there was something in the back of the school he needed to see.

Rick's eyes felt grainy from lack of sleep. He was supposed to have been off duty at seven, but had hung around the office drinking coffee and catching Dane up on the night. He'd still been at the office when the janitor, Jack McDonald, had called, and Dane had insisted he come along.

All Rick wanted was the comfort of his bed. He was too damned old to pull all-nighters. His brain felt as if it were wrapped in cotton, and he hoped like hell whatever they were walking into wasn't dangerous, because his reflexes were definitely in sleep mode.

As they rounded the side of the building, Rick smelled the familiar scent of a carcass left out in the sun, of fresh death not quite turned to decay. Any vestige of sleepiness vanished like a single drop of rain on the sun-parched ground.

"Jesus, I hope this isn't more dead cats," Dane exclaimed.

It wasn't.

It was dogs.

Five of them.

Headless and lined up in a row.

Rick identified a German shepherd and a poodle, but was unable to identify the others without their heads. He said nothing, was unable to speak around the bile that threatened to rise up in the back of his throat.

It was obvious these weren't strays. The bodies were well nourished and the poodle was clipped in a fancy style with balls on the ankles and the tail.

"Looks like they were killed here," Dane said. It was an easy assumption considering the amount of blood that stained the ground. If the sheriff tried to minimize this by saying something about teenagers getting drunk and stupid, Rick thought he might punch him in the head. Drunk and stupid was a teenage boy deciding to piss off a balcony, but it wasn't this carnage.

"The heads. They've got to be around here someplace," Dane said, his voice deeper than usual. "Let's take a look around."

The two men didn't have to walk far to find the heads, all lined up in a row beneath the shady leaves of an oak tree. Five heads, five sets of eyes staring at them in horror.

Dane let out a small gasp and stumbled backward. "The terrier on the left. That's my dog. That's my Felix." He turned and stared at Rick, his hazel eyes hollow and darker than usual. "What the fuck is happening in my town?"

Rick didn't reply, but any drowsiness he had felt earlier was gone, banished beneath the uneasy feeling that dark days were descending on the little town of Crow's Creek.

Chapter 18

Dennis and Megan Tindale lived in a tidy little ranch house painted the color of sand with hunter green shutters. The yard was neat and sported several flower beds bursting with colorful blossoms.

As Seth pulled up in the driveway, Allison felt a flutter of nervous energy take flight in her stomach. What difference did it make if her mother had had an affair? As far as Allison was concerned, it only added motive to the crime. Maybe the night before the murders, they hadn't fought about his job, but rather about an affair. Maybe that's what had driven her father into a murderous rage.

Or perhaps Hank had the affair and Joleen had found out, threatened to take the kids and leave him. Maybe that was what had set off the explosion that had ended in death.

No matter how the suppositions shifted and turned in her mind, like a game of spin the bottle, the bottle always stopped pointing with guilt at Hank. Still, if one of them had been having an affair, that put another person intimately into their lives. Was it truly possible that somebody else had been in that house on the day of the crime?

"Nervous?" Seth asked as he parked in the driveway.

"Yes, and I'm not sure why."

He turned off the engine and reached for her hand. She welcomed the warm touch, hoping it could chisel away some of the ice that encased her insides. "This all may come to nothing," he said as he tightened his grasp around her hand. "Megan may have nothing to add to what we already know."

She offered him a weak smile. "I'm not sure if this is a case of 'no news is good news' or not."

"We won't know unless we get out of the car and talk to her," he replied. He let go of her hand and opened his car door.

Allison steeled herself for whatever might come, but it was all for nothing. The Tindales weren't home.

"Sunday morning at ten thirty. Maybe they're at church," Allison said once they were back in the car.

"Why don't we find someplace nearby and have some breakfast? Maybe by that time they'll be home," Seth replied.

They found a Denny's not far from the house and settled in at a booth. Seth ordered a Grand Slam breakfast with coffee and Allison opted for a short stack of pancakes and coffee.

As they waited for their orders, Seth talked about inconsequential things, as if he knew she needed a break from thoughts and talk of Hank and the crime.

He told her a little bit about his life in Kansas City, that he lived in an apartment building downtown that had been renovated, and that he'd entertained the idea of getting married and having a family, but it apparently wasn't in the cards for him.

"Sam was all that kept me sane after Bobby's death," she replied. "I don't know where I'd be right now if it hadn't been for him."

"He seems like a great kid," Seth replied.

"He is," she agreed. She took a sip of her coffee. "You know I wasn't really crazy when I spent that year in the mental hospital." It was something she'd never admitted to anyone, not to her best friend, Michelle, not to Bobby and not to her aunt and uncle.

"Of course you weren't crazy," he replied. "You were traumatized and probably clinically depressed."

"Definitely traumatized and depressed, but I pretended to be nearly catatonic. I was mentally and physically capable of leaving the hospital a week after I arrived, but I didn't want to."

He raised a dark eyebrow. "Why?"

A small wave of shame swept through her. "I didn't want to be a part of the trial. I didn't want to deal with anything that was going on concerning the murders. I wanted to hide from it all, to avoid having to deal with it, think about it, and the mental hospital seemed like the perfect place to do that."

"And you've been hiding ever since," Seth observed.

She looked at him for a long moment, unable to help herself from noticing the dark length of his eyelashes, the strength of his jawline, the sensual curve of his lips—lips that had tasted of desire. And she wanted those lips back on hers right here, right now, to avoid the conversation she'd begun, the fact that she'd been so weak.

"I guess maybe I have been," she agreed. She broke the eye contact with him and instead stared down into her coffee cup. "Avoidance is a wonderful tool and I think my entire hometown has helped me stay in that state of mind. They've been very protective of me."

Once again she gazed at him. "I think when your investigation here is finished, I'm either going to like you a lot or I'm going to hate your guts." At that moment the waitress arrived with their orders.

As they ate breakfast, Seth once again tried to keep the conversation light and away from the reason for their drive into Goodland. Seth wished he could make her understand why he believed in Hank's innocence.

His belief was based on more than what he'd told her. It was based on hours of interviewing Hank Donovan, of staring into the man's eyes and believing he saw the truth there.

Allison had her father's eyes, intense blue and reflecting emotions like a deep pond reflected the afternoon sun. There had been times in the last couple of days that he'd looked into her eyes and lost his train of thought. The kiss they'd shared the night before had kept him tossing and turning for hours.

There was no question that she was hot. But his attraction to her was more than just a physical one. Maybe part of it was because of the awful tragedies that had shaped their lives. His father had been arrested for a heinous crime and for years Seth had hated the man. He'd hated him for what he'd done, for the shame that had descended on Seth and Seth's mother. He'd hated him as he'd never hated anyone, and he had a feeling Allison had felt that same rage for her father, that perhaps it had been that rage that had sustained her all these years.

That kind of unrelenting hatred intrinsically changed you at the core, altered what you might have been without it. Seth knew the damage that had been done to him, that the conviction of his father had written on the pages of his soul an ugliness that had never quite been erased.

The worst day of Seth's life had been when he'd realized his father's innocence, when the hatred had no place to go but inside him, where it twisted into a cancerous guilt.

"You ready to try the Tindales once again?" he asked when they'd finished eating.

Her beautiful eyes darkened, but she nodded her head and raised her chin. "Let's do it."

This time when they pulled into the Tindale driveway, a gold Ford Taurus was parked there. "They must be home," Allison said.

He could feel her tension but knew there was nothing he could do to alleviate it. What he was hoping was that if anyone knew what might have been going on in the private lives of Hank and Joleen Donovan, Megan Tindale would know. Women talked; they shared secrets and things with each other that men would never consider sharing.

This drive to Goodland might end up being a wild-goose chase, but Seth was determined to check every lead, no matter how big or how small. The break-in at his motel room had lit a fire in him, a simmer of the possibility of redemption. Seth hadn't been able to save his father, but just maybe he could save Allison's father.

They walked side by side to the front door, where Seth rang the doorbell. The sound of high heels on tile floor preceded the opening of the front door. A plump blond-haired woman dressed in a yellow blouse and black slacks looked first at Seth, then at Allison through the screen door.

She had chocolate-drop eyes and they widened as she stared at Allison. "Oh my goodness. If it isn't Allison Donovan," she exclaimed. She opened the screen and embraced Allison as tears sprang to her eyes. She held tight for a long moment, then ushered them both inside the house. "I would have known you anywhere. You look just like your mama, God rest her soul."

"Mrs. Tindale, this is Seth Walker, a friend of mine," Allison said. "We'd like to ask you some questions about my mother."

"Please, honey, make it 'Megan.' Come on into the kitchen. Dennis and I just got home from early church services and were having a cup of coffee."

Megan held on to Allison's hand, and Seth followed behind them into a cheerful kitchen with yellow gingham curtains at the window and the faint scent of fried sausage in the air.

"Denny, honey, look who is here. It's Allison Donovan and her friend Mr. Walker," Megan exclaimed.

Dennis Tindale was a tall, thin man with thick bushy eyebrows and a mouth too wide for his face. He said hello to Allison and shook Seth's hand, then excused himself and left the kitchen.

There was an offer of coffee, declined by both Allison and Seth; then they were seated at the table and Megan was gazing at Allison with tears once again in her eyes.

"Just looking at you brings back so many memories of Joleen. She was my best friend in the whole wide world. I had to leave Crow's Creek after that day. I couldn't stand going to the stores, eating at the café and knowing she was gone forever. Now, tell me why you're here after all these years and what you've been doing."

As Allison filled Megan in on her life since the murders, Seth watched Allison, a hunger building inside him. She touched him. She had a curious blend of strength and vulnerability that he found not only intriguing but also immensely appealing. He wanted to protect her from what might lie ahead, yet needed her to be strong enough to face it.

The last thing he needed to do was think about that kiss, about the fact that he wanted more from her. Taking things further with her would be unfair, not only to her, but to himself. He was here to do a job, nothing more, nothing less.

"So, what is it you want to know about your mother?" Megan asked, pulling Seth from his thoughts.

"What kind of woman was she? What kind of friend?" he asked. Allison leaned forward as if hungry to hear anything about the woman who had been her mother.

"She was a wonderful woman, a kind and loyal friend," Megan replied without hesitation. "She could light up a room just by walking in. She was the most beautiful woman in Crow's Creek and I was honored to have her as my friend."

"Was there anyone who didn't like her? Did she ever mention anyone giving her a hard time?" Seth asked.

Megan frowned thoughtfully. "There were some women who didn't much care for Joleen. Jealous and catty, they were, but it wasn't much more than that. Why? What's this about?"

"We think it's possible Hank didn't kill Joleen, that somebody else was responsible for the deaths that day," Seth replied.

A guarded look came into the woman's eyes. "Who else could be responsible?"

"That's why we're here, to see if you know who else could have committed the crimes," Seth said. He needed to break through the gated gaze of Megan to any secrets that might lurk behind. "Were you aware of either Hank or Joleen having an affair?"

Megan's eyes narrowed and she shot a quick glance at Allison, whose face held the tension of a thousand held breaths. Megan clasped her hands together on top of the table and shot her gaze out the window to a small backyard.

She remained like that for several agonizing moments, then looked at Seth. "Hank Donovan would never have cheated on Joleen. He was crazy about her and those kids, and Joleen was crazy about Hank and her kids."

"But?" Seth pressed.

Megan leaned back in her chair and released a deep sigh. "Joleen was thirty-seven when she was killed, and in the months before her death she was scared of getting old, afraid that she wasn't pretty anymore and that Hank would leave her, which of course was ridiculous, but it was what she feared." She looked from Allison back to Seth. "She was a good woman, a decent woman, but she was afraid to be alone. I think that's why she decided to have Johnny and Jenny. Allison, honey, you had started school and your mother hated being alone even during the days, when your daddy was at work. Then Johnny and Jenny got old enough to be in school all day and your mama was alone again."

Seth saw it coming, the secret that Megan Tindale had kept for her friend for the last fifteen years, a secret he knew would shatter the image Allison had of her mother, and he wished he could stop it from happening yet knew the secret was an important piece of the puzzle that might just lead to Hank's exoneration.

Megan twisted her hands together and tears swam in her eyes. "She was seeing somebody. It was only a couple of times and it didn't mean anything. It was just to fill the long hours of the day." She reached over and covered one of Allison's hands. "I'm sorry, honey. I never wanted you to know. She loved you, she loved you all, but she had her weaknesses."

Seth couldn't look at Allison. He didn't want to see the expression on her face, the hurt he knew would darken her eyes. Instead he kept his focus on Megan. "Did you tell Dane Kelly about this at the time of the crime?"

"I didn't even talk to Dane and when I heard all the evidence they had against Hank, I figured he'd come home early and somehow realized what had been going on and he snapped." She reached up and swiped at her eyes. "As far as I was concerned, there was no reason to give all those bitchy, catty women who had disliked Joleen something to talk about."

"And you don't know who it was that she was seeing?" Seth asked, still keeping his gaze averted from Allison.

"I don't have a clue. It was the one secret she took with her to the grave. I miss her. God, I miss her every day."

"Thank you, Megan, for speaking with us today," Allison said, her voice surprisingly calm and strong. It was only when Seth looked at her that he saw a raw, wrenching hollowness that pierced through his heart. "If you don't mind, I'm going to wait in the car." She was up, out of the chair and leaving the kitchen before either he or Megan could say a word.

"Where did this affair of Joleen's take place?" Seth asked. "Did they meet at a motel?"

"No. Joleen said he came to the house." She looked worriedly at the door that Allison had just passed through. "I didn't mean to upset her, but I thought you needed the truth. The truth was Joleen was a lovely woman, but she wasn't perfect and she didn't deserve what happened to her." Megan leaned forward, her eyes dark and hard. "If Hank Donovan is truly guilty, then I hope he dies in prison. I hope he dies a slow, painful death. But if he's not guilty, then you need to find who did it. You need to find him and make him pay."

Seth nodded, thanked her, then left the house and headed for the car, where Allison waited.

What price was one innocent man's freedom worth? Was it worth upsetting the people of an entire town who would rather forget about the original crime? Was it worth the pain of discovery that might taint the memory of a mother?

Seth thought about his own father and the fact that he would have done anything, risked everything, if he'd been able to get him out of prison even a day before his death.

Joleen Donovan was dead and nothing was going to bring her back, but Hank was still in prison and could be saved. Still with each footstep that led Seth to the car, he realized the question as to whether Allison would like him a lot or hate him when he left town had probably been answered. She would hate the man responsible for destroying her mother's image.

A weight of unexpected depression settled on his shoulders as he realized that he felt as if something had been broken before it had really had a chance to flourish. What was the price of an innocent man's freedom?

Leroy Grant gained consciousness in increments. First he became aware of the pounding in his head. Second he recognized that he was in his own bed, although he had no memory of how he'd gotten there. The third thing that pulled him from unconscious to fully awake was the realization that at some point during the night he'd pissed himself.

"Dammit," he muttered, and opened his eyes to the afternoon sun slashing through the window and shooting a shard of pain right through his eyeballs and into his brain.

He slammed his eyes closed against the offense and tried to remember what had happened the night before, but no matter how hard he tried, he didn't have a clue. All he knew was that he needed a shower. A man couldn't think when he'd pissed himself and his head banged like a young, eager hooker.

"Eric!" He bellowed his son's name. What he needed was a cup of strong coffee. Then maybe he'd feel like getting up and taking a shower. Maybe then he'd remember how he'd spent the past twelve hours.

"Eric," he yelled again, but there was no reply. "Where is that kid?" he muttered as he finally managed to drag himself out of bed. A glance at the clock told him it was after noon. That boy was never around when Leroy needed him.

Screw the coffee, he thought as he walked to the front window and looked outside. Damn, his truck wasn't in the driveway. There was no way Eric would have taken it, and that meant it had been left someplace else the night before.

Leroy headed directly to the bathroom, where he started the water in the shower, then stripped off his stinking, filthy clothes and tossed them into a corner. Eric could deal with them later.

Stepping into the shower stall, he leaned against the cool tile and raised his face to the hot spray, hoping some of the fog would lift and he'd remember something of his activities of the night before.

He had a vague memory of the hot night air hitting him in the face as he'd left the house, then another flash of memory of sitting at the bar at Terrible's, but there were hours in between that were missing, as was how the night had finally ended.

It wasn't the first time he'd had an alcohol-induced blackout and it sure as hell wouldn't be the last, but normally something set him off to drink himself into a blackout.

It was as he was getting dressed that he had his first memory of the night before—Eric waiting at the front door in a tux he'd picked up at the Goodwill, waiting for his ride to the prom.

Something in the hunch of Eric's shoulders, in the guarded gaze he shot Leroy over his shoulder, had reminded Leroy of Anna, the wife who'd left him so many years ago. And that had reminded Leroy of another woman.

Joleen.

He froze for a moment, suddenly remembering why he'd gotten worked up the night before. They were reinvestigating the murders. Joleen's daughter and Seth Walker were digging into the past. He'd heard the news in town the day before and it had sent him reeling. The last thing he wanted was for anyone to look too deeply into what had been going on in Joleen's life at the time of the murders.

Leroy had no illusions about his place in this town. He

was a low-life drunk who had no friends. He knew that if Allison Clemmins and Seth Walker dug too deeply, it was possible his ass would be sitting in prison, and he wasn't about to let that happen.

It was after four when Rick drove into his driveway and saw Eric Grant seated on the front porch. He'd spent the last several hours telling four families that their beloved dogs had been killed. He was beyond exhaustion and certainly wasn't in the mood for company.

But as he got out of the car, Eric cast him a friendly smile that made it impossible for Rick to tell the kid to take a hike. "You said stop by anytime," Eric said, an eagerness in his eyes that was impossible to ignore. "But, you know, if it's not cool right now, I understand."

Rick pulled the house key from his pocket and forced a smile. "I've got a half an hour or so." He figured it would take him that long to unwind from the agonizingly long day. He unlocked the front door and gestured for Eric to follow him inside.

It was only when Eric stood in the living room and looked around with interest that Rick realized that Eric was the first person who had been inside other than Rick himself.

The furnishings were basic, a sofa and an easy chair, a television and a bookcase. The walls were bare and for the first time Rick realized how little warmth or welcome there was to the place. Maybe it was because this still didn't feel like home. Home was a little boy waiting at the front door for him to return from work. Home was a woman named Holly who had once gazed at him as if he'd hung the moon.

"Nice place," Eric said. "Looks like a bachelor pad. No frills or froufrou."

"Your house didn't look like a bachelor pad," Rick replied, and indicated Eric should follow him into the kitchen. "Want a soda? I think I've got a couple in the fridge. Help yourself." Rick sank heavily into a chair at the small wooden table and watched as Eric opened the refrigerator door.

"You want one, too?" he asked.

"Sure, okay."

Eric popped the tops of the two cans, then set one in front of Rick and joined him at the table. "When my mom left, when I was young, my grandma moved into the house with me and my dad. She kept things nice. She died when I was ten, and I just wanted to keep things nice after she was gone. I think my dad believes I'm gay because I like the place clean and neat, but I'm not gay."

"It never entered my mind," Rick replied. "Not that there's anything wrong with it."

Eric took a swig of his soda. "I heard about the dead dogs. Beau was pretty upset to find out one of them was Felix."

"Everyone I talked to today is pretty upset about it."

"First the cats and now the dogs. What do you think it means? Patrick says he thinks it's the work of some weird devil worshippers."

"I don't know about that, but it's definitely the work of somebody either trying to get attention or just plain screwed up in the head."

"Maybe it's the beginning work of a serial killer. Jeffrey Don Lundgren once nailed a rabbit to a board, then beat it to death, and Peter Kurten had sex with sheep and stabbed them to death while he was screwing them."

Rick stared at the kid. How many teenagers knew about Peter Kurten, who had murdered women and children in Germany in 1929? Or about Jeffrey Don Lundgren, who had killed five people in 1989?

A faint flush colored Eric's sallow cheeks. "I told you I want to be a profiler. I spend lots of my free time using the computer in the library and doing research into the lives of criminals. It was actually Mrs. Clemmins who got me started. You know, what happened to her and her family and all. She's beautiful, isn't she?" The flush in Eric's cheeks deepened. "If I was older, I'd marry her."

The passion in Eric's eyes reminded Rick of younger, simpler days. In seventh grade he'd had a raging crush on his American history teacher. He'd spent many long hours seated at his desk with a book in his lap to hide the evidence of his uncontrollable reaction to just gazing at her.

Rick was surprised when a vision of Michelle Keller leaped into his mind, Michelle with those dancing blue eyes and the springy blond curls that just begged to be touched.

"I heard that guy Seth Walker is in town to look into the Donovan thing," Eric continued. He grinned. "I'll bet that's got Sheriff Kelly upset."

"I don't think so," Rick replied. "Dane shouldn't have anything to worry about. He's a precise man and keeps meticulous records."

"Yeah, Beau says his dad's so anal his asshole puckers when he smiles."

Rick nearly spewed soda as he laughed. "I don't know about that. He is pretty anal, but that's a good quality in a sheriff."

Eric tipped up his can to finish the soda, then got up and threw the can in the trash. "About those dogs. Maybe I could work as a sort of undercover deputy on the case," he said as he returned to the table. "If somebody at school did it, I might hear something about it. Then I could tell you."

"You think whoever did it might tell you about it?" Rick asked skeptically.

"Probably not, at least not to my face. But I'm kind of invisible at school. Most of the kids have ignored me so long, they don't even notice when I'm standing right next to them." His eyes darkened. "You'd be surprised how much stuff I hear, secrets and gossip, because I'm like the invisible guy."

Although he said it merely as a statement of fact, Rick could imagine the pain that resided behind the words. "If you hear anything, you let me know. Whoever killed those dogs needs help." Suddenly Rick's exhaustion was overwhelming. "Eric, I've enjoyed talking to you, but I've got to get some sleep."

"Oh, yeah. Sure." Eric jumped up from the chair as if terrified of overstaying and not being welcomed in again.

Rick scooted back his chair and walked with him into the living room. Eric was headed to the front door when he saw the photo. It was a small framed picture of Brian, his little face lit with a smile displaying a missing front tooth.

"Who's the kid?" Eric asked, pausing to look at the photo.

A million replies swept through Rick's exhausted brain, none of them the truth. It would be so easy to lie, to not give this teenage boy a glimpse into the unrelenting pain that never quite went away.

"He's my son." The truth eddied out of him on a sigh. "He died three years ago of cancer." The pain squeezed at Rick's lungs, pierced through him with the agony of a knife. As a cop, Rick could face off with the badasses of the world, and he'd rescued people from dangerous situations, but he hadn't been able to save his son.

Eric's dark eyes studied him for a long moment. "So, you're a father without a son, and I'm a son who has a father who most of the time doesn't remember and doesn't care that I'm alive. Life is funny, isn't it?"

He lifted his hand in a small wave, then walked out the front door. Rick stared after him and for the first time since Brian's death, he recognized that he didn't own all the pain in the world.

Rick moved to the front door and locked it, then headed to his bedroom, where he placed his gun and holster on the nightstand, then stripped down to his briefs and stretched out on the bed.

What he wanted was the sweet oblivion of sleep, but his mind whirled with thoughts of the day and Eric Grant. Although Rick was not an avid animal lover, the slaughter of first the cats and now the dogs troubled him immensely. Somebody in this small town had a very disturbed mind, and neither he nor Dane nor any of the other deputies had a clue who it might be.

There was a particular kind of criminal who liked to ingratiate himself with the officers investigating the crime. There were some who actively aided the police in the investigation.

Was Eric Grant simply a lonely young man who wanted to someday work for law enforcement and was looking for a mentor? Or was he something more insidious? Perhaps an invisible boy determined to make the people who ignored him finally pay attention?

Chapter 19

Allison didn't invite Seth in when they got back to her house. It was almost three when they pulled into her driveway. The ride home had been tense and silent and all Allison wished was that she could go back in time and forget the things that Megan Tindale had said. Several times on the drive back, Seth had tried to start a conversation, but she'd refused to play along and finally he'd given up.

She felt sick and as she murmured a good-bye to Seth and got out of the car, she realized part of it was because she'd begun to hope. Seth had made her believe that it might just be possible that her father hadn't really committed the crime. But the illumination that her father might have discovered that his beautiful wife was having an affair only added a motive to the senseless act she'd never been able to understand.

The minute she was inside the house, she wished Sam were home. The silence pressed in around her and she'd never felt so alone, or adrift in her life. She didn't want to be alone but she didn't want to talk to anyone, either.

She went into the kitchen and fixed herself a tall glass of iced tea, then carried it to the kitchen table and stared out the back window.

Was this why her aunt and uncle hadn't wanted her rooting around in the past? Had they been afraid that

Allison would find out about her mother's infidelity and be hurt?

Oddly enough Allison realized there was a tiny part of her that wasn't completely surprised by the knowledge that her mother had had an affair. She'd certainly seen the way men had looked at Joleen when the family went into town, and she'd known of the loneliness that Joleen had often complained about, the neediness she'd often displayed as she clung to Hank whenever they were together.

This new knowledge didn't diminish the fact that Joleen had been a loving and supportive mother. It merely added another dimension to the woman Allison had loved, a woman who, no matter how many affairs she'd had, hadn't deserved the price of her actions to be death.

Suddenly sick of her own thoughts, she got up and grabbed the phone. Maybe Michelle would be up for something that would keep her thoughts off her mother and the murders and Seth Walker.

"Hey, what are you doing?" she asked when Michelle answered.

"You don't want to know," Michelle exclaimed.

"Now I really want to know."

"Promise you won't laugh," Michelle said.

"Now you know that whatever you say, I'm going to laugh," Allison replied.

"I'm getting dressed for a dinner date with Wayne."

"Wayne?" For a moment Allison's mind was blank.

"You know, Mr. Kung Fu himself."

A rivulet of surprise swept through Allison. "What happened to Rick?"

"You tell me. I've made it obvious in a hundred ways to him that I'm available for something, anything with him, but I haven't heard from him. So, Wayne called this morning and asked if I'd want to have dinner with him. I told him only if we went to Emma's."

"Because that's where Rick often eats dinner. You are a wicked woman, Michelle Keller, using one man to make another one jealous."

"Yeah, well, my biggest fear is that I'll be married to Weird Wayne before Deputy Rick Solomon realizes I'm the woman of his dreams. Of course you know and I know that I'll always be Wayne's consolation prize. The real woman he wants is you."

Allison knew better than to protest. Wayne had made it clear that he'd love to date Allison. "Just don't break his heart, Michelle. He might be a little odd, but he's a nice guy."

"Don't worry, I made it clear to him that this was a we're-just-friends kind of dinner. So, what's up with you? I usually don't hear from you on a Sunday afternoon."

"Sam's over at the Blooms' and I was just at loose ends. No big deal. You go back to getting beautiful for your date and I'll see you at school in the morning. You can fill me in on all the details."

Allison hung up the phone and got up from the table, too restless to sit another minute. Maybe she'd spend a little while weeding the front flower garden. No matter how dry it got, the weeds seemed to find no problem flourishing.

She changed from her slacks and blouse into a sleeveless summer shift, knowing that even though by this hour in the evening the front yard would have partial shade, it would still be stifling.

With a fresh glass of iced tea in hand, she left the house. She set her tea on the porch, then went to the garage to get a pair of gardening gloves and a small spade. Maybe a little communing with dirt would clear her head.

She crouched down on the sidewalk and began to pull the weeds that threatened to clog the impatiens she'd planted several weeks before. With each weed she pulled, she felt her tension begin to ebb away.

There was no way Allison could judge her mother. Allison hadn't a clue what dynamics had been at work between her mother and her father at the time of the murders. She'd been a typical teenager, self-absorbed with her own little world and not privy to adult secrets.

She finished pulling the weeds and then sat on the front-porch steps and drank her tea as the sun began to lower in the west. For a moment she felt guilty about the way she'd acted with Seth on the way home from Goodland.

She was the one who had insisted she go along when he spoke to her mother's friends, and he certainly wasn't to blame for the information he'd gleaned in an effort to help her father.

A foolish effort, she thought with a touch of bitterness. He was like Don Quixote, tilting at windmills, fighting a battle that perhaps shouldn't be won. Still, she admired his single-minded focus and envied him his staunch belief in her father. She wished she shared that with him. She wished she wasn't so torn with doubt.

As she finished her iced tea, the sun sank lower on the horizon. This was the time when she wished she had somebody special in her life, someone who could share the quiet hours of the evening with her, somebody who would listen to her fears, her hopes, the dreams she wasn't even sure she possessed.

It amazed her that it was Seth that leaped into her mind. He was the man who was responsible for the doubt that suddenly seemed to shadow her life, the revelation of secrets that ripped at the fabric of her parents' marriage. Still, aside from the physical attraction she felt for him, she was drawn to him on an emotional level as well.

She'd meant what she'd said to him, that she wasn't

sure if she would love him or hate him when he finally left town. But at the moment he seemed to be the only person on the face of the earth who would understand everything that was going on in her head, and that, in and of itself, was intensely appealing.

A hot wind seemed to come from nowhere, blowing through the trees and rustling the leaves overhead. Dirt whirled in the air and dusted her face. A dog barked somewhere in the distance and an inexplicable shiver danced up her spine.

Suddenly she didn't want to be outside anymore, preferred the safety of her home. She got up, grabbed her empty glass and went inside. The taste of the dust lingered in the back of her throat. It was what she'd tasted that day when she'd gotten off the school bus. The day she'd opened her front door and walked into horror.

"A shower," she murmured to herself as she put her glass in the dishwasher. She'd take a nice hot shower and go to bed early. She hadn't slept particularly well the night before and the idea of an extra hour or two of sleep was appealing.

Half an hour later she was in her nightshirt with her teeth brushed and a book in hand. She got into bed and snuggled down between the flowered sheets, wishing only that she'd had a chance to give Sam a good-night kiss before going to bed.

It was only a few minutes after eight and she opened her book, deciding she'd read for a half an hour, then call it a night. She must have fallen asleep, for she came awake suddenly, her heart pounding the rhythm of fear.

She remained frozen, completely conscious and unsure what had pulled her so abruptly from sleep, what had caused her heart to accelerate to breakneck speed.

Her bedside-lamp illumination showed nothing different from when she'd gotten into bed. She didn't sense anyone in the house, no imminent threat.

Her heart slowed and she relaxed. Maybe it was a dream not remembered that had yanked her awake. Her book was on her chest and she closed it and set it on the nightstand. She reached to turn out the light, but froze once again as something banged loudly.

What was it?

Was it somebody breaking in?

Call for help!

Her mind scattered in a thousand directions. Don't panic. For the first time ever, she wished she had a gun, but she'd never wanted a weapon in the house with Sam, heard too many tragic stories about guns and children and accidents.

She eyed the telephone, but was reluctant to pick it up and make the call. What if it had been nothing more than a picture falling off the wall? A book in Sam's room falling over? There had been no other sound at all since that single bang.

Heart still pounding, she slid her legs over the side of the bed and stood. Surely if somebody was in the house, she'd know—she'd hear something else, sense someone near. She kept a baseball bat behind her bedroom door, and she grabbed it and held tightly to the handle as she crept out of her bedroom.

She flipped the switch in the hallway, hoping the sudden light would frighten away anyone who didn't belong or show her something silly that could be responsible for the noise she'd heard.

The first room she came to was Sam's. She flipped on the light and peered inside to see nothing amiss. The bathroom and spare room were next and again she didn't see anything that might be responsible for the noise or the crazy pounding of her heart.

By the time she flipped on the light in the living room, some of the edgy fear disappeared. Surely by now if anyone had been in the house, he would have either run away or attacked. The house was ablaze with lights and she still hadn't heard anything else since beginning the search of the house.

When she reached the kitchen, she eased her grip on the bat handle and drew in a deep breath in an attempt to control her racing heart. Whatever she'd heard must have come from outside. Her doors were still locked tight, her windows intact. She was safe and everything appeared to be secure.

A glance at the clock in the kitchen showed her it was ten thirty. She'd been asleep longer than she'd realized. She slumped against the counter as the adrenaline ebbed away.

She was about to head back to the bedroom when the sharp ring of her phone startled her. Instantly her heart was back in race mode. Who would be calling at this time of night? Sam. Had something happened to Sam? She grabbed up the receiver and whispered a breathless hello.

"Leave it alone, Allison. Leave the past alone."

It was impossible to identify the voice. It sounded odd, like a computer-mixed sound that could be either male or female, young or old. A wave of cold shock washed over Allison. "Who is this?" she demanded. A glance at her caller identification showed her that it had come in as an anonymous caller.

"Shut up and listen. Stop digging in the past or you'll be sorry, and just to show you how serious I am, check your back patio." There was an audible click as the caller hung up.

Allison held tight to the receiver as icy fear filled her. She finally forced herself to hang up the phone, then grabbed the bat in her hands once again. Her heart crashed against her ribs as she stared at her back door.

What was out there?

God, she didn't want to know—she didn't want to look—but even as she thought this, her feet moved forward, carrying her toward the door. She released her grip on the bat only long enough to flip on the switch for the outside light.

She leaned against the wall next to the door, trying to still her shaking body. The back of her neck was damp with cold sweat and for a moment she couldn't seem to catch her breath.

She closed her eyes as the voice, that horrible voice, replayed in her head. Who had made the call? Whom were she and Seth making nervous? Why would anyone care about the investigation into the past unless the person had something to fear? Unless he had something to hide?

Steeling herself, she pushed off the wall and peered out the window. She'd thought she'd prepared herself for anything, that nothing she saw out there could sicken or stun her.

She'd been wrong.

The sight of the lump of bloodied gray fur impaled to the wooden step by a knife driven through it caused her to reel backward in horror. "No," she whispered, and at the same time she crashed her hip into the corner of the table. "You bastard!" she screamed.

Bugs. Somebody had killed Bugs. Some bastard had killed her son's pet rabbit. Who could be so cruel? She felt as if a knife had been driven right into her heart, her very soul, as she thought of her son and his loss.

She dropped the bat and instead stalked over to the phone. For the moment her fear was gone, replaced by overwhelming rage. She punched in the number for the sheriff's office. Whoever did this was evil and she wanted the sheriff here to figure out who was responsible.

The dispatcher told her somebody would be right over. She hung up the phone, then picked it up once again. Seth needed to know what had happened. It was only as she punched in the number to his motel room that she realized she wasn't calling him just to tell him what had occurred, but also because she needed him here with her.

Chapter 20

Seth had just crawled into bed when the phone call came from Allison. She said nothing more than that something had happened, and asked if he could come over. Her trembling voice had frightened him and he was dressed and half out the door before she'd hung up.

The streets of Crow's Creek were deserted as he drove from the motel to Allison's house. A stiff wind buffeted his car as he stepped on the gas and ignored the posted speed limit as he raced to get to her.

What had happened? She'd refused to tell him on the phone, saying only that she needed him. As he thought of the break-in at his motel room, he wondered if something like that had happened at her place. Thank God she was apparently okay even if she had sounded shaken to the core.

He pulled up in her driveway at the same time a patrol car from the sheriff's department arrived. The swirl of the cherry lights atop the vehicle shot a new wave of panic through Seth.

He got out of the car and met Deputy Rick Solomon as he left his cruiser. "What's going on?" Rick asked.

Seth noticed the man had his holster unfastened and his hand on the butt of his gun. "I don't know. Allison called me and told me to get over here."

Seth looked worriedly toward the house. At that moment the front door opened and Allison appeared on the porch. Even from the distance and with the dim lighting he saw that her face was a shade of pale that most living, breathing people couldn't possess. Clad in a pink lightweight robe, she looked small and vulnerable.

She clung to the door for only a moment, then launched herself off the porch and into Seth's arms. He tightened his arms around her in stunned surprise. He had a brief impression of soft, unbound breasts against his chest, and the clean citrus scent of her hair, and a sharp hot desire sliced through him, a desire short-lived as he felt the tremors that possessed her body.

"Allison. Ally, honey, are you all right?" he asked. "What happened?"

"Is there somebody in the house?" Rick asked, his voice filled with urgency.

"No, nobody is inside." She took a step back from Seth and grabbed his hand instead as if needing the contact to keep her from trembling into nothing. "It's on the back porch. Bugs. Somebody killed Bugs to warn me, to stop me from digging into the past. Sam is going to be so sad, but I'm frightened."

Seth squeezed her hand and together they all headed into the house. Allison dropped her hand from his and instead wrapped her arms around herself, as if freezing. "I fell asleep reading and something woke me up. Then I heard a bang, but I didn't know what it was. I went to see, but I couldn't find anything. I was just about to go back to bed when the phone rang." She rambled as they walked through the house and into the kitchen. She paused at the doorway, her eyes large and dark as she stared at the back door.

"Who was on the phone?" Rick asked.

"I don't know. It came up 'anonymous caller.' I don't know if it was a man or a woman, but they told me to leave the past alone, then told me to look outside on the back porch." She reached up and twisted a finger through the dark strands of her hair, and a sheen of suppressed tears filled her eyes. "They killed Bugs. Oh God, Seth, they killed my little boy's rabbit."

As Rick went to the back door, Seth opened his arms and once again Allison clung to him as if he were her safety net. She didn't cry, although she continued to tremble as she hid her face in the hollow of his neck. It wasn't until Rick came back into the kitchen, his expression grim, that she released Seth and sank down at the table.

Rick sighed as he slid into the chair opposite her. "I'll take the rabbit with me when I go, but I need to ask you a few questions."

Seth sat in the chair next to her as Rick asked her to tell him again the sequence of events of her evening. As she repeated what she'd told them moments ago, Seth watched her, noting that a touch of color had returned to her cheeks and her hands had finally stopped shaking.

Seth had no idea why she'd called him to be here. When he'd dropped her off earlier, he knew she'd been upset with what Megan had told them about Joleen. He'd intended to give her some space, a little breathing room to process things.

He thought she might have called him here to tell him that she was done, that she wanted nothing more to do with the investigation or him. Her son's dead rabbit coupled with the threatening phone call might have made the cost of her father's freedom too high for her.

Rick listened carefully to her, asked pertinent questions and made notes on a small pad he'd pulled from his pocket. When she finished, he tucked the pad back into his pocket, leaned back in his chair and released a deep sigh. "It's getting damned dangerous to be an animal in this town. First the cats, then the dogs, and now this."

"Dogs?" Seth looked at the deputy curiously.

"We found five dogs beheaded behind the high school this morning. Of course that doesn't appear to be related to what happened here tonight, but the whole thing has me concerned."

He stood from the table and looked at Allison once again. "I'll be honest with you, the odds of us finding whoever killed the rabbit and made that phone call tonight are pretty slim. It's obvious you two are stirring somebody up."

"Don't you find that interesting?" Seth asked as he stood. "That we're asking questions about a fifteen-year-old crime and supposedly the guilty man is in prison, yet somebody is getting very nervous."

"Yeah, I do find that interesting," Rick replied. "And now I'm going to get the rabbit and get out of here. Who knows? Maybe whoever did this left fingerprints on the knife. I'll ask your neighbors if they saw or heard anything."

"You might as well not bother. Nobody lives on one side of me, and on the other side is Ed Jacobs and he's deaf as a rock." Allison's voice was flat.

"I'll check with him anyway. Maybe he saw something," Rick said.

Seth looked at Allison, who hadn't moved from the table. "I'm going to walk out with Rick. Are you okay?" She nodded and Seth followed Rick out the back door.

"I've got a bag in my car. I'll be right back," Rick said.

Seth watched him disappear around the side of the house, then looked down at what had been a young boy's pet, a rabbit named Bugs. He knew part of Allison's horror had to come from the fact that tomorrow she was going to have to tell her son that Bugs was dead. Seth's heart twisted as he thought of Sam.

Rick returned with a plastic bag and he pulled on

gloves to remove both the knife and the rabbit, then placed them carefully into the bag. When he was finished, Seth walked with him back around to the house and to Rick's car. "Like I told Allison, I'm not expecting to learn anything from either the rabbit or the knife. Whoever did this was probably smart enough not to leave behind any fingerprints."

He placed the plastic bag into the trunk of his car, then turned back with tired eyes to look at Seth. "I don't know what's going on here. I can't get a handle on it. But, considering that you had a break-in at the motel and with what happened tonight, if I were you and Allison, I'd be careful."

"I have no intention of stopping," Seth replied. "This just makes me believe even more that it's possible Hank Donovan is innocent and the real killer is still here in town."

Rick sighed. "God, I hope you're wrong." With a wave of his hand he got into his car.

Seth watched him pull away from the curb, then headed to the front door. When he walked into the kitchen, Allison was no longer seated at the table. The back door was open and he saw her there, on her knees with a soapy sponge in her hand, attempting to wash away the blood that stained the step.

He touched her shoulder. "Allison, stop."

She looked up at him, her face twisted with agony. "I can't. I don't want Sam to see this."

Once again his heart constricted. She looked so small, so utterly vulnerable and as if something had broken inside her. He crouched down next to her and took the sponge from her hand. "Go make a short pot of coffee or something. I'll finish this up."

She cast him a grateful look, then went back into the kitchen. Seth scrubbed the step until there was no trace of Bug's blood left, then went back inside, where he tossed the sponge in the trash and washed his hands in the sink.

Allison had made a pot of coffee and once again sat at the table. She started to rise, but he gestured her back down. "I'll get it," he said. "Just point me in the direction of the cups."

She pointed to the cabinet next to the sink. Neither of them spoke until he'd poured the coffee and joined her at the table, and then it was she who broke the silence.

"What I don't understand is why the caller couldn't have made his point by throwing a brick through my window or blowing up my car. Why did he have to do something to hurt Sam?" The tremor in her voice spoke not only of grief but also of an underlying hint of anger.

"Maybe because whoever did this knew that the way to get you to quit was not to hurt you but to hurt your son," he replied.

Her eyes changed from dark blue warm pools to glittering chunks of ice. "Then they underestimated me. When I got home this afternoon, I thought about calling it quits, about telling you to go away and leave me alone."

"I know the information Megan told us about your mother hurt you," he said with sympathy. He reached across the table, unsure whether she would take his hand, but wanting to touch her, to try somehow to ease the pain he felt responsible for causing. "And I'm sorry for that. The last thing I ever wanted was for any of this to hurt you."

She looked at his hand and slowly moved hers to grasp it. He curled his fingers around hers, and wondered how in the hell this woman had gotten to him so completely in such a short span of time.

"I know my mother loved my father. I was there—I saw it on her face whenever they were together. I heard it in her voice when she called his name. But I also know that Mom had a neediness inside her, that whenever Dad was away from her, she was miserably unhappy. Did she make mistakes? Apparently so, she was human."

She turned her head and stared out at the darkness of the night. When she finally turned back to look at him, her eyes held a steely strength, a fierce determination. "I'm not quitting. Initially when I heard that my mother might have had a lover, all I could see was that it strengthened my father's motive to kill her. But now I see what it means is that another man was intimately in our lives, a man who might have known that Johnny loved to draw and Jenny loved her stuffed dog."

Her fingers tightened on his with each word she spoke. "He might be somebody who shops in the same stores that I do, a man who smiles at me on the street when we pass or visits with me at a school activity. I want to know who he is, Seth, and I'm not quitting until I know." She released his hand and sat back in the chair.

"That means we're going to have to look at every man in town, ask questions and see what responses we get. Everyone will know that your mother was unfaithful to your father."

Her gaze skittered away from his and once again she stared out the window. He saw the tension that thinned her lips and stiffened her spine. "Maybe the price is too high," he said softly.

Her gaze shot back to his. "No. I need the truth and I need to make sure that when my father went to prison for the rest of his life, justice was done. Whatever anyone says about my mother, it can't hurt her and I won't allow it to hurt me."

The wind howled around the side of the house. Allison shivered and her eyes hollowed out. "I won't lie. I'm scared, Seth."

He wanted to take her in his arms, hold her tight and tell her that everything was going to be fine, but he couldn't do that, because he couldn't know; he wasn't sure exactly what they were up against.

At best, this maliciousness tonight was the work of a coward who simply didn't want it known that he'd had an affair with Joleen Donovan. At worst, it was the work of a cold-blooded killer who had believed himself hidden for all these years and now would do anything to make sure that he remained safe and anonymous.

Mary Kelly rolled over in bed and realized her husband wasn't in it. The wind slapped tree branches against the window and sent a mournful sound through the house.

It had been a bad day. Dane had loved that dog and finding him dead like that had sent her strong handsome husband into one of his dark, silent moods.

Before the silence had set in, he'd been angry with Beau, who had confessed to letting Felix out the night before but couldn't remember if he'd let the dog back into the house. He'd yelled at her for not noticing that the dog wasn't around first thing that morning. She rarely knew where Felix was when she got up at the crack of dawn. He could be curled up next to Dane's chair in the living room, asleep on a rug in their bedroom or in the room with Beau.

She got out of bed, and aided by the moonlight cast into the window and familiarity, she left the bedroom and walked down the hallway to find her husband. He hadn't eaten much at dinner. Maybe he'd gotten up to fix himself a sandwich or grab a hunk of the cake she'd baked for dessert.

He wasn't in the kitchen. He was sitting in the living room in his recliner, a shaft of moonlight dancing across his features. She stood for a moment in the darkness and watched him. He stared out the window, his face void of expression.

"Dane, honey, what are you doing?" she asked softly. She turned on the light and he winced and covered his eyes with the back of his hand.

"Couldn't sleep," he replied.

She walked over to his side, wanting to touch him, to stroke away the tired lines that creased his face, but there was something about his demeanor that kept her from doing so. "Is it Felix?" she asked.

"Felix and all the other dogs and those damned cats." He released a weary sigh and stared out the window. "I can't get a handle on it, Mary. For the life of me I can't figure out what the hell is going on."

"Come to bed, honey. You can't solve anything sitting up all night and stewing." She touched his arm and felt the muscles bunched in tight knots.

"You go on back to bed," he said, and moved his arm away from her touch.

"You want to talk about it?" she asked tentatively.

He turned back to look at her, his eyes cool and distant. "I don't want to talk. I just want to sit here and think by myself."

Mary tamped down the hurt that welled up inside her. She knew he didn't mean it the way it sounded. "Then I'll just go back to bed. Want the light off or on?" she asked.

"Off."

She turned out the light and made her way back down the hallway to the master bedroom. She crawled into bed and tried to still the slow, anxious thud of her heart.

Really bad things rarely happened in Crow's Creek. Oh, there were the usual things. Robberies, car accidents—old Joe Rankin had put a bullet through his own thigh in a hunting accident. There were the usual bar fights, and the Johnsons were always good for a domestic-dispute issue despite the fact that they were divorced.

Dane had always ridden with the punches, handling things with aplomb. Except for the Donovan case. And his mood now reminded her of how he'd been then.

Hopefully he could find out who was responsible for Felix's and all the other animals' deaths; otherwise it was going to be a long, dreadful summer in Crow's Creek.

She squeezed her eyes closed and tried to block out the sound of the damned wind. Always blowing, always screeching, it was enough to make a woman go insane.

For Mary, as she lay in her bed alone and thought of her husband, who had retreated away from her and into himself, it was the loneliest sound in the world.

"I should get out of here and let you get some sleep," Seth said. "You have to go to work in the morning."

Allison wasn't sure at what point she realized she didn't want Seth to leave, but as he stood and carried his empty coffee cup to the sink, she realized that not only did she not want to be alone for the rest of the night, but she wanted *him* next to her.

"I think I'll just call in sick for tomorrow." She rose and walked over to where he stood by the sink. It seemed incredible to her that in all the years since Bobby's death she hadn't wanted any man, yet she wanted this stranger who had come to town and created havoc in her life.

"Maybe that's a good idea," he replied.

"I have another idea." Her lips suddenly felt dry and her heart had begun to beat in a rhythm she barely remembered. "I don't want you to go."

His eyes darkened and sparked with heat. "Then I'll stay."

She felt as if he were looking deep inside her, seeing the adult woman that no man had ever known. She'd been a teenager with Bobby, but the desire that coursed through her blood was a burn she'd never felt before.

He reached for her then, and it was with a man's arms

that he embraced her. She molded herself to him as she raised her face to his. His mouth covered hers in a feath-erlight kiss, but there was nothing tentative about it. It was pure seduction and she welcomed it.

He stroked her hair, then ran his hands down her back. He was sure and confident, completely in control as she felt her control slipping away. Her breasts felt heavy and tingled as the kiss transformed from something soft and sweet to something hot and demanding.

She felt reckless, as if she was about to make a huge mistake and didn't care. Every point of contact their bodies made sizzled inside her, and vaguely she won-dered how that was possible, how this man could so eas-ily take her to a place no man had ever taken her with a simple kiss.

He broke the kiss and stepped back from her, his eyes glowing with a hunger she felt resonating from the tip of her head to her very toes. "Ally, make no mistake, I want you. I think I've wanted you since the first time I laid eyes on you. But you've had a rough night and I don't want you to take me to your bed because you're afraid and don't want to be alone. I want you to make this deci-sion with a clear head."

He wasn't going to let her be reckless. He wasn't going to let her have mindless passion or dramatic cir-cumstances to blame in the morning for her actions tonight.

Did that change her mind? No. She reached a hand up and placed it on his lower jaw where she felt the faint stubble of whiskers. It was at that moment that she real-ized she didn't want him here because she was afraid and she didn't want to be alone. She wanted him here with her because since the moment they met, a sexual energy had simmered between them, because the attrac-tion she felt for him had spiraled into something hot and urgent.

"I want you, Seth. It's as simple as that," she said. She could hear the rapid pulse of her heartbeat in her ear and was filled with a longing she thought she'd never felt before.

He reached up and took her hand in his, his gray eyes like molten lead. He led her to the kitchen doorway, where he paused only to turn out the light, and then continued through the living room and down the hallway.

Allison felt as if she'd entered a dreamworld, a world where there was nothing but Seth, herself and the bed where they were headed. She had no doubts, no hesitation. She had no thoughts of their future, for she knew there wasn't one, but it didn't matter.

He was in town to do a job and when that job was done, one way or the other, he'd return to his life in Kansas City and she would continue hers here in Crow's Creek. Knowing this did nothing to diminish the desire that pulsed inside her, that made her insides quiver and her legs feel weak.

When they reached the bedroom, he dropped her hand and pulled her back into his arms for a kiss that seared through any last defense she might have entertained.

She wrapped her arms around his neck and once again molded herself to him, felt the hardness of his arousal against her as his hands moved down her back to rest on her hips. His mouth possessed hers with raw, unbridled hunger as their hips began to move together in a slow grind of anticipation. When he finally took his mouth from hers, she was breathless. "I want to feel you naked against me," he said, his voice husky and uneven. His hands dropped from around her and instead moved to the tie on her robe. He pushed the robe off her shoulders and it fell to the floor just behind her, leaving her clad in the thin nightshirt and a pair of panties that she wished were red or black silk instead of white cotton.

Stepping back from her, he kicked off his loafers

and pulled his T-shirt over his head. His broad, chiseled chest gleamed in the soft lighting from the lamp on her nightstand, and then his hands went to the button fly of his jeans and her breath caught in her throat.

As he unfastened his jeans and stepped out of them, leaving him only in a pair of white briefs, she backed up to the edge of the bed, afraid that her shaking legs wouldn't hold her any longer.

"Take off your nightshirt," he said, his voice a mere whisper. "I need to see you."

His words torched a new fire inside her. Her hands trembled as they reached for and clutched the bottom of the shirt. It had been years since a man had seen her so bare, years since she'd felt so vulnerable. Drawing a deep breath, she pulled the nightshirt up and over her head and dropped it to the floor next to her robe. Instantly she crossed her arms in front of her breasts.

"Don't," Seth said. "Don't hide. You're beautiful."

She wanted to weep. It had been so long since she'd felt beautiful, since she'd felt wanted. Her nipples tautened beneath his gaze and her trembling legs gave way. She sat on the edge of the bed and in a heartbeat Seth was there with her.

They rolled onto the bed in a frenzy of tangled legs and hungry kisses. As he cupped her breasts, a current of electricity raced through her body and she cried out with pleasure. The pleasure only increased as his fingers raked over her turgid nipples.

His lips left hers, trailing kisses down her cheek and into the hollow of her throat. Smoothing her hands across the expanse of his warm, muscled back, she gasped as his tongue flicked at one of her nipples.

The pleasure was exquisite, making her wet and wanting more. Sex with Bobby had always been fast and furious, but Seth seemed to be in no hurry and his sole goal seemed to be to bring her as much pleasure as possible.

As his mouth loved the fullness of her breasts, one of his hands slid slowly down her belly. A shudder swept through her as his fingers trailed from the top of her panties down the sensitive skin of her inner thigh, not touching her where she wanted him.

He stroked up, then skipped and returned to her lower abdomen, teasing her, tormenting her as she arched her hips in response. Wanting to make him gasp, wanting to make him shudder, she reached down and ran a finger across the top of his briefs where she could feel the tip of his hardness pressing against the material.

He moaned, a deep, low guttural sound that thrilled her. She wanted him moaning; she wanted him to feel the same kind of intense pleasure that she felt with every one of his touches, each one of his caresses.

She stroked the length of him through the cotton fabric and although her intent had been to increase his desire, instead the feel of him so hard and throbbing shot a new shaft of desire through her.

"If you keep doing that, then this is going to be over before it begins," he whispered.

A small laugh escaped her. "Then we'd just have to start all over again, wouldn't we?"

"If you're trying to drive me over the edge, you're doing a very good job of it," he replied, his voice a husky growl.

She laughed again, but the laughter caught in her throat and changed to a gasp as he slid his fingers beneath her panties and found the damp center of her. Allison closed her eyes as hot sensations hissed through her.

He made a sound of impatience and pulled her panties down, where she kicked them off. He took off his briefs as well and they came back together, completely naked.

Skin against skin, heartbeats pounding, they came together in a frenzy that had her breathless, mindless. She was intoxicated with him, with his heated touch and with his clean, male scent. There was no room in her thoughts, in her heart, for anything but him.

When she thought she would go mad, when she believed she couldn't take it any longer, he moved between her thighs and his eyes glittered with wildness. His jaw was taut, the muscles in his neck corded with restraint and she felt his erection pressed against her, slowly into her.

Her body opened to accommodate him and still he held her gaze, looking at her as if she was the most important person in his world, as if he knew what he was doing to her and wanted to do it again and again.

When he was in her completely, he remained rigid, unmoving, and her need to shatter rose up inside her. She moved first, arching up against him in a silent plea. He closed his eyes then and began to move into her with slow, even strokes.

The build in her continued and she closed her eyes and cried out his name, her voice seeming to come from someplace far away. He moaned again, a wild, animal sound, and he took her mouth with his in a kiss that stirred a wildness in her.

With his moan his control seemed to snap and his thrusts into her came faster, deeper. She clung to him as the intense wave of her climax came closer, closer still. And then it was upon her, every nerve ending in her body exploded with sensation and her orgasm shuddered through her with an intensity that stunned her.

He stiffened against her, crying out her name as his arm muscles shook violently and he climaxed as well. Before she could catch her breath, he placed his hands on either side of her face and stared down at her. Gone was the wildness, the urgent hunger, that had been there moments before. Instead she saw a tenderness that pierced through to her heart.

In that instant of eye contact, in the mesmerizing depths of that sweet emotion, she felt bound to him in a way she'd never felt connected to another man. It was as if in that moment their hearts and minds, their very souls, were one.

She didn't know what scared her more—her feelings for Seth Walker or the question of what a person who killed a little boy's rabbit might do next.

Chapter 21

Allison woke before dawn, instantly aware of Seth spooned around her back. His naked body was warm and his slow, even breaths whispered against the top of her head.

She smelled him, a sleepy-male scent that was pleasant and evoked memories of what they'd shared the night before. She closed her eyes again, savoring the moment of feeling safe and secure and satisfied.

Even though she wasn't at all sure her marriage to Bobby would have gone the distance, she honored Bobby's memory. Despite his faults and his immaturity, he'd filled an important role in her life, not just as Sam's father, but as the man who'd seen her through the darkest days of her life.

A shiver tried to take possession of her. She was afraid the dark days weren't over yet. As she thought about having to tell Sam about Bugs, her heart squeezed painfully in her chest.

Realizing that she needed to call in to take the day off, she quietly slid from Seth's side. He stirred but didn't wake, and she grabbed her robe from the floor and tiptoed through the darkness of the bedroom and down the hallway to the kitchen.

She pulled on the robe and then punched in the numbers to the automated system that would let the school know she needed a substitute teacher for the day.

It was as she hung up the phone that she remembered the dream she'd had before waking up, a dream about her father. In that dream they'd been dancing, not the kind of dances Allison had done with her friends, but rather the kind of dancing Hank did with his wife.

The music she remembered was Irving Berlin's "Cheek to Cheek," and as the melody played in her head, it evoked memories of her dad's strong arms around her, the easy confidence he displayed as he led her around the room, making her feel beautiful and as light on her toes as a ballerina.

"Tomorrow night I'll dance with my girls," he'd said the night before the murders. He'd smiled at Allison. "I've got to get as much time in as possible dancing with you because it won't be long and you won't be caught dead dancing with your old man."

She'd laughed and kissed him on the cheek. "That will never happen," she'd exclaimed. "You'll always be my number one dance partner."

A piercing pang shot through her heart. There had been no more dancing after that night. Not for her mother, not for her father and not for her.

She shook her head, as if to dislodge the painful memories.

With her phone call made and dawn still not even a faint promise on the horizon, she went back to the bedroom, took off her robe and slid back into bed. Seth reached for her and drew her back into the spoon of his body. "Everything okay?" he murmured.

"Fine. I just had to make a call about taking the day off," she replied.

She relaxed against him as a faint stir of arousal unfurled inside her. Her breasts felt heavy and an electric tingle thrummed between her legs. As if he sensed her quickening heartbeat and the welling up of desire, he moved his hand to cup one of her breasts.

She felt him grow hard against her back, his sleep-warmed body tensing with his own desire. His mouth kissed the back of her neck. "I want you again, Ally," he whispered. All thoughts of what the day might bring, of old memories and dead rabbits, fled from her mind as she turned to him.

Afterward they slept again and it was almost eight when she awakened to find him gone from the bed. The house smelled of freshly brewed coffee and frying bacon, and she lay in bed for several long moments luxuriating in the idea of somebody cooking for her.

Unfortunately, she knew that although the day was beginning with sweet lovemaking and somebody else cooking breakfast, it was probably downhill after that. Today she'd have to tell her son about Bugs, and today they would begin an earnest search for the man who had been her mother's lover at the time of her death.

She went from the bed directly into the shower and discovered a damp towel that let her know Seth had been in the shower before her. Seth. She didn't know what to think about him, was afraid of her growing feelings toward him.

She'd hoped that having sex with him would be simple. Uncomplicated pleasure for both of them.

And it wasn't complicated, she reminded herself minutes later as she dried off, then dressed for the day. It didn't matter what her feelings for Seth were; it didn't matter how many times they made love or if they never made love again. Nothing was going to change the fact that he didn't belong here in Crow's Creek and she did.

She walked into the kitchen to see Seth standing in front of her stove and taking up crisp, browned strips of bacon. He was shirtless, his jeans riding low on his hips, and he was barefoot. He looked up and smiled and the warmth of that smile made her believe she could get through whatever the day might bring.

"I hope you don't mind that I helped myself," he said, and gestured to the table where two plates and silverware awaited.

"Mind? I think I've died and gone to heaven," she replied.

"Sit and I'll have this ready in a jiffy. Hope you like cheese omelet."

"I like anything that I haven't cooked," she replied.

She watched as he poured the egg mixture into the skillet, then added the grated cheese. "Do you do a lot of cooking?" she asked, and smiled as he poured her a cup of coffee and carried it to her at the table.

"Actually, I enjoy cooking. Maybe it's because I like to eat and as a bachelor I only have myself to depend on, but yes, I do a lot of cooking." He returned to the stove. "What about you?"

She took a sip of her coffee before answering. "Actually, I'm not much of a cook. Thank goodness Sam likes stuff that either comes from a box or is frozen and ready to cook. When we want a really good, nutritious meal, we either go out or go to my aunt Maureen and uncle David's house."

"You're close to them?"

"I don't know what I would have done without them." As he finished with the eggs and they began to eat, she told him how Maureen and David had taken her in after she'd gotten out of the hospital, and how they'd taken her and Sam in again following Bobby's death.

"My aunt Maureen is a tough one. She definitely wears the pants in the family. She's like a five-star general and she expects everyone to adhere to her rules. Uncle David is just the opposite, soft-spoken and with a mushy heart." She frowned thoughtfully. "They've both been upset about you, about us looking at the past again.

I think Hank's arrest broke David's heart. They were so close and Uncle David seemed to retreat further into himself after the arrest."

"Collateral damage," he said, his eyes darkening. "Whenever anyone is murdered, there's a ripple effect. The family members of the victim are changed, and the family members of the guilty. My mother never got over my father's arrest. She fell into a haze of drugs and alcohol to numb the shame of his arrest. Then when he was killed, the shame turned into a grief that killed her."

He sat back in his chair and cast her a smile that didn't quite hide his pain. "But that was then and this is now, and we have an opportunity to see that what happened to my father doesn't happen to yours. Prison life is grim, but for an innocent man it's a particular kind of hell."

She picked up her spoon and stirred sugar into her coffee cup. "And all we have to do is figure out who hated my family enough to try to kill everyone and let my father take the fall."

"It might have been hatred that killed your mother, but it wasn't hatred that killed Jenny and Johnny or that tried to kill you," he countered. "The way their bodies were left showed remorse."

"Which points right back to my father's guilt," she replied.

He studied her for a long moment. "If your father is guilty, then who is afraid of our questions? Who left the dead rabbit on your porch last night?"

She stared down into her cup, wishing she could go back to that first moment of awakening that morning, when she'd felt warm and secure in his arms. "I don't even know how we begin to figure out who my mother might have had an affair with." She shoved her plate away, her appetite gone.

"We start with a list of all the men your mother might have had contact with during her everyday activities," he replied. He got up from the table and carried their dishes to the sink. "You have paper and pencil somewhere?"

She nodded and pointed to one of the top cabinet drawers. He retrieved the legal pad inside with a ballpoint pen and returned to the table. "Your mother was thirty-seven years old. I think we need to look at anyone between the ages of twenty-one and fifty."

Allison nearly sputtered a mouthful of coffee. "That doesn't exactly narrow it down."

He grinned. "Be grateful you live in a place like Crow's Creek and not a bigger city." His grin faded. "I know it's a daunting task, Ally, but we've got to start somewhere."

"You're the first person who's ever called me Ally," she said.

"I'm sorry, should I not?"

"No, it's fine. I like it." She felt a whisper of a blush creep into her cheeks. It felt intensely personal, him calling her by a name nobody else used, and she couldn't forget how it had sounded when he'd moaned it both the night before and in the early hours this morning.

The ringing of the phone made her nearly jump out of her skin. It was her aunt Maureen. "I heard about the rabbit," she said without any other greeting. "Are you satisfied?"

Allison closed her eyes and clenched the phone. "Aunt Maureen, I'm really not in the mood for your censure this morning."

"I know, I'm sorry." Maureen's voice softened. "David wanted me to call and tell you that he has a rabbit that looks almost exactly like the one Sam had. He could bring it over this afternoon before Sam gets home from school. Maybe you wouldn't have to tell Sam what happened."

"I appreciate the offer, but I can't do that to Sam. Besides, he knew every tuft of fur on Bugs. He'd know it wasn't the same rabbit."

"It's a terrible thing, Allison. I hope you've decided to distance yourself from this Seth Walker. I'm telling you, nothing good can come from your association with that man."

Allison looked over to where Seth sat at the table staring out the window. What horror her aunt would feel if Allison told her she was not only seeing Seth but also screwing him. "I'm not backing off, Aunt Maureen. Seth and I are going forward and at this point I don't care who we upset." A new thought struck Allison. "What happened to all the things that were in the house at the time of the murders? All the furniture and the personal items?"

Maureen released a deep sigh. "When you were in the hospital, your uncle and I emptied the house. Most of the furniture was thrown away or given to Goodwill. We only kept a small amount of things. They're boxed and in a small storage unit at Benny's Storage."

"Seth and I will come by for the key to the storage unit sometime this morning," Allison said. She looked at Seth, who crooked a dark eyebrow upward.

"You won't find anything to help you there, and going through those things is only going to be painful. Allison, it's just photos and memorabilia that we thought you might want someday."

"I guess someday is now," Allison replied.

Maureen released another sigh. "I'll have the key ready when you get here."

Allison's heart softened. "It's going to be all right, Aunt Maureen. I'm going to be all right."

"I hope so."

Allison murmured a good-bye and hung up the phone.

"I take it that was the general?"

She smiled. "It was. She'd heard about the rabbit."

He frowned and glanced at the clock on the oven. "I guess the gossip pipeline in this town starts early."

"There's a storage unit that has things from the old

house. She said it's got photos and keepsake stuff. Maybe Mom kept a diary or a journal and it will be there, and maybe by going through the items, we'll find a clue to who she was seeing."

"Sounds like a good place to start," he replied. "And if we don't find what we're looking for there, then we start rattling the cages of every man in town."

"And after that?"

His eyes darkened as he held her gaze. "Then we wait and see what we've stirred up, and we hope that it isn't worse than a dead rabbit on your porch."

He had a name.

When he'd seen the morning newspaper headline, he'd nearly crowed with excitement.

THE BUTCHER OF CROW'S CREEK STRIKES AGAIN.

The headline screamed across the top of the page in bold letters, and the accompanying article talked about the beheaded cats and dogs found in Baxter's field and behind the high school. There were even quotes from the grieving pet owners

Larry Engle, who not only worked at the newspaper but also taught journalism at the high school, had written the article. He was a slight, small man with the features of a weasel and used colorful adjectives both in his writing and in his speech.

The Butcher of Crow's Creek.

The Butcher.

He liked it.

It was short and easy to remember.

The article was peppered with words like *heinous* and *evil* and with each word he'd read, his pride had grown. Gathering all those dogs and killing them hadn't been easy. It had required forethought and planning. It had been fucking brilliant. Surely somebody would admire the planning and execution of his work.

After today everyone would be talking about the Butcher of Crow's Creek. They would hide their cats and hug their dogs, hoping . . . praying that the Butcher of Crow's Creek didn't take their beloved pets.

They didn't have to worry. The animals had just been the beginning, a test of his powers, a taste of what was to come. A burst of laughter welled up inside him, but he quickly swallowed it.

He didn't want everyone talking about him for the next couple of days or the next week until another news story took their minds off the evil that walked among them.

He wanted them talking about him forever. For the most part the people in town had forgotten about what had happened at the Donovan place. The blood. The gore. The headless body of Joleen.

Oh yes, they'd forgotten, but he was going to make them remember. He was going to make them all afraid. The Donovan killings had been only the beginning and left unfinished with the survival of Allison Donovan. He'd rectify that.

Hot blood surged up inside him, flushing his face and hardening his cock. He touched himself and felt the electric tingle of a pleasure he'd never known before.

The thrill of swinging that hatchet, of the blood spurting as he took off the heads, had been unimaginable. The high he got from knowing that after this morning his name would be on the lips of everyone in town was so intense he felt half-dizzy.

This Saturday the town would celebrate Pioneer Days. There was nothing the people of Crow's Creek loved more than the day of old-fashioned fun. He hoped they enjoyed themselves. He certainly intended to make it a day to remember.

A woman and her son weren't going to survive the end of that day. He thought of the hatchet, of how it felt in his hand, how it had felt cutting through bone and muscle.

But that wasn't the sole cause of the excitement that nearly made him explode. No, it was the fact that afterward there wouldn't be a person in a hundred-mile radius that wouldn't know his name.

The Butcher.

This was the beginning of a new era for the little town, an era of horror, of fear too great to imagine. People would whisper his name with awe. They'd scream it in their nightmares.

His time of being was here and his accomplishments would far exceed what had happened in the past.

They were at the storage unit a few minutes before noon. The key burned in Allison's palm as she stared at the small metal unit that contained everything left of the life she'd once known.

"You okay?" Seth asked.

She nodded. "I'm okay. I find it hard to believe that this has been here since the time of the murders and I didn't know about it. It's just another indication of how deeply I've been in avoidance mode for the last fifteen years."

"Nobody can fault you for wanting to put this all behind you and never think about it again," he said. He offered her a small smile. "Do you hate me yet?"

Despite her tortured emotions about what they were about to do, she couldn't help but laugh. "Not yet, but don't get a big head. This isn't over yet." With a hand that trembled slightly, she unfastened the padlock and took it off the latch. The door creaked open on protesting hinges that hadn't been used in years.

A bare bulb hung from an overhead wire. Seth reached up to turn it on, and as the space flooded with light, Allison looked around. Neatly labeled boxes were stacked against both walls.

"Aunt Maureen's obsessive-compulsive personality hits again," she observed. The box marked *Jenny and Johnny* was the closest to her and she steeled herself as she removed the lid. Photos of the two were inside, along with school report cards, health records and the pictures that Johnny had loved to draw.

She picked up one of the pictures as a surge of emotion rose inside her. It was a color drawing of a fat bright sun and blue clouds and beneath the sky were stick figures of five people. Names had been written under each of them. *Mommy. Daddy. Allison. Jenny*, and *me*.

Her family. The grief that she'd barely tapped until now exploded inside her, sending her to her knees as the picture trembled in her hands. Tears blurred her vision as a choking sob escaped her.

The pain was like none she'd ever felt before, a crashing, all-consuming monster that had been building inside her for fifteen long years. Johnny's picture fluttered from her hand as she wrapped her arms around her stomach.

Seth pulled her up and into his arms and she clung to him as deep, wrenching sobs ripped through her. He said nothing, as if knowing there were no words that would halt the cascade of tears. Instead he simply held her tight until the storm passed. And it was in those moments, with his arms wrapped around her and as the grief slowly ebbed, that she realized she was precariously close to falling in love with Seth Walker.

Chapter 22

"Where were you yesterday?" Michelle exclaimed as Allison entered the teachers' lounge. "When you didn't show up for work, I tried calling your house, but you weren't there."

Allison sat at the table next to her friend and set a stack of graded papers at her side. "Somebody killed Sam's rabbit Sunday night and left it on the porch."

"What?" Michelle's eyes grew to saucer size. "Who on earth would do something like that?"

"Somebody who wanted to give me a warning not to go digging into the past," Allison replied.

"Oh my God, that's awful. How's Sam?" Michelle's eyes were filled with compassion.

Allison's heart convulsed with pain as she thought of her son and his reaction to the news about Bugs. "He spent the night at the Blooms' when it happened, so he didn't know about it until I picked him up from school yesterday. Needless to say, he was devastated. He can't understand why anyone would do such a terrible thing to a poor, defenseless rabbit. Neither can I."

"I'm so sorry," Michelle exclaimed.

Allison nodded. "So, tell me about your big date with Wayne." She needed a change of topic, anything that might take her mind off Sam and his heartbreak. "How did it go?"

Michelle took a sip of her coffee and frowned. "I felt like I was a third wheel."

"How could you be a third wheel on a date where there are just the two of you?"

"Trust me, there were three of us—Wayne, me and you."

"Me?" Allison laughed in surprise. "What are you talking about?"

"You're all he wanted to talk about. He wanted to know why you didn't date, if you had something going with Seth Walker. He wanted to know why when we all went to Crazy's you never danced. It was all about you, Allison. That man has it bad for you."

She had known Wayne was interested in her, and had tried to make it clear that she didn't return his feelings. But the idea that he'd taken Michelle out so he could learn more about her was decidedly creepy. She thought about the times recently when she'd felt like she was being watched. Was it Wayne?

She'd thought it might be Eric, and somehow it felt less threatening to believe it was a teenage boy with a crush than a grown man who should know better.

"So, if Sam was in school all day yesterday, where were you?" Michelle asked, pulling Allison from her troubling thoughts.

"We were in and out all day."

"We?" Michelle raised a pale eyebrow.

"Seth and I. I found out that there was a storage unit containing some of the items from the old house and we wanted to go through everything."

"That must have been tough."

"You have no idea," Allison replied. They had searched each box. She had been surprised at what kinds of things had brought on a new wave of grief and tears.

A plastic doll from a McDonald's Happy Meal that Jenny had loved, the coin valet from the top of her mom and dad's dresser where Allison got whatever change her father would put there as spending money.

A dried-flower corsage had reduced her to tears once again. She remembered the night her father had given it to her mother. It had been their anniversary and he'd surprised her with the rose and ribbon wrist corsage. It had still smelled faintly like her mother, a blend of gardenia-scented body lotion and the perfume she'd worn.

"Why did you put yourself through that?" Michelle asked, her eyes soft with compassion.

"We were looking to see if maybe my mother had kept a journal or a diary."

"Why?"

"Because at the time of her death we think she was having an affair, and we're trying to figure out who she was having the affair with," Allison replied.

She'd expected Michelle to be shocked, but Michelle merely looked at her soberly. "Who do you think it might be?"

Allison stared at her for a long moment. "You knew?" Michelle's cheeks stained with color. "All these years and you knew my mother was having an affair?"

Michelle averted her gaze from Allison's and instead stared down at the table. "Before the murders, one night when I spent the night with you, I overheard your mother on the phone with somebody. It wasn't your dad and I could tell by the way she was talking that it was another man."

"And you never told me?" Allison asked incredulously.

Michelle met her gaze. "I cared about you, Allison. Why would I tell you something that I knew would hurt you?"

"Did you ever tell anyone? After the murders, did you tell Dane Kelly?"

Michelle shook her head, her springy curls bobbing. "No, I didn't. I was a kid, Allison. What was I going to say? That I overheard an adult conversation that I might have misunderstood? That I had no idea who your mother was talking to, and for all I know, she was making an appointment with her insurance man or something like that."

"You should have told me." Allison stared at her friend, a sense of betrayal flooding through her as the bell rang for first period. "Dammit, Michelle, you should have told me." Her voice rang with anger.

"And when would I have done that?" Michelle stood and picked up her books from the table. "Should I have told you when you were in the hospital recovering from a split skull? Or maybe later, when you were in the mental ward and not interacting with anyone? When would have been a good time for me to destroy whatever images you might have of your mother?"

She didn't wait for a reply, but whirled on her heels and left the lounge. Allison stared after her, stunned by the sense of betrayal she felt at learning her best friend had kept this secret from her.

She got up from the table and grabbed her papers. Another thread of her life had been unraveled and Allison wondered whether, when this was all over, there would be anything left of the life she'd known.

"Hey, dickwad."

Eric turned at the sound of Beau's voice and saw his two friends hurrying down the hallway toward him. "Nice. You kiss your mother with that mouth?"

Beau flashed him a grin. "If your mother was around, I'd kiss her with this mouth."

"We're heading over to Baxter's field for a while," Patrick said.

"You wanna come or do you have a hot date with Deputy Do-Right?" Beau smirked. "I hear you and he are getting pretty buddy-buddy."

Eric felt the tips of his ears warm. "He's a nice guy. Something wrong with that?"

"You aren't going narc on us, are you?" Patrick asked, his eyes narrowing .

"He doesn't ask stuff like that and I don't tell him anything," Eric replied.

Beau slung an arm around Eric's neck and pulled him against him while he gave him a knuckle noogie on the head. "Lay off our boy, Patrick. Eric wouldn't do anything to get us in trouble." He released Eric, who rubbed the top of his head. "So, you coming with us?"

"Sure." Eric fell into step with his friends. He had nothing else to do. Nobody would miss him at home and hanging out with his friends was better than being alone.

They piled into Patrick's car, Beau in the passenger seat and Eric in the back. Beau always got shotgun. "I've got to get in all the partying I can between now and the end of school," Beau said as Patrick pulled out of the school parking lot. "My old man got me a job starting the day after school is out."

"Doing what?" Patrick asked.

"Working for Wayne at the garage." Beau's disdain was obvious in his voice. "It sucks, man. I figured I'd hang out at the pool all summer, you know, work on my tan and partying, but no, my old man thinks I need to learn how to be a grease monkey." He slammed a fist into the dashboard.

"Hey, man," Patrick protested. "Don't be breaking my car."

"Sorry." Beau slumped back against the seat. "I'm just so pissed about it. Like I really want to spend my summer hanging out with weird Wayne."

"Look on the bright side," Eric said. "Maybe you can learn enough to figure out what's knocking under Patrick's hood."

"My dad says it's cheap gas," Patrick replied.

"My old man wants me to be a mechanic—then I'll be the best damned mechanic he's ever seen. I'll be so fucking good the NASCAR people will come to me and beg me to work on their cars," Beau exclaimed.

"Success is the best revenge," Patrick exclaimed. "That's what my dad always says. He's planning on making a million dollars someday so my mom will eat her heart out that they're not still married."

Delusions of grandeur was more like it, Eric thought as he listened to his two friends talking about their summer plans. He stared out the window, his thoughts on Rick Solomon. He'd been over to Rick's place twice in the last couple of days. He would have liked to go there again this evening, but he was afraid of screwing things up.

He liked sitting and talking to Rick, who looked at him like he wasn't invisible. He'd told Eric about some of his cases when he'd been working in Chicago. They'd talked about old unsolved crimes, shared theories and debated evidence.

Someplace deep within, Eric knew he was kidding himself with his plans to be a criminal profiler. Talk about delusions of grandeur. A surge of anger welled up inside him, anger that he'd been born in the small town of Crow's Creek, rage because his mother had walked out on him and his father was a drunken handyman who'd never been a father and sure wouldn't be any help with a college fund.

Hell, he hadn't even had the money to rent a tux for prom. How was he going to afford college?

He was screwed by circumstances beyond his control, by the sheer accident of his birth, and sometimes the unfairness of it made him so angry he felt like screaming.

He narrowed his gaze as he stared out the window, his thoughts going to a dark place that would have shocked the deputy who had befriended him.

Chapter 23

It had been a hellish week and Allison was more than ready for a celebration. She stood at the kitchen sink, finishing a cup of coffee as Sam ate his breakfast.

"Are you sure he's gonna be here on time?" Sam asked for the twentieth time. "The parade starts at nine, but we're supposed to be there by eight thirty."

"Seth said he would be here at eight, and he's a man of his word. Besides, you still have to comb your hair and brush your teeth." She smiled at him. "I refuse to have my son in a parade with furry teeth and bed-head hair."

Sam grinned, a string of maple syrup shiny on his chin. "It's going to be a fun day, isn't it, Mom?"

"Absolutely. It's going to be a great day." She kept the smile on her face until Sam left the kitchen table and headed down the hallway to deal with his teeth and hair. Only then did she feel the frown creep over her features.

She desperately wanted it to be a fun day, but she'd awakened that morning with a sense of doom hanging over her. Maybe it was because she and Seth had spent the week making people uncomfortable. The questions they'd been asking around town hadn't been met kindly.

Thursday she'd been called to Sam's school. He'd

gotten in trouble for brawling with another boy on the playground. According to Sam, Brad Kincaid had said it was Allison's fault that animals were being killed, and his mom and dad had said that she and Seth were doing the devil's work.

Sam had punched the kid in the nose and although Allison had understood her son's reaction, she'd grounded him from sleepovers for the next two weeks.

With the end of school in three days, she knew Sam had entertained the idea of sleepovers with his friends almost every night, but no matter how much he'd protested her punishment, she'd been firm. She knew that the best way to parent was to be consistent and stick to her guns, no matter how much agony it caused her as his mother. Sam knew that fighting, no matter what the reason, was unacceptable behavior.

The only high point to the miserable week had been the time she'd spent with Seth. He'd kept her calm and focused and could set her to sizzling with just a look. Seth had shared dinner with them every evening and Sam had enjoyed having him around. And after Sam had gone to bed, Allison had enjoyed having Seth around. Too much.

Her heart was getting involved and she didn't know how to stop it, didn't know how to defend herself against the way he made her feel, the connection she felt to him both physically and emotionally.

If she allowed herself, she could fall in love with him. But she'd learned enough about him to recognize that much of her appeal to him had to be the case—the exoneration of her father. There was no question in her mind that Seth was trying to heal himself and using his belief in her father's innocence as the vehicle.

She hoped that no matter how this all played out, he found the redemption he was seeking, but she wasn't fool enough to allow herself to believe that the attraction he felt for her wasn't tied into the baggage of his past.

She was in the process of cleaning up Sam's breakfast dishes when the doorbell rang. "I'll get it," Sam cried. There was a thunder of footsteps; then she heard him greeting Seth.

Despite all her wishes to the contrary, her heart leaped as Seth came into the kitchen, followed closely behind by Sam. Dressed in a pair of jean shorts and a navy T-shirt that displayed every ounce of lean muscle, he seemed to heat the small confines of the kitchen.

"You look amazing," he said, making her glad that she'd chosen to wear the pink sundress that she knew showed off her figure and complemented her coloring.

"Thanks, you don't look so bad yourself," she replied.

Sam rolled his eyes. "Are you guys gonna kiss or something, or are we gonna get out of here?"

Seth smiled wickedly. "Never give a man a choice like that."

Allison laughed half breathlessly. "We're gonna get out of here." She grabbed her purse from the table. "Shall we?"

Minutes later they were in the car and headed for the staging area for the parade. "Maybe after the parade, you and I could enter the three-legged race," Sam said to Seth. "And we could ride the Ferris wheel. Mom won't ride them because she is scared of heights, but it would be cool if you'd ride it with me."

"Sam, I'm not sure Seth wants to spend the entire day doing everything that you want to do," Allison exclaimed.

Seth looked at her and winked. "Actually, I was just thinking that a three-legged race might be fun, and the Ferris wheel is one of my favorite carnival rides, but I wasn't sure who I might find to ride it with me."

"Me!" Sam replied with the brand of eagerness only a twelve-year-old boy could muster.

"I was trying to protect you, but now you're on your own," Allison said with a laugh to Seth.

Seth parked in the lot where the floats were lining up and people were rushing everywhere to get in place. "There's Mr. Baxter's wagon," Sam said, and pointed to where a tractor was in place with a wagon of hay behind it. Sam's classmates were gathered in a group as his teacher yelled to get everyone's attention.

"I gotta go," Sam exclaimed, his body vibrating with excitement.

"We'll meet you back here at the end of the parade," Allison said. "Don't leave here without us."

He nodded. "And, Mom, please don't throw a kiss at me or anything like that when we go by."

Allison laughed. "Okay, I promise I won't do that."

She watched as he ran off to join his friends, and then turned to Seth. "Shall we find a spot to stand on the parade route?"

"Sounds like a plan," he agreed.

It felt only natural that his hand reached for hers. The weather had cooperated with sunny skies but slightly cooler temperatures. Even though it was going to be hot, it wasn't supposed to be as stifling as it had been the last couple of weeks.

In the distance, in the high school football field, the lights of the carnival rides couldn't compete with the bright sunshine, but come nightfall they would glitter and sparkle against the dark skies.

Even though it was not even eight thirty in the morning, the streets were beginning to crowd with parents and friends of the people in the parade. There were also unfamiliar faces in the crowd, people who had driven into Crow's Creek to share the day of fun.

She and Seth stood on the curb in front of the hardware store, about center of Main Street. She smiled up at him. "This day always embodies the very best of Crow's Creek," she said.

He returned her smile. "You love it here, don't you?"

"I do. Despite everything that happened, this is home. It's where I've built my life and made friends. I feel like I belong here." And you don't, she reminded herself. No matter how close she felt to him, no matter how he made her heart sing, it was a temporary pleasure and she couldn't lose sight of that fact.

"I'm thinking about selling the old house," she said, surprised by her own words, but the minute they left her lips, she realized the idea had been brewing in the back of her mind.

Seth squeezed her hand, his eyes filled with a compassion that touched her heart. "Are you sure you're ready for that?"

"It's time to let go. The house is just going to go to ruin with nobody living there. It was a nice place to live and it would be a nice place for somebody else to live, to raise their families and be happy. I'll plan a day in the next couple of weeks to go take a look around and see what needs to be done to get it market ready."

Dread filled her at the idea of going back into the house where her last vision had been of her mother sitting on the sofa with her head in her lap. The scent of the blood, of death, had stung her nose just before she'd been hit in the head and cast into a dark oblivion.

"I'd be happy to go with you." Seth's deep voice pulled her from the horrible thoughts.

Once again she gazed up at him and in his eyes she saw his strength, an incredible strength that would be easy for her to fall into, to rely on. She wanted to. She wanted to tell him that she'd love for him to come with her, to be there for her as she faced the nightmare from her past.

She'd spent the last fifteen years avoiding thinking about the crime that had changed her life, hiding out in a state of denial that had masqueraded as safety and comfort. But she realized now that the only way to really let go of the past was to face it. "Thanks for the offer, but I think it's something I need to do by myself."

He nodded. "If you change your mind, you know where to find me."

At that moment from the far end of Main came the sound of the Crow's Creek High School marching band, indicating the official start of the Pioneer Days parade.

The people lining the street settled in to watch as the band came into sight, followed by the decorated floats. As Baxter's tractor rumbled into view with Sam's class in the hay wagon, Allison fought the impulse to blow her son a kiss and instead waved and shouted his name to get his attention.

He waved back and she could see the excited sparkle in his eyes despite the distance between them. The edge of apprehension that had been with her that morning since she'd first opened her eyes faded away. It was going to be a great day.

By the time the parade had finished, the air was redolent with the sweet scent of cotton candy, the savory odor of grilling hot dogs and buttery popcorn. Not only were the carnival rides busy, but also the organized activities had begun.

The next several hours were filled with laughter and fun. Seth and Sam entered the three-legged race and came in second, earning them each a red ribbon to wear on their shirts.

Seeing her son interact with Seth shot a new kind of pain through her. After Bobby had died, she'd made a conscious decision not to allow any other men in her life in a meaningful way. But had her desire to protect herself from hurt ultimately hurt her son, who obviously desperately hungered for an adult male in his life on a permanent basis?

After the races and several rides, they met up with the Blooms, and Sam went with Greg and his mother to experience some of the ride-until-you-puke rides while Seth and Allison went to the area set up for people to sit and eat lunch.

They both ordered hot dogs smothered with all the condiments, fries and sodas, then carried their food to one of the picnic tables beneath an old oak tree.

"I was willing to do the races and some of the other rides, but when Sam mentioned wanting to break his record from last year of riding the Tilt-A-Whirl twenty-two times, I knew I was out of my league," Seth said.

Allison laughed. "He'll ride that ride a hundred times, then eat too many hot dogs, too much cotton candy, and wind up with a stomachache tonight and won't understand why."

"Ah, the joys of youth."

"Thank you for all the time you've spent with him today."

Seth smiled. "It's easy to spend time with Sam. He's got a great personality and seems wonderfully well-adjusted."

"And resilient. Monday night he was brokenhearted over Bugs, but it's amazing how quickly kids can bounce back from heartache. It's too bad we seem to lose some of that trait as we get older."

"Allison Clemmins." The strident voice came from someplace behind her and Allison turned to see Bridget Altamare, using her walker like a lethal weapon as she made her way through the crowd toward Allison and Seth.

"Hello, Mrs. Altamare," Allison said in greeting.

The old woman's eyes were narrowed, nearly disappearing into the folds of sagging skin and wrinkles. "And you must be that Walker man who's causing so much trouble," she said to Seth. "I heard some fool this morning say that it was damned funny that we had no dead animals in this town until you showed up, but I don't listen to nonsense."

Allison found herself sputtering as Seth merely stared at the old woman as if she were some sort of apparition from another world. "I just wanted to tell you both that there's no point in questioning my Charlie about any affair with Joleen Donovan. For the last fifty-five years I've known where Charlie was at any hour of the day or night."

She planted the walker in front of Allison. "Your mama was a beautiful woman, God rest her soul, but my Charlie knew that if he dipped into somebody else's well, I'd have his balls hanging in a bucket. And that's all I've got to say about the matter."

She whirled the walker with a surprising agility and walked away as Seth and Allison stared after her. "Well, that was interesting," Seth finally said.

Allison giggled. "Charlie Altamare is almost ninety years old and has never made a move in his life that Bridget didn't first approve. We can definitely cross him off our list."

"Good, because she scared me more than a little bit," Seth exclaimed, making Allison laugh again.

Although there were plenty of laughs as the afternoon progressed, Allison couldn't help but notice decidedly unfriendly looks cast in their direction. Although intellectually she understood the reluctance of people to focus on a particularly heinous crime and now the possibility that the man who'd been serving a life sentence might not be the guilty party, emotionally the lack of support from her friends and neighbors hurt.

They ran into Michelle at the carousel. She sat on a bench alone, and seemed lost in thought when they approached her. Allison hadn't been able to stay angry at her best friend. Michelle had been a sixteen-year-old at the time, and Allison never doubted that Michelle's keeping that secret had come from a place of caring.

"What are you doing sitting here all alone?" Allison asked as she sat next to her friend.

"Licking my wounds," Michelle said. She smiled at Seth, who must have sensed a little girl talk was in order.

"The smell of that popcorn has been driving me crazy all day. I think I'm going to get a box. Either of you want anything?" he asked.

"Nothing for me," Allison said.

"Me, neither," Michelle replied.

Both of them watched as he walked away. Michelle sighed and turned to look at Allison. "Not only is he good-looking and has a great ass, but he's sensitive enough to go away when he needs to."

Allison smiled. "He's a great guy."

Michelle studied her features for a long moment. "You're sleeping with him, aren't you?" Allison didn't have to reply. The blush that warmed her face was her answer. "I hope you know what you're doing."

"Of course I don't," Allison said truthfully. "I didn't expect this, I didn't expect him and I certainly didn't plan it this way."

"He's going to break your heart," Michelle said with a touch of melancholy.

"I know." Allison leaned back against the bench and reached up to twirl a strand of her hair. "But I can't go back and undo things now. I can't help the way I feel about him, the way he makes me feel when he looks at me."

"I know exactly what you're talking about. I feel that way about Rick Solomon. I know it's stupid, that we only had that one date and it's ridiculous to get so attached over a simple shared meal, but I did get attached." She sighed. "And it's obvious he didn't. Unrequited love sucks. It should be against the law." She brightened. "If it was, then I could have Rick arrest me. I'd love to be handcuffed to him."

Allison laughed and dropped her hand back into her lap. "When the time is right, you'll find a man who will love you the way you deserve to be loved."

"Speaking of unrequited love, here comes the king," Michelle whispered as Wayne waved to them and hurried to where they were seated.

"Ladies," he said in greeting. "Beautiful day, isn't it?" His gaze lingered on Allison. "Are you having a good time?"

"So far it's been nothing but fun," she replied. "What about you? You enjoying the fair?"

"Absolutely. Some of my students and I are putting on an exhibition in about an hour behind the bleachers. I'd love it if you'd come and watch."

"I'll keep it in mind," Allison replied.

He remained standing in front of them as if searching for something else to say, some way to keep the conversation flowing. It went from awkward to downright uncomfortable.

The moment was broken when Sam, along with Marianne and Greg Bloom, joined them. The two boys greeted their teacher. Then as they began to chatter about what they'd eaten and the rides they had enjoyed, Wayne raised a hand in good-bye and drifted away.

"We rode the Tilt-A-Whirl twenty-three times," Sam exclaimed. "And Greg almost puked."

"I did not," Greg exclaimed indignantly, but he looked a little green around the gills.

"We were wondering if we could borrow your son again for the night," Marianne said. "George is working overtime and won't be home until sometime tomorrow afternoon."

"Can I, Mom?" Sam asked eagerly.

It would be easy to tell him okay, to let him go home with the Blooms, giving her the night alone with Seth. But she hadn't forgotten the punishment she'd imposed for his fighting in school. "Sam, you know that's not allowed for the next two weeks," she reminded him.

Sam frowned in frustration. "Couldn't you make an exception?"

What would be the harm? Allison thought. One night. A simple exception and the potential of undoing all the parenting she'd done for the past twelve years. She shook her head. "Sorry, buddy." She looked at Marianne. "Sam is grounded from sleepovers for the next two weeks."

"Then we'll just have to wait, won't we?" she said with a smile to the two disappointed boys. "But you two have the rest of the afternoon to spend time together." She looked at her watch and turned to Allison. "It's three o'clock now. Why don't we meet you back here around five? That will give the boys another two hours together before Greg and I call it a day."

"Sounds good," Allison agreed.

As she watched her son and the Blooms walk back toward the carnival rides, she saw Wayne standing by the hot dog stand, his gaze intent on her. She'd forgotten to put him on the list of her mother's potential lovers. Wayne was thirty-seven years old. He would have been twenty-two years old at the time of the murders. Even then Wayne had been working as a mechanic at the garage where Joleen took their car for repairs and maintenance.

An icy finger walked up Allison's spine, causing the hair at the nape of her neck to rise and goose bumps to appear on her arms. Was it possible he'd killed her mother and tried to kill her? Allison knew she looked a lot like her mother had at the time of her death.

Had Wayne, as a passionate young man, had an affair with Joleen that had careened out of control? That had resulted in a terrible crime of passion? Was he as harmless as Eric with a crush on her that, in the grand scheme of things, meant nothing?

Or was his interest in her something dark and malicious, a need to finish what he'd started when he'd tried to kill her fifteen years before?

Leroy hated Pioneer Days. Of course, he hated most everything in Crow's Creek. But today was the worst, when the air filled with laughter and kids ran wild as the wind. Smiles were the dress of the day and even people who didn't like one another put their differences aside to enjoy the festivities.

Leroy was hunkered down behind the bleachers, a bottle of gin in hand. He should have stayed home. He should have stayed in his bed, where happy noises couldn't reach him, where he could wallow in the misery that had felt familiar for so long.

He'd thought he could handle it today. He'd awakened that morning and decided maybe it was a day he wouldn't drink. Maybe it was a day he wouldn't remember. He'd come into town with a fragile hope that today things would be different.

For a little while they had been different. He'd arrived in town, cleaned up and sober, and started the day watching the parade, feeling for just a minute as if he was part of something greater than himself, bigger than his grief. The drums had beaten in his heart as the band had walked by, and he'd even raised a hand to wave at several of the passing floats.

Following the parade, he'd moved with the crowd to the high school football field and parking lot, where the center of the celebration took place. He'd seen Eric and his friends in the distance, but hadn't called to his son.

Leroy knew he'd been a shitty father. He neither regretted it nor reveled in it. He was merely relieved that Eric hadn't needed him, because he'd had nothing to give.

Tears burned at his eyes as he took another drink from the bottle and tried not to hear the sound of laughter that seemed to come from everywhere around him.

He would have been fine if he hadn't seen her. He might have even enjoyed the day if he hadn't caught sight of Allison Clemmins in the distance.

With her head thrown back in laughter and the sun sparking off her long, dark hair, she'd looked so much like Joleen it had sent a sharp stab of pain through him.

Joleen. Joleen. Joleen. Her name echoed with the beating of his heart and he wanted to banish the memories of her, destroy the pain that thoughts of her always evoked. And there was only one way he knew to do that.

With a small choking sob, he raised the bottle to his lips once again.

Allison sat on the edge of Sam's bed as he snuggled down beneath the sheet and released a big, wide yawn. "Today was so much fun," he said.

"It was great fun," she agreed. "And I appreciate that you didn't pout when I said you couldn't spend the night with Greg."

He smiled. "I wanted to pout," he admitted, "but I figured that would make you mad and totally ruin the whole day."

She laughed. "It's nice to know you're getting smarter as you get taller."

"You know what the best part was?" he asked.

"What's that?"

"The races with Seth. It was like he was my dad and

it was just so cool. I like him. Why don't you marry him and then he'd really be my dad? I know you like him—I can tell when you look at him. And he likes you, too."

"Unfortunately grown-up relationships are more complicated than that," Allison said. "Seth is here to do a job and when his job is finished, he'll go back to his home in Kansas City."

"He's here because he thinks Grandpa didn't do those terrible things. Do you think Grandpa didn't do them?" Sam's eyes told her what he wanted her to say, what he wanted to believe.

Allison sighed. "I don't know, Sam. I'm not sure what to believe. I'd like to think that a mistake was made a long time ago and your grandfather was sent to prison for a crime he didn't do, but I'm just not sure what's the truth."

"I hope it's true that he didn't do it. It would be nice to have a grandpa." His eyes sparkled with childish humor. "Almost as nice as having Seth for a dad."

She smiled, then leaned over and kissed him on his brow. "Don't forget we have lunch at Aunt Maureen and Uncle David's tomorrow. You know Uncle David said you could pick out another rabbit to bring home if you want to."

The sparkle left his eyes. "I haven't decided if I want another one or not. Maybe it wouldn't be fair to Bugs for me to get another rabbit to love."

"Honey, I think Bugs would like you to be happy, and if another bunny would make you happy, then that's what Bugs would want for you. Now, get some sleep, it's been a long day."

"I love you, Mom."

"I love you, Sam."

Long after he'd closed his eyes and drifted off to sleep, Allison stood in the doorway and watched him. She wished there were a way that she could keep any future heartache from him, that he'd never know a day of pain in his life.

But of course that wasn't possible. Today it was a bunny; tomorrow it would be some girl. This thought shot a pang through her as she left his doorway and went down the hallway to her own bedroom.

The wind that had been wonderfully absent all day now rustled tree branches against the house and she wished Seth were here to share her bed with her. But she didn't want to let Seth spend the night when Sam was there. She didn't want to give her son false hope that anything permanent might develop between the two of them. It was already going to be difficult enough on him when it came time to say good-bye to the man.

She got into her nightshirt and turned out the light, then moved to the window and leaned her head against the pane as she stared outside. Thoughts of Seth filled her head.

Spending the day with him just having fun had wound him more tightly around her heart. She loved not only the feel of his warm naked flesh against hers, how his five-o'clock shadow whispered against her skin, and the smoky heat of his eyes; she also loved the way he laughed, that his sense of humor matched her own and that he seemed to sense her every mood and respond appropriately.

She had proved to herself and to everyone in town that she didn't need a man in her life, that she was self-sufficient and fine alone. What she hadn't realized was how lonely she'd been, that although she didn't *need* a man in her life, there was a part of her that longed for somebody special. For Seth.

Rubbing a finger across her lower lip, she remembered the taste of him, the feel of his lips hungrily taking hers, and a liquid warmth overtook her. She hadn't realized how sexually bereft she'd been until he'd come along. She had forgotten how much joy could be found in the act of lovemaking, in the moments afterward when his arms held her close and she felt his heartbeat echoing with her own.

With a sigh of frustration, she dropped her hand from her mouth and started to turn away from the window.

But a movement by the trunk of the tree across the street caught her eye. She froze, her heart grinding to a painful halt in her chest. Aware that it would be difficult for somebody to see her standing in the darkened window, she didn't move away, but instead focused all her attention on the tree.

Had it merely been the dancing shadow of a limb that had caught her eye? Had a piece of trash been swept by the wind around the base of the tree? Or was somebody there? Hiding in the darkness of night? Watching her?

She had no idea how long she stood there, heart pounding and muscles tensed, but eventually she told herself it had been just her imagination. She backed away from the window and slid into bed, willing her heartbeat to slow to a more normal pace.

Just because you're paranoid doesn't mean somebody isn't out to get you. The words played in her head as she thought of the threatening phone call she'd received, the dead bunny left on the porch.

She'd been grateful when there had been no more phone calls throughout the week, and she'd unrealistically hoped that the single threat had been the end of things.

But as she lay in bed with her heart beating so rapidly and a taste of fear creeping into her mouth, she realized it was possible that the phone call and the rabbit had been only the beginning.

Rick walked the school grounds, along with the people who had volunteered to clean up after the day of celebration. There was nothing quite so dismal as the mess left behind after a party of major proportions.

The carnival rides were silent, their bright lights no longer electrifying the night sky. Discarded food, broken bottles and paper plates and cups littered the grass despite the trash containers provided by the city.

The wind that had whipped up wasn't making the cleanup any easier. Trash whirled in the air, making the volunteers run after the flying debris.

People could be pigs, he thought as he bent down to pick up a beer bottle. As he straightened, he saw Eric nearby, wearing plastic gloves and dealing with a mess of ketchup-smeared paper plates.

He was vaguely surprised to see him. After all, it was just after midnight on a Saturday night. He'd seen him earlier with his friends Patrick and Beau, but the other two boys were nowhere to be seen.

The kid was growing on him and that made Rick feel strangely guilty. He shouldn't care about any other kid except the one he'd lost. And yet he knew it was his refusal to let go of his grief that had driven his wife away, that made him reluctant to pursue any relationship with Michelle Keller.

An unexpected smile curved his lips as he thought of the blond high school teacher. He'd noticed her more times during the course of the day than he cared to admit.

She'd looked as sweet as cotton candy in her pink pants and top. There was a part of him that wanted to grab on to her and a stubborn piece of him that refused to reach out to anything that he felt might possibly heal his pain.

He tossed the bottle he'd picked up into the trash can and walked over to where Eric was working. "What happened to your friends?"

Eric stuck his hands in his pockets and leaned into

the wind, as if fighting the possibility of going airborne at any moment. "I guess they went home. They're not really much into doing their civic duty." The angles of his thin face were sharper in the moonlight, giving him an almost predatory look.

"How are you getting home?"

"I've got a key to Emma's Café. I just figured I'd walk there and spend the night. Then tomorrow I'll get Patrick or Beau to take me home." He tossed a handful of trash into the container. "I'll bet you're glad this is all over with."

Rick smiled. "I'm just grateful we got through the day with no lost tempers, no drunken displays of nudity and nobody getting seriously hurt. That makes it a successful day. I'm just going to take a walk around, then head home. You sure you don't want a ride?"

"Nah, I'll be fine," Eric replied.

"Then I'll see you later." Rick left Eric picking up more trash, and headed around the school building, looking to make sure nothing was amiss. As he passed the area where they'd found the beheaded dogs, he couldn't help but feel a knot of anxiety harden in his chest.

They were no closer to finding out who had killed those dogs and cats than they had been on the day the bodies had been found. He also hadn't been able to identify who had killed Allison Clemmins's son's rabbit. The neighbor, Ed Jacobs, hadn't seen or heard anything that night and there had been no prints on the knife.

Dane was equally concerned about the situation, but at the moment, they were at a dead end with no leads and no potential suspects. Rick frowned as he thought of his boss. Since the death of his dog, Dane had been unusually taciturn. He spent long hours alone in his office, with the door closed, and even when he was out of the office, his face wore an expression that forbade conversation.

Rounding the side of the building, Rick decided to check out the bleacher area, then call it a night. It had been a long day. Thankfully tomorrow was his day off. He'd sleep in, then mow the weeds that his lawn comprised and maybe kick back with a few beers and watch an action flick. These days that was as good as he expected from life.

He saw the feet first. Dirty work boots sticking out from beneath the bleachers. His first thought was that somebody had suffered a heart attack and had died. But when he leaned down and saw the face of the man on the ground, smelled the air that surrounded him, he knew it wasn't a heart attack.

Leroy Grant was stinking drunk again, passed out with an empty bottle of Beefeater clutched to his chest. Rick sighed and went in search of Eric. The idea of transporting a drunk Leroy in his car again filled Rick with revulsion. It had taken him three days to get the stink out of his car from taking him home from Terrible's the last time.

He found Eric talking to David Donovan, who was working as one of the volunteers tonight. Rick had been introduced to David and his wife, Maureen, earlier in the day. While he suspected Maureen was a champion ballbuster, he'd liked the quiet David, who smiled with his eyes and spoke in a measured, thoughtful tone.

Rick nodded to them both. "Eric, could I speak to you for a minute?" Rick didn't want to tell Eric about his father in front of David. There was no point in embarrassing the young man in front of somebody else.

"Sure. It was nice talking to you, Mr. Donovan," he said to David, then joined Rick some distance away.

On impulse Rick threw an arm around Eric's slender shoulders. Eric leaned into him, as if hungry for the body-to-body contact. "What's up?" he asked.

"We have a little problem," Rick said.

Eric's eyes darkened. "What kind of a problem?"

"Come on, I'll show you." Rick led him to the bleachers and with each step they took, he felt a tension filling Eric's body. And with that tension Rick wished he hadn't found the kid, wished he hadn't decided to show him where his father had landed in a drunken stupor.

Eric would have gone to Emma's Café and spent the night and not known. Rick wanted to kick himself. But by the time all this had added up in his head, Eric saw the feet beneath the bleacher. He went so rigid it felt as if a single blow could shatter him in a million pieces.

He jerked away from Rick and stared down at his father, and Rick could feel the rage that wafted from him. It was a wild, nearly uncontainable thing shining from Eric's eyes.

Rick identified it and understood it, had felt it himself on the night that his son had died. It was a fury against the fates who had given him a son, then had callously ripped him away, the same fates who had given a young boy a man like Leroy as a father.

"If you'll help me load him into my car, I'll see that he gets home," Rick said.

Eric turned to look at him and the rage slowly left his eyes, leaving in its wake the cold, empty eyes of a stranger. "Leave the bastard there." He whirled on his feet and walked off.

Rick stared after him until the dark night swallowed him up and he disappeared. Rick felt for the kid, but at the same time he wondered just how deep, how strong that anger ran. Although Eric had managed to tamp it down just now, what might happen if he allowed it to explode?

Chapter 24

The Butcher stood in the darkness of the night staring at the house before him. They were inside, the boy and the woman. He didn't think of them by name. He knew that most serial killers didn't think of their victims by name, but preferred to dehumanize them to make their job easier.

For the Butcher, the woman and her son weren't just victims; they were also a means to an end. A thrill kill for sure, but also the vehicle that would take him into a new realm of success.

After tonight everyone would be talking about him. His name would evoke terror in the minds of each and every person in Crow's Creek. Excitement torched through him and he raised his face to the moon, fighting the impulse to howl, to release some of the pent-up energy that vibrated inside him.

The house was dark. He knew there was no security system, nothing that would announce his arrival. He'd come prepared. He had the tools he needed to break into the house, the ski mask that would protect his identity and the hatchet that would achieve his ultimate goal.

As he stared at the house, he went over everything in his mind. Success ultimately depended on the meticulous attention to detail. It had been fifteen years since the last crime of this magnitude, fifteen years since the people of Crow's Creek had fallen into an uneasy sleep, haunted by nightmares of the Donovan family.

By this time tomorrow night, the nightmares would begin again for the good people of this small, stupid town, only this time there wouldn't be an easy fall guy to ease their fears. This time the terror would go on and on and he wouldn't be known just in this little town but all over the United States.

The Butcher. God, he loved the sound of the name, the way it rolled off his tongue.

Sweet. The rush of excitement that filled him was as sweet as any he'd ever known. Better than when he'd killed the cats, richer than when he'd killed the dogs.

It was time.

The house had been dark for quite a while. The woman and her son would be sleeping, unaware of what lay ahead. Fifteen years ago the woman had died first, then the children. Tonight the boy would be the first to die.

He circled around to the back of the house and approached the porch. The wind whipped at him, swaying tree limbs and providing a cacophony of sound that would mask his presence.

The wind had been blowing fifteen years ago, howling with a madness that had mirrored the crime. It wasn't as intense now, but still it filled him, feeding his exhilaration as he placed a piece of duct tape against the glass on the back door and used a glass cutter to remove a small section.

Not a sound. He made not a sound as he cut out a piece big enough for his hand to reach in and unlock the door. He left the glass and the duct tape on the porch, then slowly eased open the door.

Easy. So incredibly easy.

He was hard as a rock, aching with need as he stepped into the kitchen and waited for his eyes to adjust to the lack of light. The last thing he wanted was to bump into the table or a chair and rouse somebody from sleep.

This wasn't going to be perfect. Wrong time of day. Circumstances different, but he could re-create what was necessary to mirror what had happened so long ago.

He pulled his ski mask over his face, thankful that the eye slits were big enough not to obscure his vision. The weight of the hatchet felt comfortable in his hand, like an old friend, almost like an extension of him. He moved across the kitchen floor with silent stealth.

As he stepped into the living room, he saw the night-light plugged into a hallway socket, the faint glow making it easy for him to maneuver around the furniture and illuminating a path to the bedrooms.

He knew where the boy slept and in which room the woman slept. It had been easy to peek into the windows and identify both rooms. The third bedroom was a guest room with a double-sized bed and a single chest of drawers.

The first doorway in the hall was the bathroom and the one after that was the boy's room. When he reached the bathroom doorway, he laid the hatchet on the floor and drew in several deep, steadying breaths.

He'd planned this moment for a long time and soon everyone would know how meticulous, how flawless he'd been in his planning. This was his legacy, a murder that wouldn't be solved. It was the first of many.

He entered the boy's room, where another night-light burned in a socket. The boy was asleep on his back, his mouth slightly agape, and for a moment the Butcher hesitated. The children had just been at the wrong place at the wrong time.

This boy was no different, but his death was part of the legacy, a necessary piece to the plan. The Butcher flexed his fingers in his plastic gloves and approached the sleeping child.

The excitement that had danced in him since the moment he'd left the Pioneer Days celebration shuddered through him. Until this moment he hadn't been one hundred percent sure that he could do it. Different circumstances, different needs—he'd been afraid those differences would make this impossible, that he wouldn't be able to carry through with his plans.

But he heard the howl of the wind and it was as if it were speaking to him, encouraging him to fulfill his destiny. Without any further hesitation, he bent over the sleeping boy, wrapped his hands around his neck and squeezed.

It was over remarkably quickly. A few kicks and bucks, a fluttering of his eyes and then nothing. Still the Butcher continued to squeeze, remembering that the last time one had lived despite being hit over the head and strangled.

When he was certain there was no life left, no tiny little flicker that might return, he let go and straightened. He choked back a laugh of sheer exuberance, reminding himself that he wasn't done yet. Creeping from the bedroom, he went back to where he'd left his hatchet.

Time for the main event.

She never saw him coming.

She was on her stomach, sprawled like a rag doll, her breathing deep and easy in sleep. He stood right next to her bed and raised the hatchet over his head. A rush of adrenaline roared through him as he slammed the hatchet down on her neck.

Not a sound. She didn't make a noise as the blood gushed, bathing him in its sickly sweet scent. His orgasm rumbled through him, the force of it bringing him to his knees. He laughed and then he howled, the sound of it matching the wild wind that blew outside.

He got back to his feet and stared at the dead woman on the bed. It wasn't over yet. He still had lots of work to do. She wouldn't be found in her bed. No, she needed to be in the living room, seated on the sofa with her head in her lap.

He placed the hatchet on the floor and grabbed her feet. It had been good, better than he'd imagined. But he knew it could be better still.

Next time he wanted them to see him coming. Next time he'd make sure that he'd see the knowledge of their impending deaths shining in their eyes.

Chapter 25

"Can I have more mashed potatoes?" Sam asked.

"Of course." Maureen grabbed the bowl of perfectly whipped spuds and passed it to him. "According to the estimates, we had a record crowd yesterday," she said to Allison. "Everyone has been talking about what a success it was."

"I had fun," Sam exclaimed as if, in the grand scheme of things, that was all that was important.

"I think everyone had a good time," Allison agreed.

Initially the air had been tense when she and Sam had first arrived for Sunday dinner. But as the meal had progressed, the tension had fled, for which Allison was grateful.

It had taken her forever to get to sleep the night before. The thought of somebody lurking outside, staring up at her window, had kept sleep at bay. She'd vacillated between reassuring herself that it had been nothing but her imagination, and worrying that she hadn't just imagined it.

She'd awakened this morning cranky from lack of sleep and not in the mood for a subtle battle of wills with her aunt and uncle. But thankfully the meal had been pleasant, with everyone talking about the previous day's activities.

"I heard several women complaining that June Warren won the best jelly contest for the third year in a row," Maureen continued. "Of course one of the complainers was Dana McNabb, whose jelly could be used to cement bricks into a building."

Sam giggled and Allison smiled. She'd tasted Dana's jelly before. It tasted like flavored glue. "I noticed that Emma won the pie award again," she commented.

"I think the day that Emma doesn't win that award, she'll close down her business and move away in shame," David said. Although always quiet, he'd been unusually so today.

"I don't think she has to worry about that," Allison replied. "That woman does amazing things inside a perfect piecrust."

They continued to chat about the contests and prizes that had been awarded. Sam finished his meal and gave his mother the look.

"Go on," she said, knowing he was eager to head to the shed and pick out a new rabbit. He'd decided when he got here that Bugs wouldn't mind if he loved another bunny. The only difference this time was when they took the rabbit home, they were also taking home a cage they were borrowing from David until they could get to the store and get one of their own.

There was no way she was putting another rabbit into the hutch in the backyard for somebody to kill. The new rabbit would make his home in Sam's room until whoever killed Bugs was identified.

Sam left the table and headed outside, while the three adults remained at the table. "I'm thinking of putting the old house up for sale," Allison said.

"I've wondered why you haven't done it before," David said.

"I'll be happy to go up there and check things out, then talk to Doris Brubaker. She's the best real estate agent in town," Maureen said.

"Thanks, but no. I'll take care of it," Allison replied.

"I don't mind. We want to make sure it's in prime condition in order for you to get the best price. I just wish you and Seth weren't reminding everyone of what happened there." Maureen sighed. "Oh well, I'll see if Doris has any suggestions about that."

"I said I'd take care of it," Allison said more firmly.

"Maureen, for God's sake leave her alone," David added, surprising Allison. He looked at her and offered her a sad smile. "Take a walk with me, Allison. Your aunt will stay here with Sam."

Allison sat back in her chair and looked at him in surprise. "Okay. Sure."

"David, don't be a fool," Maureen said in a low voice that instantly created a ball of tension beside the mashed potatoes and roast beef Allison had just consumed. "What do you think you're doing?"

David stood and motioned for Allison to do the same. "I'm taking my niece for a walk." He took Allison by the arm. "We'll be back in a few minutes."

David's hand remained firm on Allison's arm as he led her through the living room and out of the house. It was only when they headed down the sidewalk that he dropped his hand to his side.

"Remember when Sam was little and we'd take a walk each evening after dinner?" he said.

She smiled. "And we had a terrible time keeping him in his stroller because he wanted to be a big boy and walk on his own."

David laughed, then sobered. "Your mother and father would have been so proud of you, Allison. You've done such a fine job with Sam and you're such a strong woman."

Allison laughed. "Sam was easy and certainly I've had to learn to hold my own where Aunt Maureen is concerned."

For a few minutes they walked in silence. The afternoon air was hot and smelled of burned grass, dust and the faint scent of fabric softener drifting from somebody's clothes dryer.

The tension that had knotted in Allison's stomach grew with each footstep they took. She knew her uncle hadn't brought her out in the stifling heat to tell her that she'd grown up to be a good mom and a strong woman. There was something else on his mind, something that didn't make Maureen happy. But Allison also knew David wouldn't tell her why he had her out here until he was good and ready.

They walked into the next block and came to a bench where school kids waited each morning for the bus. David motioned for her to sit, then eased down next to her.

"The worst day in my life was when your father was arrested for the murders." David's voice was soft as he stared into the distance. "Hank and I were more than brothers. We were best friends." He turned to look at her, his eyes hollow. "I knew him better than anyone. He wasn't capable of doing what they accused him of doing. I knew that. I knew it better than anyone." His voice took on strength and volume. "But I let doubts creep into my head. As I sat in that courtroom and listened to the evidence, I thought maybe he was guilty. Under the right circumstances I suppose anyone is capable of anything. But you and your Mr. Walker have given me new hope that maybe Hank was railroaded."

"So far we haven't found anything concrete that would allow for an exoneration or a new trial," she replied. "And it's possible we won't find any evidence to give him either, but we're not going to stop digging until we've exhausted every lead."

David nodded and once again stared off into space.

"I'm leaving her." He looked back at Allison. "I'm leaving your aunt Maureen."

She stared at him for a long moment in stunned silence. "But—but why?" she finally managed to sputter.

He reached for her hand and grabbed it tightly. "I think she was the one who made that phone call to you. I think she killed Sam's rabbit."

Allison gasped, feeling as if she'd been sucker punched. "Why would you think that? Why would she do that?" Someplace in the back of her mind she found it odd that her initial reaction wasn't that her aunt wasn't capable of something like that.

"Because she was afraid that you were going to destroy the facade of perfection she's built of herself in this town."

She stared at him, trying to make sense of his words. She pulled her hand from his. "I don't understand."

David drew in a deep breath and released it slowly. "Your aunt is the perfect woman, the perfect wife. That's what she wants people to believe. Everyone respects her. Everyone admires her and she was terrified that you and Seth would find out information that would taint her reputation."

"What kind of information?" Although the question fell from her lips, she felt the answer resonating inside her heart, an answer that made her feel sick. She wanted to slap her hands over her ears so she wouldn't hear the truth from his mouth. Instead she looked up and stared at him with narrowed eyes.

"She was afraid you'd find out that I had an affair with your mother."

The words shimmered in the air, like a water mirage in the desert. If I blink, they'll go away, she thought wildly. Oh God, please make them go away.

"It was a mistake," he said, as if that somehow might make it all right. "A single afternoon between two lonely people. It wasn't planned. She was having trouble with her furnace and called me to help." He leaned against the back of the bench, looking smaller, older than his years.

"I fixed the problem with the furnace and she offered me a cup of coffee. She looked so sad, so lost and so beautiful. We both knew it was a terrible mistake, but she made me feel like a man, something Maureen hadn't done in years. Anyway, it was that one afternoon and we never talked about it again. I don't think your father knew—at least I didn't think he knew until four months later when the murders occurred."

Allison stood on unsteady legs. "I need to go. I need to go home." Her uncle had an affair with her mother. Her aunt had possibly killed a rabbit and made a threatening phone call to her. Her life was exploding in front of her eyes and she had nothing to cling to, nowhere to escape the incredible pain that filled her.

"I'm sorry, Allison." David looked miserable. "I'm so goddamn sorry."

"I thought everyone in Crow's Creek was protecting me all these years, but instead everyone was protecting themselves, keeping secrets that might have saved my father fifteen years of his life, of my life." Hot tears blurred her vision, scalding her cheeks as they fell.

She turned to leave, but David caught her arm. "Allison, I just want you to know that your mother was a wonderful person, a loving woman, and what she loved more than anything else on this planet was your father and you kids. What happened between her and me meant nothing to her. It was nothing more than a temporary break from the internal loneliness that never really left her."

Myriad emotions ripped through her and they all came together to form a single question. "Did you kill her?"

His gaze didn't waver from hers. "No, and Maureen didn't do it, either. We were trapped in Emma's Café that day during the dust storm. I don't know who killed them. I wish to God I did."

She jerked her arm from his grip. "I don't want to talk to either you or Maureen again after today." She turned on her heels and headed back to the house, aware of David walking right behind her.

Maureen had called first thing in the morning after the dead rabbit had been found. How had she known about it so early? A white-hot rage filled Allison, a rage she knew she wouldn't vent today. She wouldn't talk about this while Sam was around. She didn't want him knowing that the aunt who made him mashed potatoes had also butchered his pet to save her damned reputation.

There was nothing to hang on to. The people who had been her support system, who she believed had protected her from reliving the horror of that day, had become something else, something dark and frighteningly unfamiliar.

As the house came into view, her rage increased. It was a perfect house run by a perfect woman. Maureen, the perfectionist, who cared more about her reputation than her niece and her son. Maureen, who complained all the time about David's nasty little creatures.

There was no doubt in Allison's mind that Maureen had the stomach to kill Bugs. Her aunt was nothing if not efficient when it came to taking care of problems.

Allison swiped at the tears on her face, not wanting Sam to see that she had been crying. There were so many thoughts crashing through her head, she couldn't focus on any one thing.

Had her father discovered that her mother had slept with David? Had that prompted a fight that had ended in an unspeakable tragedy? Or had David been lying about where they were on that day? Had Maureen efficiently taken care of the problem of the beautiful Joleen?

She entered the house, her heart frozen. David followed her as she stalked through the living room and into the kitchen.

"Where's Sam?" she asked Maureen, who sat at the table with the cordless phone clutched in her hand.

"He's still out in the shed."

Allison started for the back door but stopped as Maureen called her name in a plaintive tone Allison had never heard before. "Wait, I just got a phone call. I have something to tell you."

It was only then that Allison noticed that Maureen's face was as pale as a bedsheet hung out in the bleaching hot sun for too long. "What?" she asked, her heart pounding a new rhythm. Her aunt's hand shook as she raised it to her temple.

"Doris called me, wanted to know if I'd heard the news." Maureen's voice was thin, strained, and Allison's heart beat faster.

"What news?" David asked.

Maureen rubbed her temple, as if to ease the pain of a headache. She dropped her hand to the table and drew a weary breath. "Last night somebody murdered Marianne Bloom and her son."

Allison's breath whooshed out of her and she stumbled backward, her legs nearly buckling beneath her. "No." The word came whispered out of her, a protest, a prayer that somehow this wasn't happening.

"That poor little boy was strangled to death in his bed," Maureen continued, her voice growing stronger. "Marianne was decapitated and her body was left on the sofa with her head in her lap. My God, Allison, what have you and Seth unleashed in this town?"

Bile rose up in the back of Allison's throat as she

careened sideways, crashing into a chair, as wave after wave of horror consumed her. David reached out in an attempt to steady her, but she backed away from him, not wanting to be touched, afraid that she might shatter into a million pieces.

"I've got to go. Please, watch Sam. I'll be back later," she said as she backed out of the kitchen. Run, her mind screamed. Hide. Wasn't that what she did? Wasn't that how she coped with everything?

She got into her car and fumbled in her purse for her keys as her mind flashed with images. Greg dead. Marianne dead. Murdered. Like Johnny and Jenny. Like her mother.

So much blood.

There was so much blood.

Her mother sitting on the sofa with her head in her lap, her blue eyes open and staring.

She started her car engine, threw the gears into reverse and backed out of the driveway, the horrific images continuing to flash in her brain. She headed down the street, wanting nothing more than to escape.

Deep sobs wrenched from her as she thought of the cheerful Marianne and her son. Her grief clawed at her, along with the subtle hint of another, more devastating emotion.

My God, Allison, what have you and Seth unleashed in this town?

Her fault.

This was all her fault.

Somehow, someway, the questions she and Seth had been asking had stirred up a monster. This was all her fault and she had a terrible fear that this was just the beginning.

Rick stepped out of the Bloom house to get a breath of fresh air, but knew there was no way he'd get rid of the tangy copper stink of blood and death for a long time to come.

He'd seen a lot of crime as a homicide detective in Chicago, but nothing he'd experienced in that bigger city had prepared him for the scene here at the Bloom residence. Just like the Donovans. He'd seen that murder only in crime-scene photos. This one was up close and personal.

All the deputies had been called in, and behind their official vehicles lining the road in front of the house were the cars of neighbors and curiosity seekers.

George Bloom, who had found the bodies of his wife and son when he'd arrived home after working a night shift in Goodland, had been taken to the hospital and heavily sedated.

Rick swept an arm across his forehead where a trickle of sweat threatened to fall into his eyes. He turned as the door opened and Dane stepped out.

The man looked haggard. His eyes were sunken, as if they'd tried to retreat from the horror of what he'd just seen, and the lines across his forehead were etched deep into his skin.

Rick knew what was on his mind. There was no way anyone could walk into this crime scene and not think of another one. The similarities were impossible to ignore.

"Copycat? Or is it possible an innocent man is behind bars?" Rick asked softly.

Dane raked a hand through his hair and stared at the gathering crowd as if he had no idea what they were doing there. "I don't know. I'm having trouble wrapping my mind around things." He turned and stared at Rick. The yawning horror of his eyes made Rick wonder how badly the Donovan murders had affected the man. He looked lost, as if he wasn't sure how he had gotten here or what he was supposed to do.

"Dane? You okay, man?" Rick touched his taut arm.

"Fine. I'm fine," Dane replied curtly. He drew in an audible breath. "I just don't get it, I don't understand how this happened. It doesn't make sense that it's the same killer as in the Donovan case. Perps like this don't wait fifteen years between kills."

"Maybe it hasn't been fifteen years," Rick replied. "We need to check the national database, see if there have been murders like this in other areas."

"And if there haven't?"

"Then it's possible that he might have spent time in prison, or in a mental ward. Or Hank Donovan killed his wife and kids, and this is the work of a copycat."

Dane closed his eyes for a moment and his body weaved as if he might fall. Rick reached out once again, this time to grab him by the arm. He steered the big man around the side of the house, out of the sight of the onlookers and any reporters that might have shown up.

"Pull yourself together, Dane. When the details of all this get out, we're going to have more attention in this town than we want. People are going to be looking at you for answers, for assurance."

"I know. I know, dammit." Dane jerked his arm from Rick's and for the first time the dullness in his eyes receded. "Have you forgotten that I've been through this before? That I lived it fifteen years ago?" His voice cracked. "Do you have any idea how many nightmares I've had since then? How often I see those bodies in my mind?"

He leaned against the side of the house, once again looking small and slightly lost. "I hoped I'd never have to go through something like that again, but here we are." He waved a hand in dismissal. "Go on. Just give me a minute and I'll be fine."

As he closed his eyes, Rick left him there and returned to the front porch. Rick had known fellow officers in

Chicago who had a particular case that haunted them, that had cast them into deep depressions, run them into the bottom of a bottle or had them chasing the wrong end of their revolver. Rick had never had a case like that, but it was obvious to him that the Donovan murders had been that for Dane.

The crowd had grown. Two deputies worked crowd control, keeping everyone away from the scene, while two others were inside collecting evidence, although there appeared to be precious little to gather.

Whoever had done this had been thorough in cleaning up. The point of entry at the back door had yielded no fingerprints, nothing that could be used to identify a suspect. Although there was plenty of blood in the bedroom and it was obvious Marianne's body had been moved from there to the living room sofa, there didn't appear to be any physical evidence that might be of use.

They were looking for an organized killer, somebody smart, somebody who had planned well. This time there was no easy suspect as in the Donovan case. A phone call to George's workplace had let them know what time the man had left work, and the coroner had set the time of death hours before he would have arrived home.

Was Hank Donovan an innocent man spending his life in prison for a crime he didn't commit? It wasn't Rick's job to figure that out.

Rick's job was to solve this crime, two murders that Hank Donovan couldn't possibly have done. He frowned out at the people in the distance and standing near one of the deputies, he saw, was Eric Grant.

Eric, who loved all things crime related; Eric, who felt invisible among the people of Crow's Creek. He thought of the darkness he'd seen on the boy's face the night before when he'd left the high school grounds.

Rick's gut told him that whoever had beheaded those animals was also responsible for the murders. Somebody was trying to get attention. Was it possible that an invisible boy had figured out a way to make sure that everyone finally saw him?

Chapter 26

The frantic knock on Seth's motel room door jerked him up from the table where he had been pretending to make some notes but had actually been caught in daydreams of Allison.

He opened the door and the woman he'd been thinking about crashed into his arms. She was sobbing so hard, he couldn't believe she'd managed to drive. "Allison, what's wrong?" he asked with a sense of urgency. "Has something happened? Is Sam all right?"

She nodded and staggered back from him. "Sam's fine," she said through her tears. "But last night somebody murdered Marianne Bloom and her son. They were murdered just like my family." Her voice rose with hysteria. "She was left on the sofa with her head in her lap."

Shock momentarily stunned him, but Allison hit his chest with her palms, breaking the moment of stunned inertia. "What have we done, Seth?" she asked. She hit him again, wildly, out of control. "What in God's name have we done?"

He grabbed her wrists and held them tight, needing to break through her ever-growing hysteria. "We didn't do anything." She fought to free her hands from his grip, but he held on.

"We started this, we made this happen," she cried,

tears sliding down her cheeks as deep sobs shook her shoulders.

"This isn't our fault. Allison, listen to me. We didn't do this." He dropped her hands and instead wrapped his arms around her. She stood rigid in the embrace for a long moment, then with a small gasp burrowed against him.

Allison cried like she laughed, with abandon and from her heart. The sobs shook her shoulders and her tears quickly wet the front of his shirt. Still he held on, his heart aching for her as he tried to process what little he knew.

Marianne and her son murdered. By whom? At least Hank Donovan couldn't be accused of this crime. But at the moment he couldn't think about what this meant to him, to his work here. All he could think about was that a woman and her young son had lost their lives.

"I almost let Sam stay with them last night," she finally said as the sobs began to subside. She raised her head and looked at him, her eyes filled with a new kind of horror. "I almost gave in and let him spend the night." A deep shudder worked through her. "If I had, then Sam would be dead, too."

Seth stepped back from her and took her by the hand. He led her to the bed not covered with papers and notes, and sat, then pulled her down next to him and placed an arm around her shaking shoulders.

"Ally, this isn't our fault. If there's a ruthless killer in Crow's Creek, then it was just a matter of time before he killed. We can't know what prompted this. We don't know if Marianne was having problems with somebody, if George owes money or has a secret life or whatever. For all we know, despite the fact that they made it look like your family, it probably has nothing to do with you . . . with us."

Her red, swollen eyes looked at him with yearning,

with a need to believe him. "I just can't believe this is happening. I can't believe Marianne and Greg are gone." She crumpled against him and once again he held tight, wishing he could take away her pain, wishing he could magically breathe life back into Marianne Bloom and her son.

He wondered again if the price of Hank Donovan's freedom was too high. Wondered if the best thing he could do was walk away from this town and this woman now, before more damage was done.

She'd stopped crying, but she still leaned against him, as if finding some source of strength in the heat of his body close to hers. "Do they think it's a copycat killing?" he finally asked.

"I don't know." Wearily she sat up straighter. "I didn't get any real details."

"Where's Sam?"

Her features took on a hard look. "He's at my aunt and uncle's house. I need to go back and get him. I need to tell him what's happened." The hardness faded as grief once again took possession of her face. "Oh God, it was hard enough to tell him that he'd lost his pet rabbit. Now I have to tell him that his best friend is gone."

"I'm so sorry." He'd told himself when he'd first arrived in town that Allison Clemmins would have to be strong. He knew that he was going to pick old scabs, reopen wounds, and he hadn't cared much about whatever damage he left behind.

He'd been on a mission and like a soldier going into battle, he'd known there would be collateral damage and he wasn't responsible for the aftermath of his actions.

But now, with her soft curves against him, with the fruity scent of her hair filling his head, he recognized that he'd been fooling himself, that he no longer had the heart to inflict more pain on her.

"Maybe it's time we forget all this." He rubbed his hand down her arm in an attempt to warm her chilled skin. "Maybe it's time I pack up and leave here."

She stiffened and her head shot up to look at him once again. "We can't stop now," she exclaimed, the words surprising him. "What if it isn't a copycat killing? What if it's the same person who killed my family? We can't let Marianne and Greg's death mean nothing." She drew a deep breath. "I've learned some other information that I haven't had a chance to tell you yet."

"What information?"

A new tension stiffened her body as she told him about her uncle's affair with her mother and his suspicions that her aunt had been the one who had made the threatening phone call and killed Sam's rabbit.

A surge of protectiveness filled him as he heard the trembling betrayal in her voice, knew that everything she'd believed in, everything she'd trusted, had been ripped away from her.

The fact that she was here with him, a relative stranger, instead of with one of her friends, or somebody from the town itself, spoke volumes as to her emotional disconnect from the people who had raised her, the people who had surrounded her for the last fifteen years.

He'd certainly never intended to destroy her in the process of attempting to save her father, and he felt an incredible need to fix what had been broken here, but he knew that wasn't possible. Not now. Not ever.

"Do you believe your uncle? That he and your aunt were at Emma's Café the day of the murders?" he asked when she'd finished.

"I don't know. Surely if they were, somebody would remember. It was a terrible dust storm, one of those occurrences where people remember where they were. Like the day JFK was assassinated, or when the planes flew into the twin towers on 9/11."

"And do you really believe your aunt is capable of killing Sam's rabbit?"

She closed her eyes for a long moment and he ached with the obvious emotional pain that gripped her. When had this woman gotten so deeply under his skin? When had her pain become his own? He wasn't sure when it had happened; he knew only that it had.

When she opened her eyes, they were clear, with a determined glint that spoke of her inner strength, a strength he wasn't sure she realized she possessed. "Yes, I think she's capable. But what you're really asking me is if she is capable of killing my mother, of killing my sister and brother and trying to kill me."

She shrugged his arm from her shoulder and stood. She walked to the motel room window and stared outside, where the bright afternoon sunshine seemed a mockery of the darkness of their conversation.

With her back to him he was unable to read her features, to see whatever might be radiating from those telltale eyes of hers. He had never wanted to be in a woman's head like he wanted to be in hers. He not only wanted her lush lips and her sweet curves; he also wanted her thoughts and feelings.

He was in love with her. The realization hit him with a force that left him breathless. He'd blown into this town, into her life, with a mission and at this moment it all meant nothing to him. When he'd arrived in town, it had all been about him, about his needs, about his wants, but now it was about hers.

"Ally?"

She turned to face him and he knew that it would be crazy to tell her how he felt about her now, with the death of a woman and a child hanging in the air, with the betrayal of her aunt and uncle haunting her eyes.

"I don't know what to believe anymore. I don't know who to trust." She clenched and unclenched her hands at her sides. "The one thing I know for sure is that I don't want you to pack up and leave. I want you to stay and help me see this thing through. For the first time I truly believe that it's possible my father might be innocent."

Tears reappeared and clung to the length of her lashes, but she offered him a trembling smile. "If you can give me him, then I promise I won't hate you when you leave here."

"Then we see this through," he said.

She raised her hand and held it out to him, and he got off the bed and grabbed it. "And now I need to get my son and tell him that his best friend is dead." Her voice cracked and he squeezed her hand.

"I'll come with you."

"I'd like that," she replied.

He told himself it didn't mean anything, the fact that she needed him now. He'd be a fool to believe that whatever relationship they'd built could withstand whatever lay ahead.

He had the feeling that eventually, when this was all over, he'd be only a reminder of the darkest days Crow's Creek had ever known. And the worst part was he feared that the darkness that had fallen onto the small town was only going to get deeper and more profound.

The funeral for Marianne and Greg took place four days later on a hot Thursday afternoon with most of the town present for the somber occasion. Although a white canopy had been erected to provide shade, the air inside the enclosure was stifling and filled with the sickly sweet scent of flowers and a faint odor of sweat.

Allison had thought her tears had been spent since the day of the murder, but as she stood next to Seth and listened to Reverend Taylor's eulogy, new tears chased themselves down her cheeks.

Sam and the other students at the school had attended a memorial service the night before. Today he was spending the afternoon at the house of another of his friends. She didn't think it was necessary for him to be here for the burial after he'd said his good-byes to his friend the night before.

He'd been devastated by the news of the deaths and Allison had spent the previous day sitting at the kitchen table with Sam, working on a scrapbook dedicated to his friend.

Those hours of looking at pictures of Greg and Sam, of placing them into the scrapbook and talking about the fun they'd had together, had begun a healing in Sam.

Seth had been a big help, too. He'd taken Sam to a movie, had shared quiet man-to-man talks with him about life and death, about friendships and loss. Allison would be forever grateful for Seth's support in helping her son deal with the tragic situation.

She wasn't the only one fighting tears as the eulogy went on. George Bloom was a shell of the man he'd been before. Held up on either side by two men who looked like brothers, he was like a marionette whose guide strings had been cut.

Dane Kelly also looked like a man shattered. Clad in a perfectly pressed khaki uniform, standing next to his wife and son, he looked like he'd aged a decade in the past four days. His skin was sallow and his eyes were sunk so far into his head he looked like a man being eaten from the inside out.

According to the official reports and the local gossip, there were no leads in the case. No potential suspects had been identified and for the first time that Allison could remember, doors were locked at dusk and suspicion hung darkly in everyone's eyes.

Rick Solomon stood at one of the poles of the canopy. Although not in uniform, he was obviously on duty. His gaze swept the crowd with focused concentration and his body held the poised tenseness of an animal ready to spring.

Was the killer here? Masquerading as a friend? A neighbor? Why had Marianne been killed and left on the sofa like Joleen? Was it the same killer? Allison's head ached with the questions that whirled around and around, tumbleweeds of thoughts blowing through her brain.

David and Maureen were present, standing next to each other but not touching, not speaking. More than once throughout the ceremony Allison had felt the weight of her uncle's gaze on her, but she'd refused to return the gaze.

She hadn't spoken to either of them since she'd picked up Sam from their place. Before Allison had told Sam about the murders, she'd had him pick out a new bunny to bring home. Sam had named the bunny Muffin and he now slept in the cage David had provided. The bunny had helped somewhat with Sam's grief, giving him a furry friend to hold while he'd cried.

Maureen didn't try to catch her eye. She stood rigid, with her head held high, an island of that steely strength that Allison had once admired and now hated and feared just a little bit.

Wayne stood just behind them, his head lowered as if he might be silently weeping for the dead.

Finally, the ceremony was over and most of the crowd headed for their cars, as if afraid to linger, afraid that the next somber ceremony might be their own.

Seth took her by the arm, a gentle touch that found its way to her heart, as had so many things he'd done over the past four days. "You ready to go?" he asked.

"Not yet. I want to speak to Dane before we leave." She had yet to tell the sheriff what she'd found out about her mother's affair with her uncle and David's belief that it had been Maureen who had made the threatening phone call to her and killed Sam's rabbit.

"Sure you want to do that?" Seth asked.

"You mean throw my family members under the bus?" She looked up at him and offered him a forced smile. "I won't protect them. Dane needs to know the information. If there is a link to what happened to my family and what happened to Marianne and Greg, then he needs to know all the ugly details that we've learned over the past couple of days."

She broke the eye contact with Seth and instead turned to look across the cemetery to the area where her family members were buried. Surprise electrified her as she saw a figure of a man kneeling down at one of the grave sites.

Who was it? And why would he be there? She stepped away from Seth and on impulse broke into a run. "Ally? What are you doing?" Seth called after her, but she didn't stop.

She was halfway there when the man turned his head and saw her coming. She recognized him. Leroy Grant, and he was definitely at her mother's grave. His eyes widened and he rose to his feet as she got closer. He took off running.

"Hey, wait! Leroy," she yelled, but he didn't stop.

By the time she reached her mother's grave, Leroy had disappeared from her sight. She stopped then and leaned over to catch her breath, aware that not only was Seth approaching but Rick and Dane as well.

She was about to straighten when she saw it—a single red rose on her mother's grave. Her heartbeat quickened once again. Why would Leroy Grant put a rose on her mother's grave? What did the drunken odd-job man have to do with Joleen?

"What's going on?" Dane asked once the men had caught up with her.

"I want to know why Leroy Grant was here on my mom's grave." She pointed to the rose. "And I want to know why he'd put a flower here."

Dane frowned. "Who knows why that drunk does anything that he does?"

"I want you to bring him in for questioning," Allison replied. "I want to know where he was at the time of my mother's murder. And while you're at it, check out my uncle David and aunt Maureen's whereabouts that day. He and my mother had an affair and Maureen knew about it."

Dane stared at her in surprise, then swept his hat off his head and wiped his sweaty forehead with the back of his arm. "Look, Allison, I hate to be blunt, but right now I don't have time to waste on a crime that happened fifteen years ago. I've got to stay focused on what happened four days ago." His eyes narrowed as his gaze went from her to Seth.

"Maybe I should be asking the two of you where you were four nights ago," he said.

"What?" Allison gasped.

"You two have every motive in the world to commit a murder like this in order to exonerate your father," he said.

"You can't really believe that we'd do something like that," she protested.

"No, I don't." He set his hat back on his head. "But I'm telling you right now every single person in this town is a suspect and I won't rest until I find out who is responsible for Marianne and her son's death. That takes precedence over anything else, including the mystery of why Leroy Grant would put a flower on your mother's grave."

He didn't wait for a reply but turned on his heels and stalked away. Rick shifted from one foot to the other and shook his head. "He's under a lot of stress. People are scared and he isn't sure how to allay their fears. I'll check into Leroy's connection with your mother and I'll get back with you."

Allison watched as he turned and followed in Dane's path. Then she returned her attention to her mother's headstone and the single rosebud lying there.

"Don't jump to conclusions," Seth said softly.

A humorless laugh escaped her. "When did you learn to read my mind?"

"At the moment it's an open book." He slid an arm around her waist.

She leaned into him, her heart heavy. "It was bad enough to find out my mother had slept with Uncle David. But Leroy?" A shudder worked through her. "How could a woman love her husband and her children yet sleep around?"

"We can't know what drove your mother, what needs she had or what fears."

"I could never be like her," Allison said.

"Not everyone has your inner strength of character. Your mother wasn't a bad woman. She was maybe just a weak woman. We're all weak at times. I'll confess that I've slept with some women for all the wrong reasons."

She crooked an eyebrow as she gazed at him. "I hope I'm not on that list." She'd meant to inject some levity that might unknot the coil of tension in her stomach.

He reached out and slid his hand to her cheek, his palm warm against her skin. "No, Ally. I slept with you for all the right reasons." There was a longing in his gaze, a heat in those amazing gray eyes of his, that only increased the tight coil of the tension inside her.

He dropped his hand from her face and stepped back from her. "Come on, let's get out of here," he said with a roughness in his voice. "I'm sick and tired of death. Let's go do something to celebrate life."

* * *

He was one of the last people to leave the funeral. The sound of mourning still rang in his ears, but it was the underlying terror he'd felt radiating from everyone that fed his soul, that made him want to crow.

He was smarter than all of them. The only thing they'd managed to figure out was that the sharp weapon that had killed Marianne Bloom was probably the same that had been used on the slaughtered cats and dogs.

For the past four days the headlines in the *Crow's Creek Chronicle* had screamed his brilliance. THE BUTCHER STRIKES HORROR. THE BUTCHER IDENTITY STILL A MYSTERY. NO LEADS AND THE BUTCHER STILL AT LARGE.

The story had even been picked up by the wire services. He'd made the national news two days in a row. For the last four days he'd been riding a high the likes of which he'd never known before. It was only now as the mourners left the service, that he felt the crash coming, the high seeping away to leave him empty.

He wasn't ready for the high to end. He wanted to feel it forever, but he knew he needed to take some time, let the initial horror fade, before creating more.

Besides, it was fun to sit back and watch the deputies and the good sheriff twist in the wind, sweat with the realization that they were chasing somebody smarter, more cunning than any criminal they'd ever chased before.

Everyone had believed the terror had ended with the Donovan murders, but now they knew that had been only the beginning. He was responsible for the terror that filled the eyes of every woman in town. He was responsible for the men who looked at one another with a touch of suspicion.

And he couldn't wait to do it again. As the emptiness filled him, the need to act grew like a wildness inside him. It was only when he saw Allison Clemmins and Seth Walker heading for her car that a sweet rush of adrenaline filled up the empty spaces inside him.

The one who had survived.

The one who had gotten away.

Chapter 27

"Nothing in the national database to match the search criteria, no physical evidence to lead us in any direction. I've got neighbors turning on neighbors and women calling me at all hours of the day and night because they hear a noise that frightens them." Dane slammed his empty coffee cup down on the top of his desk and looked at his deputies in frustration.

"I don't want a single one of you talking to any reporter. I see you doing that, you'll be fired immediately. I want every one of you out on the streets assuring the good people of this town that we have everything under control."

It was the day after the Bloom funerals and Dane looked as if he hadn't slept in a month. All of them were feeling the pressure. They couldn't even agree if it was the same person who had killed the Donovan family or a copycat.

Dane was leaning toward a copycat killer, but Rick knew he wasn't exactly emotionally uninvolved in the case. If it wasn't a copycat murderer, then that meant he had made a tragic mistake fifteen years before and had helped put an innocent man behind bars.

"Get out of here, all of you," Dane said. "And don't forget your reports at the end of the day. I want everything in goddamn triplicate."

"Jesus, I not only got my wife all over my ass—I've got Dane chewing on it," Will Stanton, one of the other deputies, said as he and Rick stepped out of the building and into the heat of the day. "If I fart on duty, I feel compelled to write it into my report."

Rick laughed, although it really wasn't funny. "I know what you mean. He's definitely more than a little obsessive-compulsive when it comes to writing things down. Where are you headed?"

"I guess I'm gonna stroll down Main Street and try to exude quiet confidence. What about you?"

Rick frowned thoughtfully. "I'm not sure where I'm headed." But he did know. He just didn't want anyone else to know. Minutes later he was in his car and headed to the outskirts of town.

Although Dane had been adamant that he didn't have the time or the energy to focus on whatever issues Allison and Seth were raising concerning her family's murder, Rick wasn't convinced that the two crimes weren't somehow connected. All he had to do was find that connection and maybe he'd have the answer as to who was responsible.

Tumbleweeds darted across the street in front of him as he turned onto the dirt road that led to the Grant house. It bothered him that Leroy had been at the cemetery yesterday. It bothered him that the man had placed a rose on Joleen Donovan's grave.

He could find no notes to indicate that Leroy Grant had been interviewed following Joleen's murder. The man had been completely off the radar of the investigation, but he'd jumped onto Rick's radar the day before.

He had no idea what he'd find when he got to the house, no idea if Leroy would be drunk or sober, if he'd even be capable of explaining his actions from the day before.

And then there was Eric. Eric, who had left the high

school grounds the night of the murders with darkness shining from his eyes; Eric, who had no alibi for the time after he'd left. It was impossible that Eric had been responsible for the Donovan murders. He was only a year old when those murders had taken place.

But was it possible that Leroy had an affair with Joleen, an affair that prompted Eric's mother to leave town, to leave him behind? Was it possible that Leroy killed Joleen and the kids in a crazy, drunken rage and somehow Eric had found out about it? And had that somehow thrown Eric into the same kind of killing rage?

"You're reaching, Solomon," he said aloud as he parked the car in front of the run-down ranch.

He didn't want Eric to have anything to do with any of this. It was strange, but his growing relationship with Eric had filled some of the empty spaces inside Rick. Somehow Eric had made him remember the precious moments he'd spent with Brian, without evoking the killing pain that had been there before.

He was healing. Oh, thoughts of Brian would always come with pain and with the million regrets that a man could have for things not said, time not spent, but Brian had been filled with life and with love and ultimately Rick knew that his son wouldn't have wanted him to stay sad for the rest of his life. Brian had always hated seeing his daddy sad.

If Leroy was guilty of something worse than placing a rose on a dead woman's grave, then Rick had no idea how that might change his relationship with Eric. Although there didn't appear to be any love lost between father and son, the dynamics of family were never clean and simple.

He got out of the car and approached the house. Before he reached the porch, Leroy stepped out, a shotgun pointed at Rick. "Don't come any closer," he said. "And don't touch your gun or I swear I'll pull the trigger." Leroy's voice shook, along with the barrel of the gun.

Rick froze, heart pounding. "What in the hell are you doing, Leroy? Put the gun down before somebody gets hurt."

"I figured sooner or later you'd come for me, but you aren't gonna arrest me for something I didn't do."

"Do I look like I'm here to arrest you?" Rick held his hands out to his sides. "Is Eric home?"

"Eric?" The barrel of the gun lowered slightly. Terrific, instead of shooting him through the heart, if he pulled the trigger, he'd shoot off Rick's balls. "He's around here somewhere. What do you want?"

"I just came to ask you some questions. Put the gun down, Leroy. For God's sake, if I'd wanted to arrest you, I could have done it Saturday night when you were passed out under the bleachers at the high school."

Sweat beaded up on Leroy's forehead and trickled down the sides of his face as he stared at Rick. Finally, he lowered the gun and set it on one of the splintery wooden chairs on the porch. It was only then that Rick managed to draw a full breath.

"Come on, then," Leroy commanded, and gestured him to the porch.

Rick approached cautiously, with his hand on the butt of his gun, although it wasn't necessary as Leroy plopped down in one of the other chairs, enough distance away from the shotgun to alleviate the last of Rick's concern.

"What questions do you want to ask me?" Leroy asked. He rubbed a hand over his unshaven cheeks, and although his eyes were bloodshot, he didn't appear to be under the influence.

"You were at the cemetery yesterday."

"Yeah, what about it? Last I heard, it was a free country." Leroy leaned back in the chair and eyed Rick with a touch of wariness.

"You put a rose on Joleen Donovan's grave. Why would you do that?"

Leroy stared at some point beyond Rick's head. "I just felt like it, that's all. I didn't think anyone was paying attention to me until Allison started chasing me."

"Why did you run?" Rick asked.

Leroy focused his gaze back on Rick. "Because I didn't want to talk to anyone."

Rick moved the shotgun onto the floor next to him and sat in the chair opposite Leroy. "You're going to have to talk now. What's your connection with Joleen Donovan?"

"Don't think you're going to pin that murder on me. I know folks are talking like Hank Donovan might be innocent now, but I'm not going to be the fall guy here."

"I'm not looking for a fall guy. I'm looking for the truth. What was your relationship with Joleen Donovan?"

"I did some work for her, some odd jobs, and she treated me better than anyone in this fucking town, even my own wife." His eyes filled with tears. "She talked to me like I was a real man. She listened to me and I could make her laugh. She had the best laugh in the whole world." He used the back of his arm to swipe at his eyes.

"Were you sleeping with her?"

"Hell no." The words exploded out of him as he leaned forward, nearly toppling out of the chair. "No," he repeated. "But I would have. I was crazy about her, and the day she was murdered was the day the only thing worthwhile in my life was taken away." He began to weep.

A movement at the front door caught Rick's attention and he saw Eric standing just inside the screen door. It was obvious from the look on his face that he'd heard his father's words, words that had spoken of just how little Eric meant to his father. Eric turned away from the door and disappeared into the house as Rick's heart squeezed with the boy's pain.

"Where were you on the day of the Donovan murders?" Rick asked Leroy.

Leroy sucked up his tears and wiped the snot from his nose with the back of a sleeve. "I was at the hospital with my wife and Eric. He had an earache and he wouldn't stop crying. We took him to the emergency room around two that afternoon. We were there when the dust storm hit."

He squeezed his eyes closed, but tears once again trekked down his cheeks. "The next day when I heard about the murders, all I could think of was if it wasn't for that earache, I would have been at the Donovan place." He opened his eyes and stared at Rick. "I could have saved them. I could have saved *her*." He rose on unsteady legs. "I need a drink. Are we done here?"

Rick nodded and Leroy went into the house, where Rick knew he would disappear into the bottom of a bottle. Rick rose and grabbed the shotgun. He'd take it with him back to the sheriff's office. If Leroy wanted it, he could pick it up there. As an officer of the law, he didn't like the idea of leaving the weapon with a man who he knew would be stinking drunk in the next couple of hours.

He'd reached his car when he heard footsteps behind him and turned to see Eric approaching, Eric, the boy who had paid with a lack of father love for having an earache when he'd been a baby.

"He didn't kill them," Eric said. "He's a drunk and he's totally pathetic, but he's not a killer."

"I didn't consider him a serious suspect, but I needed to ask the questions," Rick replied.

Eric shoved his hands into his shorts "It must be something in the genes."

"What?"

Eric shrugged. "My old man was crazy about Joleen Donovan and I'm crazy about her daughter. Weird, huh? But I know what I feel for Mrs. Clemmins won't come to anything. I'm not sure my dad realized the same thing with Joleen Donovan."

"Eric, I've got to ask you a question."

"What's that?" The boy looked at him with clear eyes, eyes that reminded Rick of his son's.

"Where did you go after you left the high school grounds the night your father was passed out under the bleachers?"

Eric's eyes flared with surprise. "I told you that night that I was going to Emma's, and that's where I went. Oh, I get it. Teenage misfit, abandoned by his mother and resented by his father. All the baggage necessary to make a serial killer, except for the fact that I'm not."

Rick wasn't completely convinced, although he didn't want to believe Eric was responsible for any of the madness that had gripped the town. Still, Eric was extremely bright, organized and obsessed with these kinds of crimes.

"I don't know who killed the Blooms, just like I don't know who killed those animals," Eric continued. "I want people in this town to see me, but not for doing stuff like this."

Rick nodded. There was nothing else he could do here. Until they had a lead, some evidence, no arrest would be made and the hysteria of the people would increase.

Minutes later as he drove back to town, his thoughts turned to Michelle Keller. She'd been on his mind a lot over the last couple of days, but he hadn't picked up the phone to call her. He was afraid he'd let it go too long, that she wouldn't be interested in pursuing anything with him.

Besides, he had a crime to solve, a crime that would require long hours and his total concentration. He'd procrastinated too long and would once again have regrets for what he hadn't done, what he wouldn't do.

Chapter 28

The summer vacation had started with the tragedy of the Bloom murders and although almost a week had passed since that horrible day, Allison still felt emotionally fragile.

Over and over again she thought about how close she'd come to losing Sam, how close she'd come to dismissing the fact that he was grounded, and letting him go to the Blooms' to spend the night.

Not only that, but she'd been having nightmares of the day her family had been murdered. She awakened each morning with the horrifying visions still in her head, visions of her dead mother, who, before the nightmare was over, transformed into Marianne Bloom.

The week had brought no break in the case and no break in the dry heat that had gripped the area. She stood now at her back door and stared out at the dying grass. Spring wasn't even officially over yet and already everything looked as brown and dead as in late summer.

"Mom?"

Sam's voice came from the kitchen doorway and she turned to see him standing in his pajamas, his hair pointing in all directions. "Good morning," she said. "Ready for some breakfast? I thought you might like some French toast this morning."

"Hmm, sounds good." He slid into his chair at the

table. "Is Seth coming over? I was thinking maybe we could play some catch or something."

Seth. His very name caused an explosion of warmth inside her. She didn't know how she would have gotten through the last week without him. He was the only one who could understand all the emotions she'd felt for the last week, and every minute she was away from him, she felt as if a piece of her were missing.

That worried her. It worried her a lot, but more than that, Sam's growing relationship with Seth worried her. In the past two weeks he'd had enough loss in his life to last a lifetime. If she continued to allow Seth to be such an important part of Sam's life, it would be just another loss for him to deal with. It was time to put the brakes on, for her sake, but more importantly for Sam's sake.

"No, Seth isn't coming over today. I think you and I need to spend some quality time together." She opened the refrigerator door and took out the eggs and milk, ignoring the look of disappointment that flickered across Sam's face.

"So, what are we gonna do?" he asked, as if doubtful that she could come up with anything remotely entertaining.

"I thought maybe we'd go to Emma's for lunch, then drive out to the house where I grew up and see what kind of shape it's in."

Sam perked up. "That sounds cool. I'd like to see where you grew up."

"And how do you feel about maybe doing some cleanup there?" She beat the eggs with milk and dipped a slice of bread into the mixture.

"What kind of cleanup and what's in it for me?"

She laughed. "I don't know and maybe a new PlayStation game."

"Cool. Okay, I'm in," he said.

As Allison cooked the French toast, she and Sam chatted about what they might find at the old house.

"Maybe there will be bats in the attic," Sam said with that glee that boys always got in their eyes when they talked about creepy, crawling things.

"Goodness, I hope not," she replied. "I don't even want to think about bats, let alone see one."

"Or maybe there's a family of raccoons living inside now," Sam continued. "Don't worry, Mom. If there are any wild animals inside, I'll protect you. I'll use my karate and scare them away."

Allison laughed again. "I feel much better knowing I have you for protection."

After breakfast Sam went back to his room to make his bed and shower for the day. Allison was cleaning up the dishes when the phone rang. It was Seth. "Good morning." His smooth, deep voice seemed as intimate as a caress.

"Good morning to you, too," she replied, and steeled herself against the warmth that swept through her.

"How are you doing?"

"I'm okay." She carried the cordless phone to the table and sat. "Rick Solomon stopped by last night to tell me that Leroy Grant had a big crush on my mother, but it was nothing more than that. He also told me he'd questioned my aunt about the rabbit and the threatening phone call, but she denied having anything to do with it."

"How does that make you feel?"

"Like she's a liar," she replied.

"I'm sorry, Ally. If I hadn't come here, this all would have stayed under the rug." There was genuine remorse in his voice.

"Oh, I have a feeling with or without your presence here eventually I would have figured out the truth about their character flaws."

"On a lighter note, I was thinking maybe the three of us could see a movie this afternoon and maybe grab a pizza for dinner. I know Sam's been wanting to see that new Disney movie that's showing right now."

She squeezed the phone more tightly against her ear, a lump rising up in the back of her throat. "Seth, we can't do this anymore." Her initial intention was to tell him that today she'd made plans for herself and her son. She hadn't expected to say the words that fell out of her mouth. She closed her eyes against the pain they created inside her.

The words were met with a long silence. "What are you talking about?" he finally asked, but she had a feeling he knew exactly what she was talking about.

She drew a weary breath. "I think I've given you everything I can concerning the case of the murder of my family. I can't do any more to help you, and you can't do anything else to help me, and I can't let you get any closer to my son."

She swallowed against a rising emotion. "This was never supposed to happen. We were never supposed to happen."

"But we did," he replied with a fierceness. "Allison, when I came here, I was driven by my need to find one man innocent and see him freed. Somehow I thought in doing that, it would relieve the guilt I'd carried around about my not believing in my father's innocence. It was all about me. But at some point in this process, it became all about you. I don't know if your father will be freed or not, and suddenly that's not what's most important to me. I've fallen in love with you, Allison. I've fallen in love with you and your son."

They were exactly the words she hadn't wanted to hear because they forced her to face what was broken inside of her. And she was broken; she just hadn't realized it until now.

"Oh, Seth, don't love me," she answered softly. "I don't want to be in love. I don't want to invite another man into my life." Her heart squeezed painfully tight in her chest and she could scarcely talk around the lump in her throat.

"Ally, don't let the man who killed your family also destroy your ability to love and be loved. And don't allow your fear to keep love out of your son's life."

She closed her eyes, wishing she could close her heart against his words, against him. If she was going to hate him, it should be now when he forced her to examine the real damage that had been done to her when her father had been arrested and a piece of her heart had been irrevocably broken.

"I just need some distance, Seth," she finally said, hating herself for not being able to completely break it off, hating herself for wanting him to break through her fear and fix her.

There was a long pause. "Okay," he finally said. "I'll give you some distance, but I'm not going away, Ally." He hung up before she could reply, and she wasn't sure whether she was pleased by his words. All she knew was that Seth Walker had become too intimate, too much a part of her support system, her very sanity, and she needed to pull back and find her own strength again.

The Butcher watched her leave her house with her son at eleven thirty. He'd been tailing her for the past week, seeking the right time to make his move. But Seth Walker had become an irritation of major proportions, always around her, staying into the wee hours of the morning at her house.

He followed her to the café, where she and her son went inside and took a booth. He took a table nearby and ordered a double cheeseburger and fries. As he ate, he watched her, trying to imagine how she'd look with her features twisted in terror as she realized she hadn't escaped her fate after all.

He felt itchy inside, his need to act growing more and more intense with each passing minute. This morning for the first time since the Bloom murders, the newspaper headline hadn't been about him.

That was fucking unacceptable. He didn't want a day to go by that everyone wasn't thinking about him, worrying about him, wondering who was next.

He dipped a French fry into a pool of ketchup and thought of the blood that had spewed from Marianne Bloom. It had been slick and warm. The only thing that had been wrong about the kill was that she hadn't seen him coming. He'd cheated himself by striking at her before waking her up, before allowing her to turn over and see him with the hatchet raised over her.

Allison would see him coming. God, the very thought of her seeing him, recognizing what was about to happen, filled him with an itch, an excitement that he could scarcely contain.

He motioned for the waitress. "Can I get a refill on the soda?" he asked.

She grabbed his glass with an undisguised look of exasperation and stalked off to the counter. She returned a moment later and slammed the full glass down harder than necessary.

"Thanks, I appreciate it," he said, and gave her one of his nicest smiles. The bitch didn't know it, but she'd just made his list. He knew she was a single mother, had a little girl who would die in her bed just before he cut off the bitch's head.

Marianne might have been the first, but Allison wouldn't be the last. Oh no, he planned on being around a very long time.

Chapter 29

"You have got to be stuffed," Allison said to her son, who had managed to put away a burger, fries and a shake, then top it off with a large piece of chocolate pie.

"I'm just building up my strength," he said. "You know, for the work we might have to do at the house."

Seth loved her. Throughout the meal his words had played and replayed in her mind. He'd fallen in love with her. And she loved him, too. Was she going to be a fool and turn her back on a man who made magic when he looked at her with those smoke gray eyes? A man who not only gave her strength but also recognized the strength she had on her own?

She didn't want to be one of those women who ended up living alone for the rest of their lives, bitter with regret and aching with loneliness. She didn't want that loneliness to burden her son as he grew up and made a life of his own.

How often did fate drop a man in your life who fit so perfectly? What she had to figure out was if her love for him was somehow tied to what he'd come here to do. Did she love him because he'd given her the hope that maybe, just maybe her father was innocent? That maybe the man who had rocked her in his arms, the man who had loved to dance with his girl, was nothing more than another victim?

"Mom?" Sam's voice held a wealth of impatience. "Hello? Anybody home?"

"Sorry, I was daydreaming," she replied. "Are you ready to get out of here?"

He nodded and together they left their booth and headed to the cashier, where Allison paid for the meal. As they walked outside, Allison caught her breath against the heat. "Maybe we should stop at the convenience store and grab some bottled water to take with us," she said as they headed for her car.

She paused at her car door, that prickly uncomfortable sensation making her look around uneasily. There were few people on the street and she saw nobody who seemed to be paying any attention to her.

It was then she realized the wind was gone and the air held an unnatural stillness. Surely that was what made her feel uneasy, the absence of the wind.

She unlocked the car door and she and Sam got inside. A quick stop at the convenience store and they were on their way to the house on the hill, the place she hadn't been to in fifteen years.

She felt ready to face it, to face the memories, both good and bad, that she knew returning there would bring. If nothing else, Seth had made her recognize that it was time to make peace with the past, to let go of the house and the memories that had kept her trapped, unable to truly move forward in her life.

Sam hummed beneath his breath as they drove away from town, oblivious to the emotional turmoil building up in his mother the closer they got to the house.

It's just a structure, she told herself. Although evil had happened there, the house itself had been an innocent victim as well as the people who had died that day.

"Once we get the house sold, you'll have a tidy sum of money in your college fund," she said.

"That's good, because I think I want to be a lawyer

like Seth, and he told me that means going to school for a long time. I wish he lived here in Crow's Creek. Even if you and him didn't get married or anything, it would be cool if I could see him every day."

"That would be nice," she agreed.

She tensed as she turned into the long drive that led to the house. "Why is there a gate?" Sam asked as they pulled up in front of the barrier.

"Aunt Maureen had the gate put up because nobody lived here and she didn't want people breaking in or anything."

"How are we going to get through?" Sam asked.

"I have the key." Allison shut off the car and pulled her key ring from the ignition. She'd had the tiny padlock key on her key chain for the last fifteen years and had never used it.

As she unlocked the gate, she looked toward the house. The house itself looked smaller than she remembered. Maybe it was because the surrounding trees had gotten so big.

She opened the gate, then returned to the car and drove through. She parked in front and as Sam grabbed the bottled water and a broom and dustpan from the backseat, she got out of the car and stared at the place where she'd spent the first sixteen years of her life.

The sun had faded the paint from white to gray and the front door hung crookedly from its hinges. The overall air was one of abandonment. Tall weeds and brush had taken the place of a lawn and Allison made a mental note that the first things that would need to be done were mowing and painting.

"It looks pretty sad," Sam said as he came to stand next to her.

"A coat of paint will make it look happy again. Come on, let's go inside."

Her heart began a rapid beat as she approached

the door, remembering the last time she'd turned that knob.

The porch creaked beneath their feet, and her hand trembled as she reached out to unlock the door. As she turned the knob, she once again noticed the stillness in the air, as if Mother Nature held her breath in anticipation of something happening.

The door opened with a groan of rusty hinges and she stepped into the living room. No visions assailed her, no horror swept over her and she released a small sigh. The room was empty except for the dust that covered the hardwood floor.

Sam leaned the broom against the wall and set the bottled water and dustpan on the floor. "It doesn't look too bad, Mom," he said. "Can I look in the other rooms?"

"I'll give you the tour," she said. They started in the kitchen and she shared with Sam some of the memories the room contained. Birthday parties and holiday meals had taken place in this room. It had always been a place of laughter, of warmth, and those memories filled Allison with a bittersweet happiness.

From the kitchen they went down the hallway to the four small bedrooms. It was in Jenny's and Johnny's tiny rooms that she felt the first stir of deep, abiding grief. Sam seemed to sense her sadness, for he grabbed her hand and looked up at her with a surprisingly adult gaze. "I'm sorry, Mom. I hope you're not going to cry."

She smiled and sucked back any tears that might have thought about falling. "It's just sad to think about my little brother and sister."

"They would have been my aunt and uncle."

She nodded. "And they would have loved you so much. Johnny loved to draw and he probably would have done art projects with you. Jenny liked animals, stuffed and real. She would have probably lived on a farm with all kinds of animals or she would have been a veterinarian."

"I'm sorry I never got to meet them," Sam said, and squeezed her hand.

"Me, too," Allison replied around the lump in her throat.

When they reached the room that had been her bedroom, the conversation lightened as she told Sam how the room had been decorated with posters and a bright pink bedspread with purple and green throw pillows. "I listened to the Beatles all the time," she said.

"Beatles? Who are they?"

As Allison explained about the singing group from Britain, they returned to the living room. "Why don't you sweep up this floor while I make some notes about what needs to be done around here?" She pulled a notepad and pen from her purse.

"Okay," Sam agreed.

Allison slid to the floor, unmindful of the dust she knew would probably coat her butt when she stood, and began to write down all the things that would make the house more marketable.

The first item that made her list was paint, both inside and out. She was pleased that although the faucets had run with rusty water, they'd all worked. She didn't think it would take a ton of money to get the place market ready, but emotionally she was pleased to realize she was ready to let go of this house.

She didn't know who had killed Marianne and Greg Bloom. She didn't know if her father was guilty or innocent. She had no idea if there was a future with Seth. But at this moment, the one thing she was certain of was that she was ready to move away from the tragic events of her past, and selling this house was the first big step in doing that.

* * *

It was too good to be true. Allison and her son back in the place where it had all begun. The Butcher stood behind a tree in the front yard of the old farmhouse and felt the rolling, screaming waves of excitement rushing through him.

It was fate that had placed them here, had placed him here. He had everything he needed to complete what had been left unfinished fifteen years before.

It would be a new horror for the town, another jewel in his crown. There would be no question about his skill, his cunning, his overwhelming brilliance after today. It would be not only the people in Crow's Creek who knew his name, but also people all over the United States, maybe even all over the world.

He left the tree and made his way stealthily to his car, which was parked up the road and hidden by brush. His hatchet was there, along with his ski mask, some rope and duct tape.

This time nobody was sleeping. He would have to be even smarter to take on two of them while they were awake. But he was up to the task. He was the best. The best! His cock hardened as adrenaline pumped wild and hot inside him.

The victims were in place. He was well prepared.

The only thing that was missing was the wind.

Chapter 30

The minute Allison and Sam stepped out on the porch to leave the old farmhouse and return home, she saw it—the ominous rolling black wall of a dust storm. It filled the sky in the distance, like dark billowing smoke driven by a tremendous force beyond the horizon. Allison had seen the natural phenomenon only once before in her life, and that had been on that terrible day fifteen years ago.

"Wow!" Sam exclaimed. "Awesome."

She touched her son's shoulder. "Come on, let's get back inside. We'll have to wait it out inside," she said. The last thing she wanted was for the two of them to be in the car when the storm struck.

They moved off the porch and back into the house, where Sam ran to the window with a southwest view. "It's getting closer," he said, a hint of fear deepening his voice. What had initially appeared awesome to the twelve-year-old obviously no longer seemed so awesome.

Allison moved to stand behind him and placed her hands on his slender shoulders. "I know it looks kind of scary, but it's just wind and dust."

She stared beyond Sam to the approaching maelstrom and, almost hypnotized by the boiling, swirling sight, went back in time, back to when she'd been sixteen years old and on her way home from school.

It had been Ellie Gordon who had seen it first. She'd squealed in horror as she stared out the window, but nobody paid much attention to her because Ellie squealed about something all the time.

It was only when Jennifer Landers, Ellie's seatmate on the bus, had screamed as well that everyone looked out the window and saw the boiling brown mass descending upon them.

Chaos ensued. The girls screamed and the boys darted from window to window as the bus driver, Mrs. Johnson, yelled for all of them to calm down, to sit down. As the dark cloud approached, the bus began to rock from the force of the wind and the sky darkened, turning the sunny day into night.

Mrs. Johnson pulled the vehicle off the road and parked as the brunt of the storm hit them. Tumbleweeds and other debris struck the side of the bus as the wind screeched like a banshee.

"It's the end of the world," Ellie screamed, tears coursing down her face. "God's wrath is coming down on us all. Oh, sweet Jesus, forgive me for my sins and deliver me from evil."

"Shut up, Ellie," one of the boys shouted.

"Yeah, it's just a dust storm," somebody else added.

Mary Layton, one of Allison's best friends, who was seated next to Allison on the bus, laughed and grabbed Allison's hand. "Everyone knows the last time Ellie prayed was when she thought she was pregnant and prayed for a period."

Allison laughed, too, but she squeezed tight to Mary's hand until the storm passed and the sun once again began to shine.

"Show's over," the bus driver said, and started the engine to finish delivering the students to their bus stops.

There was one stop where Ellie got off; then it was time for Allison's stop. She climbed off the bus and waved to her classmates and noticed that the black cloud of dirt had moved northward.

The first thing she was going to do when she got inside was take a shower. Even though the bus windows had been up, the dust had seeped in through the minute cracks and crevices of the bus and swirled in the air. She felt grimy with it. She smiled as she thought of her little sister and brother in the house with her mom.

She'd bet her mother had spun a story to ease the fears of the two young kids, and the way she knew her mother, it would have been a story about a princess saved from the evil dust monster by a handsome prince. If there was one thing Joleen Donovan loved, it was telling fairy tales where dragons were slain and princesses and princes lived happily ever after.

The porch was covered with a layer of dirt as she climbed the stairs to the front door. She couldn't wait to get inside and tell her mom she'd aced her English test, that Bobby had asked her to go to the prom and that silly Ellie had thought the dust storm was the end of the world.

She'd had no warning of what was to come, no sense of foreboding about the horror that awaited her.

"Mom?" she called as she flung open the door. She took three steps into the room and saw her mother seated on the sofa. Joleen wore her favorite pink-flowered duster and was sitting where she always sat to watch *General Hospital.*

Her head. For a moment Allison couldn't make sense of it. Joleen's head wasn't where it belonged. Rather than being on her neck, on her shoulders, it was in her lap. It was only then that Allison smelled it, the rich copper scent of blood, the raw, ugly scent of death. She opened her mouth to scream, but never released a sound of her horror as she was struck over the head from behind and knew no more.

"Mom! You're hurting me!"

She slammed back to the present with Sam wiggling to escape the biting imprints of her fingernails in the tops of his shoulders. She dropped her hands and backed away from the window. "I'm sorry, honey. Move back. I don't want you standing in front of the glass."

She tasted the tangy flavor of blood and realized she'd bitten the inside of her mouth as she'd remembered that day. What had happened to Mary Layton? Funny. Allison had never seen her again after that day on the bus when they'd held hands and laughed, not knowing the nightmare that Allison would face.

The storm now fell upon the little farmhouse. The room darkened and the house began to creak and groan beneath the onslaught of the wind. A thud sounded against the outside wall. "What was that?" Sam asked, his eyes wide, as they stood in the center of the living room area.

Probably a poor bird, disoriented from the storm, she thought, but she didn't speak the thought aloud. Sam was so softhearted he'd want to go outside and see if the bird could be saved. "Just trash or something picked up by the wind," she replied.

"How long will this last?" Sam asked, and shot a worried glance back toward the window, where it was almost as dark as night.

"Not long." At least that's what she hoped.

"Will we be safe here?" His forehead furrowed with little lines of worry.

She offered him a reassuring smile. "We should be fine. This old place might look a mess, but it was built strong. Why don't you show me some of those karate moves of yours?" she asked. "You have all this space." She gestured around the empty room and then forced a smile. "And you have me as a captive audience."

She needed something, anything, to take her mind off

the dust storm. The memories it evoked in her tried to take hold of her once again, to pull her back to that day when her entire world had exploded apart, when a killer had beaten her home and taken from her everything that she loved.

As Sam began his first series of movements, her head was filled with the vision of her mother's milky blue eyes, of that single moment when she'd tried to make sense of what had happened. In a single instant just before she'd been struck unconscious, she'd seen blood everywhere, as if a crazed painter had tried to turn the room red. This room, right where she and Sam stood. Her mother had been murdered here, along with her little brother and sister.

And she should have died as well. The killer had meant for her to die.

She smiled and nodded at her son as her mind filled with the horror, and the wind shrieked around the farmhouse like a loosened wild beast. It will be over in a minute, she thought. The storm will pass and we'll go back to our house, back to our lives, and we won't ever come here again.

"That's great, Sam," she said as he finished up a series of moves. She glanced toward the window, where there was no change in the darkness of the sky. How long could it last? She already felt as if she'd been trapped in this house of death for an eternity.

She and Sam both jumped as the front door flew open and a swirl of thick dust entered like an unwelcomed guest. Allison took two steps toward the door to close it when he appeared in the doorway, a man in jeans and a T-shirt and wearing a ski mask. In his hands he held a hatchet.

For a moment, she thought he was a horrifying phantom from her past, a specter of evil conjured up from her imagination. But as he took a step forward, his boots rang on the wooden floor, and as Sam gasped and ran to her side, she knew he wasn't from her imagination.

He was real.

He was death.

She'd escaped him fifteen years ago and now he was back to claim her.

Chapter 31

Seth entered Emma's Café just after one for lunch. He really wasn't hungry but was sick of his own company and the silence of the motel room. He'd been unsettled since his conversation with Allison that morning.

Nothing like baring your heart, your soul, to a woman only to be told that she needed some distance. It had the same result as a swift kick to the balls.

After he'd caught his breath, he'd sat on the bed and stared at the papers he'd accumulated in an effort to gain her father's freedom. There was no real smoking gun, nothing concrete that could be used to free Hank Donovan. Even the Bloom murders didn't point to his innocence, only the probability of a copycat killer at work.

Was that why she'd needed some distance? Because he hadn't been able to accomplish what he'd come here to do? Or had he misinterpreted her feelings for him?

The café was unusually quiet. People weren't going out the way they had been before the Bloom murders. Seth slid into an empty booth and picked up the menu, although by now he pretty well knew it by heart.

He ordered a club sandwich, chips and a glass of iced tea, then leaned back and tried not to think about Allison and Sam, but it was an impossible venture.

Thoughts of her filled him up. He hadn't misinterpreted anything. She loved him. He knew it. He saw it in the softness of her eyes, in the way even the most casual touch they shared lingered for a moment too long.

He couldn't imagine spending the rest of his life without her, without Sam. The boy had grabbed on to his heart as effortlessly, as indelibly as his mother had.

Seth had spent most of his life alone, nursing a guilt that had encased his heart, keeping himself emotionally uninvolved as he focused on a mission that he now realized wouldn't have healed him even if he had succeeded.

His healing had come with the curve of her lips as she smiled at him, in the way she sighed his name when they made love. He loved her and he knew that she loved him, too.

When she'd told him that the two most important men in her life had betrayed her, she'd said it half jokingly. But her father's arrest and Bobby's death had scarred her perhaps more deeply than she knew.

It was fear that kept her from reaching out for the love he had to offer her, the fear of being hurt again by any man she allowed into her heart.

He didn't intend to walk away from her. Somehow he had to figure out how to break through that fear, how to reach that amazing, vibrant woman inside and assure her that they belonged together.

She was going to have to send him away with stronger words than that she needed some distance. And he wasn't going to give her an easy out by letting her talk to him on the phone. If she intended to send him out of her life, she was going to have to tell him in person; she was going to have to look into his loving eyes to do so.

Suddenly the last thing he wanted to do was to be sitting in Emma's Café alone. He knew her plans had been to go to the old farmhouse this afternoon and that's where he wanted to be.

He threw enough money on the table to pay for the meal he wasn't going to stay to eat, then started to walk toward the front door. He heard the wind before he reached the door, a screeching noise audible above the clatter of silverware and the voices of the patrons.

He stood at the door and watched day turn to night as thick dust filled the air. It was an awesome sight.

"Would you look at that?" the waitress who had taken his order said as she moved to stand next to him. "I've never seen anything like it before."

"I have," an old man replied. "Looks like it did fifteen years ago, the day the Donovan family was murdered."

A sense of disquiet filled Seth as he stared out the door. He told himself there was no reason for concern, but a growing urgency made him want to run outside, jump into his car and drive to the farmhouse.

He told himself he was being silly, that there was nothing to worry about. Besides, he'd be a fool to go out in the storm. He couldn't even see the other side of Main Street. There was no way he'd be able to drive to the farmhouse.

He'd have to wait it out. He just hoped the alarm that made him feel half-sick with anxiety was nothing.

Chapter 32

Allison stared at the man in front of her, her heart smashing so hard against her ribs that she felt half breathless. She grabbed the broom and held it out before her, knowing it was an ineffective weapon against his hatchet, but needing something between them and the man.

Although she was afraid for herself, she was absolutely terrified for Sam. Whatever it took to save him, that's what she'd do. She'd die to protect him.

She knew if that happened, if she died here, Seth would see that Sam was okay.

And in that instant, of knowing that she would trust her son to Seth, her heart opened to all the love she felt for him. But she couldn't think about that now.

"Sam," she said in a low, trembling voice. "I want you to run out the back door. Now, Sam." She didn't wait to see if her son obeyed, only prayed that he did as she lunged forward with the broom in front of her.

The man easily sidestepped her thrust and swung the hatchet, missing her by mere inches. A sob escaped her as she heard the faint bang of the back door. Thank God, Sam had done what she'd asked. He'd run.

The masked man laughed, a low rumble of such pleasure it raised the hairs on Allison's arms. "What do you want?" she screamed, and scrambled back from him, the broom still held defensively in front of her.

"You."

The word reverberated in the air. He laughed again and she frowned. That laugh sounded familiar. But where had she heard it before? She couldn't think. She couldn't place it.

"Who are you?" Her hands were slippery with perspiration as her attention stayed focused on the wicked-looking weapon he held in his hand.

"The Butcher. I'm the Butcher of Crow's Creek and I've come to finish what was started fifteen years ago." He took a step toward her and laughed as she cringed and jabbed with the broom.

Again she was struck by the fact that she knew his voice, had heard it before, but her heart pounded so fast, so furiously, she was dizzy and couldn't put her thoughts together. All she knew was that she was in imminent danger and she had to find a way to escape.

She tried not to think about Sam out in the wind, in the blinding dust. At least he wasn't in here, facing this madman, who seemed to be taking pleasure in toying with her.

He swung the hatchet again, the blade catching the end of her broom and nearly whipping it from her hands. She gasped and held tight, knowing that without the broom there would be nothing standing between her and death.

It was a standoff. Panting, she faced him and he stared back at her, his eyes gleaming bright through the eye slits of the mask. "Why are you doing this?" she asked. Her voice sounded eerie to her own ears, thin and reedy and filled with terror.

"Because I can," he replied.

A sob ripped from her. "Did you kill my family?" She had to know. Had he been the one who had killed them, then let her father take the fall?

"It doesn't matter if I did or not. I'm going to kill you

just like I did Marianne Bloom. Then I'm going to go outside and hunt down your son and strangle him like I strangled Greg."

He spoke the words as matter-of-factly as if he were explaining that he was going to the store to buy a gallon of milk. The only difference was the faint, sick vibrating energy that pulsed from him.

She saw the bunching of his arm and leg muscles, and sensed that he was about to attack. She knew it was only a matter of time before he'd be able to knock the broom out of her arms, only a matter of time before the hatchet would connect with some part of her body.

As he sprang forward, she threw the broom at him and raced down the hallway and into the bathroom. She slammed the door and turned the lock, sobbing wildly as her pounding heart threatened to explode out of her chest.

It was only then she remembered. The bathroom was windowless. She was trapped. She backed away from the door and hit the sink cabinet with her back. She stared at the locked door, the only sound that of her ragged breathing.

Had her mother seen him coming? The man with the hatchet? Oh God, Allison had never been so afraid in her life. She didn't want to die. She wanted to see Sam grow up. She wanted to meet his girlfriends and be at his wedding. She wanted to spoil his children and grow old with Seth.

Seth.

Her heart cried out to him, for him and for all the love she'd miss. It was utter tragedy that in the moments before her death her heart opened to embrace her love for Seth.

Too late.

Tears burned her eyes as deep sobs sent her to her knees.

Too late.

The hatchet hit the door. She screamed as wood splintered. Oh God. Oh God. There was no way to stop him. He laughed, the sound of madness. "Might as well unlock the door and meet your fate," he said.

She froze as she finally recognized the voice. But it made no sense. He couldn't have killed her family. He would have been a baby at the time of those murders.

As the hatchet once again slammed into the door, another scream ripped from her. But she knew that just like on the day Jenny and Johnny and her mother had been murdered, nobody could hear her screams.

"That was awesome!" Patrick exclaimed as the dust began to thin. He looked at Eric in the passenger seat of his car. "Wasn't that awesome?"

Eric nodded and drew a deep, ragged breath. It hadn't been the storm that had frightened him but rather the fact that they were parked just off the country road, and he'd been afraid another car wouldn't see them and would plow into them.

Wind still buffeted the car, but the visibility was improving with each passing minute. They'd been driving aimlessly, wasting the hot day in the confines of the air-conditioned car and talking about summer plans, girls and anything else that popped into their heads.

"I guess it's over," Patrick said as he started the engine of his car. He refastened his seat belt and was about to pull back on the road when something slammed into the side of the car where Eric sat.

Both of them yelled and Eric turned to see Sam Clemmins at his window. The boy's face was twisted in terror as he banged on the glass. "What the hell?" Patrick said as Eric rolled down the window.

"He's gonna kill her," Sam cried. "He's got a hatchet and he's going to kill my mom."

Eric opened the car door and bolted out. He grabbed Sam by the shoulders. "Who? Who's going to kill your mom?"

Sam whipped his head back and forth. "I don't know. He had on a mask. You gotta do something. She's up at the old farmhouse."

"Get in the car," he commanded the boy, then leaned down to look at Patrick. "Call the sheriff." As Patrick took out his cell phone, Eric took off running.

Not Mrs. Clemmins. Not Allison. He couldn't let anything happen to her. His heart banged as he ran faster than he'd ever run in his entire life. She was one of the few people who had been kind to him, who had taken time to listen to him when he talked, who had made him feel special.

He couldn't let anyone hurt her. He loved her. And even though he knew nothing would ever come of that love, even though he was smart enough to recognize that it wasn't real love but rather a crazy crush, that didn't change the fact that if anything happened to her, a piece of him would die.

A hatchet. Sam had said the man had a hatchet. That meant it was the Butcher who had her. Still, he wasn't afraid for his own safety. All he could think about was Allison.

The wind whipped around him as if trying to slow him down, but Eric, who had never been particularly athletic, fought on with the strength of a linebacker.

When the house came into view, he didn't hesitate. He took the porch stairs two at a time and burst through the front door. For a moment he thought he was too late. There was nobody in the living room.

"Mrs. Clemmins," he yelled. "It's me, Eric."

"Eric! Run. Run, Eric." Her muffled voice came from somewhere in the back of the house.

He raced forward and turned to go down the hallway

and that's when he saw him. The masked man with the hatchet. In an instant Eric processed what he saw, the broad shoulders, the slender waist and hips, the boots on his feet. He knew those boots.

Confusion fluttered through him. "Beau? What in the hell are you doing?"

Beau pulled off his ski mask and stepped away from the door he'd been standing before. From behind the door Eric could hear Allison crying, yelling for Eric to run.

"I'm not the sheriff's boy anymore. I'm not Dane Kelly's kid. I'm the Butcher of Crow's Creek." He approached Eric, the hatchet hanging at his side. "You shouldn't have come here, Eric. I've got work to do."

A million thoughts flitted through Eric's head as he stared at his friend. Why hadn't he seen it? After all the research he had done on serial killers, how had he missed the fact that his best friend had become the terror of the town?

Eric had always thought he was the invisible man, the one that nobody really saw, nobody really paid any attention to, but Beau's words made him realize that Beau had been the invisible one. He'd often complained that in this town he was nothing but the sheriff's kid, that few people rarely called him by his proper name.

"You killed those cats and dogs?" Eric asked.

"And the Blooms." Beau's eyes glittered. "You can't imagine what it's like, Eric. You can't imagine the power, the kick. Everyone is afraid of me. Everyone is talking about me."

"You know I can't let you hurt her," Eric said.

Beau smiled. "You can't stop me." Without warning he swung the hatchet. Eric tried to leap back, but the weapon caught him on the outside of his leg just above the knee. It cut deep. Blood shot out and the white-hot pain sent all rational thought out of Eric as he fell to the floor.

Unconsciousness flirted with him, dark shadows ebbing and flowing in front of his eyes. He dry heaved as the pain seared through him He was vaguely aware of Beau standing above him. "You shouldn't have tried to be a hero, buddy. I'll be back for you after I take care of her."

In a desperate attempt to stop him, Eric reached out and grabbed his boots. Beau tripped and fell to his knees, muttering a curse as he kicked at Eric's head.

As a boot connected with his forehead, he saw dancing stars and tears filled his eyes. They weren't tears of physical pain; rather they were the tears of a boy who had desperately wanted to be a hero, but ultimately was just going to be another victim.

Rick sat in the passenger seat of Dane's car as the two drove at breakneck speed toward the old Donovan place. The call from Patrick Johnson had come in minutes before and Rick only prayed they didn't arrive too late.

The details were sketchy, but they had enough information to know that Allison Clemmins was in mortal danger from a masked man with a hatchet. It was him, the Butcher of Crow's Creek, and Rick prayed they were in time not only to save Allison but also to arrest the murderer who terrorized the town.

"I'll tell you right now. I intend to shoot first and ask questions later." Dane held the steering wheel so tight his knuckles were white and his eyes burned with a sick fever.

"I just want him in custody," Rick replied. "Maybe this will answer the question of Hank Donovan's innocence."

"There was never any question in my mind where he's concerned. I'll go to my grave thinking that he's guilty," Dane replied.

The two men fell silent. They were only minutes from the farmhouse. Would it be too late for Allison? Would they be too late to catch him? Don't let it be Eric, a little voice whispered inside him. He didn't want it to be the teenage boy who had worked his way into Rick's heart.

"We go in fast," Dane said as the farmhouse came into view. "Our first goal is to protect lives. Our second is to get the son of a bitch responsible."

Rick nodded as adrenaline fired through him. By the time Dane stopped the car, Rick was out with his gun drawn and ran up the porch steps.

He heard the screams as he went in through the front door. Screams coupled with the sound of splintering wood. But it was the sight of Eric, unconscious and crumpled on the floor, his leg bleeding from a horrendous wound, that momentarily halted him in his tracks.

"Jesus Christ," Dane muttered from behind him. "Sheriff's department," he yelled. "Put your weapon down and come out with your hands up." Both he and Rick pointed their guns in the direction where the screams were coming from.

Stunned surprise electrified Rick as Beau stepped out of the hallway and into the living room, the hatchet held in his hand. He glanced over at Dane, whose face had gone as pale as a corpse.

"What are you doing here, boy?" Dane's thick voice indicated his enormous strain.

A door creaked open and Rick saw Allison step out into the hallway. He gestured to her not to come any closer. The situation was still volatile.

"My name isn't *boy*," Beau replied fiercely. "You can call me the Butcher." He seemed not a bit concerned that two men held guns pointed at him. "I wasn't sure I could do it at first. That's why I killed the cats. Then when I killed Felix, I knew that I could kill anything, anyone."

"Why?" The word ripped from Dane's throat.

Beau cocked his head and gave his father a sly grin. "Because I'm just a chip off the old block."

"What the hell are you talking about?" Dane's voice vibrated and Rick saw that the hand holding his gun trembled.

Beau laughed derisively and shook his head. "You and your notes. Everything you've ever done in your life is written down on paper. I found your notes in the basement, Dad, behind the loose brick in the wall. I read all about what you did here fifteen years ago, how you killed them."

Rick wasn't sure who gasped louder, himself or Allison. He stared at the man who'd been his boss, the man who was sworn to protect and serve the people. On Dane's stark, white face, Rick saw the truth.

"Don't you get it? Now I know how you felt that day, the rush, the thrill. Like God. Didn't you feel like God when you killed them? That's the way I felt. We can feel it again now. We can be a team." The words rushed out of Beau, like the wind screaming around the house. "You and me. We can go down in history together."

Dane stared at his son and heard the wind blowing like it had done that day fifteen years before. Somehow it had always felt that the events of that day had happened to somebody else. He'd managed to maintain a distance from the horror. But now it all rushed back to grab him by the throat, twist in his stomach, burn in his heart.

He'd loved her.

Joleen.

He'd been willing to give up his wife and son, to give up his position as sheriff and go away with her. He'd been so certain that she'd felt the same way about him. But she hadn't. She'd laughed at him, told him he was a foolish boy, that she wasn't about to leave her husband and her family.

The hatchet had just been lying there and he had no real memory of picking it up, of swinging it at her with such force. As he stood facing his son, the taste of dust filled his throat and the sound of the wind filled his head with a rushing noise, and for the first time in fifteen years Dane Kelly really saw what he had done.

And as he stared into his son's eyes, he recognized what he'd spawned. "You're wrong, boy. What I felt that day when I murdered Joleen and those kids was sickness and remorse. There was nothing thrilling about it."

He smiled, a soft smile. "I love you, Beau." The trembling in his hand stilled as he pulled the trigger and shot his son between the eyes.

Allison screamed and Rick whirled his gun to point it at Dane. "Jesus, Dane. Put your gun down," Rick yelled. "Put your goddamn gun down!"

Dane looked at Allison. "I'm sorry. I never meant for it to happen. It just all went crazy that day." He moved his gaze to where his son lay dead on the floor, and the wind screamed and the taste of dust choked him. He recognized his son for what he was, but more importantly he looked at himself and acknowledged what he was. Without hesitation, he raised the barrel of the gun to his mouth and pulled the trigger.

Allison stared at Rick, too stunned to speak, too stunned to move. Rick returned her stare, his eyes radiating the same emotion. Dane? Dane had killed her family?

Too much information crowded in her head, making it difficult for her to sort through it all. "Sam?" Her son's name came out of her in a whisper.

She saw Rick's Adam's apple bob as he swallowed, visibly shaken by what had just occurred. "Sam's okay."

She sucked back a sob; then the stunned inertia that had gripped her broke as she remembered Eric. She ran to his side and fell to her knees. "He's still alive. We need an ambulance." She picked up Eric's hand in hers and squeezed tightly. "Hang in there, Eric. We're going to get you help."

She had no idea whether he could hear her. She looked up at Rick. "He tried to save my life. We have to save him." Tears began to course down her cheeks as Rick got on his cell phone, calling for an ambulance, then calling for backup.

He crouched next to Eric and when he looked at Allison, tears were in his eyes. "He's a good kid. He's got to be all right."

The front door flew open and Seth flew in, his eyes wild and crazed until his gaze found her. He closed his eyes and opened his arms and Allison ran to him.

As he wrapped her tight in his arms, she felt the deep shudders that coursed through him, the raging of his heartbeat against her own. For the first time in what felt like an eternity, she felt safe.

His hands moved down the length of her back, as if checking to make sure there was nothing missing, nothing hurt. He finally released her enough to look down at her. In his eyes she saw, not only his fear of losing her, but the enormous love he had for her, a love she intended to grab on to with both hands, with all her heart.

"Still needing some distance?" he asked, his voice thick and husky with emotion.

"Absolutely not. I love you, Seth Walker, and somehow we're going to figure it all out." She burrowed back into his arms as she heard the sound of sirens in the distance.

She finally broke away from him. "Sam? Where's Sam?" She needed to hug her son, to hold him as tightly as Seth had just held her.

"He's okay. He's outside with Patrick Johnson," Seth replied.

She looked at Rick, who nodded, and she ran for the front door. When she reached the porch, she heard him. "Mom!" he cried. He ran toward her, his face and hair covered with dust, and he launched himself into her arms.

Allison held him tight, relishing the scent of him, the feel of his wiggly warmth in her arms. It was only then that she began to cry once again.

"It's okay, Mom," Sam said as he patted her back. "I'm okay and so are you."

She finally released him. "Yes, we are." She became aware of Seth standing just behind her and she reached out a hand for him. "It's over," she said as Seth's hand grabbed on to hers. "It's really and truly over. Dane Kelly killed my family and Beau killed the Blooms."

At that moment an ambulance pulled up along with two other patrol cars. Paramedics and additional deputies rushed inside, and in almost no time a stretcher was carried out with Eric on it.

He was conscious and as Allison rushed to his side, he gave her a loopy smile, probably due to whatever drugs the paramedics had dripping through the IV tube.

"Eric, I can't believe how brave you were. You're my hero," she said.

"Cool," he said. "I just didn't want him to hurt you." His eyelids looked heavy and the words came slowly. "I'm not going to ask you out on a date again. That's lame." He looked over her shoulder to where Seth stood. "I can tell you like him and that's cool." He drew a deep sigh. "Someday I'll find a girl my own age and she'll love me."

Allison smoothed his hair away from his face. "You're going to be fine, Eric. And when word gets out of how brave you were here today, I have a feeling you're going to have to fight the girls off."

Again he gave her a crooked grin. "I'm not going

to fight too hard, okay?" He closed his eyes and was whisked into the back of the awaiting ambulance.

As the vehicle pulled down the driveway, Allison felt a strange peace rush through her. There would be a million questions in the days and weeks to come. People would discuss Beau and Dane over lunch at Emma's, while standing in line in the supermarket. Law officers would try to understand what went wrong, what had made a killer, not only of one of their own, but of his son as well.

At the moment Allison didn't care about any of that. All she cared about was that she had her son on one side and the man she loved with all her heart on the other. She'd survived and in that survival she realized exactly what was important. In the end, being strong enough, not only to be loved, but to love was all that mattered.

Rick came out of the house, still looking shell-shocked. He approached the three of them. "I'm going to need statements from you and Sam," he said to Allison. "It's going to take a while to sort all this out, but it sounds like once it is sorted out, your father will be a free man."

"Can I take them home now?" Seth asked. He placed one arm around Allison's shoulders and the other around Sam.

Rick nodded. "I'll be in touch."

They got into Seth's car and it was only then that Sam spoke again. "Seth, I know you have a life in Kansas City, but I don't think it's as good a life as you could have here with my mom and me."

"Sam," Allison protested, but it was a weak one.

"Well, it's true," he exclaimed. "We could love you more than anyone else, Seth. Mom would make a good wife. She doesn't cook a whole lot, but she cleans good and she makes my dirty socks smell nice."

Seth laughed. "You've sold me, Sam. Now all you have to do is sell your mom on the idea."

As Sam began eagerly extolling Seth's virtues, Seth grinned at Allison. "Do you hate me now?" he asked softly.

She laughed, the joy inside her filling up every dark corner that had ever existed. "I'm going to show you later tonight exactly how I feel about you, and when I'm finished, you'll be begging for a little distance."

Those smoke gray eyes of his flamed hot, filling her with a welcome heat. "Promises, promises," he murmured under his breath, and stepped on the gas pedal to hurry them into their future together.

It was almost seven when Rick finally left the Donovan farmhouse. The bodies had been taken away, reports had been written and there was nothing left to accomplish.

He got into his patrol car, but didn't start the engine. He'd gotten word an hour ago that Eric had been through surgery for the wound on his leg. Although it would be a long time in healing, the kid was going to be just fine.

He was still having trouble wrapping his mind around the fact that Dane had killed the Donovan family and that his son had committed additional murders.

The death of Beau at his father's hand had been almost as shocking as Dane eating the business end of his gun. Later Rick would try to figure out what he might have done differently in the situation, if he could have saved either life.

At the moment he had a new appreciation for life. His pride in Eric was huge. The kid had shown the kind of bravery, the kind of decency, that spoke of the cop he might someday eventually become. One way or another, Rick would see to it that he got to go for his dream of being a criminal profiler.

He started his car engine and thought of Brian. His

son would be pleased by whatever he could do to help Eric. That was the kind of kid Brian had been and Rick had done his son a disservice by checking out of life.

On impulse, he picked up his cell phone and dialed Michelle Keller's number. She answered on the second ring, and the sound of her bright, cheerful voice lifted the pall that he'd carried on his shoulders since walking out of the farmhouse.

"Michelle, it's Rick Solomon. I was wondering if this Friday night you'd like to come to my place for dinner." He held his breath, wondering if it was too late for him, for them.

"Ah, lawman, I thought you'd never ask," she replied.

Epilogue

Seth and Sam sat in the car as Allison got out of the passenger seat and stood staring at the prison walls before them. At any minute her father was going to walk out of there, finally a free man.

It had been almost three months since that day at the farmhouse. That day hadn't been the last of the tragedies Crow's Creek had seen. Two days after the deaths of Beau and Dane, Mary Kelly had swallowed a handful of sleeping pills and had never awakened. The day after that, Leroy Grant had left Terrible's and crashed his truck into a tree trunk, instantly dying. His blood alcohol content had been three times the legal limit.

David Donovan left his wife for parts unknown. Maureen put the house on the market and also left town. The house was still for sale and rumor had it that Maureen had moved to a small town in Missouri and had gotten a job with the mayor's office.

In the wake of the tragedies, more heroes had been born as the town came together in unity. Rick Solomon had petitioned the court to become Eric's legal guardian, and the owner of the hardware store had started a college fund for the boy.

To everyone's surprise Patrick Johnson's parents had reconciled and were now living as a happy couple.

Wayne Fenton had opened a second karate school in a nearby town and had quit his job as a mechanic.

The notes that Beau had talked about just before he'd been killed had been found in the Kelly basement behind a loose brick. They were a full confession of what had happened that dark day at the Donovans' place, and they, along with Rick's reports, had begun the wheels of justice turning to gain Hank's freedom.

Best of all, Seth had moved from Kansas City to Crow's Creek and he and Allison had gotten married in a quiet ceremony with only Sam, Rick and Michelle as witnesses. Seth had opened a law practice and Allison would return to her teaching position when school started again in two weeks.

"Do you think he's going to like me?" Sam asked as he leaned over the seat behind Seth.

"What's not to like?" Seth replied. "You're smart, you're funny and you aren't half-bad-looking when you've got your hair combed. He's going to love you, Sam. I have high standards and I love you."

Sam touched his shoulder. "Me, too."

I love you were words spoken often between the three of them. They knew how fragile life was, how important it was to embrace each and every moment and let the people you cared about know how you felt.

Seth directed his focus back to Allison, who stood at the front of the car, her body tensed as she waited for her father to appear. She looked especially beautiful today, with her long dark hair loose around her shoulders, wearing a blue sundress and white sandals with dainty heels.

This was the final piece in making her whole, reuniting with the father she so desperately needed.

And then he was there, standing in the distance with a plastic bag in his hand. Seth's heart filled his chest as he watched Allison start the walk toward her father. As

Hank saw her, he dropped the bag and opened his arms. She ran to him and they hugged.

"Want to see magic?" Seth asked Sam.

"What kind of magic?" Sam asked.

Seth rolled down his car window and hit the button on the CD player. The music of Irving Berlin's "Cheek to Cheek" blared from the car.

He leaned back in the seat and fought happy tears as he watched the woman he loved. With the sun shining down on them, Allison finally danced with her father.

Read on for a sneak peek at
Carla Cassidy's next chilling
romantic suspense,

Up Close and Personal

Coming from Signet Eclipse in October 2009.

The three detectives stood in the master bath, where they believed the killer had first approached Betsy. "She was in the bathtub, relaxing with a glass of wine," Jordan said thoughtfully. "And then he appeared and startled her; she dropped her glass and grabbed her robe, and he made her walk into the living room and sit on the chair."

Jordan frowned as she tried to reconstruct the scene in her head. "He had to have had a weapon other than a knife."

"Why? What makes you think so?" Ricky asked.

"There were no defensive wounds on Joann, and, at least at first glance, there are none on Betsy. Why did these two women allow themselves to go docilely with a man without at least trying to fight back? They allowed themselves to be tied to a chair without protest?" She shook her head. "It just doesn't make sense. There had to have been a gun."

"It's a theory," Anthony replied.

"And why did he leave numbers at Joann's feet and not at Betsy's?" she asked, although she knew none of them had an answer.

"Maybe it's not the same killer," Ricky offered.

"It's the same," Jordan replied flatly. She felt it. She knew it, and the evidence pointed to the same killer.

"Ricky, why don't you check the master bedroom and the desk drawers in the kitchen to see if you can find an address or appointment book that Betsy might have kept."

"It's possible this has nothing to do with your reunion," Anthony said. "Both of them might have gone to the same hairdresser or had their nails done in the same place."

"That's what we'll need to figure out—how the killer ties into both women's lives," she replied, although Jordan felt in her gut that it was the high school reunion that had brought a killer into their lives.

"Hey, anybody home?" John Lindsay's voice called down the hallway. He'd been drinking. Jordan could hear it in his voice before she saw his face.

"Shit," she exclaimed, and hurried out of the bathroom with Anthony and Ricky close at her heels.

She met John and Adam in the hallway. Adam's ebony features were taut with tension as John gave them all a loopy grin. "What are you all looking at me for," he asked. "Let's catch this mother."

"I met him in the driveway as I was coming in," Adam explained.

The idea of John behind the wheel of his car was appalling. "Take him home, Adam," Jordan said.

"Whaddya mean? I'm working here," John protested. "I don't wanna go home." His words were slurred and his eyes bloodshot. He wasn't just tipsy; he was totally plowed.

"You're drunk, John. I can't let you compromise the scene. Let Adam drive you home. There will be another case on another day for you." Although she was angry with him, she couldn't help but feel a deep compassion for the man who had so recently lost his wife.

"Come on, buddy. Let me take you home," Adam said, and grabbed John by the elbow.

John's eyes flared wide and he stiffened with belligerence. As senior detective on the scene, Jordan prepared herself for a battle, but instead of fight, John seemed to fold into himself. He leaned against Adam as tears filled his eyes. "I screwed up. Sorry."

"I'll take care of him," Adam said, and the two men went down the hallway toward the front door.

"Somebody should talk to the sarge," Ricky said.

Jordan whirled around to look at him. "Don't you dare say anything. I'll handle the situation. For God's sake, he just lost his wife. Cut him some slack."

"It's one thing to cut him some slack. It's another to have a drunk stumbling around at a crime scene," Ricky said, a flash of irritation in his blue eyes.

Jordan felt her anger rise and tried to tamp it down, not wanting friction on the team. "Ricky, you have a lot to learn about teamwork. John's one of our own. We don't run to the brass with every problem. We take care of one another. Now let's get the crime scene boys in here and get to work."

As she strode back down the hall to the living room, she knew something was going to have to be done with John, but it wasn't going to be done today. Right now they had a scene to process, notes to be taken, and that was just the beginning.

"I'm going upstairs to talk to the husband," she said.

"I'll come with you," Anthony replied. "Ricky, you stay down here with the CSI team."

"I'm trying really hard with him," Jordan said as they climbed the stairs. "But that kid gets under my skin more than anyone has in a long time."

"He still has a lot of things to figure out. By nature he doesn't seem to be a team player, but he's exceptionally bright. He'll figure it out. But he's right about one thing—we do need to do something about John."

"I know," she agreed.

She opened the bedroom door, and it was obvious that Dr. Ralph Baker was a mess. He lay across the king-sized bed, staring up at the ceiling with eyes that were nearly swollen shut from crying.

The officer sat in a chair next to the bed. As Jordan and Anthony walked into the room, the officer stood and nodded, then left, closing the door behind him.

"Dr. Baker, I know this is an extremely difficult time for you, but we need to ask you some questions," Anthony said.

Dr. Baker closed his eyes, as if the very idea was overwhelming.

"Is there somebody we can call for you?" Jordan asked. "A friend or relative you'd like to be here with you?"

"No, there's nobody." Wearily, as if the effort were far too great, he pulled himself to a sitting position on the edge of the bed. "I need to be with my kids." He gazed at the detectives, torment darkening his eyes. "How am I going to tell them that their mother is gone? Jesus, how do I explain something like this to them—to anyone?" He broke into a torrent of weeping.

Jordan and Anthony waited patiently until he pulled himself together once again; then they began the arduous task of getting as much information from him as they could.

He'd arrived home after spending the weekend in St. Louis and had found Betsy. It was obvious she was dead and he'd immediately called 911. He hadn't touched anything and had sat on the porch while waiting for the police to arrive. The last time he'd spoken to Betsy had been late Friday afternoon. He hadn't tried to call her again because he'd been busy with his conference.

As he gave them this information he sobbed off and on, appearing to be a bewildered, grief-stricken husband. The only thing worse than interviewing a family member of a victim was having to give notice of death to unsuspecting family members. Both those parts of the job sucked, Jordan thought as Dr. Ralph sobbed so hard he began to retch.

Anthony led him into the bathroom across the hall from the bedroom, and the good doctor upchucked all the fine conference food he'd eaten for the past three days.

When he came back into the bedroom he was the color of a bleached sheet, and Jordan had a feeling they would get nothing more of substance from him tonight. "We'll have one of our officers take you wherever you need to go for the next couple of days," she said.

He gazed at her blankly, as if he hadn't considered that he wouldn't be able to stay here. Minutes later he left with an officer who would help him to notify Betsy's parents.

They would need to talk to him again, but Jordan knew the next few days would feel like hell for him. They had plenty of other things to do before they sat down to take a comprehensive statement from Ralph.

"Jordan, Anthony, I've got something to show you," said Willie Anderson, one of the crime-scene techs. He led them into the living room. Betsy's body had been taken away.

"We didn't notice this until just a few minutes ago." He picked up a large piece of glass that had been broken from one of the display cabinets and held it up for them to see. Numbers written in blood, the same numbers that had been written at Joann's feet.

"I guess now we know for sure that we're working with the same perp," Anthony said.

Jordan stared at the numbers.

2468.

2468.

Joann. Betsy. 2468. Her heart thundered as realization struck her.

"It's not twenty-four sixty-eight," she said.

"What do you mean?"

"It's two, four, six, eight. Who do we appreciate?" She stared at Anthony. "It's a cheer. Joann, Betsy—they were both cheerleaders. Oh God, he's killing cheerleaders."

Anthony stared at her for a long moment. "You were a cheerleader with them."

"Head cheerleader," she replied, her voice sounding as if it came from some distant place. Her mind raced over the past two weeks, all those times when she'd felt somebody watching her.

She'd thought it was that creep Parker Sinclair. But what if it wasn't? What if it had been the killer checking her routine, watching her habits, seeking the time and place where she would be most vulnerable?

Waiting.

Watching.

Two, four, six, eight. The chant resounded in her head to the frantic beat of her heart as she realized she could very well be marked as the next victim.